Isle of Dogs

Isle of Dogs

PATRICIA CORNWELL

LITTLE, BROWN AND COMPANY

A *Little, Brown* Book

First published in the United States in 2001 by G. P. Putnam's Sons

First published in Great Britain in 2001 by Little, Brown and Company

A CIP catalogue record for this book
is available from the British Library.

HARDBACK ISBN 0 316 85859 5
C FORMAT ISBN 0 316 85860 9

Printed and bound in Great Britain by
Clays Ltd, St Ives plc

Little, Brown and Company (UK)
Brettenham House
Lancaster Place
London WC2E 7EN

www.littlebrown.co.uk

To Friend and Publisher,
PHYLLIS GRANN

Isle of Dogs

One

Unique First fit her name like a glove, or at least this was how her mother always put it. Unique came first and was one of a kind. There was no one else like her—and this was a damn good thing, to quote her father, Dr. Ulysses First, who had never understood what genetic malignancy blighted his only child.

Unique was a petite eighteen-year-old with long, shimmering hair that was as black as ebony, and her skin was translucent like milk glass, her lips full and pink. She believed that her pale blue eyes could mesmerize whoever looked into them and that by casting as little as a glance at someone she could bend that person's mind to fit her Purpose. Unique could haunt someone for weeks, building up unbearable anticipation until the final act, which was a necessary and frenzied release, usually followed by a blackout.

"Hey, wake up, my car's broke down." She knocked on the window of the Peterbilt eighteen-wheeler that was parked all by itself at the Farmers' Market on the fringes of downtown Richmond. "I'm wondering if you got a phone?"

It was 4:00 A.M., pitch dark, and the parking lot was poorly lit. Although Moses Custer knew very well that it wasn't safe to be out here alone at this hour, he had ignored his usual good judgment after fighting with his wife and storming off in his truck, where he intended to spend the night, alone and missing in action, out by the vegetable stands. That would sure show her, he always thought when their marital routine turned ugly. He opened the door of his cab as the knocking on the glass continued.

"Lordy, what's a sweet little thing like you doing out here at this hour?" Moses asked, confused and drunk, as he stared at the creamy, delicate face smiling at him like an angel.

"You're about to have a unique experience." Unique said the same thing she always did right before she moved in for her Purpose.

"What'chu mean?" Moses puzzled. "What unique 'sperience?"

The answer came in a legion of demons that kicked and pounded Moses and ripped at his hair and clothes. Explosions and obscenities erupted from hell, and fire seared his muscles and bones as savage forces beat and tore him to shreds and left him dead and drove off in his truck. Moses hovered above his dead self for a while, watching his mauled, lifeless body on the tarmac. Blood streamed out from under his head as rain smacked down, and one of his boots was off and his left arm was at an angle that wasn't natural. As Moses gazed down on himself, a part of him was worn out and ready for Eternity while another part of him regretted his life and grieved.

"My head's ruined," he moaned and began to sob as everything went black. "Ohhh, my head's ruined. Lord, I ain't ready! It ain't my time yet!"

Complete darkness dissolved to a floating airspace from which Moses watched pulsing emergency lights and urgent firemen, paramedics, and police in yellow rain slickers with reflective tape that glared like white fire. Flares hissed on wet pavement as a heavy cold rain fell, and voices were excited and loud and made no sense. It seemed people were yelling at him and it frightened Moses and made him feel small and ashamed. He tried to open his eyes, but it was as if they had been sewn shut.

"What happened to the angel?" he kept muttering. "She said her car broke down."

Unique's car was fine and she drove around downtown for a couple of hours, listening to radio newsbreaks about the mugging and hijacking at the Farmer's Market and the speculation that it had been committed by the same gang of highway pirates that had been terrorizing Virginia for months. But this time Unique enjoyed the afterglow a little less than usual. She could have sworn that old black truck driver was dead, and she was irritated that her accomplices had been in such a hurry to run off that they had robbed her of a complete release. Had it been up to her, she would have finished what she started and made sure the truck driver never talked again.

But she wasn't worried about cops paying her any mind as she cruised around in her white Miata at this strange hour. Part of being Unique was not looking like what she was. Part of being Unique was not looking at all like what she did. She was so certain of her invincibility that she pulled off at Fred's Mini Mart, where a police car was parked.

Unique could spot an unmarked car from a block away, and she slipped inside the store as she eyed the handsome young blond man who was paying for a quart of milk at the counter. He was wearing jeans and a flannel shirt, and she searched for any sign of a gun and detected a bulge at the small of his back.

"Thanks, Fred," the blond plainclothes cop said to the man at the cash register.

"You bet, Andy. I've missed seeing you. This whole last year, it's like you dropped off the damn planet."

"Well, I'm back," Andy said, pocketing his change. "You be careful. There's a really bad gang out there. We just had another truck driver hit."

"Yeah, no shit! Heard it on the radio. How bad did they mess him up? I guess you worked the scene."

"Nope. Off duty. I heard about it the same way you did," Andy replied with a trace of disappointment.

"Well, me—I agree with what the newspaper's saying about it being a hate crime thing," Fred said. "From what I hear, the leader's a white dude and all the victims so far are black, except for that female trucker a couple months back. But then, I think she was a minority, too, if you know what I'm saying. Not that I'm a big fan of dykes, but that was pretty horrible. Seems like I read somewhere she had a stick shoved up her and was cut . . . Oh!" Fred exclaimed, startled, as Unique appeared out of nowhere and set a six-pack of Michelob on the counter. "You slipped in so quiet, sugar, I didn't know there was nobody else in the store!"

Unique smiled sweetly. "I'd like a pack of Marlboros, please," she said in a small, soft voice.

She was very pretty and dressed neatly all in black, but her boots were scuffed and they sure were dirty, and she looked as if she had been caught in the rain. Andy noticed a white Miata in the parking lot when he got back in his unmarked Caprice, and he had scarcely driven off when the delicately lovely girl with the strange eyes climbed into the Miata. She followed him through downtown, all the way to the Fan District, and just as he slowed down to see if he could make out her license plate, she turned off on Strawberry Street. Andy had an odd feeling that he couldn't place, and as he returned to his small row house and fixed a bowl of cereal, he had the eerie sensation that he was being watched.

Unique knew how to stalk anybody, including a cop, and she stood across the street in the deep shadows of trees and watched Andy's shadow move from room to room eating something out of a bowl. Several times he parted the curtains and looked out at the vacant, still street. She cast her gaze in his direction and imagined the power she was having over his mind. He was feeling uneasy and sensed Something, she believed, because Unique had been around for a very long time and could trace her most recent possession back to Dachau, Germany, where she had been taken over by a male Nazi. Long before that—she had divined from tarot cards—she had been The Adversary and had eyes all over her body.

Andy parted the curtains again and by now was unsettled enough to carry his pistol everywhere he went inside his house. Maybe he was out of sorts because it really bothered him when a bad case went down, like Moses Custer, and Andy wasn't part of the investigation. It depressed and frustrated him to hear on the news that the trucker was kicked, stomped and beaten, and left for dead, and Andy hadn't been anywhere around to see things for himself and make a difference. Or maybe he was in a dark mood simply because he had been up all night and was excited and scared about what lay ahead.

A ndy Brazil had been waiting for this day for an entire year. After endless hours of bone-aching work, he was at last launching his first installment of a special series of essays that in several hours would be posted on an Internet website he called *Trooper Truth*. The project was both ambitious and unlikely, but he had been quite determined when he first approached his boss about it inside her formidable office at Virginia State Police headquarters.

"Just hear me out before you say no," Andy had said, shutting her door. "And you've got to swear you'll never tell anybody what I'm about to propose."

Superintendent Judy Hammer had gotten up from her desk and been silent for a moment, looking like a publicity portrait of power as she stood in front of the Virginia and United States flags, her hands in her pockets. She was fifty-five years old, a striking woman with keen eyes that could penetrate body armor or empower a crowd, and her smart business suits could not hide a figure that Andy had to resist openly staring at.

"All right." Hammer had begun her characteristic pace around her office as she considered what Andy intended to do. "My first reaction is—absolutely not. I think it would be a big mistake to interrupt your law-enforcement career so soon. And I'll remind you, Andy, you were a cop in Charlotte for only a year, then a cop here in Richmond for only a year, and you've been a state trooper for barely six months."

"And during that time I've written hundreds of crime columns for area papers," he'd reminded her. "That's my most important accomplishment, isn't it? Hasn't your major agenda been to use me to inform the public about what's going on and what the police are doing about it or, in some instances, not doing about it? The whole point has always been to enlighten people, and now I want to do that in a bigger way and to a bigger audience."

Andy's was an unusual career and always had been. He'd gone into journalism right after college and had gotten involved in law enforcement as a volunteer, riding with police and writing eyewitness pieces for the city newspaper. This had been in Charlotte, North Carolina, where Hammer had been chief at the time, and she had eventually hired him as a sworn officer who enforced the law while continuing to write crime columns and editorials. Hammer had allowed him this unprecedented opportunity because she was in an unusual position, too, having been given a grant by the National Institute of Justice that allowed her to take over troubled police departments and straighten them out. She had always seen beyond boundaries and had become Andy's mentor, faithfully bringing him with her as she moved on in her career, but as he sat in her office and watched her pace, he sensed that his plan struck her as ungrateful.

"I appreciate everything you've done for me," he had said to her. "I'm not turning my back on you and disappearing."

"This isn't about my worrying that you're going to disappear," she had replied in a way that made him feel that if he vanished for months she wouldn't miss him in the least.

"I'll make it worth your while, Superintendent Hammer," he promised her. "It's time I have more to say than just who robbed who or how many speeders were caught or what's the latest crime wave. I want to put criminal behavior into the context of human nature and history, and I believe it's important, because people are only getting worse. Can you help me get a grant or something so I can pay my bills while I do the research and write and take flying lessons—?"

"Who said anything about flying lessons?" she had interrupted him.

"The aviation unit's got instructors, and I think I could be much more useful to you if I had my helicopter pilot's license," he'd explained.

Hammer let him have his way, perhaps because she realized he was going to leave her anyway. He could launch a website as a special, classified project while he continued to work for her, she said, but the condition was that he had to remain anonymous, because Governor Bedford Crimm IV, who was an aristocratic, autocratic, impossible old man, did not allow Hammer to disseminate information to the public without his approval. Clearly, whatever Andy wrote could not be directly connected to the Virginia State Police, but at the same time had to reflect favorably on it and encourage the public to support it. She had added that Andy had to be available for emergencies, and if he wanted to learn to fly, he could work that out on his own schedule.

He pushed his luck by asking, "Will I have a travel budget?"

"For what?" Hammer asked. "Where are you going?"

"I'll need funding for archaeological and historical research."

"I thought you were writing about human nature and crime." Hammer had begun to resist him again. "Now what? You're flying helicopters and globetrotting?"

"If I discuss what's wrong with America today, I need to show what was wrong with it when it got started," he'd explained. "And you need more pilots. You've already had two quit on you in the past three months."

A ndy sat at the table in the dining room, which had become his hopelessly cluttered office, and typed his password into his computer and opened a file. After twelve months of arduous research and writing, and flying lessons and ground school, he was desperate to get out and chase lawbreakers and investigate violent crimes from both the ground and the air. He was eager for people to read what he had to say, and often he fantasized about riding or flying with other troopers or working a scene and overhearing people talk about what they had read on the Trooper Truth website that day. No one would have a clue that

Trooper Truth was in their midst gathering even more information from their comments. Only Hammer knew the truth about Trooper Truth, and she and Andy had been meticulously careful to protect his identity.

When, for example, he had done archaeological research and traveled as far away as England and Argentina gathering facts, he never let on that he was a journalist-cop doing research. He was simply a twenty-eight-year-old man who was doing graduate work in history, criminology, and anthropology. It was the first undercover job Andy had ever had, and it still amazed him that no one bothered to check on whether he was actually enrolled in a university graduate program or was even who he said he was.

Although Andy was not the sort to stare into the mirror and see himself the way others did, he was aware that he had many gifts in his favor. He was tall with a sculpted build, and his features were so perfectly proportioned and refined that as a boy he had been teased for being *pretty*. His hair was light blond, and his blue eyes changed with his thoughts and moods very much like the sky reflecting shifting clouds and light. He could look stormy or peaceful or extremely intense. His intellect was quick and facile, and his words could shine like silver and be just as hard when necessary.

It had never been difficult for Andy to get what he wanted because people, as a rule, were drawn to him or at least mindful that he was a presence they could not dismiss. He also worked hard to compensate for the emptiness of his early years. His father had been murdered when Andy was a child, leaving no one but an alcoholic mother who never acknowledged that her son was special or decent, but rather exiled him to a lonely realm of relentless preoccupations and fantasies.

Had he not grown up that way, he could not have endured the isolation that was necessary for him to explore and write what the world was about to read. But now that the moment had come, he felt as disturbed and gloomy as the morning beyond his windows. Heavy clouds hung over the city. As a vein of lightning pierced the dark dawn, it occurred to him that it would be a terrible omen if the power went out and his computer crashed. He was startled out of his preoccupations when the telephone rang.

"At least you're awake," Judy Hammer said without so much as a good morning. "I'm—"

"I thought you were going to call me out in emergencies," he interrupted her. "I wish you'd let me know about the truck driver at the Farmers' Market."

"You weren't needed," she said.

"Same M.O.? Was he cut on?"

"I'm afraid so. Several cuts to his neck with what looks like a razor, but none of them lethal," she replied. "Apparently, the assailants left in a hurry, and he came to long enough to call nine-one-one. The reason I called is, I'm waiting, Trooper Truth," Hammer let him know. "I thought you said your website was going up at six-thirty. That was five minutes ago."

It was her way of telling him *good luck*.

A BRIEF EXPLANATION

by Trooper Truth

The rich early history of the U.S.A. is based largely on eyewitness observations described in letters, true adventures, testimonies, maps, and books published in the early seventeenth century. Most of those original accounts have been lost forever or are silently maintained in private collections. Other historical documentation, sadly, was stored in Richmond and burned up during the Civil War so Northerners could rewrite the facts and convince schoolchildren the world over that our country really got its start in Plymouth, which is simply a lie.

That lie and others should come as no surprise. So much of what we know as "fact" in life is, in truth, nothing more than propaganda or a well-meant reflection on how events and people are perceived by those with a bias and poor vision. Tales pass from lips to lips, from news story to news story, from e-mail to e-mail, from politicians to us, from witnesses to jurors, and eventually we are led to believe all manner of things that are grossly distorted if not patently false. This is why, as I begin to have these conversations with you, the reader, I will rely on my own primary research and experiences, and focus on science and medicine, which have neither imaginations nor personalities nor politics nor grudges.

DNA, for example, frankly doesn't care if you did it. DNA doesn't care if you didn't do it. DNA knows exactly who you, your parents, and your children are, but has no opinion about it and no interest in being a friend or getting your votes. DNA knows it was you who left seminal fluid in someone, but is neither judgmental nor voyeuristic about how or why that deposit might have occurred. So I am far more inclined to trust DNA than the defendant on the witness stand, and it is a shame that DNA is too busy working crimes and pedigree disputes to reconstruct the history of the United States. If DNA had the time, I suspect we would find that most of what we presently believe about the past is tainted, perhaps shockingly so.

Since DNA isn't available to serve as our narrator in this series of essays, I will do the best I can to tell you what I have discovered about the beginning of English America, in hopes that it will serve as a metaphor for who we are and what has become of our society. The story begins with a small but significant turn of events on the docks of London, December 20, 1606, when thirty-six mariners and one hundred and eight settlers said painful goodbyes and no doubt comforted themselves in alehouses on the *Isle of Dogges*, as it was spelled on a 1610 map of London.

The settlers and the mariners who would pilot the ships to Virginia descended the Blackwall stairs to the docks, where these brave adventurers, who wanted more in life, including gold and silver, boarded the *Susan Constant*, the *Godspeed*, and the *Discovery*, and began their historic voyage to the New World by being stalled in the mouth of the Thames for six weeks. Records cite the reason for the delay as either no wind or wind that blew in the wrong direction.

If any of the stranded settlers looked back toward the alehouses and experienced a change of heart, we know nothing about it, but the math indicates that no one jumped ship. During the voyage, one settler died in the Caribbean, possibly from heatstroke, and on May 14, 1607, when the three ships finally tied up at Jamestown Island on the north shore of the James River in Virginia, one hundred and seven settlers disembarked. Soon after, three settlers were killed by Indians, and in July, the ships sailed back to England for supplies, leaving one hundred and four settlers to fend for themselves.

Their number dwindled quickly and dramatically as the mariners and Captain Newport made the endless voyage back to England. There, I suspect, the men restored themselves and made plans in Isle of Dogs alehouses and at the Sir Walter Raleigh House while the settlers waited for supplies and tried to develop peaceful relations with the Indians—or Naturals, as the settlers called the Native Americans—by giving them bits of copper and trading other trinkets for tobacco and food.

No one thus far has been able to give me a definitive explanation for why the settlers and the Naturals had such an inconsistent relationship, but I suspect the answer lies in human nature, which inspires people to overpower others and to be touchy, bigoted, selfish, greedy, deceitful, and to beat up innocent people and steal trucks. Nor could anybody tell me why the Isle of Dogs was named such, and I can only speculate the obvious: The name may refer to *sea dogs*, since it is known that many Elizabethan sailors and pirates patronized the alehouses while resting from where they had been or waiting to sail out to wherever they were going.

I will go into great detail about pirates soon enough, for they certainly were a powerful presence when America was trying to get started, and we still have a problem with them today on our highways and high seas, although the pirates' mode of transportation, equipment, and weapons have dramatically evolved over the centuries. It is unfortunate, I'm sorry to tell you, that modern pirates have the same personality and modus operandi as pirates of old. They remain cruel-hearted cutthroats whose creed is *dead men tell no tales*, thus justifying their seizing of ships and tractor trailers and murdering everyone in sight. Lest Virginians assume their history is untouched by such despicable character disorders, let me remind you that the Chesapeake Bay once bristled with pirates, and Virginia's Tangier Island openly traded with and hosted them and, as legend has it, was visited by Blackbeard himself.

Isle of Dogs

As I begin sharing truths with you, the reader, I hope you will reflect upon your own life and try very hard to put at least one other person's needs and feelings before your own this day. Just as objects in the mirror are closer than they appear, so The Past rides our bumper along life's highways and may, in fact, be inside the car with us. Who we are is who we were and the more things change, the less they do, unless we start with our hearts.

Be careful out there!

Two

Governor Bedford Crimm IV knew nothing about the Trooper Truth website until his press secretary, Major Trader, came to see him at 1:00 P.M. and set the "Brief Explanation" on the governor's antique burlwood desk.

"Are you aware of this, Governor?" Trader asked.

Governor Crimm picked up the computer printout and squinted at it. "What is it, exactly?"

"Good question," Trader grimly answered. "We've all known it was coming, but there's been no way to check it out or anticipate its spin on things because Trooper Truth is a fake name. And there appears to be no way to trace this renegade trooper through the Internet."

"I see," the governor pondered as he strained blindly to pick out a word or two. "Am I to assume he's one of ours? Oh," he added, pleasantly surprised when Trader served him a chocolate brownie on a small Wedgwood plate. "Why, thank you."

"Made fresh this morning from only the finest Belgian chocolate. I'm afraid I ate far too many of them, myself."

"That wife of yours certainly can cook," the governor said as he ate half the brownie in two bites. "I bet she doesn't use mixes. Or did we already discuss that?" He ate the rest of the brownie, unable to resist anything chocolate.

"Everything from scratch."

"A strange phrase, I've always thought," the governor considered as he wiped his fingers on a handkerchief. "What is *from scratch*?"

"Ingredients. It has to do with—"

"Tsst, tsst." The governor made his familiar hissing noise, which meant he did not want an answer to the question, but simply was expressing curiosity. "On with things," he impatiently added.

"Yes," Trader said. "Trooper Truth. There's no one on the state police force with the last name of Truth, and no one over there claims to have any idea who Trooper Truth is. But prior to the posting of this first essay"—he indicated the printout—"there have been numerous promotions of the Trooper Truth website and when it was going to be launched. Whoever the person is, he's well versed enough in the Internet to make sure his marketing ploys and ads have shown up everywhere you can imagine."

Governor Crimm picked up his nineteenth-century magnifying glass, which was English and made of ivory. Peering through the lens, he made out enough of the essay's contents to get interested and slightly offended.

"It's been clear for a while that this Trooper Truth individual is based in Virginia or at least wants to point the finger at Virginia," Trader indignantly went on as the governor slowly read. "I've got a file on what he's posted on various bulletin boards and sent out in mass e-mailings. He seems to have access to every governmental e-mail address in the Commonwealth, which is one of the reasons I am sure he's an insider, a turncoat, and a troublemaker."

"Well, I like what he has to say about America starting in Jamestown and not Plymouth," remarked the governor, whose family had been in

Virginia since the American Revolution. "I'm mighty tired of other states taking credit for what we've accomplished. But I don't approve of his implication that history is untrustworthy. That's going to step on some toes, now isn't it? And what's this about pirates?" He steadied the magnifying glass over Blackbeard's name.

"Very troublesome. I'm sure you heard the news this morning?"

"Yes, yes," the governor said, distracted. "Do we have any further information on that?"

"The victim, Moses Custer, was beaten severely and doesn't remember much and was babbling a lot about a unique experience with an angel whose car had broken down. But after continued questioning by the state police, he sobered up and seemed to recall a young white male with dreadlocks who shouted obscenities when he flung open the Peterbilt's tailgate and discovered thousands of pumpkins, which he and his gang no doubt had to unload quickly and in secret into the James River. The guy, uh, Custer, had the same weird cuts as some of the other victims."

"I thought we were doing our best to play down this pirate business," the governor seemed to remember. "Didn't I order Superintendent Hammer not to release any statements to the press about anything without our approving it first?"

"You certainly did. And so far, we're managing to keep the sensational details out of the media."

"You don't suppose Trooper Truth intends to keep blabbing about our pirate problem on the Internet, do you?"

"Yes, sir," Trader replied as if he knew this for a fact. "We can rest assured his website is going to open a can of worms, because by all appearances, it's an inside job and I fear your administration could be blamed if things really get ugly."

"You might be right. I get blamed for most things," the governor confessed as his stomach rumbled and his intestines lurched into activity like worms suddenly exposed to daylight. He wished Trader had not mentioned a can of worms.

Crimm's constitution just wasn't what it used to be, and very often he felt like hell. Last night he had endured yet another formal dinner at the executive mansion, and since he was hosting some of his biggest financial supporters, the mansion's director had decided it was important to serve Virginia food and wine. As usual, this had meant ham from Smithfield, baked apples from Winchester, biscuits made from an antebellum recipe, and wines from Virginia vineyards.

Crimm's digestion simply couldn't tolerate any of it, especially the apples, and most of the morning he had been seeking out the most convenient, secure toilet inside the Capitol, until he finally gave up on cabinet-level meetings and retreated to his office, which had thick walls and a private bathroom he could use without Executive Protection Unit state troopers posted outside the door. As if all of that wasn't bad enough, the wine had given Crimm a sinus headache.

"It doesn't make sense why I have to serve, much less drink, inferior wine," the governor bitterly complained as he slowly moved the magnifying glass over the printout.

"I beg your pardon?" Trader looked confused. "What wine?"

"Oh, you weren't there last night, I guess." Crimm sighed. "We ought to serve French wines. Think about how much Thomas Jefferson loved French wine and all things French. So why would it be such an egregious break from tradition to serve French wines in the mansion?"

"You know how critical people are," Trader reminded him. "But I totally agree with you, governor. French wines are much better, and you deserve them. However, someone will say something and no doubt it will be widely publicized and costly to your reputation. Which brings me back to Trooper Truth. This article is only the beginning. We have a loose cannon on our hands and somehow must stop whoever it is or at least have some say-so about it."

The governor could have done without the cannon reference, too, as he slowly made out words and scarcely listened to his press secretary, who was a meddler and an irritation. Crimm was not clear on why he had ever hired Major Trader or even if he had. But Trader certainly wasn't Crimm's cup of tea, at least not anymore, assuming he ever was. The press secretary was a fat slob who was far more interested in big meals, big stories, and big talk than he was in being honest about anything. The only good thing about Crimm's failing eyesight was he could scarcely see people like Trader at all anymore, even when he was in the same room with them, and thank God for small favors, because the sight of Trader with his fleshy jowls, ill-fitting suits, and long, greasy strands of hair combed over his bald pate was increasingly repulsive.

"... *objects in the mirror are closer than they appear,*" the governor slowly read out loud as he peered through the magnifying glass. "*So The Past rides our bumper along life's highways and may even be inside the car with us* ..." He glanced up and gave Trader a huge eye. "Hmmm, now that's an interesting thing to consider."

"I have no idea what it means, if anything." Trader was irritated that the governor would consider anything beyond what he, the press secretary, recommended.

"It's like a riddle," the governor went on, intrigued, moving the magnifying glass over the essay as if he were reading a Ouija board. "You remember the Riddler in *Batman*? All of these little riddles hinting at where, when, and how the Riddler was going to strike next, but Batman and Robin had to decipher the riddle first, of course. This Trooper Truth fellow is giving us a clue about something, about what he's going to do next or maybe about what *I* ought to do next. Something about *life's highways.*"

"Speaking of that ..." Trader seized the opportunity to move on to a subject that he might be able to control. "Speeding continues to be a serious problem, Governor, and it's occurring to me that if we emphasize speeding to the voting public, we can divert any unwanted attention away from pirates."

"Speeding on *life's highways*. Maybe that's what he's getting at. Maybe that's the riddle," the governor said, fascinated by his own deductions. "But I wasn't aware that speeding had gotten worse."

It hadn't. But Trader wanted to tug the governor's attention away from riddles. Crimm was known to make inane, inappropriate statements about whatever his latest whim, curiosity, or observation was, and it would not be good at all should he indicate that a riddle or the Riddler was influencing his executive decisions.

"Citizens are complaining that they're forced to exceed the speed limit even in the slow traffic lane because of aggressive motorists riding their bumpers and flashing their headlights," Trader spun his latest fabrication. "And we can't have state troopers every other mile waiting with radar guns. Not to mention, there are escalating incidents of road rage because of these jerks who want to go ninety miles an hour and don't care who they cut in front of."

"People aren't scared enough. That's the problem." The governor was halfway listening as he began to decipher what Trooper Truth had to say about DNA. "You know, he's right about trusting technology instead of human beings. Maybe we can figure out a way to make the public believe we have some new advanced technology that will catch them speeding even if there's not a trooper in sight."

The governor suddenly began to believe with religious conviction that this was the riddle Trooper Truth was hinting at. It was damn time to scare the public into behaving! Detectives and district attorneys did it daily by threatening suspects with DNA even if there was no DNA recovered or if the analysis of it wasn't helpful. So why shouldn't the governor start scaring people, too? He was weary of being nice. What good did it do?

"We have all these new helicopters," he told his press secretary. "Let's scare the hell out of people with them."

"What? You want helicopters to find speeders and buzz them?" Trader didn't like the idea in the least, especially since he hadn't thought of it first.

"No, no. But I see no reason why we can't use them to check speeding from the air, pretend they've got fancy computers to do that, then the pilots radio troopers on the ground to go after the bastards." The governor's intestines were crawling again, as if they had some place to go in a hurry. "All we've got to do is post warning signs on the roads out there, and people will be scared into believing they'll be arrested, even if there isn't a helicopter or trooper within ten miles."

"I see. A bluff."

"Of course. Now, you go to work on that right away." The governor needed to end the discussion instantly. "Get back with me on the proposal and we'll issue a press release before the day is out."

"Using aviation to catch speeders is not a good idea," Trader warned him. "It's going to hurt your rating in the polls and create an explosive situation . . ."

Governor Crimm's gut was already creating an explosive situation, and he shot up from his leather chair as he ordered Trader out. Moments later, as Crimm sat behind a closed door with the fan going, he wondered who Trooper Truth really was and if there might be a way to influence what he posted on the Internet. How helpful it would be if the governor could get a thoughtful, philosophical person to disseminate Crimm's ideas and beliefs. Crimm reached for the portable phone on the shelf near the toilet paper.

"Who's this?" Crimm asked when a man answered.

"Trooper Macovich," came the hesitant reply from the Executive Protection Unit's outpost in the basement of the executive mansion.

Thorlo Macovich recognized the governor's voice immediately and hoped the governor didn't recognize his. Or maybe if he was lucky, the governor had already forgotten the incident that had occurred in the mansion's billiards room the other night. It was also possible the governor hadn't seen it, because he couldn't see much of anything these days. But that youngest Crimm daughter would remember Macovich, all right. He had never seen anyone pitch such a fit over losing a game of pool—yelling obscenities and ordering Macovich to stay in the basement and never come upstairs again, which was seriously interfering with his duties.

"Trooper Truth . . ." Crimm started to say as a cramp doubled him over.

"You all right, sir?" Macovich was surprised and alarmed. "Woo, what's that noise?"

"You got any idea who this Trooper Truth person is?" The governor could barely talk.

"No, sir. But everybody's sure talking about him. What's that? Sounds like somebody ripping bubble wrap. You sure you're all right, sir? Wooo, it sounds like somebody's shooting a gun in the Capitol! It ain't safe! I'll be right there . . . !"

"No! Don't come here," the governor blurted out as gasses pushed against his organs, struggling to escape. "Find out who Trooper Truth . . . who he is. Make that your mission, you hear me? And tell the kitchen staff I want a light supper tonight. For God's sake, no apples or ham. Maybe seafood."

"From Virginia, I guess, sir." Macovich was relieved. Clearly, the governor didn't remember him.

"As long as it's not shad roe."

"Don't believe they catch shad roe this time of year. I can fly a state helicopter to Tangier Island and pick up fresh blue crabs, if that would please you, sir," Macovich added with reluctance because he hated going to Tangier Island. "And maybe trout."

"That's it!" the governor said, startled both by an idea and what sounded to Macovich like a deflating hot air balloon. "We'll start with Tangier Island! You troopers can put the first speed trap over there. Did you know they used to welcome Blackbeard on that island? Bunch of pirates, that's what they are. Well, I'll show them."

"They don't have posted speed limits on Tangier," Macovich pointed out, and he wasn't clear on what speed traps the governor meant. "Most of them Tangierians ride around in golf carts, sir. Or in little boats. And they already don't get along with the rest of Virginia. You mind if I ask what speed traps you're talking about?"

"We don't have a name for it yet." Governor Crimm mopped sweat off his face as his gut continued to play against him in a loud, painful percussion. "Forget the seafood. You can just pick it up when you paint the speed traps on the island first thing tomorrow. Now listen here, Trooper, get up with Trader and he'll brief you. We're going to make life's highways safe again, just like Trooper Truth said in that riddle on his website."

Macovich did not recall noticing a riddle on the Trooper Truth website, or anything at all that might have compelled the governor to decide that speed traps should be set on a remote island in the Chesapeake Bay with a population of less than seven hundred people. Macovich sure didn't want to be dragged into anything that had to do with Tangier Island, where there wasn't a single African American resident. In fact, when he was ordered to fly there to pick up seafood, he got the distinct impression that he was the only African American the Islanders had ever seen, except for ones on TV and in the catalogs the mail boats brought in.

Macovich left the mansion and lit up a Salem Light as he walked around Capitol Square, not especially eager to have a word with the press secretary about this or anything else. That son of a bitch Major Trader couldn't be trusted, and everybody knew it except the governor. Wooo, Macovich worried from inside his cloud of smoke. If the state police started picking on those Tangier people, there was going to be nothing but trouble.

"Let me ask you something," Macovich asked as he walked into Trader's office. "You ever been to Tangier Island or even met a Tangierian?"

"It's not the sort of place I would visit." Trader was perched over his keyboard and eating a chili dog that one of his assistants had brought him for a snack. "How many times do I have to tell you to take your sunglasses off when you're inside a building or it's after dark? I've worked very hard to change the image of all you troopers so the public doesn't perceive you as a bunch of thick-headed brutes." He gobbled up half of the hotdog in one mouthful and dribbled mustard on his stained, unfashionable tie. "Just because you're plainclothes EPU and fly around in helicopters doesn't mean you can go against protocol and make everybody look bad."

"Wooo, we're gonna look bad, all right," Macovich retorted, leaving his sunglasses on. "We go roaring into that island with our big helicopters and start handing out speeding tickets, those people are gonna do something about it."

"I believe that would be a mistake." Trader wiped his flabby lips with a greasy napkin and strategized quickly. The governor had yet to inform him that the first speed traps would be set on Tangier Island, but he wasn't about to let Macovich sense as much. "We'll lock every one of them in jail," he added as if he had already given much thought to the consequences should the Islanders rebel.

"Oh, now that's a good one, Mister Press Secretary," Macovich said, sarcastically. "Let's lock up the entire island of fishermen, women, and children. Not to mention all the old folks. We've got highway pirates running around loose out there beating the shit out of innocent truck drivers and smuggling dope into Canada, but we gonna make sure none of them Tangierians go too fast in their golf carts."

Trader licked his fingers and wiped them on his voluminous trousers. "I wouldn't push my luck, if I were you," he snipped. "Not after you cheated at pool the other night. Naughty, naughty."

"I didn't cheat!" Macovich bellowed so loudly that other state employees poked their heads out of offices up and down the hall.

"The First Family certainly thinks you did, and it's just fortunate for you that the governor has more important matters on his mind," Trader retorted haughtily. "I'd hate to be the one who reminds him that you aren't very popular in the mansion these days. You certainly wouldn't be the first EPU trooper to find himself back in uniform, riding around in a car all day and night."

"Well, Superintendent Hammer ain't gonna do that to me, 'cause then who's gonna fly the governor's old, blind ass around, huh? Who's gonna fly the First Family's lazy big asses around, huh?"

"Would you please lower your voice?" Trader raised his.

Macovich stepped closer to the faux colonial desk, his sunglasses glaring at Trader. "In case you've forgotten," Macovich snarled, "we're down to two helicopter pilots 'cause First Lady Crimm runs 'em all off." Macovich turned to walk out, then spun back around. "And guess what else, Trader? Life ain't no big plantation anymore, and one of these days you're gonna wake up and find yourself smack in the goddamn middle of *Gone With the Wind*!"

Unique First had never seen *Gone With the Wind* or read the novel, but she could relate to the expression. She had always been able to disappear without a trace, and as a child had discovered that if she rearranged her molecules while trespassing or breaking into her neighbors' homes, she would become invisible. She followed the cobblestone of Shockhoe Slip and slipped inside Tobacco Company, an upscale restaurant and bar in a renovated old tobacco warehouse not far from the river. Unique sat near the piano and ordered a beer and began to smoke as she relived last night.

Acting as a decoy for the highway pirates was getting boring, if she were to be honest about it. The road dogs she had begun to associate with months ago were small-minded and stoned most of the time. Their leader, in particular, was frying his brain with booze and pot and was so out of it that Unique no longer bothered having sex with him. She tapped an ash and signaled the waitress to bring another beer as she felt the stare of a woman sitting alone at the bar.

"You from out of town?" the woman asked, and her strong energy and hot eyes registered clearly on Unique's sexual radar.

"In and out," Unique evasively replied with her sweet smile.

"Oh." The woman got up and marveled over this pretty woman's unique way of expressing herself. "Mind if I join you?" She set her beer down on Unique's table and pulled out a chair. "My name's T.T., which is really funny now that this Trooper Truth stuff is all over the place. You won't believe it, but people who know me and even strangers all of a sudden got this crazy notion that my initials T.T. stand for Trooper Truth, and just because I wrote for my high school newspaper, I'm supposedly Trooper Truth but don't want anybody to know!"

Unique held T.T.'s gaze and sipped beer.

"Well, I'm not," T.T. went on. "But I wish like hell I was because that's the new mystery in this town: Who is Trooper Truth? What's the truth about Trooper Truth? Like he's Robin Hood or something. You got any guesses? And you sure have amazing hair. You must brush it all the time."

"I don't know," Unique replied as T.T. bounced her foot and fidgeted nervously like a schoolboy with a crush. "My car's broke down. Maybe you could give me a ride home?"

"Sure!" T.T. said. "Hey, no problem. Man, you got such a quiet voice.

Sorry about your car. Man, that's such a bitch when your car fucks up, you know?"

T.T. continued to rattle on as she smacked a ten-dollar bill on the bar and put on her leather biker's jacket. She usually wasn't this successful when she tried to pick up women, but it was about damn time her luck changed. T.T. worked for the state and had to wear dresses and other feminine attire in the office, where no one knew the truth about her private life. So the only opportunity she had for assuaging her loneliness was to dress the part and hang out in bars at night and on weekends. This was expensive and largely unproductive, and her hands were shaking with excitement as she let Unique into her old Honda.

"Which way?" T.T. asked as she pulled out onto Cary Street.

"Let's go down to the dock, you know, off Canal. I love looking at the river. We'll walk on Belle Island," Unique replied in her tiny, hushed voice as her Purpose, as she thought of it, throbbed inside her and a slow burn of ancient rage began to consume her brain.

Minutes later, she and T.T. got out of the Honda and stood along the water, the chilled September air blowing Unique's hair like black fire. There wasn't another person around and it vaguely penetrated Unique's spell that T.T. was incredibly stupid to wander off with a perfect stranger, and how dare she just assume that Unique was of her persuasion and would be interested. How incredibly stupid the other ones had been, too. Unique took T.T.'s hand and they walked over a footbridge that led to Belle Island, where Union soldiers had been imprisoned during the Civil War. The island was densely wooded and cut with bike paths and trails. Unique pulled T.T. behind a tree and began to kiss and fondle her into a frenzy.

"I want you to have a unique experience," Unique whispered as she dug her tongue in T.T.'s mouth and slipped a box cutter out of a pocket.

Three

Major Trader had served in the Crimm administration long enough to realize several things. First, the governor did indeed have a lot on his mind and was therefore easily persuaded to endorse a policy or suggestion that differed from his original conception. Second, as if he weren't already confused and almost blind, he was forgetful and easily distracted, especially if his bowels acted up. Third, Trader was best served if he stole good ideas and blamed other people for bad ones.

As Trader sat in his office, looking out the window at Macovich's cloud of smoke retreating across the graceful Capitol grounds, he considered the governor's positions on various agendas and reminded himself that Crimm had been pounded repeatedly for transportation problems throughout the Commonwealth. Traffic continued to be impossibly congested and motorists were getting increasingly hostile in northern Virginia. Roads and bridges were falling apart. Trains did not always run on time or at all and were overcrowded, and nobody liked to fly anymore. The governor was blamed for all of it and more.

Although Trader did not intend to give Macovich credit for warning him about the people of Tangier, Trader was certain that the governor's latest notion about speed traps on the island was going to be met with stinging resentment, and it was therefore probably best to give someone else the credit. He jotted some quick notes on a pad of paper, wondering what the new initiative should be called. He tried Speed Check Aviation Regulation but decided SCAR wasn't quite what he was looking for, but he was rather pleased with SCARE, which could be an acronym for Speed Check Aviation Regulation Emergency. Yes, he thought, that could work very well. SCARE would make the governor's point about scaring people into behaving, and Emergency hinted to the public that the governor believed that stopping speeders on Tangier Island and elsewhere was a matter of life and death. No matter what Trooper Truth leaked about pirates, the public wouldn't pay any attention, because citizens would be in a lather about speed traps. Trader tried the governor's private line.

"Yes?" Crimm sounded weak and bleary.

"I think I've come up with something. How would SCARE work for you?" Trader tapped his pen on his notepad. "It certainly sends the message you want. Just imagine SCARE painted on signs across the Commonwealth."

Crimm's rump was raw. He was shaky and soaked in cold sweat, and as he tried to remember what he and Trader might have talked about right before Crimm's terrible gastrointestinal eruption, all the governor could piece together was something about Trooper Truth's riddle.

"You mean, scare him into revealing his true identity?" The governor sat down in his big leather chair, picked up the magnifying glass, and discovered a new pile of memos and news clips. "Now where did those come from?"

"Where did what come from? You mean the SCARE signs?" Trader was befuddled, which was fairly routine when he talked to the governor.

"Oh, I see." It was a figure of speech, of course. "I suppose you're talking about scaring Trooper Truth into telling the truth about who he is. I suppose he could be a she. I don't feel well and really can't discuss this further."

"I was talking about the speed traps." Trader hated it when the governor cut him off. "We have to come up with a name for the program and I thought SCARE would do exactly what you were hoping . . ."

"Nonsense!" The governor suddenly remembered the gist of their earlier conversation. "If you call something SCARE, then everybody on Tangier Island will know the point is to scare them and they'll suspect it's an empty threat. Come up with a name that sounds more bureaucratic and rather meaningless, then the Islanders will take it seriously."

"Well, those Islanders are going to be difficult, as I've already said." Trader took credit for warning the governor. "Just remember, you heard it from me first. So don't blame me if there's controversy."

"If I look bad, I most assuredly will blame you."

"As you should," Trader said. "But don't let my warning stop you from laying down the law, Governor." Trader had long since mastered the art of doublespeak. "I think we should send a helicopter down there immediately and try out our program. Don't you?"

"We send helicopters down there anyway to pick up my seafood. So I don't see why not."

"That's exactly my point," Trader agreed.

Trader hung up and scribbled on his notepad for an hour, trying every combination of meaningless words he could conjure up or find in the thesaurus. By the end of the afternoon, he came up with VASCAR, which stood for Visual Average Speed Computer, more or less, and implied that if a motorist was visibly speeding, then an objective non-human device—a computer—would decide if the person was guilty by calculating the average speed he was going when he moved from point A to point B. Points A and B would be white stripes painted across pavements that could easily be spotted from the air. Trader was certain the acronym would be appropriately confusing and bureaucratic enough to strike fear in the hearts of all. Most important, he would make sure that any public outrage would be directed at the state police, and not the governor or him.

This is brilliant, he happily thought as he logged on to the Internet, using an alias screen name. A scheme was rapidly unfolding in his mind, and there was much to do. He pulled up the Trooper Truth website, his pulse breaking into a gallop. Nothing excited him more than his own cleverness and skills at manipulation. He would make sure the news of VASCAR raced through cyberspace and alerted people around the world that Virginia would not tolerate speeders and never had, and that the Commonwealth was a big bully that sent in powerful helicopters to persecute an island of quiet watermen, few of whom owned cars. He would see to it that citizens were furious and complained directly to State Police Superintendent Judy Hammer, thus diverting transportation criticism and pirate problems away from the governor and, of course, away from Trader.

Hammer was new, not a Virginian, and therefore an easy target. Trader didn't like her anyway. Superintendents in the past had always been burly, tough men from old Virginia families, and they understood pecking orders and paid appropriate respect to the press secretary, who ultimately controlled what the governor thought and what the public believed. Hammer was a disgrace. She was a blunt, confrontational female who often wore pants, and when Trader had met her the day she was interviewed for the superintendent's position, she had looked right through him as if he were air and hadn't laughed at or even noticed his off-color anecdotes and jokes.

Trader's fingers paused on the computer keyboard, and then he began to compose an e-mail:

Dear Trooper Truth,

I read your "Brief Explanation" with great interest, and hope you can address the concern of an old woman like me who never married and lives alone and is afraid to drive because of all the crazies on the road, including those awful pirates!

But I certainly don't think the answer is speed traps and helicopters that go roaring after honest citizens! VASCAR is going to start another civil war, and I hope you will address this in your next essay.

Sincerely,
A. Friend

Trader didn't intentionally put a period after the A, and he didn't notice the typo as he hit SEND NOW. He realized his mistake when he got a response moments later:

Dear Miss A. Friend,
Thank you for your interest. I'm very sorry you are lonely and afraid to drive. That makes me sad, and please feel free to write me any time. What is VASCAR?

Trooper Truth

Major Trader decided he might as well be Miss A. Friend from now on, and he fired off another e-mail:

Dear Trooper Truth,
I'm so pleased you would take the time to answer a lonely old woman. Superintendent Hammer knows what VASCAR is. It was her idea. I'm surprised you haven't heard all about the speed traps she's going to put on Tangier Island and can't help but suspect she got the idea from your "Brief Explanation." I applaud you for influencing her to make an example of people who once were in bed with pirates and now take advantage of tourists.

Sincerely,
Miss A. Friend

Trader chortled as he dashed off a memo to Hammer. It was brief and confusing, and was accompanied by a press release that was to be circulated immediately, on orders of the governor.

W hat the hell is this?" Hammer asked when her secretary, Windy Brees, handed her a fax from the governor's office that informed her of a new speed monitoring program called VASCAR.

"New to me," replied Windy. "What a stupid name. I mean, it doesn't mean anything, if you ask me, except it reminds me of NASCAR – the National Association for Stock Car Racing – and I bet the governor didn't think about that. Just another example of not looking before you leak."

Hammer read the memo and press release several times, furious that the governor would implement a state police program without conferring with her first.

"Goddamn it," she muttered. "This is the stupidest thing I've ever heard of. We're going to start using helicopters to monitor how fast drivers are going? And the first target is Tangier Island, the news of which is to remain classified until white reflective stripes have been painted on what few roads they have out there? Get the governor on the phone for me immediately," Hammer ordered Windy. "He's probably in his office. Tell whoever answers that it's urgent."

Windy returned to her desk and rang up the governor's office, knowing it would do no good. The governor never returned Hammer's calls and had not met with her once since he appointed her. Windy had learned to fabricate elaborate excuses for her inability to get the governor to respond to Hammer. "One thing's for sure," Windy often told the other secretaries and clerks when they were outside on smoking breaks, "a stitch in the hand is worth two in the butt," which was her way of saying that by fudging to her boss, Windy was taking preventive measures so she didn't get her ass kicked when she had to tell Hammer that the governor, as usual, couldn't be bothered with his female state police superintendent.

Windy's acquaintances and colleagues had long since stopped correcting Windy's malapropisms, and by now, no matter how badly she

mangled a cliché, most people knew what she meant and, in fact, became vague about what the cliché was supposed to be and ended up
reciting the mangled ones. This was maddening to Hammer, who was repeatedly subjected to her staff *writing off into the sunset* or accusing someone of *marching to a different color.*

"Superintendent Hammer?" Windy hovered in the doorway. "I'm
sorry, but the governor can't be reached at the moment. Apparently,
he's in transition."

Hammer looked up from a stack of reports and memos she was reviewing. "What do you mean, he's in *transition?*"

"Traveling somewhere. Maybe even walking back to the mansion. I'm
not sure."

"He's in *transit?*"

"Or on his way there, I guess." Windy got more tangled up in her fib.
"But I don't think anybody can reach him right now, to cut to the point.
So it's not just you."

"Of course it's just me!" Hammer looked at the VASCAR memo
again, wondering how she would handle the administration's latest and
perhaps most damaging lamebrain decision. "He's not going to talk to me
and you can stop trying to make me feel better about it."

"Well, it's not nice of him." Windy put her hands on her hips. "And I
hope you won't get mad at me just because of how he treats you. It's not
fair to shoot the messenger."

Kill the messenger, Hammer irritably thought. You *shoot* the piano
player and *kill* the messenger. My God, I can't stop thinking in clichés!
And I hate clichés!

"One of the men I was dating last month told me that the only reason the governor appointed you is because he's always getting bad press
about all our highway problems and needs someone he can pass the
scapegoat to," Windy said, "and I don't think you should blame yourself
for that or take it personal."

Hammer could not believe she had inherited such a hairball for a secretary. If only it weren't so difficult to fire state employees. No wonder
the last superintendent had retired early with a heart condition and

Parkinson's disease, but what the hell had been on his mind when he hired Windy Brees? For starters, how do you get past her name? And it should have been apparent the first time she opened her mouth that she was an embarrassment and incompetent, a perky little idiot caked with makeup who minced about, tilting her head this way and that in an attempt to appear submissive and cute and in need of powerful men to take care of her.

It was past 6:00 P.M., and Hammer packed up her briefcase and headed home. She drove through downtown feeling certain that VASCAR was going to ruin her career and there didn't seem to be a thing she could do about it. Was it merely coincidental that the very day Andy launched a website that was supposed to make the state police look good, the governor had decided to launch a program that would make the state police look bad? Was it mere chance that Andy had rather much slammed Tangier Island by indicating that it had once been a nest for pirates, and now the governor was going after the Islanders? Not to mention, she was desperately short of helicopter pilots and the few troopers left in the aviation unit needed to spend their time looking for criminals and marijuana fields, as opposed to tracking speeders on a tiny island or elsewhere.

Hammer brooded about Andy as she continued working herself into a state of fulminating paranoia. She should never have allowed him to write his Internet essays uncensored. But that had been part of the agreement.

"I'm not doing it if you edit me," he had told her last year. "One obvious reason for anonymity is that no one knows what Trooper Truth is going to say or has any control over it, otherwise the truth would be lost. If you read my essays before they're posted on the Internet, Superintendent Hammer, then I know very well what you'll do. You're going to start worrying about criticisms, blame, and political problems. That's what bureaucrats focus on, unfortunately. Not that I'm calling you a bureaucrat."

"Of course that's what you're calling me," she had said, deeply offended.

And maybe he was right, Hammer dismally thought as she followed East Broad Street toward her restored neighborhood of Church Hill. Maybe she *was* turning into a bureaucrat who was far too consumed by what people thought and said about her. What had happened to her firm but diplomatic way of dealing with complaints and demands from the public?

She called Andy on her cell phone. "We have a potential emergency," she told him. "The governor wants to put speed traps on Tangier Island and all hell's going to break loose."

"I heard about it," he said.

"How?" She was startled.

"I wish you had said something to me," Andy added in frustration as he sat in front of his computer, going through the hundreds of e-mails Trooper Truth had gotten so far this day. "I didn't even have a clue until Miss Friend sent me an e-mail. I may need an assistant. I'll never keep up with all the mail I'm getting," he declared as his computer announced *you've got mail!* four more times.

"VASCAR wasn't my idea, for God's sake!" Hammer replied. "And who is Miss Friend? The focus right now should be on these outrageous hijackings and assaults—not on speeding! Andy, I need your help with this. We've got to figure out what to do."

"There's only one thing to do," he said as he typed. "I'll go to Tangier Island myself and paint a speed trap and see what the response is. Better I should do it than someone else, and I can use Trooper Truth to counter any negativity directed at you and the state police, and I'll show the public what a bad idea VASCAR is, and maybe the governor will drop the damn program and let us work real crimes. All I need is a couple cans of reflective, fast-drying paint, a brush, a helicopter, and a little time to appropriately revise tomorrow's essay on mummies."

"What the hell do mummies have to do with anything?" Hammer protested.

Mummies

by Trooper Truth

Like most people, I grew up watching mummies in horror films. Having done a lot of archaeological research of late, I can tell you, the reader, that these terrifying depictions of a living dead person bound in strips of cloth aren't accurate—or fair.

Mummies can't hurt us unless they spread an infectious disease from antiquity, which isn't likely, although I suspect you could suffer an adverse respiratory reaction after inhaling layers of dust in a creepy, cold place. I suppose you could injure yourself while looking for a mummy or find yourself lost deep inside a pyramid and die of thirst and starvation, or you could certainly encounter a grave robber and get into a violent altercation.

In death investigation, the term *mummy* refers to a dead person whose body has been exposed to extreme cold or aridness. Instead of decomposing, the body dries out and can remain in this state of preservation for decades or hundreds of years. This type of mummy, which typically shows up in cellars or the desert, is not a true mummy, but you can rest assured that anthropologists and others will refer to dried-out bodies as mummified because the term is here to stay. I will admit that it probably sounds better for an expert witness to say a victim was mummified than to admit that the poor soul was shriveled up and dried out and looked like a skeleton covered with shoe leather.

The word *mummy* is derived from the Arabic word for bitumen, which in the original Persian form meant *wax*. So *mummy* is a substance such as bitumen, which is a type of asphalt used in Asia Minor, and *a mummy* is a person or animal that has been preserved by artificial means, although it would not be accurate in modern times to refer to an embalmed body as a mummy. The reason for this is simple. Bodies embalmed with formaldehyde are not necessarily well preserved. If you dig up an embalmed body a hundred years later, depending on where it was buried, you are probably going to find that the dead person isn't as well preserved as a thousand-year-old Egyptian mummy.

In our society, we do not fill the embalmed person's belly with pure myrrh, cassia, and other perfumes, nor do we stuff bitumen into the limbs or steep the body in the mineral natron for seventy days before tightly binding it in strips of flaxen cloth that are then smeared with gum, which is what the Egyptians often used instead of glue. A modern embalmed body is not placed inside a human-shaped wooden case that is leaned up against a wall inside a cool, dry sepulcher.

I'm not saying that you couldn't preserve your dead loved one in this ancient manner, assuming you are able to find a trained scribe to mark the body for the embalming incision and then a practitioner called a *ripper up* to assist with a sharp Ethiopian stone before he flees because the Egyptians considered it a crime for anyone to physically violate the dead, even if the ripper up was legitimately hired to do so, according to the Greek historian Diodorus. And assuming you're willing to pay for it, a deluxe embalming in the Egyptian fashion costs about one talent of silver, which is approximately four hundred U.S. dollars, depending on inflation and the exchange rate.

Not so long ago, my interest in mummies led me to Argentina where scientists were in the midst of doing numerous tests on them, such as MRIs, CAT scans, and DNA needle biopsies. I got in touch with *National Geographic* to see if I might be allowed to visit the mummies, and I was told, "Okay," as long as I didn't say a word about it until after the cover story was published.

It was a cool, bright morning when I arrived in Salta, a city in northwestern Argentina that has become a center of archaeological investigations of Inca and other pre-Columbian Indian cultures. There I joined the archaeologists who had headed the expedition on an Andean volcano peak on the Argentine–Chilean border, where they had discovered three perfectly preserved five-hundred-year-old mummies of Inca children who had been offered as ritual sacrifices and buried with gold, silver, and pots of food. The archaeologists took me in a Jeep along a dusty road to Catholic University, where a small building had been turned into a temporary laboratory that was heavily patrolled by guards armed with machine guns. Grave robbers, like pirates, have remained a constant threat to our society, even in remote locations.

As I watched the archaeologists carry the first small bundle from a freezer and set it on a paper-covered examination table, I realized that unwrapping the frozen remains of two Inca girls and a boy who had been killed half a millennium ago was not unlike my working car accidents and violent crime scenes. The major difference is that in archaeology, the artifacts and causes of death are studied with no thought of bringing anyone to justice, but rather to interpret a mysterious and elusive past, which in this case was that of a people who had no written language but revealed their history through elaborate textile weaving and art. I confess that I didn't care much about diseases, diets, costumes, and customs, but was preoccupied with whether the Inca children had been unconscious, due to altitude and ritual alcoholic drinks like *chicha* (corn beer), when they were buried alive.

I wondered what the two girls and boy thought when they were dressed in fine woven outfits, feathered headdresses, and jewelry, and taken by processions up 22,057 feet to the summit of Mount Llullail-laco. I hoped they didn't know what was happening when they were wrapped in cloth and placed sitting up in deep graves that the Incas finally filled with rocks and earth in hopes that the gods would be pleased.

I can still envision the faces of those three murdered children, especially the boy, who was possibly around eight years old when he was dressed in fur-trimmed moccasins and a silver bracelet, and sent on his journey to the Afterlife with two extra pairs of sandals and a sling for hunting. His expression was one of distress and protest, and his knees were drawn in a fetal position, his ankles tightly bound with cord. I suspected he had been alert and none too happy about his role in religion, and I had a bad feeling that he resisted and was awake as he was smothered with soil and stone. The girls, possibly eight and fourteen, were not bound and looked rather placid, but oddly, one of their graves had been struck by lightning, and when the little mummy was unwrapped in the makeshift lab in Salta, I could still smell the odor of burned human flesh. It seemed to me that the Almighty had let the Incas know that He wasn't pleased in the least about their burying little children alive.

Not much ever changes, I'm sorry to say. Continuing to research our past, I spent time at the Jamestown excavation site and made pilgrimages to Great Britain, trying to connect the First Settlers with those who had gotten stalled in the Thames. I explored Isle of Dogs downriver mud, marshes, bars and car parks, and the Millennium Dome that rises like a giant poached egg spiked with gold-painted cranes, but I could find no trace of John Smith or his fellow travelers and not one living person who could remember a thing.

Nor did anyone in the pubs and alehouses I visited seem remotely impressed with the little-known fact that Tangier Island has an Isle of Dogs connection because Tangier was discovered by Captain John Smith in 1608.

What I'm leading up to, my new reader friends, is unfortunate news.

Isle of Dogs

Tangier Island has been discovered again, and not just by tourists interested in crab cakes. Unseemly people in power have decided to use the simple Islanders to make political points, and this is unfair, regardless of the watermen's tainted pirate past. I will address this in unvarnished detail soon.

Be careful out there!

Four

ammer closed the Trooper Truth file in frustration and befuddlement. What did Andy think he was doing? What did mummies and Jamestown have to do with current problems in Virginia and crime?

This was all most inappropriate and destined to cause nothing but problems, she thought as she slammed a drawer shut and wished someone knew how to make decent coffee in this place. How was she supposed to feel after reading his mummy essay?

It was a few minutes past eight and everyone at headquarters, it seemed, was reading Trooper Truth and the comments were an audible buzz in offices up and down the halls. Hammer had been shocked and unnerved when she'd heard *Billy Bob in the Morning* talking about the mummy essay on the radio as she was driving to work.

"Hey! Guess what we're gonna do! We're gonna start a contest right here on *Billy Bob in the Morning*. Our listeners out there can call us up with a guess about who the real Trooper Truth is. Cool? And whoever gets it right wins a special prize that we'll figure out later. Wow! Look at that! Our switchboard's already lighting up. Hello? This is Billy Bob In The Morning. You're on the air, and who's this?"

"Windy."

Hammer couldn't believe it when her secretary's high-pitched voice had drifted out of the car radio. Based on the poor connection, Hammer assumed Windy was calling on her cell phone, probably from her car as she drove to work.

"So tell us, Windy, who's Trooper Truth?"

"I think it's the governor, only he probably has a ghost pen."

Hammer fussed with paperwork at her desk, her ear trained toward Windy's adjoining office. The minute the secretary blew through the door and dropped her lunch bag on the desk, Hammer jumped up from her chair and swooped in on her.

"How could you do such a numbskull thing?" Hammer demanded. "And what the hell is a ghost pen?"

"Oh!" Windy was thrilled but a bit taken aback by Hammer's ire. "You must have heard me on the radio! Don't worry, I just said I was Windy and didn't give my last name or say where I work. What ghost pen? Oh yeah. You know, someone who gets someone else to secretly write for him, probably because he's not a good writer."

"I think you have ghost writer and pen name mixed up," Hammer said with controlled fury as she paced in front of Windy's desk and then thought to shut the outer door. "Don't I have enough trouble with the governor without you calling up a goddamn radio station and accusing him of being Trooper Truth?"

"How do you know he's not?" Windy touched up her lipstick.

"This isn't about how I know or don't know anything. It's about indiscretion and poor judgment, Windy."

"I bet you know who Trooper Truth is," Windy said coyly, giving Hammer a little flutter of heavily mascara-coated eyelashes. "Come on. Tell me. I just bet the band you know exactly who he is. Is he cute? How old is he? Is he single?"

Before this moment, Hammer had given little thought to what it might feel like if people started asking her if she knew who Trooper Truth was. It wasn't her nature to lie unless an arrest or confession required it, or she was leaving for a trip and hid the suitcases and assured Popeye she'd be right back. Why Hammer would think of Popeye this very moment was hard to say, but images of her beloved Boston Terrier, who had been stolen during the summer, knocked Hammer hard and forced her to retreat into her private office, where she shut the door and took deep breaths. Tears welled up inside her.

"Hammer," she brusquely said when her private line rang.

"It's Andy."

She could barely hear him and sniffed loudly, steadying herself.

"We've got a terrible connection," Hammer said. "Are you on the island?"

"Roger. Just letting you know we landed at oh-eight-hundred. . . . I'm on Janders Road. Figured that might be a good one . . . not as heavily traveled as . . . and . . . stupid . . . who cares . . . ?"

"You're breaking up, Andy," Hammer said. "And we've got to talk about this morning's essay. I can't believe it. This can't continue. Hello? Hello? Are you there?"

The line was dead.

"Dammit!" Hammer muttered.

Tangier Island had no cell antennas and few of the watermen used cell phones or the Internet or cared a whit about Trooper Truth. But it wasn't lost on any of the Islanders that a state police helicopter had chopped in from the bay and landed at the airstrip only an hour ago. Ginny Crockett, for one, had been looking out her window ever since. She took a moment to feed her cat, Sookie, and when she returned to the living room of her neat, pink-painted house, she saw a state trooper in his gray uniform and big hat painting a wide, bright white line across the broken pavement of Janders Road. The inexplicable and ominous stripe began right in front of The What Not Shop on the other side of weeds pushing up through broken pavement and was headed straight for the family cemetery in Ginny's front yard.

Water ran coolly in her crab farm's three steel tanks just off the porch in the shade of crab-apple trees. Peelers—as blue crabs in the process of shedding their shells are called—were out of season and would not be looking up at tourists with resentful telescope eyes the rest of this year. But that didn't stop Ginny from posting a sign and charging tourists a quarter to take a peek at the big jimmy, or male crab, she kept in one of the tanks. In fact, she had named the crab "Jimmy," and so far he had earned her twenty dollars and fifty cents. Maybe that trooper was only pretending to be painting the road so he could spy on her. The authorities were always snooping, it seemed, to find out if people like Ginny were paying taxes on the revenue their entrepreneurial activities earned.

The Islanders had learned over the decades that tourists would buy anything. All you had to do was nail together a little wooden box, saw a slit in its top, set it somewhere, and post a notice saying what you were selling and giving its price. The most popular items were recipes and street maps written and drawn by hand and photocopied on colorful paper.

Ginny walked to her chainlink fence to get a closer look at the trooper working his way across the street with a wide brush and a can of special paint that, based on what Ginny could make out on the label, promised to be waterproof, to dry quickly, and to glow in the dark. He was a young, handsome fellow moving slowly in a crablike fashion, and to give him credit, he didn't appear to be enjoying himself very much.

"You hadn't orte do that!" Ginny complained that no one should be painting up the road. "It ain't fittin'!" she added loudly in the odd, musical way the people of Tangier have expressed themselves since emigrating from England centuries ago and remaining in a tightly closed population on their speck of an island.

Andy fixed dark glasses on her and noticed right off that she had the worst dentures he had ever seen. When he had stopped off in The What Not Shop earlier to buy Evian, he had noticed two other island women inside, and they also had terrible dental work.

"Does your island have a dentist?" Andy asked the old woman who was watching him suspiciously from the other side of her chainlink fence.

"Ever week he come in from the main," she reluctantly replied, because the dentist was a sore subject and all her neighbors tended to deal with it by denying what was obvious.

"The same one been coming here for a while?" Andy asked from his squatting position on the street. He had stopped painting for a moment.

"Yea. One and the same been coming to Tanger for so long, I disremember when," she replied, more self-conscious than unfriendly now, her lips crinkled like crepe paper around big, fakey teeth.

"There are a lot of bad dentists out there," Andy said gently. "Everybody I've seen here so far has clearly had an astonishing amount of dental work, ma'am, and although it's none of my business, maybe you folks ought to consider getting a different dentist or at least having the one you use thoroughly investigated."

His comment and his bright, perfect, natural teeth cut Ginny to the wick, which was Tangier talk for saying something went deep and caused excruciating pain. It wasn't that the Islanders didn't quietly gossip at gatherings about the visiting dentist. But without him, they would have no one.

"I don't suppose you read Trooper Truth," Andy said to her as he resumed painting the stripe. "But he has some interesting things to say about facing the truth and, in fact, demanding truth. But the only way you get truth, ma'am, is to stare what you fear straight in the eye, whether it's a mummy or a shifty, harmful dentist."

Ginny was unnerved and had no idea what to make of this young trooper with his kind ways that didn't seem to fit with his threatening uniform and his trespassing and violating the road in front of her house.

"Now, don't you be throwing off about the stripe like you ain't paintin' it right afore my very eyes," she declared, changing the subject.

"I'm not," Andy said. "I have to paint this speed trap—on the orders of the governor, ma'am."

Ginny had never heard of such a thing and was instantly inflamed.

There were fewer than twenty gas-powered land vehicles on the entire island, most of them rusting pickup trucks used for hauling things. Pretty much everybody either walked or got around on golf carts, scooters, mopeds, or bicycles. Tangier was less than three miles long and not even a mile wide. Only six hundred and fifty people lived here, and why would the governor care if one of them got a little frisky in his golf cart? Life was slow on the island. Roads were barely wider than footpaths, few of them paved, and one wrong turn could send you headlong into a marsh. Speeding on land had never been a community problem, and in fact, Ginny had never heard of the mayor or the town council taking up this particular issue.

"Well, theys many a road on the main and you don't need to be a painting up ours. Doncha stop that? Afore you're going to catch it, young feller!"

Andy wasn't sure what the island woman had just said to him, but he detected a threat.

"Just doing my job," he said, dipping the brush in the paint can.

"What happen you drive over it?" Ginny pointed at the wet painted line on the road.

"Nothing yet," Andy explained in an ominous tone, in hopes he might encourage the woman to complain and provide him with a few good quotes for the next Trooper Truth essay. "I've got to paint another one exactly a quarter of a mile from this one. Then when our helicopters patrol the island, the pilots can time how long it takes for a vehicle to get from stripe to stripe. VASCAR will tell us exactly how fast you're going."

"Heee! Jiminy Criminy! They going to bring NASCAR here to Tangier?" Ginny was shocked.

"VASCAR," Andy repeated, and he was thrilled that Virginians might confuse VASCAR with NASCAR. "It refers to a computer that knows if you're speeding."

"Then what?" Ginny still didn't understand, and her mind was roaring with stock cars and drunken fans.

"Then a trooper on the ground goes after the speeder and gives him a citation."

"What he gonna to recite at us?" Ginny envisioned the young trooper in his big hat and dark glasses sternly reprimanding some poor Tangierman on his bicycle, probably pointing his finger, trying to scare him as the trooper recited something like one of those Miranda warnings Ginny was always hearing about on programs she picked up on the satellite dish that was surrounded by glass balls and other yard ornaments.

"A ticket," Andy went on in a stern voice. "You know what a ticket is?" His paintbrush found the edge of the pavement, mere inches from Ginny's fence and all the dead family members whose headstones were worn smooth and tilting in different directions. "We write you a ticket and then you go down to the courthouse and pay a fine. Cash or check."

He knew very well that Tangier Island did not have a bank, and a check, in this old woman's mind, was what the Coast Guard was always doing or what the tourists got when they ate the crab cakes and corn pudding at Hilda Crockett's Chesapeake House.

"How much you make us pay when we get warranted, if we do?" Ginny was getting increasingly alarmed.

Andy stood up and stretched his aching back as he struggled to decipher what the woman had just said to him. Then he recalled his visit to The What Not Shop right before he had started painting the stripe and overhearing two Tangier women whispering about him and saying something about someone being warranted and that they couldn't fathom who had done what, but it was probably *that Shores boy who live cross from the school. He's got more mouth than a sheep and here his daddy's poor as Job's turkey. That's right, Hattie. Durn if his daddy don't foller the water even when it's the dog days while that Mr. Nutters a his can't be learned nothing. Spends all his time progging, he does. Well, I swanny, Fonny Boy ain't neither smarter than a ticky crab, Lula.*

So *warranted*, Andy figured, must mean getting arrested, and according to Hattie and Lula, there was some island kid named Fonny Boy Shores who wasn't much help at home, had a smart mouth, didn't study, and preferred to spend his time wading along the shore and looking for things with a stick instead of contributing honest wages to his poor family.

"Fines for speeding depend on how many miles over the limit you were going," Andy informed the unhappy island woman.

He didn't let on for a moment that he thought it was appalling to hand out citations based on ground speed checked from the air. Planes and helicopters had neither radar guns nor good views of license tags, and he could just imagine a pilot calculating the speed of a northbound white compact car, for example, and radioing a trooper in his marked car to go after the offender. The trooper would roar out from behind shrubbery in the median strip and flash and wail after the most likely northbound white compact car, selecting the vehicle from a scattered pack of white compact cars whizzing along the interstate. What a waste of Jet-A fuel, taxpayers' money, and time.

"It's three dollars for every mile over, plus thirty dollars for court costs," Andy summarized. "What's your name, by the way?"

"Why you want to know for?" Ginny backed up a step, threatened.

"Do you ever use the Internet?"

She stared mutely at him.

"No, it's not something you catch fish with," Andy said, slightly frustrated and disappointed. "I don't guess you have PCs or modems out here." He glanced around at small clapboard houses that lined the deteriorating road and eyed several golf carts bumping along in the distance. "Never mind about the Internet," he added. "But I would like to know your name, and if you give it to me I can e-mail it to Trooper Truth so he can quote you and let the world know what you think of the governor's new speed trap initiative."

Ginny was baffled.

"It might bring more tourists to your crab tanks." He pointed at them. "Those quarters add up, don't they?"

"It's well and all if I get me a quarter now and again," Ginny said, trying to dilute her private tax-free enterprise. "But this time of year, there are neither pailers to show for a quarter, and all I got is a jimmy right in the tank there. Now, he's a right big feller, but times is slow and soon enough strangers will take thesselves other places and won't be coming here."

"You never know. Nothing like publicity. Maybe things will pick up a bit." Andy tried to coax her into giving him her name. "People read about your big jimmy and they'll line up to take a look."

Ginny gave in and told the trooper who she was because she sensed he wasn't a revenuer but had other legal matters on his mind, and quarters did add up. A lot of people these days, it was her observation, didn't think twice about tossing away quarters, dimes, and nickels and, of course, pennies. Not that she was fond of pennies, not hardly. Everyone on the island was always trying to unload their pennies on their neighbors. The little brown coins circulated nonstop and it had gotten to the point that Ginny recognized individual pennies, and knew she'd been had when she shopped for groceries and was given an inordinate number of familiar pennies for change.

"I don't want neither pennies," she was constantly chiding Daisy Eskridge, the cashier at the island's only market.

"Well, now, honey, I'm not trying to put them on you, but I have to give 'em out," Daisy replied last time Ginny complained. "Leastways I do since Wheezy Parks was in here buying some flour and soap and give me mor'n four hundred pennies. I said I'd give her tick, but she was of a mind to chuck her pennies, and I can't be fitting all them pennies in my drawer, Ginny."

Ginny was still annoyed with Wheezy, who always refused to buy things on credit and was the island's biggest offender when it came to passing unwanted pennies. There was a pervasive and shameful rumor circulating along with the pennies that Wheezy was opening the money boxes late at night and exchanging her pennies for quarters, nickels, and dimes. Then, to make matters worse, the conniving woman was always getting rid of the rest of her pennies at every opportunity. Why, Wheezy probably had most of the silver change on the island—probably stashed in socks under her bed.

"So, Ms. Crockett, ten miles over is thirty dollars plus court costs." The trooper was explaining a very complicated legal process, and Ginny drifted away from pennies and focused on him again. "Fifteen is reckless driving and the person could go to jail."

"Lordy! You can't throw us in the jail!" Ginny protested.

She was right, but not entirely. No one could be locked up on the island, which had neither a courthouse nor a jail. This clearly meant that anyone caught speeding would be deported to the mainland. The suggestion of such a thing excited primitive fears throughout the island the instant Ginny hurried down Janders Road and cut over to Spanky's Place, where Dipper Pruitt was spooning out homemade vanilla ice cream for three quiet Amish tourists in long dresses and hairnets.

"They's gonna lock all us in the jail on the main!" Ginny exclaimed. "They's gonna turn the island into a racetrack!"

The Amish women smiled shyly, counting out coveted silver change from tiny black purses, placing one shiny coin at a time on the counter, making not a sound. Ginny didn't see tourists from Pennsylvania often, and always marveled at the way they dressed and acted and how pale their skin was. They could sail for hours on the Chesapeake Breeze or the Captain Eulice ferries and walk around the island all day without getting sunburned, windblown, or cold. They never helped themselves to porch rocking chairs, sat on gravestones, looked in the crab tanks without paying, or made comments about the exotic way the Islanders talked. Ginny had never heard a single Amish person complain about Tangier's ban of alcohol or the early curfews that discouraged nightlife and swearing and made sure the watermen were home with their families and in bed early. If all strangers were like people from Pennsylvania, Ginny and her neighbors might not resent them quite so much.

"God-a-mighty! Who say we going to the jail?" Dipper wanted to know as she rinsed off ice cream paddles in a basin of tepid water. "And what they say we did?"

"Going too fast in the golf carts," Ginny replied as the Amish women silently walked back out into the cool, damp morning. "The police is painting stripes to warrant each and ever one of us with helichoppers. By and by they gonna make us leave for good so they can have NASCAR and make a barrel!"

Within the hour, the entire fleet of white work boats the Islanders called bateaus was speeding back in from the island's guts and criks and the wide-open Chesapeake Bay. Small outboard motors hissed and sputtered like radiators as the watermen worked the throttles to the limit, responding to the threatening news about jails and NASCAR and the trooper's insulting comments about the Islanders' dental work. A spotter plane was diverted from its quest for schools of fish bait and began circling Janders Road at a low altitude, careful not to get too close to the rusting crane that rose from the south hook of the island, near the waste-treatment plant and the airstrip made of dredge.

Fortunately for Andy, the paint dried almost instantly, and therefore the growing crowd of unhappy women and children armed with garden hoses and buckets of water had little effect on his work. But he was getting nervous and having second thoughts about stirring up the locals to get them to offer truthful opinions for the sake of his essays. Maybe he shouldn't have let Trooper Macovich wait in the helicopter. Maybe this assignment was too dangerous to carry out alone. Andy hurried up with the stripe he was painting in front of the Gladstone Memorial Health Center, where Dr. Sherman Faux was drilling another tooth in Fonny Boy's mouth.

Five

Governor Crimm's morning was not going well so far. He had gotten lost on his way down to breakfast and ended up in one of the mansion's parlors again, where he sat patiently in a Windsor chair waiting for Pony, the butler, to pour coffee from the antique spout lamp into the chamber stick on top of the nearby Chippendale lowboy. Crimm had misplaced the silver magnifying glass that he faithfully kept on the marble fireplace mantle in the master suite.

"Where am I?" he said, just in case someone might be nearby. "I don't want ham this morning and I must have my coffee. Pony? Come in here immediately! Why is it so chilly? I feel a draft."

"Oh dear!" First Lady Maude Crimm's voice floated into the parlor. "Is that you, Bedford?"

"Who the hell else would it be?" the governor thundered. "Who took my magnifying glass? I think someone is taking it on purpose so I can't see what everybody is up to."

"You always think that, dear." Mrs. Crimm's heavy perfume entered the room, and her bedroom slippers whispered across the Brussels carpet. "There's no conspiracy, precious," she lied as her blurry form bent over and kissed the top of his balding head.

There was a conspiracy and the First Lady knew it. She had an incurable addiction to collectibles, and her husband's failing eyesight and the Internet had, at long last, granted her ample opportunity to succumb to her vice. Most recently, Maude Crimm hadn't been able to resist trivets, for example, and over the past few months, she had procured scores of them with turned handles, cherubs, lacy circles, tulips, grapes, scrolls, and "God Bless Our Home," some of them cast iron, some brass. When she was pecking away on the computer earlier this morning, while the governor was snoring in bed and clenching his teeth, she had come across a wonderful buffed star-and-braid trivet that she could not stop thinking about.

Her philosophy about shopping was to exercise restraint now and then by walking away from whatever she wanted, whether it was a new dress or a trivet, and see if the desired item continued to call out to her. If it did, then the purchase was imminent and meant to be. Her husband did not share her philosophy and she had learned to keep her acquisitions out of sight, a task that was getting increasingly easier. All the same, his blind peregrinations throughout the mansion were becoming a great concern. One of these days, she feared, he was going to walk into one of the linen closets and clank into the growing stack of antique trivets on the heart-of-pine floor. The First Lady did not need another one of her husband's tirades. He hadn't yet gotten over her last collecting spree, when thirty-eight early nineteenth-century wick trimmers and a rare Monarch Teenie-Weenie toffee tin were delivered to the mansion. Of course, this was over a period of several days. Mrs. Crimm was clever enough not to order everything at once and to stagger the deliveries with Federal Express.

"Did you check the Lafayette Room?" Mrs. Crimm asked her husband. "Sometimes your magnifying glass ends up in there on the Sheraton chest next to the oil lamp. I believe I may have seen it near the two-part mirror the other day, now that I think of it."

"Why would it end up in the Lafayette Room?" the governor sullenly responded. "We only let other governors and former presidents sleep in there. Someone's hiding it from me. What is it you don't want me to see around here?" he demanded as he got up from the spindly old chair.

"You know I never want you to not see anything, dear," she replied as she led him out of the parlor. "However, I did happen to read that dangerous Trooper Truth this morning. I don't suppose you've seen what he put on his website again?" she added to divert his attention.

"What?" the governor followed her and bumped into a tilt-top tea table in a sitting room, jostling a finger lamp. "Did you print it out?"

"Of course I did," Mrs. Crimm gravely said. "Since you can't find your magnifying glass, I'll have to read it to you. But I fear it will aggravate you, Bedford, and upset your submarine again."

The governor did not appreciate his wife's openly discussing his submarine, which was their pet name for his constitution.

"Who's here?" he asked, squinting about, making sure no one was within earshot.

"Nobody's here, precious. Just you and me and we're almost to the breakfast room. There, turn right and watch out for the lithograph. Oops! Here, I'll straighten it."

He heard something scrape as she rearranged the lithograph he had just knocked with his large nose.

"I bang my head on that damn thing one more time," he threatened as he shuffled into the breakfast room and groped for a chair. "What is it of, anyway?"

"William Penn's treaty with the Indians." Mrs. Crimm shook out a linen napkin and tucked it into the collar of her husband's dress shirt, which was buttoned crooked and did not match his paisley suspenders, green velvet vest, or striped necktie.

"This is not Philadelphia and I fail to see why William Penn should be inside the mansion," the governor said. "Since when did that happen?"

Clearly, he had forgotten his wife's fleeting passion for lithographs, if he had ever known about it. The governor sighed as Pony materialized with the coffee pot.

"Good morning, sir," Pony said as he poured.

"No it's not, Pony. No, indeed. The world's going to hell in a handbasket."

"It most certainly is, sir," Pony agreed with a sympathetic nod of the head. "I tell you, I thought the world already went to hell in a handbasket a long time ago, but I was wrong. I sure was. Things is just getting more messed up, that's right. It's enough to make a man want to run down to the church and beg God Hisself to please, please help us out of our misery and forgive our sins and our enemies and make people behave. What wrong with folks anyway?

"You know, the other day when them caters showed up for that big dinner of yours?" Pony went on. "I was minding my own business getting them tea and I heard one of 'em say to the other, 'I wonder if I could take one of these little teacups that's got the Com'wealth of Virginia on it. What you think?' 'I don't know why not,' the other one say. 'You pay tax, don't you?' 'I sure do,' say the other lady cater. 'And nothing in here belong to the Crimm family anyhow. It belong to all of us.' 'Well, if that isn't the God's truth. It belong to us.'

"Then," Pony went on, getting more animated as his tale wore on, "both them caters stuffed their teacups in them big handbags of theirs, can you believe that?"

"Why on earth . . . ?" the First Lady sputtered in shock and disgust. "Why didn't you stop them, for heaven's sake! I certainly hope they didn't take the handleless cups and saucers, those lovely pearlware ones with the Leeds floral design."

"Oh, no, ma'am," Pony assured her. "It was the ones with handles and the Com'wealth logo on 'em in gold."

"You shouldn't be serving tea to caterers, to begin with," Mrs. Crimm reprimanded Pony. "And certainly not in official tea cups. Caterers are common workers, not VIP guests of the mansion, oh dear me." She looked at the governor for support as he slopped coffee on the table cloth and missed the saucer when he set down the cup. "We really must stop being so generous with the public, Bedford. Why, I suppose next thing, some taxi driver or toll collector will show up at the guard gate and demand a private tour which includes tea in official china!"

"The mansion doesn't belong to us," the governor reminded her, and dark thoughts crowded together like unfriendly people on an elevator as the door to his patience slid shut and his mood began to descend. "Any person off the street could come here and ask for a tour, if the truth be known. But that doesn't mean we have to do it or that they can make us. The public doesn't know this is their legal right and I'm not about to tell them. Now read that damn essay to me, Maude."

He was desperately hoping there would be another riddle today that might guide him through the thickets that seemed to be closing in on him from all sides.

"Mummies," she said, peering over reading glasses and scanning the printout. "You know, I've always been rather frightened by mummies, too. I had no idea anyone else felt the same way. But what is all this about Tangier Island? It's the second time Trooper Truth has mentioned it. What's going on out there, Bedford?"

"Would you like grits or hash browns with your eggs?" Pony politely inquired.

"I didn't know we were having eggs," the governor replied.

"I told him poached eggs," Mrs. Crimm informed her husband as she smoothed her dressing gown over her ample lap. "I thought that might be soothing. Nothing like bland food when your submarine's out of sorts."

Governor Crimm's mind, like his constitution, was submerging without any clear direction. He scarcely heard another word his wife said or read as he moved closer to a suspicion that soon enough became a conviction. There was an encrypted message in what Trooper Truth had written about mummies, and Crimm suddenly remembered that as a child, he had called his mother "Mummy."

Lutilla Crimm had conceived her oldest son in a wealthy section of Charlottesville called Farmington during a terrible snowstorm. Crimm dimly conjured up what he could remember hearing about that event, and it seemed that when his father would get annoyed with his wife, he would make snide asides to little Bedford about never allowing a woman to run and ruin his life.

"They're full of mendacity, women are," Bedford's father would say when the two of them were carrying in logs for the wood-burning stove or shoveling snow off the brick sidewalk in front of their imposing brick house that rose before a backdrop of mountains. "They'll sweet-talk you, son, and make you think they're right desperate to have sex with you, then when they've got you wrapped around their fingers and saddled down with kids, guess what?"

"What?" Bedford had begun giving voice to what would become his most frequently asked question.

"What?" echoed his father. "I'll tell you *what!* They'll suddenly announce that the ceiling needs to be replastered or the molding is crumbling or there are cobwebs hanging from the chandelier, right when you're in the middle of . . ."

"Oh," Bedford replied as he dumped split logs into the bin by the stove.

"Let's just put it this way," his father went on while his wife worked on a needlepoint in her parlor upstairs. "Half of you was scattered over the quilt, son. That's probably why you're a runt with bad eyesight."

"What exactly did Mummy say?" Bedford had to know the truth. "Was she asking about the ceiling or the cobwebs?"

"Neither one. Not that night. She sat straight up in bed and said, 'Why, I don't believe I fed the cat.'"

"Had she?" young Bedford inquired, and he would never forget his dismay at learning that he would forever be visually impaired, short, and homely—all because of a cat. "Why would Mummy suddenly think of the cat at that precise moment?"

"That's exactly what I mean about women, son. They think of all kinds of things at that precise moment because they want to create a diversion." His father shoved a log into the wood stove and sparks flew up in protest. "Your mummy knew exactly what she was doing when she brought up the cat."

Since then, Bedford Crimm not only hated cats, but he also carried a pain in his heart and was deeply insecure because his mummy had committed interruptus during his conception, thus spilling much of his vitality on the quilt. She could not possibly have loved her quickening son much, Bedford mused unhappily as he picked at a poached egg he could scarcely see and groped for the pepper mill and continued to tune out his wife, who was having a stressful conversation with Pony about people who have been struck by lightning. Crimm believed he had put his unfair childhood behind him when he had become powerful in politics, and now Trooper Truth had brought it all back.

A miasma of paranoia and anger leaked through Crimm like a noxious gas, and his submarine went into alert. Somehow Trooper Truth knew the truth about the mighty governor's shameful start in life and the last thing Crimm needed was for others to find out. Oh, of course Trooper Truth knew! He knew everything. Why else would he have mentioned mummies in his essay?

"This is an outrage!" He slammed his fist down on the table and a silver candlestick toppled over into the butter dish.

The breakfast room froze in silence.

After a moment, a startled Maude Crimm said to him, "My goodness! It's a good thing that candle wasn't lit, dear, or the butter might have caught on fire. Real butter is animal fat and will burn just as easily as lighter fluid."

"Not quite as easy as that, ma'am," Pony voiced his opinion. "But don't want to take no chances." He picked up the candlestick and wiped it off with the napkin draped over his arm. "Don't want no fires in the mansion. This place would go up in flames quick as a dried-out broom, old as it is."

"Here we are talking about lightning and people's homes and clothing burning up, and then a candlestick lands in the butter," the First Lady said in a hushed, ominous tone. "I hope that's not a sign."

"Emmm emm." Pony shook his head and clucked his tongue. "I sure do hope you're right. Don't need no sign like that."

"What sign?" the governor came to and instantly thought of VASCAR and the signs Major Trader intended to post throughout the Commonwealth. "Get Trader on the phone," Crimm ordered Pony. "Tell him I want a briefing immediately on how things are going on Tangier Island. We should have that speed trap painted by now. And ask Trooper Macovich if he's figured out who Trooper Truth is yet. I'm going to find that scoundrel and silence him before he does any more damage! I don't give a hootenanny about the First Amendment!"

He pounded the table again, and Pony caught the candlestick just in time.

T.T. had not caught on to anything just in time, and Unique was certain T.T. had been more than dead by the time Unique had walked back across the footbridge last night and eventually driven off in her Miata. Even so, Unique felt a strong urge to check things out. Her memory of what had transpired after she and T.T. had gotten to the island was patchy and vague, but based on the amount of blood on her clothing she saw when she finally returned to her shabby downtown apartment, Unique had a pretty good idea of what she had done to that presumptuous, ugly woman who had been so bold as to think Unique would be interested in her or was her type at all.

She parked near Belle Island and set off in tennis shoes, carrying a Polaroid camera for what would appear to be a brisk morning nature walk. In the light of day, the island looked very different, and it took Unique a good twenty minutes to find the brick ruins where she apparently had dragged T.T.'s nude body, although Unique had no recollection of having done anything after she slashed the young woman's throat from ear to ear. Unique's pulse picked up and she felt a surge of power, excitement, and sexual arousal as she stood just inside crumbled brick walls and stared at the mutilated, bloody body lying face up in the mud.

T.T.'s eyes were partially open and dull, and her hair was clotted with blood and dirt. It disgusted Unique to think she had ever touched her lips or any part of her. She squatted and took photographs from every angle, so she could clearly remind herself of the event later without running the risk of having the film developed in a shop. She was a little surprised when she leaned in for close-ups and detected the faint scent of T.T.'s cologne, which brought back memories of a scream and then a gurgling sound as T.T. clutched her neck while Unique kicked her head before slashing her breasts and carving the name Trooper Truth across her belly. Unique was impressed that she had been clever enough to add the Trooper Truth bit. T.T. had wished she was Trooper Truth, and now she was.

"You got what you wanted," Unique said softly to the cold, gory body as she headed back to the footbridge.

She was long gone in her car when T.T.'s office began calling her home number to see why she hadn't shown up at work that morning. Unique was cruising past the blond undercover cop's row house when two women taking a walk with their babies in strollers discovered the appalling sight in the brick ruins on Belle Island at the very moment Pony pretended to discover the governor's missing magnifying glass.

Pony knew how out of sorts the governor got when he couldn't find one of his eccentric optical aids, and although the First Lady had given Pony strict instructions that he was not to make it easy for her husband to see while he was home, because of the trivets, Pony decided he needed to do something quick. He dipped into a pocket of his crisp white jacket and withdrew the silver magnifying glass, which he silently set inside a pewter compote.

"Well, I'll be!" he exclaimed. "Look what I found. Here's your magnifying glass, sir. Why you putting it in the compote for?"

Maude Crimm gave Pony the dirty look he deserved for defying her directive. She met the governor's enlarged right eye as he peered through the magnifying glass and scanned his surroundings.

"Where in thunder are the girls?" he inquired as he realized that his daughters were not sitting at the table.

"Oh, I told them they could sleep a little late this morning," their mother replied. "They stayed up late watching TV and are worn out.

Isn't that something? Your magnifying glass was in the compote. Bedford, you need to keep better track of it, dear."

"From now on, it doesn't leave me," he threatened as his wife stiffened. "From now on, I intend to see what's going on under my own roof, you hear me? I wasn't born yesterday. Oh no, I wasn't. I was born in 1929 and am no fool." He pointed a stubby finger at his wife. "You're hiding something from me, Maude."

"I most certainly am not," she lied as she worried about the trivet she had found on the Internet that morning.

Governor Crimm pushed back his chair and got up with the napkin still tucked into his collar like a misplaced cape. For the first time in his marriage, he began to entertain the suspicion that his wife might be having an affair. There could very well be another man in the mansion right this minute, and that's why someone had deliberately tucked his magnifying glass in the compote. He imagined all the men out there who would jump at the chance to sleep with a First Lady, especially his, and the governor's submarine lurched violently.

"So that's what this is about!" he declared from the arched doorway as his daughters' thick, tired feet sounded on the stairs.

He had her figured out, all right. Of course, he knew what she was doing, and he imagined her casting her bosomy, moist spell on other men. While Crimm anguished over erotic, unseemly images, the First Lady thought of her growing stash of trivets in the linen closet and panicked. Her husband somehow knew about them. Pony, meanwhile, decided it was time to brew fresh coffee and vanished without a sound as Mrs. Crimm's eyes filled with tears and her daughters' loud, slow approach drew nearer.

"Oh, will you ever forgive me, Bedford?" Mrs. Crimm begged and sniffed.

His magnifying glass caught the edge of the napkin and he yanked it out of his collar and flung it to the floor, his worst fear realized.

"Just tell me how," he said as cramps seized his submarine. "How did you find them? The phone book? Dinner parties?"

"Never at dinner parties." She was stunned that he might think she would go to a dinner party and steal a trivet. "I would never do anything that low. Nor do I need to," she added somewhat indignantly. "I found them on the Internet, if you must know. You can find anything on the Internet these days, and the temptation has been overwhelming. Oh Bedford, I just can't help myself. No matter how ashamed I feel, I know it will happen again. I suppose there are much worse flaws I could have."

"There is no worse flaw you could have! And Pony must be in on it, too," the governor said breathlessly as his submarine cut through the dark, convoluted surface of his well-being, the periscope up and spying on the enemy, which in this case was his unfaithful wife. "That scoundrel Pony had to know what you've been doing since he's here waiting on you hand and foot all day. And I doubt they've been sneaking into the mansion at night. Please don't tell me they have! That would be the most vile of degradations if you've been sneaking them in at night while I'm sleeping in the same bed! Go back upstairs this instant!" he ordered his daughters. "We're having a fight, and you know we never fight in front of you!"

"Never at night," Mrs. Crimm swore as her daughters' heavy footsteps sluggishly shuffled around and thudded back upstairs. "After I get them, they always arrive the next morning, sweet husband, and I've been hiding them in a linen closet."

"Well, you can rest assured I'll check every linen closet the moment I arrive home today," the governor thundered, and he would have checked now, but his submarine was in distress and headed straight for a mine. "And if I find them there—or even one—that's it. I mean *it*."

"You won't," she said, dabbing her eyes and calculating where she could hide the trivets after she snatched them out of the linen closet the instant he left. "I promise on my life. You can check the linen closets all you like forever, my dearest, and they'll have nothing in them but linens. All of our pretty linens, neatly pressed, folded, and stacked."

The governor broke out in a heavy cold sweat as the first explosion reverberated through his hollow organs in an awesome, foul wave and rolled with gathering momentum toward his orifice. Bedford Crimm IV's submarine armed its torpedoes and slammed shut its sphincter muscle hatch as he fled with great commotion to the nearest powder room.

Six

Once a week, Dr. Faux took the ferry to Tangier Island, where he donated his time and skills to people who had no local physicians, dentists, or veterinarians. It was his mission in life, he often said, to help the less privileged watermen and their families, who were unaware of his unusual billing practices and creative coding that routinely defrauded Virginia's Medicaid program.

Dentists, Dr. Faux thought, had no choice but to supplement their incomes at the expense of the government, and he sincerely believed that subjecting the Islanders to unnecessary or shoddy or fake procedures was only fair in light of his great sacrifice. Who else would come to this forsaken island, after all? Well, nobody, he reminded everyone he worked on or pretended to work on. He adjusted a lamp and moved a mirror around Fonny Boy's back molars.

"Seems to be a lot of commotion out there," Dr. Faux commented, deciding that the tooth he had just filled would require another root canal. "Now Fonny Boy, I strongly remind you to cut back on the soda pops. How many a day are you drinking? Be honest."

Fonny Boy held up five fingers as Dr. Faux looked out the window at all the women and children washing a mysterious painted stripe on the street.

"Entirely too many," he admonished Fonny Boy, who was fourteen, tall and lanky, with windblown sun-bleached hair and a nickname he had earned because of his funny habit of shirttailing and progging—or wading about with a stick or net, not in search of crabs but treasure. "You're clearly more susceptible to cavities than most folks," Dr. Faux pointed out the same thing he did to all of his island patients. "So I think you should at least switch to diet drinks, but preferably water."

Fonny Boy had spent most of his life on and in the water, and for him to drink it would be like a farmer eating dirt.

"Nah, I can't drink it," he said, and his numb lips and tongue felt ten times their normal size. "I'm so swolled up, I'm likete choke!"

"What about bottled water? They have some really good ones these days with fruit flavors and lots of fizz." Dr. Faux continued to stare out the window. "Why does that spotter plane keep circling overhead? And who is that soaking wet trooper with a paint bucket and a bottle of Evian and why is everybody chasing him down the street? Well, while I've got you doped up, I may as well adjust your braces."

Dr. Faux paused to jot down several codes and notes on Fonny Boy's thick dental chart.

"Nah!" Fonny Boy protested. "That gives my mouth the soreness. The braces, they are good enough save for the little rubber bands always flying out for neither good cause."

Fonny Boy had never wanted braces in the first place. Nor had he been happy when the dentist had insisted on pulling four perfectly good teeth earlier in the year. Fonny Boy hated going to the dentist and often complained to his parents that Dr. Faux was a picaroon, which was the Tangier word for pirate.

"He gave me a look at a photo of his car," Fonny Boy had said just the other day. "He got a huge black Merk and his lady got one, too, only of a different color. So how come he can have cars so dear if he works on ever one of us for neither money?"

It was a good question, but as usual, nobody took Fonny Boy seriously, and in part this was because of his nickname. His neighbors and teachers found him amusing and peculiar and loved to trade tales about his poking through the trash-strewn shore for treasure and his uncontrollable compulsion to make music.

"I swanny," Fonny Boy overheard his aunt Ginny Crockett comment after a recent Sunday prayer meeting. "He has a mind that ransacking the shore's gonna land him a barrel a silver dollars. Heee! His poor mom's always blaring at him, and I can't say as I fault her. She's done all what she can for that boy, and on back of that, I wish he's keep quite on the juice harp."

"I'm a die! He totes that juice harp everywhere and sure plays a pretty tune." Ginny's friend said the opposite of what she meant, because it was everyone's opinion that when Fonny Boy played the harmonica, which was constantly, he made nothing but an awful racket.

"His daddy ought to give him the dickens, but he's always bragging on that boy," Ginny replied, and in this instance, she meant exactly what she said, because Fonny Boy's father was hellbent on believing that his only son was the envy of the island.

"Soon as we get these braces off," Dr. Faux said as he pulled on a new pair of surgical gloves that would be billed for three times their value, "I'm going to recommend crowns for eight of your front teeth. You up for a little blood work this morning?" he added, because Dr. Faux had discovered there was quite a market for selling blood to shady medical researchers who were doing genetic studies of closed populations.

"Nah!" Fonny Boy jerked in the chair and gripped the armrests so tightly his knuckles blanched.

"Not to worry about crowns, Fonny Boy. I'll use precious alloys and you'll have a million-dollar smile!"

Just then, the old black telephone rang inside the clinic. The phone dated from the days when cords were covered with cloth insulation, and as usual, there was a lot of static.

"Clinic," Dr. Faux answered.

"I need to talk at Fonny Boy," a male voice said through loud crackling and humming over the line. "He thar?"

"That you, Hurricane?" the dentist asked Fonny Boy's father, who went by the nickname Hurricane because he had a temper like one. "You're due in for a checkup and cleaning and blood work."

"Let me talk at Fonny Boy afore the devil flies in me!"

"It's for you," Dr. Faux said to his patient.

Fonny Boy got out of the chair and took the receiver as he swatted at a lethargic fly. "Yass?"

"Look a' here! Lock up the door tight as an arster!" Fonny Boy's father said urgently. "Don't turn the dentist out! Now and again we got to do things for cussedness, honey boy. It's all what we know to do in a situation like this one here. That dentist mommucked up your mouth again?"

"Yass! He wouldn't do nothing to me, Daddy!" Fonny Boy said, which was *over the left* or talking backwards and meant, of course, that the dentist intended to mangle Fonny Boy's mouth badly.

"Well, don't you be out of heart," his father said, encouraging his son not to be depressed or discouraged. "We gonna give him a dost of his own medicine and make the example of him, and break the police of going on us all the time. We are all kin together, honey boy. Now you keep quite and we'll be right thar!"

"Oh my blessed!" Fonny Boy exclaimed as he sprang to the door and locked the deadbolt with the key hanging behind a painting of Jesus shepherding lambs.

He was not entirely clear about why he was supposed to trap Dr. Faux inside the clinic, but that durned dentist deserved what was coming and it was exciting that something was happening. Tangier was very boring for its young, and Fonny Boy had dreams of finding his fortune and one day leaving for good. He peered out the window at a crowd of watermen marching up the road in military formation, some of them armed with wooden oars and oyster tongs.

"Sit in the chair thar and mind your step!" Fonny Boy ordered the dentist.

"I need to get the cotton out of your mouth," Dr. Faux reminded his patient. "You need to sit in the chair, then I'll sit in it after we're finished, if you want." Dr. Faux supposed the lidocaine had agitated Fonny Boy and precipitated a transient nervous disorder.

Even the most experienced dentist couldn't be sure how certain drugs might affect some patients, and Dr. Faux always inquired if the person had any allergies or adverse reactions to medications. But the Islanders were so rarely sedated or subjected to even the mildest anesthesia or mood-altering substances, except for the alcohol they weren't allowed to drink, that Dr. Faux's patients were rather virginal and perfectly suited for blind studies with placebos and other concoctions that various pharmaceutical companies wanted the FDA to approve and were happy to donate to Dr. Faux for experimental purposes. The dentist slid gloved fingers around inside Fonny Boy's mouth, fishing for the cotton.

"You didn't swallow it again, did you?" Dr. Faux worried.

"Yass."

"Well, you may be a little constipated for a few days. How come you locked the door and what did you do with the key?"

Fonny Boy felt his pockets to make sure the key was safely in his custody. It was not. What did I do with it? he thought, his eyes darting around the examination room as feet and angry voices sounded from the street. Excited, Fonny Boy popped the dentist in the nose, not with malice, but with sufficient force to draw blood.

"Ouch!" Dr. Faux cried out in surprise and pain. "Now why did you do that?" he asked as the watermen yelled for Fonny Boy to unlock the door.

"I can't!" he yelled back to them. "I ain't got holt of the key! I disremembered where I put it at!"

"Why did you hit me?" Dr. Faux was shocked and upset as he dabbed his nose with a tissue.

Fonny Boy wasn't sure, but it seemed important to prove himself

through violence. He rather much liked the idea of the watermen seeing that he had used force to subdue the dentist. Certainly, his father
would be pleased, but Fonny Boy just wished he could recall what he
had done with the key as the commotion outside intensified.

"He-ey! You have to broke the door!" he shouted to the angry mob.

The watermen did and thundered inside, waving their oars and tongs.

"Down with Virginia! Down with Virginia!" was their furious battle cry. "You daren't go back to the main, Dr. Faux, hear? You're wer
prisoner!"

"You're going to catch it!"

"That's right! That's right!"

"Heeey thar, Dr. Faux. How feels it, you being the one stuck in that
thar chair?"

"Give him the dickens!"

"I did!" Fonny Boy said, full of himself. "I scobbed him right in the
nose and down he went ass-over-tin-cup!" he boasted.

"We should yank out ever one of his teeth! Look at all the teeth a'
ours he always a' pullin'!"

"Take him potting, we should! And tie 'im up good and feed 'im to
the crabs!"

"And that ain't no way to go, I tell you!"

"Durn it, if it ain't what he got comin'! Hear?"

"Wait a minute!" Dr. Faux protested loudly enough to briefly silence
the watermen as he cowered in the dentist's chair and rubbed his nose.
"I do hear! And what I'm hearing is first you're mad at Virginia, and now
you've suddenly turned on me! Make up your mind!"

"We mad at ever one of you on the main," someone decided. "There's
neither one from the main who don't take our advantage."

"Well, if you're fully decided on kidnapping me," Dr. Faux thought
quickly and with fraudulent intent, "then your plan will only work if you
send notice to the governor. Otherwise, no one will know I'm here and
what good will it do to lock me up? And as for your unfair and ungrateful accusations about how I've taken care of your dental needs, I

must point out that I have come here for many years with nothing but goodness in my heart, and without me you would have no dentist at all."

"Better none than you."

"My wife, she would still be with all her teeth. And I get the ache in my tooth when it gets right airish out. A tooth you fixed!"

"Well, maybe we should have another mind about this." One of the watermen had second thoughts and leaned his oar against a wall. "We don't want neither trouble."

"Exactly," Dr. Faux agreed. "You watermen are projecting. You're furious with the governor, and I can't say as I blame you. Clearly, you're being persecuted and discriminated against as usual, and I'm not sure what these painted lines are about, but they weren't put there with your best interest in mind."

"Nah, neither interest that might be a good turn for us."

"Don't listen to him talking at us!" It was Fonny Boy who took charge. "He's of the main, and how did it come to us that the troopers and him are here at the same time? He's spying, he is!"

"I'll swagger! What's in your head to make you notion him spying on us, honey boy?" Fonny Boy's father asked with growing anger and resentment.

"Spying on potting and drudging and then he go telling untruths about jimmies and sooks and arysters. Soon enough, they'll make the law that we have no business follering the water," Fonny Boy declared without the thinnest fabric of evidence.

"This one thar let on that to you?" Fonny Boy's father asked as he jerked his chin at the dentist.

"Yass. Durn if he didn't!"

"What words did he put to you?"

Fonny Boy shrugged, his yarn running aground, but the seed had been planted.

"Can't be taking no chances," another waterman spoke up.

"Nah."

"Nah. That's right."

"The governor already's cut our crabbing to the wick, and now that arster drudging is pretty near on us, what if are toldt to leave that off, too? Why, there'll be nothing in our pockets, neither a red cent."

"It ain't fittin'!"

"Nah. For sure it ain't!"

"I say we let 'im make one call over the phone and talk our intentions," Fonny Boy's father suggested in a wild, angry voice.

"Who's he gonna call for?"

"I say he talk at the state police, that's what. They was the ones who painted on the street out thar. And maybe the dentist is spying for the police on part of the gov'ner."

Dr. Faux was handed the old black phone, and after calling directory assistance and going through a series of transfers, he got Superintendent Judy Hammer on the line and prayed she wouldn't think to run a record check on him.

"Who is this?" Hammer asked, and she could hear angry murmuring in the background.

"I'm a dentist from the mainland," a voice replied. "I take care of Tangier Island and am here now and in a passel of trouble because your trooper painted stripes on Janders Road and the governor is taking over the island so he can turn it into a racetrack."

"What in the world are you talking about?" Hammer asked, and she almost hung up on the so-called dentist, who clearly was a whacko, but then decided that maybe she ought to hear him out. "The stripes are a speed trap and part of the governor's new VASCAR program."

"If you don't remove the stripes immediately and sign an agreement that prohibits the state police, coast guard, and others from ever molesting the Islanders again, they're going to keep me as a prisoner against my will!"

"Who is this?" Hammer asked again, taking notes at her desk.

"I'm forbidden from giving you my name," the voice said.

"Down with Virginia!" someone with a strange accent cried out in the background.

"Neither body here voted for the gov'ner, as I recollect it."

"We ain't done nothing but fish our floats and make an honest living, and what we come home to? Stripes on the street and him, the dentist, pulling out ever one of our teeth!"

"I haven't pulled out every one of your teeth!" the dentist objected with his hand over the phone, but Hammer heard him and everybody else anyway.

"All right," Hammer said in an authoritative voice. "Just what exactly do you want us to do? I'm confused."

Her question was followed by silence on the line.

"Hello?" she asked.

"We're all wore out with being interfered," she heard someone say. "Talk at her and say to pass at the gov'ner that we was having a right good time of it before his meddling, and what we want is our own independence from Virginia!"

"Yass!"

"That's right! Neither more revenuers or police coming on the island! We'll take our own independence!"

"Neither more money going to tax! Neither a penny!"

"And no more telling us to hold down our catch!"

"Yass!"

"Well, you heard them," the dentist said to Hammer. "No more fishing restrictions, state taxes, policing, or interference. Tangier Island wants to secede from Virginia, and," he added, lowering his voice in a conspiratorial way, "the ransom for my release is fifty thousand dollars in unmarked bills that you are to express mail to P.O. box three-sixteen in Reedville. Please meet these demands immediately. I'm a hostage in the medical clinic and have already been beaten and am bleeding and my life is in danger!"

Before Hammer could respond to what she interpreted as madness and blatant extortion, the dentist hung up on her. She tried to find Andy to no avail and left him a voice mail explaining what had happened.

"Your mummy essay has caused considerable damage," she added at the end of her recorded message, "although I can't say as fact that anyone on the island read it. But you certainly have set the stage for making people believe that Tangier Island is being persecuted by Virginia and you'd better do something to set the record straight, Andy. Call me."

Andy did not get the message until late that night because after he and Macovich had flown back to Richmond, Andy had quickly thrown together a secret mission that had required a disguise and a borrowed civilian helicopter. He had spent the rest of the day on Tangier Island, gathering information, and when he finally got home, it was close to midnight. He played his voice mail and returned Hammer's call, waking her up.

"My God," he said. "I had no idea! If only I had known before now."

"Where the hell have you been?" Hammer's groggy voice came over the line.

"I can't tell you," Andy said. "Not now. I know that may seem rude and unfair, but I've been doing research and investigating a matter that I really don't have time to discuss at the moment. But suffice it to say that when I outlined the essays I planned to write for the website, my agenda did not include Tangier Island or dental fraud, so I've been busy— very busy—trying to find out everything I can about the Islanders, and I've got to get off the phone and start writing . . ."

"Andy!" Hammer was wide awake and offended. "You can't keep secrets from me! Where have you been all day? Have you heard the news? Apparently not," she added with emotion. "A woman was viciously murdered on Belle Island and the killer carved your name on her body!"

"My name? What the hell do you mean, my name?"

"I mean Trooper Truth."

"Someone carved *Trooper Truth* on her body?" Andy was shocked and amazed. "What . . . ? What . . . ?"

"I don't know what the hell what or anything else. But I think it might be a damn good idea to scrap this Trooper Truth shit and return to normal police duties before any more damage is done."

"You can't blame me for what some deranged killer did! As awful as I feel about the victim, I had nothing to do with her death and I promise to help in any way. Listen, we had an agreement and you promised,"

Patricia Cornwell

Andy reminded her. "And don't forget what I said a year ago when we discussed all this. If you tell the truth, the forces of evil don't like it, and shit happens. But in the end, truth will prevail."

"Oh, for God's sake!" Hammer replied unkindly and with impatience. "Please, don't subject me to any more of your naive philosophizing!"

"That hurts," Andy said, stung and disappointed, but more determined than ever. "Read Trooper Truth in the morning and maybe we'll talk."

A BRIEF HISTORY OF TANGIER ISLAND

by Trooper Truth

Although it may wish it wasn't at the moment, Tangier Island is part of the Commonwealth of Virginia, and was happened upon in 1608 when John Smith and seven soldiers, six gentlemen, and a doctor of Physicke were exploring the Chesapeake Bay in a three-ton open barge.

While searching for fit harbors and habitations, they found themselves in the midst of many isles, which they named the Russell Isles. When they crossed the bay to the eastern shore, they found themselves confronted by two grim, stout Naturals, or *Salvages*, as Smith called them, who bore long poles with bone heads.

"Who are you and what do you have in mind?" the Salvages boldly demanded in the language of Powhatan, called such because this was what the great chief Powhatan, father of Pocahontas, spoke.

Smith answered them in their own language, which impressed the Salvages considerably, and I pause here to digress a moment about the importance of communication, which certainly is a timely issue in light of what happened yesterday on the very island (Tangier) that John Smith discovered. No government, including Virginia's, should make laws and take initiatives that affect a people who speak backward. If an Islander says, for example, "Well, this is a nice one," or "It ain't rainin' none," he may mean quite the opposite, depending on his speech tune, as native Tangierman David L. Shores explains in his definitive work *Tangier Island: Place, People, and Talk*.

Now, in the old days, if an Islander meant the opposite of what he said, then he would signal as such by adding, "over the left," which obviously meant he was talking backwards. He would say, "It ain't rainin' much, over the left," which was only fair if he really meant it was raining like hell. Not so anymore. Only those intimately acquainted with the Islanders' use of inflection and facial expression might detect what was really meant when, as another example, a waterman says, "I have neither interest in going" or "That's a poor arster."

"What you're getting at, I guess," said my closest friend, who from now on I will refer to as my *wise confidante*, "is if the Islanders' reaction to the VASCAR speed traps was, 'Well, this is nice!' then what they probably meant was that the speed traps aren't nice at all and they're really pissed off about them. Based on what you've told me, clearly, the island woman Ginny Crockett was annoyed, even if she talked backward to the police, correct?"

"Exactly my point," I agreed. "The governor shouldn't do anything to or on that island without a full comprehension of backward talking. And it's pretty clear to me that the governor's administration is quite skilled at backward thinking, but not backward talking. And they've just done a brilliant thing."

"And you just had a forceful inflection in your voice and an exaggerated high pitch and prolonged your syllables while jerking your chin and raising your eyebrows when you said *they've just done a brilliant thing*. Does that mean you really meant the opposite?"

"Ah! I was testing you to see if you're catching on," I replied. "It's not what you say, but *how* you say it."

"I'm wondering if John Smith might have had a similar difficulty when dealing with the Salvages," my wise confidante mused. "Perhaps the Salvages talked backward as well."

"Well, you can be sure that how they said things was often much more important than what they said," I replied.

After a friendly visit with the Salvages, Smith set sail again, following inlets and the coast, when suddenly *an extreame gust of wind, rayne, thunder, and lightening happened, that with great danger we escaped the unmerciful raging of that Ocean-like water,* in Smith's words. Barely escaping with their lives, they sought shelter on one of many islands that Smith named the Russell Isles.

Setting sail again, they were struck by a second storm that blew their mast and sail overboard and almost sank them as they frantically bailed out the barge. For two days, they waited out the tempestuous weather and searched for water to drink on an uninhabitable spot that Smith named Limbo Island. Finally, they repaired their sails with the shirts off their own backs and headed home to Jamestown.

Most scholars seem to believe that Tangier is one of the Russell Isles. But I asked myself after studying several old maps and a modern flight chart: Is it possible that Tangier might really be Limbo, and might this explain the Islanders' tendency not to mean what they say or say what they mean? I don't think historians can completely rule out the possibility any more than I can offer much of a case for it. But if you look on a Washington sectional flight chart, you will see that Tangier and Limbo Islands are only a few minutes helicopter flight apart.

To investigate this further, I decided to fly a helicopter to Jamestown and from there record the exact coordinates were Smith to sail from Jamestown to Tangier and then return to Jamestown and sail to Limbo. Note the geographic coordinates, which I shall supply here for Jamestown, Tangier, and Limbo as they were displayed on my GPS when I hovered over each island. After you study the chart, I will explain the significance:

	JAMESTOWN ISLAND	TANGIER ISLAND	LIMBO ISLAND
LATITUDE	37° 12.47	37° 49.51	37° 55.75
LONGITUDE	76° 46.66	75° 59.87	76° 01.58

Clearly, Tangier and Limbo are not at all far from each other. So the hypothetical case I make is if you, the reader, imagine Smith and his men in the open barge with terrible rains, thunder, lightning, and zero visibility, how could Smith be so certain that when he thought he sought refuge on what he named Tangier Island that he really wasn't on Limbo Island instead? I know with reasonable certainty that had I been flying in such conditions after a nip or two of Wild Turkey, perhaps I could have ended up on Limbo as easily as anywhere else.

Whether Tangier is really Limbo will never be known. I doubt if John Smith were here today that even he could tell us. But I have no doubt that if Smith visited Tangier in modern times, he would feel as if he were in Limbo, even if he weren't.

If Tangier is really Limbo, then I personally wish the name had stuck. I believe Limbo Island could have developed a strong and specialized market in attracting tourists who are neither here nor there and would like to go somewhere in the middle of nowhere and do nothing about anything for a while. I also don't think the governor of Virginia would have bothered ordering speed traps painted on the streets of a place named Limbo, nor would the people of Limbo have cared one way or other.

Be careful out there!

Seven

Andy could measure Hammer's impatience by the rhythm of her fingers drumming her desk. This moment, she was tapping out a loud staccato on her ink blotter as Andy briefed her on Tangier Island and how the uprising was connected to the Tangiermen's past, because he had no reason to know at this moment that his comments about dental malpractice had riled up the Islanders just as much as the speed trap had.

"Most of those people probably don't even know their past and have never heard of John Smith," Hammer countered from behind her desk, which afforded a fine view of the circular drive in front of headquarters and flags fluttering from tall poles.

"I wouldn't underestimate them, and I'm just trying to give you a little background," Andy replied, sweating beneath his uniform and dreading what Hammer was going to say about his latest Trooper Truth essay.

"My point is, the Islanders are programmed to think people are picaroons out to steal their island from them and everything on it—very much the way the Native Americans felt when the English sailed to Jamestown and started building their fort."

"Picaroons?" Hammer frowned.

"What the Islanders call pirates."

"Oh, God," she groaned.

Windy Brees suddenly wafted into Hammer's office with an excited look on her made-up face and a UPS package clutched in her bright red-painted fingernails.

"Holy heavens to Betsy!" Windy exclaimed. "You'll never guess what happened!"

Hammer never liked it when her secretary made her guess. "Just tell me," Hammer said with an edge of impatience.

"We've got more trouble than you can poke a snake at!" Windy breathlessly said. "Some dentist who works on those Tangierians is missing! He went to the island yesterday as usual, and his wife told the Reedville police that he never came back on the ferry, and when the clinic was called, some strange-talking boy said the dentist was being held hostage until the governor makes the island an independent state. Or something like that."

"Yes, I am already aware of what's happened. Apparently, the Islanders are holding him hostage in the medical clinic," Hammer said.

"The clinic?" Andy said as a very bad feeling crept over him.

"So the dentist told me when they let him make a phone call," Hammer explained. "But I don't know his name. He said he couldn't give it to me."

"Sherman Fox," Windy filled her in. "It's a weird spelling." She glanced at her notepad. "F-A-U-X."

"It's Faux," Andy corrected her.

"It's fo'? Fo' what?" Windy puzzled.

"Never mind," Hammer abruptly said. "Andy, did you happen to see this dentist when you were painting the speed trap yesterday?"

"No," he replied, neglecting to mention that when he had returned to the island later, wearing a disguise, he hadn't seen the dentist, either, but had probably been within twenty feet of him because one of the places Andy had visited was the medical clinic.

He needed to tell Hammer about his secret mission, but he thought it wise to wait until she was in a better mood.

"A large group of watermen were marching down Janders Road," he added, "and I'm not surprised because the Islanders have a long history of resentment and isolation. And as much as I admire Thomas Jefferson, he didn't help matters by ordering all the Tangier boats snatched and supplies cut off during the American Revolution. Here he is saying this to his own people and treating Tangier like an enemy country, as if the island wasn't part of the very Commonwealth he governed . . ."

"Well, I'm afraid Mister Jefferson isn't available to help us out!" Hammer curtly cut him off as she rose from her chair.

"Maybe that's best, based on how he handled the island last time," observed Andy, who had barely escaped on the awaiting Bell 407 helicopter when the watermen chased him down Janders Road, across several footbridges and through countless wetlands, and finally onto the tiny airstrip, where Trooper Macovich was waiting in the helicopter and, thank God, had already started the engine.

"We've got to go back," Andy told a frantic Macovich as he took off, skipped the hover, and sped away.

"You out of your damn crazy-ass mind?" Macovich's voice sounded loudly in Andy's headset as a rock pinged off a skid. "We ain't going back! Those nutcakes are throwing things at us! Let's just hope they don't hit a rotor blade!"

They didn't, because the 407 was very powerful and soon enough was well out of range.

"Well, the thing is, I didn't finish," Andy tried to explain as he watched the angry mob shrink to the size of ants.

"Man, you didn't finish painting the speed trap? Shit. That's just too bad," Macovich said. " 'Cause I ain't going back there unless it's to buy crabs for the guv. If you ain't buying something, you'd better not go back, either, unless you want to end up crab bait."

"That's fine," Andy assured him. "I think there's a serious case of dental fraud going on down there, but I'll take care of it myself."

Andy had not ended up crab bait, nor had he been foolish enough to return to the island in the same helicopter that clearly was marked STATE POLICE. He had been shrewd enough to get a buddy of his at the local charter service to let him use an unmarked Long Ranger . . .

"Andy!" Hammer stopped pacing and stared accusingly at him. "Are you with us, or did you already leave without letting me know?"

"I'm sorry," he apologized. "I was just thinking about the Islanders and how their true feelings about us come out when we aren't buying seafood or souvenirs. They were actually throwing rocks at the helicopter as we flew off."

"How awful!" Windy said with overblown emotion. "You could have been killed. I mean, throwing rocks at a helicopter is a little more serious than *sticks and bones will shake like stones but words will never hear me*, now isn't it?" She certainly wished Andy were older and would ask her out one of these days. "I don't ever want to visit an island where they throw rocks and talk inside out."

"I see you read Trooper Truth this morning," Hammer wryly commented as Andy feigned ignorance.

"Wouldn't miss him for all the eggs in China," Windy gushed. "I sure do wish he'd put a picture of himself on his website. I'm just dying to know what he looks like."

"He probably looks like a nerd." Andy pretended to be critical and jealous of Trooper Truth. "You know how most of these computer jockeys are. And I'm getting sick of hearing Trooper Truth this and Trooper Truth that. You'd think he's Elvis."

"Well, I don't think he's Elvis. And I no longer believe he's the governor using a ghost name, either," Windy announced. "Not after what I read this morning. If the governor was Trooper Truth, then he wouldn't criticize the governor, because that would be the same thing as criticizing himself and . . ."

"What else do we know about the kidnapped dentist?" Hammer interrupted as she started pacing the carpet again and wished she could tie Windy's tongue in a knot.

"He was born in Reedville and has been volunteering out there on Tangier Island for more than ten years, although he doesn't like to admit it to anyone, so the police said his wife said," Windy answered. "Because it wouldn't help his practice back home if patients knew he got most of his experience from working on Tangierians. But at least he understands how they talk and he thinks like one."

"How do you know what he understands or thinks?" Hammer was quite opposed to assumptions and found herself surrounded by them constantly.

"You know what they say about birds in a pod," Windy reminded her. "Everybody on that island thinks alike, and he'd have to think like them to work on their teeth. The Reedville police also mentioned that this Dr. Fox doesn't have an address, only a P.O. box, and his wife claims there are no photos of him because he hates to have his picture taken. Also," she gusted through the information, "he doesn't have his social security number on his driver's license or anything else, and all of his phones are answered by machines, and when he takes family vacations to exotic places, he never tells anybody where he's going."

"I think we need to run a few checks on him," Andy suggested, as if the idea had never occurred to him before this minute. "Sounds to me like he's hiding something. What about his lifestyle? Money?"

"Gobs of it," Windy said. "The police told me he has this big, huge house and all these cars and private schools."

"How do the police know what his house looks like if they can't find an address for him?" Andy inquired.

"Oh, Reedville's a small place and everybody knows where everybody else lives. Besides, a huge house like his right on the water sticks out like a sore nose on your face."

"I did think it more than a little suspicious when he said the Islanders were demanding fifty thousand dollars cash, which was to be sent to a

Reedville P.O. box." Hammer continued to pace. "He also said that they were demanding all restrictions lifted."

"I see," Andy said. "So they're trying to extort our lifting the freeze on crab licenses."

Hammer absently snatched memos off her desk and glanced through them, hopeful that the governor might finally have returned one of her phone calls. But no. There was not a single message indicating he had tried to reach her or even knew she had been trying to talk to him for months.

"And I'm sure they expect us to remove the speed traps and prevent NASCAR from coming. They think we're going to turn the island into a racetrack," Andy informed Hammer.

"So I understand. How the hell can they think such a thing?" Hammer's voice rose. "The island couldn't possibly hold a hundred and fifty thousand fans. There would be no place to put the cars and no way to get them or the drivers or pit crews on and off the island. Not to mention, no beer or cigarette sponsors want their stock cars and people like Dale Earnhardt, Jr., and Rusty Wallace on a track where alcohol and tobacco are considered sins. And Tangier's barely above sea level, meaning the track would flood. Why the hell did you tell them NASCAR is coming, Andy?"

"I didn't. I was explaining VASCAR, not NASCAR, and this island woman got the names mixed up, just like a lot of people are doing."

"Well, I'm quite sure they'll demand we get rid of the crab sanctuary, too." She continued obsessing about the governor and his avoidance of her. "They've not forgiven us and never will for deciding most of the Chesapeake Bay is off limits to watermen." One part of her talked on while another part of her got angrier with the governor. She had no doubt that were she younger or a male, the governor would be calling her constantly. "We'll have to give the sanctuary back or unsanction it or whatever the legal process might be."

"Superintendent Hammer?" Windy seeped back into the discussion like an unpleasant draft. "I tried the governor's office first thing when I got in and he's in meetings again and not talking to anybody at all."

"Bullshit," Hammer said, eyeing the small, brown paper-covered package Windy was holding. "Is that for me, and who is it from?"

"Yes. The return address is Major Trader. Would you like me to open it?"

"Has it been x-rayed?" Hammer asked.

"Yes, yes. You know us, we never judge a box by its cover." Windy ripped off the paper. "Oh look! Homemade chocolates with a note that says . . ." She held up a small card and read, *"Best wishes, Governor Crimm."*

"That's strange," Andy commented, knowing all too well that Crimm never gave Hammer the time of day, much less presents. "I think I'd better take these."

"What for?" Hammer asked, perplexed.

"Because it's damn suspicious and I intend to look into it," Andy said.

"Now Windy," Hammer decided, "that will be enough for now." She motioned for her secretary to leave and not say another word. "Call the governor's office and see if you can get him on the damn phone."

Windy looked disappointed and unhappy at being banished, and she sure did wish her boss's poor little dog hadn't disappeared. Hammer was hardly ever in a good mood anymore. Andy gave Windy a little wink to cheer her up as she left.

"The Islanders don't care about the sanctuary," Andy said as he tucked the chocolates into his briefcase. "It wouldn't make sense for them to care about it because they don't fish in those parts of the bay."

Hammer actually knew very little about fishing or the laws pertaining to it. The fishing industry did not fall under the jurisdiction of the state police, but was the business of the Coast Guard unless fishermen committed serious crimes on roads or highways, which was exactly what had just happened when they marched down Janders Road and kidnapped the dentist and threatened treason. She tuned out the part of her that was fussing with the governor.

"Explain this sanctuary stuff to me," she said, sitting back down at her desk. "And everything else about why the Islanders don't like Virginia."

Andy informed her that Tangier Island had become increasingly hostile toward the rest of the Commonwealth when a recent General Assembly passed a number of bills that were entirely in favor of crabs and not the watermen who chased after them. It was true, however, that crab stocks were in serious trouble.

"A waterman brought in to testify before the legislators back in January admitted that the number of crab pots required to snag a hundred blue crabs had climbed from ten to fifty," Andy explained. "And last year, hard-crab landings dipped below thirty million pounds and the downward trend is continuing."

Harsh words such as "fully exploited," "overcapitalization," and "overfishing" were fired at Buren Stringle, the head of the Tangier Island Watermen's Association and the island's only police officer. Legislators set a lower limit for the number of crab pots the watermen could toss into state waters. Subsequently, a Blue Crab Advisory Commission was appointed, and it further tightened the restrictions by declaring that all pots would be tagged, thus making it easier for the marine patrol to count them and see who was cheating. The sanctuary was expanded to cover four hundred and sixty-five square miles of water at least thirty-five feet deep from the Maryland line to the mouth of the Chesapeake Bay near Virginia Beach—a crafty political move that would allow a million more pregnant crabs to safely reach vital spawning grounds.

"In truth, the sanctuary does no good at all," Andy summarized to Hammer. "The area of the bay deemed off limits happens to be a deep trough that would require extraordinary lengths of rope for every crab pot dropped in the water. The watermen have been keeping this bit of intelligence to themselves, and so far no one on the mainland, except possibly me, knows that Tangier Island has no interest in the new sanctuary or is the least bit opposed to it. Meanwhile, pregnant crabs continue to travel to their usual spawning grounds, indifferent to their new protection and not entirely aware of it."

"Okay. So forget the sanctuary idea," Hammer decided with disappointment. "But I can't think what real leverage we have, Andy. The way you've described it, Virginia really doesn't care much about the plight of the watermen, and the watermen aren't really that interested in Virginia's concerns, either."

"The root of all problems," Andy commented. "Nobody cares."

"Let's don't become cynical."

"What we need is some good ol' fashioned community policing," he said. "And I can do that through Trooper Truth."

"Oh no," she warned. "No more . . ."

"Yes!" Andy countered. "Let's at least give it a chance. Trooper Truth can ask his readers to help with our cases."

"Including Popeye!" Windy was suddenly in the doorway. "Oh, wouldn't that be wonderful if we could get Trooper Truth to ask for help finding Popeye?"

"What?" Andy asked, shocked. "What do you mean, *find* Popeye?"

Pain passed through Hammer's eyes.

"Don't be mad at me," Windy said to her. "I know you think I just let the cat out of the box, but maybe we can find Popeye. Maybe it's not too late, even if she did disappear months ago when you let her out to potty."

"That's enough, Windy," Hammer said again. "Please leave and shut the door."

"Well, okay, but I'm sending Trooper Truth an e-mail right away and telling him about Popeye."

She left and shut the door. Hammer sighed.

"How could you?" Andy whispered, outraged and deeply saddened by what had happened and that Hammer had never told him. "How could you not call me the minute Popeye disappeared?"

"You were off on one of your research trips, Andy," Hammer said in a defeated way. "And I don't know why else, but, well, I just haven't wanted to talk about it. There's nothing that can be done. Hold on." She held up a hand. "Now what is it, Windy?" she said to her secretary, who had just opened the door.

"Richmond Detective Slipper is on the line," Windy announced.

"Thank you." She waited until Windy shut the door again and shot Andy an ominous look as she picked up the phone and said, "Hammer."

She listened and scratched down notes for what seemed a very long time and Andy could tell by the expression on her face that she was being told something serious and unpleasant. In fact, she looked a bit unnerved.

"As I told you yesterday," she finally said, "the word is, nobody knows who he is. But I wouldn't be so quick to assume that just because the name Trooper Truth was . . . Yes, right. Of course, you have to follow every lead, and of course I'll let you know, and please keep me posted." She hung up and turned upset, anxious eyes on Andy. "The detective on the murder case—the woman found on Belle Island. She's been identified."

"Who?" Andy asked.

"Trish Thrash. A twenty-two-year-old white female who went by the nickname T.T. Apparently she worked for the state and was a closet lesbian who was known to pick up other women in area bars . . ."

"What do you mean, *Trish Thrash?*" Andy asked, baffled and upset.

Hammer went on to explain that Trish Thrash was the victim's name and that the city police believed the homicide was hate-related and committed by a male, possibly by whoever Trooper Truth was.

"That's insane!" Andy blurted out at the top of his voice. "I was . . . Well, I couldn't possibly have . . ."

"Of course you didn't do it!" Hammer replied as she got up and began pacing at top speed. "Jesus Christ! I knew this was a bad idea! And no more writing those goddamn . . . !"

"*No!* You can't punish me for what some other asshole did." He jumped up from his chair and grabbed her arm, not roughly but firmly enough to make her stop pacing and look at him. "Listen." He lowered his voice. "Please. I'll . . . I'll get this straight and see what I can do to help. I've never heard of Trish Thrash and don't see how this can possibly be related to me or Trooper Truth or anything that has to do with . . . Well, let's just hope the Richmond police don't do anything as stupid as releasing that detail about Trooper Truth to the media."

He was beside himself. If he was forced to reveal Trooper Truth's true identity, then not only would a year's work end up in the trash, but

Hammer would be in hot water with the governor for allowing one of her troopers to publish uncensored by her and especially by the governor.

"Maybe I can somehow reassure the governor that Trooper Truth isn't some deranged killer," Andy thought out loud. "And I'll get my readers involved in helping solve problems and bringing about justice in the Thrash case and others."

"What we need is to get word to the governor that we have an urgent situation on Tangier Island," Hammer replied in frustration. "Not talk to him about a murder that's not even our jurisdiction!"

"Maybe I can track him down for you," Andy suggested as Trooper Macovich walked into the office and overheard the tail end of their conversation.

"He always eats at Ruth's Chris Steak House on Wednesday nights," Macovich said.

"You two find him," Hammer ordered, adding to Macovich, "and maybe he won't remember you and the pool incident. For God's sake, whatever you do, don't play pool again."

"Wooo," Macovich agreed, shaking his big head. "Don't you worry. No way I'm ever playing with that girl, not for no reason."

"Don't play with anyone in the mansion." Hammer wanted to make sure Macovich was clear on this.

He frowned a little behind his dark glasses. "But what if the governor orders me to?"

"Let him win."

"Woooo. That ain't gonna be easy. He can't see nothing, Sup'intendent Hammer. Half the time, he don't even hit the cue ball. You know, he catch a little flash of white and go after it with his stick. And last time I was there, I set down a Styrofoam cup on the side of the table and he smack my coffee all the way across the billiard room."

"You shouldn't be putting your coffee down on furniture in the mansion in the first place," Hammer told him.

"I didn't think he saw me do it," Macovich said.

Eight

Dr. Faux was tied up in a chair and blindfolded by a bandanna that smelled like brackish water. Not especially frightened, he was mostly irritated and terribly inconvenienced. As time passed, his hopes for a speedy release and fifty thousand dollars cash were beginning to fade. He was no longer sure what the Islanders' intentions were, but they were not known for being violent.

In fact, as far as he knew, the biggest crime in the history of the island was the theft of a safe from Sallie Landon's house several years back. She had had her life's savings in it, and everybody on the island had chipped in so she wouldn't have to depend solely on the original recipes she sold in the little box she had nailed to a telephone pole near the post office. The crime was never solved.

Dr. Faux's captors had moved him out of the examination room and into an unknown location inside the clinic where he could hear bicycles rattle past an open window that allowed a constant flow of humid air to circulate flies and mosquitoes. It would do no good for him to call out for help because the entire population was in on the conspiracy and seemed to have turned on him. For the first time in the better part of half a century, Dr. Faux had time to reflect upon his life. He sighed as he pondered lost opportunities and his unwillingness to become a missionary to what was then the Congo. God had called Sherman Faux, and little Shermie had basically hung up on the Great Creator and then refused to answer at all anymore. At last, God was punishing Dr. Faux, more than likely. Here the dentist was imprisoned on a tiny, remote island out in the middle of nowhere, and unless he came up with a clever plan, his Medicaid scamming days might very well be over.

"I'm sorry," Dr. Faux told God. "I had it coming. Kind of like Jonah saying he wasn't going to Nineveh, so you said 'Guess again' and had that big whale swallow him up and spit him out on Nineveh, after all. I ask you not to make me wake up and find myself in the Congo, God. Or Zaire, as it was called last I heard. It's bad enough to be where I am right this minute."

Fonny Boy was sitting on the floor, leaning against a wall inside the medical supply room. He was hot and itchy from insect bites and already weary of guard duty, but when the dentist had started praying out loud, clearly oblivious to Fonny Boy's presence, he had slowly lifted anchor and puttered away from his favorite fantasy of pulling in a crab pot and finding a treasure chest in it that was filled with gold and jewels. His obsession with sunken ships was probably the only reason he could force himself out of bed every summer, holiday, and weekend morning at two o'clock when his father woke him up and they headed off to the docks in the golf cart. As Fonny Boy ate a fried oyster or crab breakfast sandwich, he would imagine himself hauling up a crab pot and finding it was snagged on a sunken picaroon ship, or maybe one of the crabs would be holding on to a gold coin or a diamond.

There were several self-published legends of the island that most of the gift shops sold, and Fonny Boy had read them all because of his interest in maritime history and salvage. His favorite story was of an incident that occurred in February of 1926 when strange winds and tides lowered the shallow waters of the bay just offshore and revealed the hulk of an old rotting ship, a picaroon ship, Fonny Boy was sure, because a battle-ax was found along with fine china and other artifacts that the watermen quickly sold to a visiting antique dealer from New York.

Unfortunately, the waters rose rapidly and the ship was never seen again. Fonny Boy had done the math. If the picaroon ship had survived several centuries in the bay, then certainly another quarter of a century or so wouldn't have made that much difference. It was still out there somewhere, but unfortunately, no one remembered exactly where it was sighted during that long-ago cold winter.

The other possibility Fonny Boy entertained was that the sunken ship might be a Spanish one that in 1611 stopped at Old Point Comfort in what is today Hampton, Virginia. The ship might have been sent by King Phillip III of Spain to spy on the people of Jamestown and see what they were up to. Other historians believe the Spaniards were, in fact, searching for another vessel that had sunk in the area. Why go to all that trouble unless there was treasure on the ship that sank? Fonny Boy reasoned. There wasn't much going on in the new English settlement except the people were hiding inside the fort to avoid the Naturals, who were very fickle, from what Fonny Boy had read—one minute bringing the settlers maize, the next minute greeting them with a storm of arrows.

Fonny Boy had always taken sides with the Naturals. He supposed that to the Naturals, the settlers were rather much like the strangers the Islanders tolerated most of the time but didn't particularly trust or like. Why was it that strangers were always looking down on people who were Naturals or local? Strangers ought to be called Unnaturals and should be pitied because they are the ones who need taxi rides and don't know the best place to eat or how to grow corn and have to pay a quarter to peek at peelers, as if molting blue crabs were some exotic creature like a panda bear or an anaconda.

Dr. Faux had fallen silent as the sun slipped into the Chesapeake Bay and restaurants and gift shops closed sharply at six. Although the dentist couldn't see because of the brackish-smelling bandanna, he could feel the temperature dramatically shift as night began to cloak the island and a cold front blew in. It was clear he would not be going anywhere anytime soon. No one, including the Coast Guard, visited Tangier after dark, when fog rolled in and obscured the eroding shore and what was left of the airstrip. Only the watermen's work boats could move about freely when conditions were poor, but that did Dr. Faux not a bit of good, since he knew from experience that the Islanders were stubborn and not inclined to change their minds. No one was going to let him go home, perhaps ever.

"You keep me here tied up like this," Dr. Faux said out loud, because he thought he had heard a stirring inside the room a few minutes ago, "then who's going to take care of your teeth? That you in here, Fonny Boy?"

"Yea." Fonny Boy's answer was followed by several blows on the harmonica.

"I would like to know what the plan is, if you don't mind telling me," the dentist said.

"Depends on the gov'ner," Fonny Boy repeated what the watermen had discussed among themselves after taking the dentist hostage. "If the stripes stay on the road, then there is no hope for you. We had wer fill of Virginia and are sick and tard of the way we is treated and don't want to go to the jail for speeding in the golf carts and don't want NASCAR building a racetrack so they can make a barrel. And we plan to really fix you for what you done to wer teeth, making out that you care when it ain't so!"

"NASCAR?" Dr. Faux was stumped. "Have you ever been to a NASCAR race, Fonny Boy?"

"Yea!" he exclaimed, lifting his eyebrows and tightening his jaw, meaning he was talking backward and saying *no*.

"Well, I can't tell if you mean yes or no, but I assure you, NASCAR has no intention of coming here and there is no barrel of money to be made from stock-car racing or anything else on this island."

"The police say so. And if the gov'ner don't do what he orte do and stop steering us up, we going to set out all the bateaus and form a block-ate around the island and raise a flag with a jimmy on it and burn up the Virginia flag! And you made a barrel here on Tanger, now ain't that right, Dr. Faux?"

"You're going to raise a flag with a male crab on it and commit treason?" Dr. Faux was shocked and persisted in sidestepping the boy's accusations about the dentist's honesty. "That would cause another civil war, Fonny Boy. Do you realize the serious consequences of such a hostile act?"

"All I know is we had wer fill," Fonny Boy said with defiance and a bit of a swagger in his voice.

"Well, I tell you, son, I've visited your island for many years," Dr. Faux confessed. "And it's no coincidence that I don't choose to live here. My point is, if you want a chance in life, Fonny Boy, you've got to do the smart thing, which in this case is listening to me."

"Listening to you is not much count," Fonny Boy replied with a few toots on the harmonica, not letting on that his interest was snagged by what might just prove to be a transaction of some sort.

"Listening to me has plenty of value. Because doing the smart thing might just give you an opportunity. Maybe there's something special out there for you, Fonny Boy. But if you go along with these people that have me locked up in here, there's a good possibility you'll end up in trouble and spend the rest of your life on this tiny, eroding island, selling crabs and souvenirs and playing the harmonica. You got to help me get out of here, and if you do, maybe I'll take you with me back to Reedville and you can work in my office and learn to drive a real car."

"If I carry you to shore, what you gonna do? Throw silver dollars at me?" Fonny Boy asked sarcastically as he blew out an unrecognizable rendition of "Yankee Doodle."

"You know what a recruiter is?" Dr. Faux said smoothly. "Well, I'll tell ya. I could put you to work going around and finding needy children whose teeth require a lot of work their families can't afford. You bring them in to my Reedville clinic and I'll give you ten dollars for every kid.

When you learn to drive, I'll find you a car. We don't have to come back here to this impoverished little island ever again."

Fonny Boy had a lot to think about and it was time to head home for supper. He walked out of the storage room, shutting the door hard to make sure the dentist heard him leave, and failing to inform him that water and a tray of food would be delivered momentarily. Fonny Boy felt a pinch of guilt as he got on his bicycle and pedaled away from the clinic, still working on "Yankee Doodle." Maybe he should have been a little kinder to Dr. Faux and told him food and drink were on the way. Maybe he should work harder to do what he had been taught in church, but getting involved in military and mutinous activities sharpened Fonny Boy's edge.

He felt a bit feisty and in a mood to commit mischief and mayhem. He played his harmonica loudly and rode his bicycle faster than usual, speeding up full tilt when he crossed the two painted lines on Janders Road. Fonny Boy pumped furiously through chilly air and moonlight, scarcely acknowledging his aunt Ginny, who was headed to the clinic in a golf cart.

"Heee!" she called out to him as they passed each other in the road. "Doncha play the juice harp in the evening! You gonna drive the neighbors star-crazy!"

Fonny Boy tooted out a loud, rebellious reply and wished he hadn't swallowed the cotton again. Last time, it had clogged him up for a week, moving through his guts and criks with the slow purpose of a glacier until finally working its way out when he was in the bateau with his father, not a toilet or land in sight.

When Ginny walked into the storeroom moments later carrying a tray of crab cakes, hot rolls, and margarine, Dr. Faux was praying again.

". . . Amen, dear Lord. I'll get back to you later. That you, Fonny Boy?" the dentist asked hopefully. "Lord have mercy, it's freezing in here. Where'd this winter weather come from all of a sudden?"

"Blowed in from they bay. I got supper and water."

"I need to use the bathroom." Dr. Faux was embarrassed to talk this way in front of a woman whose mouth he had excavated and exploited for years.

Ginny said "yea," as long as he promised to return to the folding chair and didn't mind her tying him up and covering his eyes with the bandanna again.

"If you tie me up and put on the bandanna, I won't be able to eat," Dr. Faux complained as Ginny freed him and he squinted in the dim light of the storeroom.

"I'll sit right here without you don't come back from doing your business, and on the back of that, I didn't come over for to tell you nothing." It was Ginny's way of saying she'd leave him alone while he used the toilet, unless he tried something sneaky, like escaping, and in addition, she had no intention of giving him any sort of information.

While the dentist headed to the bathroom, she settled herself on a box of free antibacterial soap samples and ruminated about the speed traps, NASCAR taking over the island, and what the trooper had suggested about the Islanders' criminal dental care. She and several other women had convened at Spanky's and set out to spread the word to the entire Tangier population by posting signs on chainlink fences and all the shops and restaurants. They had even told the ferryboat captains, who promised to incorporate the NASCAR news and dental fraud alerts into their guided tours as they carried visitors back and forth between Crisfield and Reedville.

Dr. Faux returned to his folding chair and asked Ginny how her dentures were holding up.

"The same," she said. "And now and again I feel a bit squamish from when you pulled them last teeth the other week. I spewed up the evening 'fore last."

"If you're feeling nauseated and throwing up, it must be a bug of some sort," Dr. Faux misinformed her. "And it sounds to me like your new dentures are clacking a little bit."

"When the cream wores off, they do."

"Well, if you need another tube of adhesive cream, you can pick up one while you're here." Dr. Faux hungrily ate a crab cake. "They're in the middle cabinet in the examination room."

Ginny silently watched him eat and began to struggle with deep resentment that was inching toward hate. She was a solid church woman and knew that hate was a sin, but she couldn't seem to help herself as she watched the greedy, indifferent dentist stuff food into his mouth.

"I always thought you was the best I ever knew at teeth, Dr. Faux," she finally blurted out. "But now I seen you for the truth, and you learned me we shouldn't trust neither one neither more. We're of a mind what things you been doing on us. I'm just so out of heart about it, and was thinking as much when I was renching the dishes right afore I brung your dinner. We gave you all what we could, mostly food and good words, when you come here to help us, and then what you did! Why bimeby, you got aholt of each and ever one of us and mommucked up our mouths so you could get mor'n you was supposed to from the gov'ment!"

"My dear Ginny, you know that's simply not so," Dr. Faux said in a cajoling tone. "For one thing, government officials audit dentists constantly and check for things like that. I could never get away with it, even if it would ever enter my mind. And I swear and kiss the Bible," he tossed out one of the Islanders' favorite exclamations, "that what I'm saying to you is true!"

"That's all over!" Ginny declared, indicating she'd heard enough of his tales.

Huh, Ginny bitterly thought. A cold day in Heck it would be when some government agent took the ferry out here and tried to poke around in the Islanders' mouths, looking to see if certain work had really been done or was necessary. She tried to pray away the hate in her heart by reminding herself that were it not for Dr. Faux, she wouldn't have dentures or adhesive cream or free samples of mouthwashes. She supposed she would have no teeth of any sort, except for the real ones that Dr. Faux had claimed he had no choice but to extract because of abscesses, root fractures, bad enamel, an overbite, and she forgot what else.

"I don't want to hate neither one," she silently prayed, but reality settled on her like a huge stone she could not push away.

The truth, of course, was that she had been rather shocked to discover she had such major dental problems, but she had trusted Dr. Faux. The truth was, that up until a few years ago, her teeth were fine and people were always talking about her pretty smile. Why, she hadn't had a cavity since childhood, and then suddenly, she didn't have a single tooth left in her head. The more she brooded over this as she locked up the clinic and headed down the dark street, the more she began to entertain a host of poisonous thoughts about Dr. Faux. How many times had he told her that all of the Islanders were born with bad teeth and Tangier Disease due to *inbreeding*? How many times did she hear yet one more tale about someone's fillings falling out or a root canal going bad or a crown that looked like a piano key cracking smack in half for no good reason?

Huh, she thought with gathering agitation and grief as she crossed the painted lines on Janders Road. Maybe they ought to hold Dr. Faux hostage until all of his teeth fell out. Maybe he ought to have clacking dentures that didn't fit right and caused a lot of gum soreness and missed meals. Maybe he ought to spy an ear of sweet corn and feel overwhelmed by nostalgia and loss, or be embarrassed when it sounded like he was playing the castanet while he talked on the phone.

"Honey, you look a norder! Why, you're sob wet!" Ginny's husband noticed that she was sobbing as she rushed inside the house and slammed the door.

"I want my teeth!" she cried out hysterically.

"You remember whar you laid 'em last?" he asked, as he began walking around, looking for the glass jelly jar she usually soaked her dentures in. "Well, I swanny!" he suddenly said as he put on his bifocals. "Durn if they're not in your mouth, Ginny!"

An Historical Footnote

by Trooper Truth

At a glance, it may not seem entirely honest of me to call this digression a footnote, because it should be plain to the reader that the text is not preceded by a number, nor is it at the bottom of a page.

However, a footnote doesn't have to mean a reference designated by a number that we find in works of nonfiction, textbooks, and term papers. A footnote can also indicate something of lesser importance. For example, it could be said that until a few years ago, Jamestown was nothing more than a footnote in history, since most people believed that the U.S. really began at Plymouth and that's why we celebrate Thanksgiving. Although schoolbooks still devote scant attention to Jamestown, at least our nation's first lasting English settlement has made it into accepted educational writings and is not relegated to a footnote, literally.

In the high school textbook *The American Nation*, I'm pleased to report, Jamestown is discussed on pages 85 and 86. Sadly, however, my 1997 edition of the *Encyclopaedia Britannica* offers only an eighth of a page on Jamestown and leads one to believe that there is nothing left of the site except replicas of the ships the settlers sailed on from the Isle of Dogs. The replicas are actually about a mile west of the original fort and are part of what is called the Jamestown Settlement, which is also a replica, I reluctantly point out, but worth visiting as long as you realize that the first settlers did not construct the twentieth-century buildings, restrooms, food court, souvenir shops, parking lots, and ferry, any more than they sailed on the fabricated ships moored in the river.

I find it rather embarrassing that when you visit Jamestown, there are numerous signs directing you to the Settlement and only one or two that point you in the direction of the original site. So you can choose to visit the fabricated Jamestown or the real one, and many tourists choose the former because of the conveniences, possibly. Of course, when the Settlement was built, it was believed that the original site had eroded into the river, which explains why Virginia thought a fabrication was the best the Commonwealth could offer.

"The point is," I said to my wise confidante, "people accept as truth things that are fabrications or at the very least can't be proven," and I went on to give my wise confidante the example of how Tangier Island supposedly got its name.

The story goes that when John Smith discovered the uninhabited island we now assume is Tangier but may in fact be Limbo, he was vividly reminded of a town called Tangier on the south side of the Strait of Gibraltar, in North Africa. He was thus inspired to name the new island in the New World Tangier Island, which seems an apocryphal tale to me.

"Tangier Island bears no resemblance to Tangier, North Africa," I explained to my wise confidante, "and it makes me wonder if Smith was engaging in a little backward talk, assuming he ever uttered a word about any place called Tangier."

" 'Ye spy the isle there?' " I said he might have asked while he was exploring in his barge. " 'It is most pleasant and does cause me to think of Tangier,' " I said he might have added with noticeable inflection and facial expression because he meant quite the opposite and was making a joke.

There are other theories that Tangier Island was named after Tangier,

Morocco, based on information that some British soldiers stationed in Tangier set sail for America with their Moorish wives and settled on an island in the Chesapeake Bay some people believe was Tangier when the English military withdrew its garrison from the Moroccan city in 1684. However, years later, people who called themselves "Moors" and lived in Sussex County, Virginia, denied that their Moorish ancestors had any connection to Tangier Island.

Who knows what is true? In fact, no one seems quite certain when Tangier was first inhabited, but there are accounts of patents of land being granted as early as 1670, and a much-disputed Tangier tradition has it that in 1686, John Crockett settled on a rise and raised livestock, potatoes, turnips, pears and figs, and eight sons. The island began to flourish and gained the attention of warring factions during the American Revolution, when the British demanded supplies from Tangier, and the rest of Virginia responded by blockading the island and passing along severe threats from Virginia Governor Thomas Jefferson.

Meanwhile, pirates seized whatever they wanted and burned down the house of an Islander named George Pruitt as they cruised about, terrorizing a people who were too few and unarmed to defend themselves. As if that wasn't bad enough, a boy named Joe Parks II was snatched by the British, conscripted and carried away, and all Tangier youth were forced into hiding. The Islanders had little choice but to decide it was better to openly trade with the enemy than to have their crops, property, and loved ones seized, and they began selling commodities to the British, to other Americans and pirates, and simply flew whatever flag was appropriate, depending on who was in the area. This survival technique has endured down through the centuries, and to me explains why the Tangier people of today suffer tourists on the island and ply them with crab cakes, trinkets, T-shirts, taxi service on the golf carts, and misinformation.

Dear readers, I'm asking you to interact with me by helping enforce the Golden Rule. Please! If any of you have suffered any suspicious or bad dental work performed by one Dr. Sherman Faux of Reedville, e-mail me as soon as possible. And if anyone happens to know the whereabouts of a female Boston terrier named Popeye, please let me know immediately! Like the dentist, the innocent dog has been spirited away and is possibly being held hostage somewhere. Unlike the dentist, Popeye has never hurt or taken advantage of anyone and doesn't deserve what has happened to her. If you have information about these crimes or any others—especially the recent vile murder of Trish Thrash—please get in touch.

Be careful out there!

Nine

Major Trader was hunched over his keyboard like a turkey buzzard when Trooper Truth's latest essay went up on the website at exactly three minutes past seven this Wednesday morning.

"What sort of nonsense is this?" Trader exclaimed out loud to no one but himself. "Naughty, naughty, Trooper Truth. We'll see about you mucking up the Commonwealth's revered history and asking the public to snitch for you!"

Trader bit into a jelly doughnut and wiped his thick fingers on his flannel pajamas as his wife stirred about in the kitchen, clanging cookware, rummaging and rooting through a cluttered cabinet for the frying pan.

"Do you have to make so much racket?" Trader yelled from his office on the other side of the spec house he and his wife would soon sell for a handsome profit.

Trader was very clever with his investments and had become a wealthy man over recent years. His modus operandi was simple. He would buy a lot in an exclusive neighborhood that did not allow spec houses. He would build a house, live in it for one year, then sell it, claiming that his position with the governor necessitated privacy and security, both of which were somehow violated, forcing him to move yet again. Although the neighbors had his scam figured out, no one could prove that he was really building a spec house, even though each of the ten homes he had sold so far were identical and rather generic. Pointed letters from the neighborhood association had been ineffective and completely ignored, and Trader's pattern had become an addiction.

He loved moving. Perhaps it provided the only drama in his otherwise artificial, mendacious life. Several months out of every year Trader ordered his wife about, supervising her packing and cracking the whip over his contractor's spinning head, goading him into escalating the building schedule, all the while yelling "Hurry up! Hurry up! We've got to move in two weeks and the new house had better be ready! Don't you screw with me!"

"But we haven't even put the wiring in yet," the contractor had pleaded with Trader just last week.

"How long can that possibly take?" Trader fired back.

"And you haven't picked out paints yet."

"Just use the same damn eggshell white you've used on the other ten houses, you fool!" Trader yelled over the phone. "And the same off-white Burbur carpet, you idiot! And the same brass Williamsburgy light fixtures, you ninny! And the same pulls and door knobs from Home Depot, you meathead!"

It was vital that Trader play a sovereign role when he was in his own castle. The rest of the time, he was a toady for the governor and no one could possibly understand how hard that was on a man's ego unless he had experienced it firsthand. *Do this, do that. Use a different word. Rewrite that paragraph. Oh, I changed my mind. Let's tell the press this instead. Where's my magnifying glass? Leave my office now! I'm not feeling well.*

At least Trader's demanding and unrewarding career had taught him the value of manipulation, revenge, and profiteering. Thanks to the Internet, it wouldn't be long before he would be a self-made millionaire if his latest investment scheme was successful.

"Major? You haven't told me which you'd like for breakfast. Sausage or bacon? Raisin toast or muffins? Grits with or without cheese?" his wife yelled from the kitchen as cookware clanged.

"What are you doing in there? Practicing percussion for the goddamn symphony?" Trader yelled back. "I want it all."

Thank goodness their kids were off in boarding school and college and Trader didn't have to listen to their noisy nonstop feet and grating voices. His wife was disruptive enough, and sound certainly carried in their new house just like it had in the other ten. Trader was getting close to fifty, and if all went according to plan, he could retire soon and focus on cyber crimes. Trader frowned, deep in thought, as he read the latest Trooper Truth essay again and then composed a provocative anonymous e-mail.

Dear Trooper Truth,

I am the great-great grandson of a Confederate spy, so maybe it is in my DNA (ha ha) to be unable to resist leaking intelligence. I say ha ha because I knew you would appreciate my witty reference to DNA since you have written about it before. I happen to have reason to know that the governor has no intention of trapping any speeders on Tangier Island. He could care less. His true motivation for launching VASCAR there was to create a mess that someone else would be blamed for. I'm sure you'll want to mention that in your next essay. By the way, I was very sorry to hear about Popeye. Has it occurred to you that maybe someone stole the helpless little dog for a reason? And if someone has information re: Dr. Faux or anyone else, is there a reward?

Sincerely,
A. Spy

As usual, Trader did not intend to place a period after the *A* in *A Spy*. As usual, he clicked on the SEND NOW key before he could make the correction. The spec house filled with the greasy aroma of frying meats as he waited for Trooper Truth to get back to him.

"Breakfast is ready!" his wife shouted from the kitchen at the same moment his computer announced, "You've got mail!"

Dear Mr. A. Spy,

    Citizens should be willing to tell the truth without being paid! And if you know anything about Popeye's disappearance, you'd better tell me, or else!

                                  Trooper Truth

"Well, well," Trader muttered with a gleeful smile. "I do believe I struck a nerve."

"Did you say something, Major?" his wife screamed over water drumming in the cheap metal kitchen sink.

"Not to you!" Trader thundered as he composed another e-mail.

Dear Trooper Truth,

    I have heard rumors about who the dog's owner was. Can that be a coincidence? You know, not everybody likes that woman, who shouldn't be in the position she's in to begin with. It's a man's world, right? By the way, does she have an unlisted address? I'm wondering how the dognappers found her house. And yes, citizens should be handsomely rewarded for helping the police.

                                    Sincerely,
                                    Mr. A. Spy

Andy was enraged as he tapped out a message back to A. Spy.

Dear Mr. A. Spy,

It is not a man's world in the least, and if Popeye is the victim of some sort of political intrigue, I suggest you tell me what you know this minute. Don't make me warn you again. And where her owner lives is none of your business. I'll get back to you about the reward.

Trooper Truth

Andy sent the e-mail and waited for Mr. Spy to answer him. But the storm of e-mails flying into Andy's cyberspace box were from other readers. Mr. Spy had signed off and was taunting him, Andy decided with mounting fury.

He couldn't stop thinking of the times he had played with Popeye and had been licked by her. He could almost feel her sleek tuxedo coat and the baby softness of her pink belly, and how well he remembered the comforting sound of her toenails clicking across the hardwood floor back in the days when he had been a frequent visitor of Hammer's.

Andy reached for the photo album on top of a stack of research books. He was going to find that dog if it was the last thing he did. He was concerned for Hammer's safety, too. She did, in fact, have an un-listed address and was extremely careful to keep her personal life top secret. Only the police, her professional associates, and a few of her neighbors knew where she lived, and she never talked about Popeye or allowed the media to take the dog's photograph. So how did the dog thief find Popeye unless the crime was, as A. Spy suggested, an in-side job?

"Please be alive, Popeye," Andy muttered as he found his favorite photograph of Popeye—the one of her in a Little Red Riding Hood win-ter coat. "Please don't forget about Superintendent Hammer and me. We'll find you! I promise! And just wait and see what I do to the son of a bitch who stole you!"

He scanned the photograph into cyberspace, and instantly, the image of Popeye filled his computer screen. He opened up his website program and typed in the caption: "Missing. Have you seen Popeye? Big reward offered!" If people were so lacking in character that they needed money to do the right thing, then Andy would play their little game. He edited the caption to say "HUGE REWARD offered," and of course, the expected bogus responses came in immediately. People claimed to have seen Popeye wandering along the shoulder of the Downtown Expressway or in an alleyway or crying in the back seat of a suspicious car. If the price was right, other people wrote, they would give Trooper Truth clues about where Popeye was and why.

There was an outpouring of sympathy, too. Hundreds of readers offered their own sad stories of pets they had lost since childhood. It was the most mail Trooper Truth had gotten so far, and Andy spent the entire day at his dining-room table trying to answer it and hoping that someone would come forth and say, "Hey, I took the dog because my kids wanted one and I couldn't afford it. So I'll meet you in some secret place and give Popeye up for a price." Or maybe someone would write, "Look, it was a setup. Someone who hates Superintendent Hammer told me all about the dog and gave me the address and a small amount of cash. I realize now it was a mean, heartless act and I will be happy to give Popeye back as long as I don't get in trouble and am rewarded."

Sadly, there was no e-mail about the murder of Trish Thrash, or T.T., except for a short note from someone named P.J., who claimed that she used to play softball with T.T. and knew for a fact that T.T. would never willingly go to Belle Island with a man.

Have you lost your mind?" Hammer said to Andy over the phone at 6:00 P.M. "I thought you were supposed to write only anti-crime essays. It's bad enough that you're straying from mummies to pirates, but now you're pretending to be the SPCA!"

"Do you want me to take Popeye's picture off the website?" He tested her. "I certainly can, but I thought giving it a shot couldn't hurt anything.

Maybe she's still out there and someone will be tempted enough by the reward to give her back."

"I just don't know if I can stand seeing her in that sweet little red coat every time I log on to your site," Hammer confessed sadly.

"When people avoid looking at pictures, it indicates that they haven't healed. That's why I never tear up photos of old girlfriends. If I can look at them now, then I'm okay. If I can't bear to look at them, then I'm not okay," Andy said.

"Well, leave her picture on the site, then," Hammer said. "I'll just have to get used to it. And you're right, Andy, if there's any chance Popeye might be found, we have to do everything we can. I thought you were supposed to stake out the governor tonight." Her tone turned all business again. "And I'm not sure it was a wise thing to criticize him again in your Trooper Truth essay. By the way, who is this so-called *wise confidante* you keep referring to?"

"Having a wise confidante gives me license to have dialogue and expository conversations," Andy replied.

"Well, I don't know who the hell *she* is, but no one is supposed to know you're Trooper Truth, especially in light of this awful murder." Hammer was brusque with him. "So I certainly hope you haven't blown your cover over some so-called wise female confidante. And if you have, I have a right to know about it, even if I'm not the least bit interested in your personal life. Please don't tell me it's Windy."

"Windy?" Andy was offended and changed the phone to his other ear. "I should hope you would think I have better taste than that."

Hammer ended the conversation, which had gone on far too long, and hung up without saying goodbye. Andy sent one final e-mail, but this time he used his own screen name:

Dear Dr. Pond,

Just wondering if you've gotten those toxicology results yet? Remember, this is an extremely sensitive case, and I appreciate your keeping all details strictly confidential. And no, I can't fix your recent reckless driving ticket. I suggest you go to driving school on a Saturday that is most convenient for you, and the points will be taken off your record.

Thanks and good luck,
Trooper Brazil

He logged off and put on his uniform, and within the hour was parking at Ruth's Chris Steak House on the city's south side, where he met Trooper Macovich, who had piloted the First Family in for dinner. The two of them sat in Andy's car and watched the steak house's front door, waiting for the governor to emerge.

"What's it like flying them?" Andy asked as he gazed out at the gleaming Bell 430 helicopter that was painted gun metal gray with dark blue stripes down the sides and the seal of the Commonwealth on the doors.

"Wooo, I can tell you for a fact, it ain't all it's cracked up to be," Macovich replied. "Just a damn good thing the guv didn't recognize me when I flew them here, 'cause I thought for sure that ugly daughter of his was gonna say something about playing pool and then the cat sure would be outta the bag. But she was too busy getting into the snacks in that little drawer under the backseat, you know? I sure do hope she don't say nothing when they come out, though." Macovich lit a Salem Light and turned his dark glasses on Andy. "So now that we're sitting here man-to-man, how 'bout you tell me what you did to get into so much trouble. I mean, everybody's wondering why Hammer put you on the bricks for an entire year."

"Who said I was put on the bricks?" Andy asked with a touch of defensiveness.

"Everybody say so. The word on the street is you got in big trouble for something or maybe had a fight with Hammer."

"I was getting my pilot's license and several additional ratings."

"I know it didn't take you no forty hours a week for a whole year to learn how to fly. And your ratings took what? Maybe two, three weeks each? So what was you doing the rest of the time? Just running women and watching TV?"

"Maybe."

"You gonna tell me what you did to get suspended?" Macovich persisted.

"No," Andy said sullenly, deciding he might as well allow the rumor to persist because no one, including Macovich, could know the truth about Trooper Truth.

"Well, no one would guess you'd have a messed-up life. Anybody looking at you would think you're the happiest son of a bitch in town," Macovich added with a prick of jealousy.

"We need new pilots." Andy changed the subject. "Right now, you and I are the only ones left."

Macovich followed Andy's gaze outside to the big helicopter and began to entertain a suspicion.

"I bet you want to fly the governor," Macovich accused him from behind a cloud of smoke.

"Why not? Seems to me you could use a hand," Andy nonchalantly replied as he instantly decided to approach the governor on the matter. "The First Family certainly ought to have more than one pilot, and what the hell do you do when it's not VFR conditions?" he added, referring to Visual Flight Rules, which meant that weather conditions were good enough to fly by sight instead of instruments.

"Find some excuse for why the helicopter can't take him wherever it is he wants to go," Macovich replied. "I usually tell him there's a maintenance problem or radar's down."

"You've got a four-thirty and you only fly in pretty weather?" Andy couldn't believe it. "That thing was made to fly through clouds. Why do you think it's got auto-pilot, IIDS, and EPHIS? Not to mention that smooth-as-silk rotor system. Hell, you could roll that bird like an F-sixteen. Not that I'm recommending it," Andy was quick to add, since it was illegal to perform acrobatics in a helicopter. "But I have to admit, I did roll it on the simulator down in Fort Worth when I was at the Bell

Training School. Slowed down to about a hundred knots, pointed the nose down at two thousand feet, pushed the cyclic all the way to the right, and around I went."

The idea of being upside down in a helicopter gave Macovich a bad reaction and he inhaled as much smoke as he could to calm his nerves. "You one crazy ass," he said. "No wonder you got suspended. Unless"— it suddenly occurred to Macovich—"you really wasn't suspended but are up to something. On some secret project. Wooo!"

"Speaking of secrets," Andy artfully dodged and deflected, "I wonder who Trooper Truth is."

"Yeah, well, you ain't the only one," Macovich replied. "The governor wants to know something fierce, and he's ordered me to figure it out. So if you got any ideas, I sure would 'preciate your passing them on."

Andy didn't reply.

"I'm curious, myself," Macovich went on. "How'd he know about Tangier Island and what we was doing out there, huh? I read all about it in one of his columns on that web of his. It's like he was there watching the whole thing."

Andy said nothing, because he did not want to lie. Macovich turned his dark glasses on him as yet another suspicion hovered over his thoughts.

"You ain't Trooper Truth, are you?" Macovich pressed him. " 'Cause if you are, I promise to keep it a secret, long as you understand I got to tell the governor."

"Listen, what makes you think I wouldn't tell the governor myself if I knew who Trooper Truth was?" Andy sidestepped the question.

"Hmmm. I guess that's a good point. If you knew, you would tell him and take all the credit," Macovich considered.

"Why wouldn't I?"

"Then who you think it is? I know it's passed through my mind that maybe Major Trader's doing it."

"Not hardly," Andy said. "Trader can't tell the truth. So he couldn't possibly be Trooper Truth, now could he?"

"You're probably right." Macovich blew out a cloud of smoke. "You also right about us being short of pilots."

"Why do they keep quitting?" Andy wanted to know.

Macovich decided he had said enough. He was already in trouble with the First Family. No point in making matters worse, and he was worried that Andy might prove to be a threat to him. That white boy sure was smart—a lot smarter than Macovich. Andy didn't even have to think hard about anything before he made a comment, and sometimes he used words that Macovich didn't know.

"So, I bet when you was in school, you was one of those book-worms," Macovich said as envy crept into his tone and compelled him to find a way to put Andy down. "Bet you lived in the library and all you did was study."

"Hell, no. I never studied," Andy said, not adding that he had sailed through college in three years and loved learning so much that he never considered his schoolwork *studying*. "All I wanted to do was get out and get on with things."

"Yeah, no shit." The cloud of smoke nodded.

Machovich had suffered through one year of a technical college where he grew to strongly resent his father's ambition that his oldest son would one day hold down a respectable job at Ethyl Corporation, mak-ing solvents. Macovich moved out of the house his freshman year and joined the Army, where he learned to fly helicopters, and then moved on to law enforcement. A couple months back, he gave his father a framed autographed picture of the First Family, just to rub it in a little bit. Mrs. Crimm had written a nice personal inscription on it that said, "First Lady Maude Crimm."

A cigarette butt sailed in a perfect arc and landed on the pavement, where it glowered like an angry eye.

"All I gotta do is say one word to the guv about you flying as my co-pilot and he take care of you," Macovich bragged without the slightest intention of facilitating helicopter flying or anything else for Andy— except trouble, maybe. "That's assuming he don't remember me. Now if that pool shark daughter decides to make a fuss, then I might be best off speaking to him another time. Wooo, I'd better light up quick before they come out."

For a brief instant, the smoke cleared enough for Andy to remember that Thorlo Macovich was the biggest black male he had ever met.

"Now, it ain't the guv who mind people smoking." Macovich lit another menthol cigarette. "But the First Lady—wooo." The smoke shook its head. " 'Member that interview she did in the paper the other Sunday on *tertiary smoke*? I mean, how?" The cloud of smoke went on and on. "What? I inhale, then I blow it in your mouth, then you hurry and locate a third party and blow it in their mouth?"

"You'd better blow it somewhere quick," Andy said as he worked out a plan. "Here they come."

Ten

The most malignant smoke in Virginia was not generated by Salem Lights but by a highway pirate named Smoke, who had been consummately evil from birth. His lengthy rap sheet of crimes as a juvenile ranged from truancy to setting cats on fire to malicious wounding and homicide. Although he had finally been brought to justice in Virginia several years earlier, he had managed to break out of a maximum-security prison by forming a noose of sheets and pretending to hang himself from his stainless steel bed.

When prison guard A.P. Pinn noticed Smoke slumped over on the floor, a noose around his neck, bug-eyed with his tongue protruding, Pinn threw open the cell door and rushed inside to see if the inmate might still be alive. Smoke was, and he jumped up and smashed a food tray against Pinn's head. Then Smoke quickly dressed in Pinn's uniform and sunglasses and walked out of the penitentiary without detection. Pinn had gone on to write a book about his ordeal and published it himself. *Betrayed* had not sold very well, and Pinn turned to hosting a local cable show called *Head to Head with Pinn*.

Smoke watched *Pinn Head*, as he called the show, every week to make sure there were no leads on his disappearance or any suspicion that he was the leader of a pack of road dogs. In a way, it disappointed him that Pinn had never so much as alluded to him except to mention that *being trayed* had traumatized Pinn and no one can relate to what it's like to be smacked in the head with meat loaf and instant potatoes until they have had it happen at least once.

Pinn's show had gotten under way and Smoke and his road dogs were gathered in their stolen Winnebago, which was parked behind pine trees on a vacant lot in the north side of the city. Smoke pointed the remote control and turned up the sound as Pinn smiled into the camera and talked with Reverend Pontius Justice about the Neighborhood Watch program the reverend had just kicked off in Shockhoe Bottom, near the Farmers' Market.

"Look at that motherfucker," Smoke said as he gulped down an Old Milwaukee. "He thinks he's something."

Pinn was dressed in a double-breasted shiny black suit, a black shirt and black tie and obviously had bleached his big teeth. When Smoke had known Pinn in the pen, the guard had worn thick tinted glasses. Now he must have contact lenses that caused him to squint a lot.

"What does he think this is? The Academy Awards? I can still see the knot on his head from where I hit him with the tray." Smoke pointed.

"He always had that bump on the back of his head," said Cat, the most senior road dog. "See, he didn't use to shave his head and put wax on it like he does now. So the bump shows up. Man, he got one shiny head. Need to wear sunglasses to even look at it." Cat squinted through cigarette smoke and tapped an ash into a beer can.

"What kinda wax you think he use?" asked another road dog named Possum, who was puny and unhealthy-looking and tended to stay in his room during the day, watching TV with the lights out. "Bee wax, you think? Hey, maybe he use Bed Head. 'Member that dude I bought the gun from? I ask him how he got his head so shiny and he say he use Bed

Head that he got in New York in one of them Cosmetic Centers, and it cost like twenty bucks. It's in a little stick you gotta push up from the bottom and then rub it on your hand like dod'rant . . ."

"That fucker putting dod'rant on his head?" said a third road dog, Cuda, which was short for Barracuda. He stared blearily at Pinn's polished scalp.

"Shut up!" Smoke turned up the volume again.

He was getting excited because Pinn was warming up to the very subject Smoke had been waiting to hear about.

". . . In your book *Betrayed*," Reverend Justice was saying from his overstuffed chair next to a plyboard wall painted to look like a bookcase next to a cheery fireplace, "you went on at great length about how neighbors got to be neighbors instead of just living in the neighborhood. I believe I'm quoting correctly."

"Uh huh, I said that."

"So if we love our brothers and sisters and keep an eye on them coming and going, the neighborhood will change."

"Uh huh. Yeah, I might have said that."

"Did you have this philosophy before you got banged in the head?"

"I don't recall. Might have." Pinn sat straighter in his chair and stared into the camera as he fondled the satin tie he had bought at S&K for nine-ninety-five. "I do know I was being neighborly when I checked on that dead inmate, and next thing I know, I'm unconscience on that hard cement floor. He took my uniform and everything in it." Pinn was getting riled by the memory and it was becoming difficult for him to look serene and wise. "You 'magine that? How would you"—he pointed his finger at his TV audience—"like it someone smack you aside the head and left you naked, implying to the prison population and other guards that maybe you had a male honey who done something to you, 'cause you was found face down with nothing on!"

The reverend was turning pale and beginning to sweat under the hot lights. "That's what forgiveness . . ." He tried to cut Pinn off.

"Forgiveness my ass! I ain't forgiving that punk. Hell, no. I find him one of these days and then we see who smacks who." He glared into the camera, staring straight at Smoke. "And let me tell you, someone knows where that snake in the weed is. You seen him, you call this toll-free number at the bottom of the screen and we send you a reward." He repeated the number several times. "He go by the street name of Smoke and is a plain-looking white boy with dreadlocks and what he calls a beard that got about as much hair as a possum tail."

"Hey!" Possum objected, tossing an empty beer can at the TV.

Smoke pushed Possum off the ottoman and ordered him to shut up. "You bust that TV and I'm going to bust your head!"

"Now I don't know what Smoke is wearing these days 'cause last time I seen him he was in an orange jumpsuit, but he's a young white male 'bout twenty-one or -two and mean as a snake," Pinn went on. "I guarantee he ain't doing nothing to help the neighborhood. Not hardly no way! Now you listen up." He searched the faceless audience behind the camera. "You want some snake in the weed slithering around your neighborhood?"

"We will absolutely keep an eye out in the neighborhood," Reverend Justice promised with a nod as he mopped his face with a handkerchief. "Sure is a lot of meanness out there. Just look at this most recent awful case of Moses Custer getting beat on and his Peterbilt being hijacked right there next to the pumpkin stand."

"He take the reefer or just the cab?" Pinn was momentarily distracted by the terrible story.

"I didn't take no reefer." Smoke made a pun to the TV. "Wish it *had* been full of reefer, though, instead of fucking pumpkins. What you want to bet Pinn Head's this Trooper Truth dude? Maybe he's the idiot writing all that shit on the Internet."

"Yeah, he did," the reverend said, nodding. "A Great Dane reefer," which was trade talk for the top-of-the-line freight van that had been filled with pumpkins and hitched to the Peterbilt eighteen-wheeler truck. "I visited Moses in the hospital." The reverend shook his head sadly. "That poor man look like a pit bull got hold of him."

"What he say they did to him?" Pinn was getting edgy. He didn't like it when a guest was better informed than he was.

"What make you think he Trooper Truth?" asked Possum, who was computer literate and responsible for checking out the Trooper Truth website every morning to see if there was anything on it that Smoke ought to know about.

Possum also handled all Internet transactions, which included searches for eighteen-wheelers that might be parked somewhere with a FOR SALE sign, and news stories about truck shows, truck rodeos, truck accessories and parts, farmers' markets, piracy, smuggling, Canada, and a few of Possum's own special interests such as the *Bonanza* Fan Club and any related conventions that he would, undoubtedly, never get to attend. There was a large volume of e-mail, too, of course, from Smoke's criminal contacts, most of whom remained anonymous.

"Moses was sleeping in the Peterbilt," Reverend Justice was saying, "when all a sudden this angel came to give him a unique experience, then next thing he knows, all these demons are throwing him down on the pavement, where they start kicking and beating on him and cutting him up."

"He not have the doors locked?" Pinn said with a hint of judgment, for it was his habit to find fault with the victim whenever possible, and he was already reaching a verdict that Moses Custer might never have been attacked by demons, pirates, or anything else had he bothered to lock his doors.

"I guess not, but that don't mean he's to blame." The reverend gave Pinn a severe look.

"Hey," Cuda piped, "maybe he say what hospital he in and we go finish him off!"

"Naw, I don't think Pinn Head's Trooper Truth," Possum voiced his opinion. "Not unless he write a lot better than he talk. I think Trooper Truth the po-lice just like his name say he is. 'Cause he always talking about pirates and DNA and shit, and we better watch out he don't come after us 'cause he sure do have a way of finding out things and you already been locked up before." He looked at Smoke. "And there's a 'scription of you going around, so maybe we be better off just quittin' being pirates and maybe go get jobs at the Foot Locker or Bojangles or something . . ."

"Shut up!" Smoke screamed at him as the RV's aluminum door opened and Unique walked in carrying something in a plastic trash bag.

"I need some money," she said to Smoke. "You still owe me."

"Listen here, you concerned viewers out there." Pinn was pointing his finger at the camera again, once more fixated on his own ordeal. The hell with Moses Custer or anyone else. "You see a plain-looking white boy with dreadlocks, you call me right now."

"See, I told you there's a 'scription!" Possum exclaimed.

"He say anything about that queer girl who just got killed on Belle Island?" Unique asked as she stared at the TV.

"What queer girl?" Smoke asked with a yawn.

"No, but Trooper Truth did on his web, but he didn't say nothing about her being queer," Possum volunteered. "He's asking the public for tips."

Unique thought this was very funny. There were no tips. She had been invisible when she left the bar with T.T., so it wasn't possible that anybody had seen Unique and could offer tips to Trooper Truth or anyone else. Of course, becoming invisible was not without its downside. Unique had finally realized that rearranging her molecules when she pursued her Purpose was probably the reason she didn't remember much after the fact. And reliving her cruelities was the best part.

"Pick up the phone right this minute." Pinn repeated the telephone number at the bottom of the screen. "You tell the truth and we get him, I send you five hundred dollars. This is A.P. Pinn for *Head to Head with Pinn*. Good night," he beamed.

"Maybe we should go out and see what's around," Cat suggested, thoroughly bored by the TV show and the local news that followed. "I get the car out from under the tarp and we can go huntin'."

"Yeah," grunted Cuda. "We're almost out of beer and I got one smoke left. Man," he got up, stretching and strutting. "Maybe we find that Custer son of a bitch and kill him in the hospital before he keep snitching on us."

"He doesn't know anything more about us," Smoke snapped at Cuda. "And if you'd killed him to begin with," he added to Possum, "we wouldn't have to worry about it."

Possum had drunk too many beers while they were out cruising for a prize the other night, and his aim had been a little off, much to his secret relief, and as best he knew, the bullet he had fired had struck Moses in the foot and knocked his boot off. "I still think we should find him," he agreed, contrary to his true feelings. "I'll get him smack in the head this time." He pretended to be as cold-blooded as Smoke by pulling a nine-millimeter pistol out of the back of his relaxed-leg jeans and pointing it at the TV, as if it were a hospital bed.

"You shoot the TV, you little shit, and you're next." Smoke jumped up and grabbed the gun and pointed it at Possum's head, snapping back the slide.

Possum swallowed hard, his eyes wide with terror as he begged, "Smoke, don't. Please! I was just kidding, you know?"

"I need my money," Unique said in her quiet, soft voice as her eyes began to blaze and her Purpose began to create that unbearable tension inside her Darkness.

Smoke ignored her, laughing as he shot a hole in the floor. The ejected shell pinged against a lamp and he tossed the pistol back to Possum. "Or maybe I'll shoot the damn dog, since you seem to like her so much. In fact, bring her in here."

"No!" Possum cried out. "Please, Smoke. You can't go shooting that little dog! And I don't like her, either! I can't stand that stupid dog, but we need her! So don't go wasting a bullet on her yet!"

"I'm gonna shoot her eventually," Smoke said. "Or set her on fire, even better. But not until I'm ready to get that bitch Hammer. I'll show her for getting me locked up. Her and that fucker Andy Brazil!"

Possum reluctantly retreated to his bedroom, where he was shocked to see a photograph of Popeye in a red coat filling his computer screen. The real Popeye was sleeping on Possum's bed and noticed the scanned photograph of herself the instant Possum woke her up.

"Shit!" Possum whispered. "We can't tell Smoke about this!" he warned Popeye as he picked her up and she began to shake with excitement and fear.

Trooper Truth somehow knew that Popeye had been dognapped and was still alive! He was looking for her and encouraging the world to help him out. Of course, Popeye knew very well that Trooper Truth was Andy, because she had overheard many private conversations between Andy and Popeye's owner when the website was in the planning stages. Then Andy had suddenly disappeared, and next, Popeye had.

"I ain't gonna hurt ya, little girl," Possum was whispering in her ear. "But Smoke's mean. You know how mean he is, and we gotta make sure he don't know Trooper Truth's offering a reward for you and got every-body joining some big posse to come find you, just like on *Bonanza*."

Popeye didn't need to be reminded of how mean Smoke was, and she would have traded her favorite stuffed squirrel for a chance to sink her teeth into his ankle. She would be forever traumatized by the mem-ory of that unguarded moment when her owner had let her out the front door and gotten distracted by the stove, which she wasn't sure she had remembered to turn off. It all happened so fast. Her owner ran back into the kitchen while Popeye was sniffing grass near the side-walk, and then a black Toyota Land Cruiser suddenly roared up the street and slammed on the brakes and Possum was calling Popeye's name and holding out a treat.

"Come here, Popeye, you good little girl," Possum said as if he were the nicest human in the world. "Look what I got for you!"

Next thing Popeye knew, she was snatched up and thrown into the back of the Land Cruiser, which was driven by that vicious monster, Smoke. Popeye was sped away to the Winnebago, where she had been ever since, and every night she dreamed about her owner, who Smoke said was dead. For a while, Popeye hadn't believed him, but by now, she had resigned herself to the probability that her owner was gone from this earth, because if she wasn't, certainly she would have found Popeye by now and sent Smoke to jail for the rest of his rotten life.

Possum held Popeye tightly and carried her back into the living room. Possum had learned to fake many things, including his feelings. He was careful to act as if taking care of their canine hostage was an inconve-nience. He never let on that he and Popeye had bonded, and that the dog was perhaps the only warm spot of love in his life, except for the television reruns he watched while the other road dogs slept. Popeye cowered in Possum's lap and licked his hand.

"I told you not to lick me!" Possum lied to Popeye, who by now understood the ugly act Possum put on when Smoke was around.

"Maybe it's time we get a message to Hammer that we've found her dog," Smoke said as he handed Unique cash and she silently left. "So she'll meet us somewhere, and when she does, I blow her fucking head off and Brazil's, too."

"Yeah," Cuda said. "You been saying that for months, Smoke. And I keep saying to you, what if she brings other troopers with her? And what if this Brazil guy gets off the first round? I 'member you telling us last time you got in a tussle with him, you ended up in jail, so he must be The Man."

"He's not The Man! I am! Maybe we just kill everybody who shows up, including *you*," Smoke cruelly taunted Popeye. "Lock that ugly dog back in your room and send an e-mail to Captain Bonny and ask him when the hell we're gonna make our move and use the damn dog to get the fuckers," he told Possum. "I'm tired of waiting!" he said to everyone. "Go get the car!" he ordered Cat.

Possum logged on to the Internet, clicked on FAVORITES and pulled up Captain Bonny's egotistical, self-promoting, self-serving website, which featured a fierce woodcut of Blackbeard on the home page. Possum went to the *How To Contact* section and pecked out the following message, which was the opposite of what Smoke wanted:

Dear Captin Bonny
 Us pirates ain't ready to make the Big Move yet. I'll let you know.

Yours truley,
Pirate Possum.

Major Trader just happened to be eating a banana split in his spec-home office when the e-mail landed. He was becoming annoyed with Pirate Possum and whoever his felonious, crude mates were. Trader had faithfully leaked information to the pirates and kept them out of the news for many months and so far had gone unrewarded. He had better be taken care of appropriately just as soon as the pirates made their so-called Big Move, which Trader had assumed all along was a big move of cocaine, heroin, and guns across the Canadian border.

He typed out an e-mail.

Dear Pirate Possum,

It was good to hear from you as always. But let me remind you that when I orchestrated the dognapping of Popeye so you could set up an ambush of Superintendent Hammer, the deal was that I would be handsomely rewarded. I have been patient for months, and now my terms have changed! I am demanding not 50% but 60% of the booty, paid in cash and left in a waterproof suitcase at a location of my choosing. Let me remind you that if you don't come through for me, I will be forced to use force.

Sincerely,
The Notorious Captain Bonny

Eleven

The black front door of Ruth's Chris Steak House slowly opened, and Governor Crimm and the First Lady emerged from the former plantation house, pressed upon from all sides by serious EPU troopers in neat suits. The Crimms' four daughters—all unmarried and over thirty—fell in behind their important parents and were sealed off from the rest of society by yet another wall of troopers at the rear of the procession.

Macovich quickly tossed the cigarette and unfolded himself like a stretcher as he worked his way out of the car while Andy smoothed down his dark gray uniform, checking to make sure that his clip-on tie, pepper spray, handcuffs, tactical baton, extra magazines of ammunition, pistol, and whistle were in place. He realized it might not be a good idea to bring up Tangier Island or Hammer in front of so many sets of eyes and ears. Certainly, it would make Hammer look bad if her troops knew that the governor never returned her phone calls or met with her. And based on the way the governor was walking, Andy wasn't confident that he was entirely sober.

"Look, it's possible the governor might remember you or the daughter you upset might say something," Andy said, falling in stride with Macovich as the distinguished party approached. "So I think it best I take him aside. I think he's a bit drunk."

Macovich had no intention of helping Andy have a private audience with the governor, especially if the governor had a buzz on and was happier and more generous than usual. The last thing Macovich needed was for Andy to end up the governor's pet in addition to being Hammer's pet. Macovich had been trying for years to gain special status and even affection from the governor, all to no avail, and the pool incident certainly hadn't helped matters.

"Wooo, I wouldn't try it," Macovich tried to discourage Andy. " 'Specially if he's drunk. He's one mean man when he's drunk."

Macovich felt a little guilty about lying and stepping on Andy, but Macovich couldn't help himself. He feared he had leveled out on his professional climb to success, and if he wasn't shrewd and territorial, he would find himself working security in a shopping mall one of these days or maybe flying grumpy racist businessmen around for a helicopter charter service. But to Macovich's surprise and annoyance, Andy completely ignored Macovich and walked right up to the governor and shook his hand.

"So the military's protecting me now." The governor seemed pleased, recognizing dimly that the person before him was a tall male in uniform, and therefore was either Army or National Guard. "I like that."

The three oldest Crimm daughters fastened their attention to Andy like leeches at a blood-letting, while the fourth daughter, whose arrested adolescence was annoyingly apparent, smacked gum. Governor Crimm smiled, patting for his magnifying glass, which he had attached to his pocket-watch chain to insure that his beloved optical aid did not find its way into the compote again. A huge eye peered through thick glass, scanning to see who might be watching his generous overtures toward the young soldier.

"The more protection the better, I always say," the governor commented. "What's your name, soldier?"

"Andy Brazil. I'd like to be one of your pilots, Governor. If that would be all right with you. Maybe I could have a moment of your time to discuss it."

"Bet you want to be executive protection, too."

The governor had heard this before. Every state trooper he had ever met wanted to be EPU, just as most federal agents wanted to be Secret Service. It was all about power. It was all about being close to the throne. He also vaguely made out that Andy was a handsome fellow, well built but not a big wall of muscle like the other men and women who protected the First Family. Andy's was a useful body that could dance around trouble instead of barreling right through it, and the governor fancied that Andy might make a decent son-in-law for at least one of the Crimm daughters. Then it dimly penetrated his overburdened, inebriated mind that he wasn't so sure he was inclined to trust his wife around such an attractive and charming young fellow.

Despite her swearing to tell the truth and even placing her left hand on the Crimm family Bible, the First Lady had not convinced her husband that she hadn't been hiding adulterous men in the mansion's linen closets. Yesterday, Crimm came home for lunch unannounced and discovered Pony on his hands and knees wiping a linen closet floor with a rag.

"What are you doing?" the governor demanded as he fumbled for his watch chain and the magnifying glass dangling from it.

"Just putting a little furniture polish on the hardwood," Pony said, nervously rubbing oil into the scratches the trivets had left on the heart-of-pine flooring. "I've been meaning to get around to it, sir. Just now did. There's some nice split pea soup cooking in the kitchen, if you want some."

"Does it have ham in it?" The governor peered through the magnifying glass at the scratched old wood. "How did the floor get gouged like that? It looks like someone wearing hobnail boots was hiding in the closet or maybe someone wearing tap shoes."

"I think it's maybe from the vacuum cleaner," Pony suggested as he covered the scratches as quickly as possible. "I keep telling the house-keepers not to put the vacuum cleaner in the linen closets. I'm afraid the pea soup does have ham in it. I didn't know you'd be coming home for lunch or I would have made sure they didn't put ham or even a ham bone in it, sir."

Just as Pony was explaining all this, the governor detected a clanking sound as someone hurried downstairs. Crimm hurried, too, but wasn't fast enough to catch the source of the odd noise that he now suspected was a man wearing either spurs or armor, and his fears about his wife began to scream inside his psyche. Was she playing strange dress-up games with unknown men she picked up on the Internet? He imagined her in erotic poses with virile young suitors dressed in nothing but spurs or a helmet with a plume or perhaps both. Maude and her lascivious lovers would have loud, metallic sex and maybe use magnets to enhance their perverted pleasure before she suddenly noticed the crown mold-ing and cobwebs and began withholding favors from these cybermen the same way she had been denying the governor for long years. For all he knew, Andy Brazil was part of the plot. How did the governor know that Andy hadn't already met Maude on the Internet and wanted to fly the First Family because he really wanted to fly Maude?

"You'd have to be a state trooper before you can be EPU," the governor told Andy in an autocratic, unfriendly tone.

"I am a state trooper, Governor. And we're short of pilots," Andy added to the First Lady, because by nature he was inclusive and did not treat the wives of others as appendages.

"Seems like it's always the same pilot these days," she said, irritated by the reminder as she frowned at Macovich.

Where had all her pilots gone? As she recalled, there had been plenty of them earlier in the year, and she supposed that the problem must be that ball-breaking woman who was the new superintendent of the state police. Trader had horrible things to say about her. What was her name? A tool of some type. How appropriate. A sledgehammer? No, not quite.

Mrs. Crimm strained to remember. Sledge. That was it. Superintendent Sledge. Maybe it was time for the First Lady to send a pointed note to her and demand more pilots, and Mrs. Crimm fondly thought of her favorite saying, *Variety is the spice of life*, and recited it out loud.

"Pardon?" Andy was baffled.

"I'm just wondering if you agree," the First Lady said to him.

Andy sensed he was being tested and replied, "In most cases. But not always. For example, I don't wear a variety of clothes to work. Always a uniform. And I very much like the state police uniform and am happy to wear it every day, so variety is not an issue with me."

"What?" The governor picked up on his wife's secret code and was shocked she would be so blatant, and he imagined her having sex with this Andy fellow, who probably would have nothing on but a duty belt. "Variety most assuredly is not the spice of life or anything else," Crimm thundered. "Life is all about faithfulness and serving your master. And what do you mean by *spice?*" He glared through his magnifying glass at his unfaithful wife.

"Dear, calm down," said the First Lady, who suddenly recalled that she had hidden her stash of trivets in the spice cabinet, and perhaps it was best not to allude to spices again. "I told you not to eat all that sour cream and butter. You know what it does to your submarine." She was confident this would divert his attention. "Why, all that animal fat and all those dairy products are just fuel oil for your submarine, and spices aren't the problem because there were no spices on your dinner, other than all that salt you poured over everything. We avoid spices for good reason, now don't we? And we won't mention them ever again for fear you'll make associations that will excite your submarine and send it plunging into turbulence that could end terribly with blown gaskets and leaking seals and silt billowing up from the bottom of your constitution. Now, Trooper Brazil—what an exotic name, are you South American? Have you met Constance, Grace, and Faith?"

The First Lady stopped short of the fourth daughter, the youngest, and the least attractive woman in the parking lot.

"And what about you?" Andy asked the ignored daughter, halfway expecting her name to be Sloth or Gluttony, based on her appearance and demeanor.

"What's it to you?" She violently chewed a massive wad of bubblegum, and Andy was struck by her bluntness and lack of charm. "And I saw you get out of your unmarked car." She scowled at him. "What good does it do to drive an unmarked car and then wear a uniform? How retarded is that?"

"You don't sound like you're from around here." Andy overlooked her poor manners as he tried to place her loud drawl. He also didn't intend to reveal that Hammer insisted Andy drive an unmarked car since he was an undercover journalist and she preferred that he draw as little attention to himself as possible.

"I was born in Grundy, in the coal mines," the rude daughter replied.

"You most certainly were not." The First Lady was appalled. "I was carrying her during a whistle-stop campaign up there on the western Virginia border where we toured several coal mines," she informed Andy as the governor continued to scan through his magnifying glass, in search of the helicopter, while the EPU huddled around him and his family in the dark, waiting for orders. "But she was born in a hospital just like all of my daughters," Mrs. Crimm added indignantly, giving the so-far nameless girl a warning glance.

"Can always use another pilot, I suppose," Governor Crimm despondently said, wishing he hadn't eaten so much and humiliated that the First Lady had mentioned his submarine in public.

There were times when Bedford Crimm regretted his life. In Virginia, governors can't succeed themselves, so he always had to wait four years before running again. For twenty years, he had been recycled through his arcane, antiquated, ridiculous state system—commander in chief for a term, then back to the private sector for another term, then back in the mansion again. The White House was smaller and more distant by now. Governor Crimm was over seventy, vodka went straight to his head, and his poorly wired submarine was almost never on course anymore.

The EPU troopers were getting restless. A crowd was gathering. Andy was no fool. He knew that an added bonus to flying the governor would be that the closer he could get to him, the more information he could gather for his Trooper Truth essays.

"Governor," Andy said, "Let me just say again that I'd be honored to fly you and your family around in a new helicopter, and although I don't need to be EPU, I will protect you at the same time. I don't suppose I could have a moment to talk to you privately?"

Macovich was seething, but nobody could tell, because troopers were taught never to register what was going on inside them. His only consolation as he watched Andy eclipse him on this crisp September night was that Macovich knew that horrid youngest Crimm daughter's name very well. Wooo, he sure did. He had never spoken to her, not even when he had beaten her in pool, but he always kept his eye on her behind the dark mask of his sunglasses.

Her name was Regina, pronounced the British way, and this was part of what was wrong with her, if you didn't include her unfortunate obesity and broad, homely face. It was well known among the troopers that Regina had inclinations that did not coincide with the First Lady's relentless attempts to matchmake her undesirable daughters.

"Trooper Brazil's not a great pilot," Macovich whispered to the First Lady, deciding the best way to protect his turf was to set Andy up. "But he's single and been pretty down lately. I think he's lonely."

"How sad!" the First Lady whispered back. "Why, I'll just invite him to the mansion!"

"Oh, now that would be mighty nice, ma'am," Macovich replied as if it were the most magnanimous thing he'd ever heard.

Andy Brazil had no idea what he was getting himself into, Macovich thought with a thrill of vindication. The pretty white boy was going to have the stuffing ripped out of him just like the straw man the flying monkeys carried off, following the orders of their supervisor, the wicked witch of the west, or wherever she was from.

"Well, I guess we should go," the governor decided as his submarine plunged into murky bile spewed out by his gallbladder. "I'm not feeling well and should never have eaten that Belgian fudge cake that Trader had couriered to the restaurant and sent to the table," he added as Andy's antenna went up. "It's true, Maude, I need to cut back."

Macovich and his fellow troopers led the First Family away to the helicopter under a cloak of protective darkness as Andy got out his cell phone. He would call the steak house immediately and insist that any leftover fudge cake be sealed in a plastic bag right away. Suddenly he remembered he had promised Hammer to tell the governor about the situation on Tangier Island. The helicopter's engines ignited and the four blades began to turn as Andy ran toward the chopper.

"But Governor!" Andy shouted, "Superintendent Hammer has urgent news and must talk to you!" His words were scattered by rotor wash.

"I smell cigarettes!" the First Lady went off like a smoke alarm as she held on to her stiffly sprayed hair, protecting it from the sudden wind.

"Not me," all of the troopers said at once.

Smoke and his road dogs were watching all this from behind the tinted glass of the black Toyota Land Cruiser that had been stolen in New York and through a series of transactions had ended up in Smoke's possession with new plates and the vehicle identification number filed off. The pirates had been cruising when they happened upon Bellgrade Shopping Center, where Ruth's Chris Steak House was tucked back behind old trees, and they couldn't help but notice the huge helicopter sitting in the grass.

None of the highway pirates had ever seen such a thing, and when the throttle was turned up to full power, Smoke and his crew gawked at beating blades and landing lights blazing as trees whipped in hurricane-force gusts.

"Shit," Smoke exclaimed. It was rare he showed emotion other than anger and hate. "Would you fucking look at that!"

Cuda, Possum, and Cat sat in awed silence, the chopping of the blades thudding their eardrums and exciting their blood like lust.

"I wonder how hard it'd be to fly one of those things," Smoke said.

"You imagine what we could do with something like that? Fuck trucks! Shit, no one could ever catch us and we could deliver the goods ourselves in half the time from here to Canada, get the middle man out of the way."

The helicopter lifted, flooding wildly swirling grass with dazzling light, and through an expansive passenger's window, Smoke could just make out one of the Crimm daughters ripping open a bag of junk food, maybe chips. Then he noticed someone else. Andy Brazil was trotting back to his unmarked car. It turned Smoke to molten lava to see that son of a bitch again. When Andy had been a city cop, he and Hammer had been responsible for catching Smoke and putting him in prison. Not a day had passed in Smoke's cell when he hadn't entertained sadistic fantasies about what was in store for those two cops.

"Well, well, well," Smoke said, as the helicopter rose above trees and thundered into the sky. "Look who's here. Maybe I ought to blow his motherfucking brains out right now."

"Whose brains?" Cat tore his eyes away from the bright light churning up the night. He followed Smoke's vindictive stare to a blond trooper climbing into an unmarked car.

"Why you want to blow his brains out now, man?" Possum protested as Smoke put the SUV in gear. "Don't go be doing something like that with all these police around! You crazy or what? You wanna do that, I'm getting outta the car."

Possum was riding up front, and when he grabbed the door handle, Smoke backhanded him across the face. Cuda and Cat shrank into their seats, getting smaller and falling silent. They despised Smoke but had nowhere else to go, and were in too much trouble by now to do anything but stay in their present employment. Both Cuda and Cat had started out in street gangs, which were a dime a dozen these days. Being a pirate was like being the Mafia, Cat reassured himself as he didn't move or blink in his seat in the Land Cruiser. Nobody messed with Smoke and his road dogs, and they went after bigger prizes than just ripping off people and ATM machines and doing drive-by shootings for fun. The other day, Smoke had taken his crew to Cloverleaf Mall and bought all of them brand-new Nikes and all the pizza and french fries they could eat in the food court.

So he wasn't all bad. Possum was trying to make himself feel better, too. But he was tired of being smacked around by Smoke and worrying about him hurting or killing poor little Popeye. When Possum was growing up, his daddy used to smack him around, too, and do awful things at the dinner table, stabbing steak knives into the wood and throwing food across the room. His daddy liked to shoot rabbits and send the dogs after them so he could have the pleasure of watching the small, shrieking creatures torn to bits. Possum began to stay in the basement, dropping out of school to watch TV in the dark. Over the years, he stopped growing and crept up from the basement only late at night to raid the refrigerator and the liquor bottles after his parents had quit fighting and gone to sleep.

Possum had never caused any kind of trouble until he was able to see in the dark and sunlight hurt his eyes. Then he began to venture out of the basement after midnight and walk around Northside's Chamberlayne Avenue, looking dreamily at cars gliding past and normal people out—people who could come and go as they pleased and didn't have to spend their days in the basement listening to their daddy tear up the house and beat on their mama and torture animals.

One morning at about 2:00 A.M., Possum was malingering in the parking lot of Azalea Mall, eyeing the ATM and hoping someone had forgotten to get their cash out of the little slot he was shoving a Slim Jim down, and a Land Cruiser pulled up. Possum started running, but Smoke was too fast for him. Next thing, Possum was tackled to the pavement and a white boy with dreadlocks was sticking a gun to Possum's head and ordering him into the Land Cruiser. Possum had been a road dog ever since, and sometimes he missed the basement and thought about his mama. Once—and only once—he had called her from a pay phone.

"I got me a good job working at night," he told his mama. "But I can't say where, Mama, 'cause Daddy would come get me, you know. You doing all right?"

"Oh, honey, sometimes it ain't so bad," she said in that defeated, depressed tone Possum knew so well. "Please come home, Jerry," she added, because Possum's real name was Jeremiah Little. "I miss you, baby."

"Don't you be worrying none." Possum got a big lump in his chest as he talked inside the graffiti-scarred phone booth. "I gonna get enough money to get you out of there and we go live in some nice motel where he ain't never gonna find us!"

The problem with his plan, Possum had since learned, was that Smoke kept the prize money to himself. He gave cash to his dogs as needed and wouldn't allow them to accumulate any on their own. Possum got plenty to eat and all the alcohol and pot he wanted. He wore nice basketball shoes and huge jeans that were always falling off. He was equipped with a pager, a cell phone, a handheld Global Positioning System, a gun, and his own room in the RV. But he had no savings and it was likely he never would. He thought about this as his face stung and the inside of his lip bled. Possum missed his mama and realized that Smoke was even worse than Possum's daddy.

"You can't be killing him right now," Possum tried to reason with Smoke. "It's better we wait and make the Big Move. Then we can blow away all them motherfuckers at once, including Popeye."

Smoke turned back onto Huguenot Road and sped off. "Don't worry, I ain't taking Brazil out tonight in front of all these people. But I'm going to get him bad when the time's right—just like I'm gonna get that bitch Hammer. Hey. Maybe I'll feed her fucking dog to a pit bull and leave the carcass in her yard."

"You do that, you ain't got nothing to fuck with her about no more," Possum said with feigned nonchalance. "That dog the biggest prize you got, Smoke. You know that lady cop do anything to get that dumb dog back, right? So you gotta play your cards and be patience. Maybe you could use that dog to get Hammer and Brazil at the same time. What you wanna bet Brazil knew Popeye and don't like it none, either, that the dog disappeared, huh?"

"Yeah. I'll set both of them up. Fucking yeah. At the same time!" Smoke tried to follow the helicopter that was fast moving out of sight toward the lit-up city skyline. "Then we'll take them to the clubhouse," as he referred to their RV, "and I'll have a shitload of time to really make them hurt bad before I blow their brains out and throw their fucking bodies in the river."

The road dogs knew that Smoke's specialty as a child was to bury rabbits and chipmunks alive, jump on frogs, trap birds and throw them out windows, and do other unspeakable things to helpless creatures. It wasn't lost on Possum that Smoke had christened each of his road dogs with an animal's name, as if to imply what he would do to them if they ever got out of line.

"Yeah, set 'em up." Possum pretended to sound mean-spirited and tough. "And maybe kill some other people, too," he added. "And maybe tell Cap'n Bonny we ain't paying him nothing and he tries to mess with us, we shoot him and throw him in the river, too."

"Shut up." Smoke smacked Possum on the ear. "I gotta find out where they park that helicopter, then we're gonna take it. Maybe hot-wire it."

"You don't got to hot-wire it," Possum dared to offer as his ear rang with pain. "I seen something 'bout them on the Discovery Channel. All you do is push a button, they start right up. Then you lift this little handle and steer with a stick."

"Driving a helicopter ain't the same as driving a truck." Cat broke his silence. "I don't know if we could pull it off."

"Find out where the state police airport is," Smoke ordered his road dogs. "Look it up on the GPS."

Unique didn't need a GPS to find her way around, nor did she have one. Smoke did not supply her with special weapons and equipment, although she could get anything she wanted from him, if needed. But Unique had her own special techniques that radiated from her Darkness where the Nazi dwelled deep inside her soul. As she drove her Miata along Strawberry Street, she felt weightless and airborne. She was flying through the night, her long hair streaming behind her and the wind cool on her delicately pretty face. She parked a block from the blond undercover cop's row house, not having a clue that he was Andy Brazil—the very cop that Smoke had just been talking about.

Unique had not known Smoke back in the days when Andy and Hammer had arrested him, and therefore she had never seen or met either one of them, to her knowledge. Were Unique not controlled by evil, it might have seemed a remarkable coincidence that she was stalking not only Smoke's enemy, but also Trooper Truth, and had no clue. But in fact, nothing that happened in Unique's life was coincidental or accidental. She was guided by her Purpose, which had directed her to leave the trash bag on the undercover cop's porch and tape an envelope to his front door.

Twelve

Overlooking the city from the top of one of Richmond's seven hills was a historic row house that Judy Hammer had taken great pains to restore and furnish impeccably. She was paying bills at her antique rolltop desk, the lights of the city spread out beyond the window in a comforting circuitry that reminded her she had a tremendous responsibility to Virginians and had become a role model to women throughout the nation.

All the same, it was no easy matter finding eligible men when one is creeping closer to sixty and carries a gun in her Ferragamo handbag. Hammer was feeling lonely and discouraged and had been terribly unnerved by seeing the photograph of Popeye on the website. It had also been another bad day in the news. A woman was suing McDonald's for allegedly having been burned by a pickle from an improperly constructed hamburger. Then a legally blind man and his brother tried to burglarize an apartment, and the pair made the tactical error of deciding the blind brother would be the lookout. Not to mention the people who were getting blood clots from flying coach and the local police who were dredging the James River again for guns, since most suspects claimed they tossed their weapons off bridges after committing their crimes.

Hammer was a little surprised that she hadn't heard from Andy by now. She worried that the silence might indicate a failed connection with the governor. Perhaps he and Macovich had been unable to make contact, or if they had, the results were not helpful. Just as these thoughts were making the rounds in her mind, the telephone rang.

"Yes," she answered curtly, as if she hated for anyone to bother her.

"Superintendent Hammer?" Andy's voice traveled over the line.

"What is it, Andy?" Hammer said.

He was driving east on Broad Street, where surly teenagers lingered on corners and in front of boarded-up buildings, glaring at the unmarked car with all of its antennas and hidden blue lights.

"I'm not too far from Church Hill," Andy said as he kept up his scan of shifty-looking people. "If it's not inconvenient," he bravely pushed ahead, "maybe I should drop by and tell you what's going on."

"Fine," Hammer said and hung up without saying good-bye.

Hammer did not have the genetic coding to tolerate a waste of time, and as she got older, her resentment of remote communication intensified. She could not abide the clangor of the phone when someone entered her airspace uninvited. She loathed voice mail and played it as quickly as she could before deleting it from her life, usually long before the message ended. Two-way radios were a nuisance and so was e-mail—especially *instant messages* from *buddies* she did not choose, who barged right into her cyberspace without being invited. Hammer just wanted quiet. At this stage in her life's journey, people were beginning to make her tired and she was noticing how rarely communication relayed anything that mattered.

"Tell me what's going on," Hammer said when Andy was scarcely inside the front door. "Did you mention to the governor that Tangier Island is holding a dentist hostage and has declared war on Virginia because of the damn speed traps and NASCAR and possible dental fraud?"

"I didn't get a chance," Andy reluctantly admitted as he settled on the sofa. "I don't think he recognizes anyone visually, either. He thought I was military and had no idea who Macovich is. I'm just wondering if that's the root of his problem, Superintendent Hammer. Maybe he's legally blind and hasn't seen you since you were sworn in because he never saw you to begin with."

Hammer had never considered this. "That's ridiculous," she decided.

"With all due respect . . ."

She raised a hand to silence him. Whenever anyone led off *with all due respect*, she knew damn well she was being lied to and was about to be dissed or annoyed. "Just say whatever it is, and cut the respect crap," Hammer told him.

"Someone needs to inform him that he has to do something about his vision," Andy made the point. "Maybe you should."

"If I ever talk to him, I'll tell him that and more," Hammer said impatiently.

Andy made her feel old. His very presence aged her by years, and she had begun reacting with avoidance and wasn't especially warm to him anymore. She had been a strikingly handsome woman all of her life until she'd turned fifty-five, when it seemed to her she instantly accumulated body fat and wrinkles. Her upper lip began to disappear overnight, her hair began to thin, and her breasts began to shrink, all within days. Andy, meanwhile, only got handsomer every time she saw him.

It wasn't fair, she thought.

"Are you all right, Superintendent Hammer?" Andy asked. "You seem angry and kind of out of sorts all of a sudden."

"Just the mention of the governor puts me in a foul mood," she evasively said.

It was so fucking unfair, she silently complained. Men Hammer's age dated women Andy's age, women who thought bald heads, weathered skin, thick glasses, decreased muscle bulk, migrating hair, special pumps and pills to help raise the level of intimacy, and snoring were somehow a bonus. Oh, how women had been brainwashed, Hammer raged on in silence. Young women bragged to each other about how old their lovers were.

Just the other day, Windy Brees had been smoking a cigarette outside in the headquarters parking lot when Hammer overheard her telling a friend about Mr. Click. Hammer had briskly walked past Windy and the friend, staring at the pavement, loaded down with files and her briefcase, pretending she was unaware of the conversation. But Windy had a voice that carried, and the entire state police force heard every word.

"How old is Mr. Click?" Windy's young female friend had asked enviously.

"Ninety-one," Windy had proudly replied. "I'm just smitten. All I do is wait by the phone." She held up her cell phone and sighed, wishing it would trill.

"But it's not on," the friend had observed. "You have to push in the power button and turn it on, otherwise it won't ring if he calls." She dug her own cell phone out of her purse and demonstrated.

"Well, I'll be!" Windy had exclaimed with renewed hope. "I wonder if he knows to turn his on? Because whenever I call his cell phone, I always get this same voice that says he's not available, and it depresses me, because I worry he isn't available in general and that's why I've not heard from him since late last night."

"I may as well take matters into my own hands," Hammer decided. "I can't wait for the governor to see me while a dentist is held hostage on an island that has declared war on Virginia. Nothing good can come from this, Andy. We must intervene immediately."

"With all due respect," Andy started to say, but caught himself. "Superintendent Hammer," he started again, "Governor Crimm is a proud man who is addicted to power. If you go over his head, he won't forgive or forget it. He may not recognize it, but he'll deeply resent your getting all the credit."

"Then what the hell do we do?"

"Give me forty-eight hours," Andy boldly promised. "I'll somehow get an audience with him and inform him of all the facts." He paused as he thought of Popeye and how empty Hammer's house seemed without the little dog. "I posted a photo of Popeye on the home page of my website . . ."

"I saw it," Hammer replied. "And you should have asked me first, now that we're on the subject."

"I'm not going to give up on her," Andy said.

Hammer's eyes filled with tears that she quickly blinked back.

"I know how much you miss her," Andy went on, touched by her sadness and determined to make her talk to him about her feelings. "And I know how much you hate it when I do things without permission, but I'm not a rookie anymore, Superintendent Hammer. I have a mind of my own and a pretty good sense of what I'm doing. It seems you're always irritated with me and have no appreciation of anything I do."

Hammer wouldn't look at him or respond.

"To be honest," Andy went on, "you seem miserable and mad at the world most of the time these days."

Hammer was silent. Andy started to get up from his chair.

"Well, I don't want to invade your privacy," he said, sensing that the last thing she wanted was for him to leave. "But I guess I'll head out and not disturb you any further."

"That's a good idea," Hammer said, abruptly getting up. "It's late."

She walked him to the door as if she couldn't wait for him to leave.

Andy glanced at his watch. "You're right. I need to go," he said. "I have to finish my next essay, you know."

"Do I dare bring up the subject?" Hammer asked as she walked him out to the front porch, where a tart fall breeze rustled trees that were beginning to turn the first hues of yellow and red. "Will there be more salient comments from your wise confidante?"

"I don't have a wise confidante," Andy said with surprising sharpness as he went down the steps and passed through the gentle glow of gaslight lamps. "I wish I did," he tossed back at her as he unlocked his car. "But I've yet to meet anybody who fits that description."

He drove back home feeling out of sorts, and he was startled and suspicious when he climbed his front steps and saw a trash bag on the mat and an envelope taped to his door. There was nothing written on the plain white envelope, which looked like the generic kind available in any drugstore, and the black plastic trash bag clearly had something in it. Andy's law-enforcement instincts instantly went on alert, and he touched nothing and got on his cell phone.

"Detective Slipper," a voice answered after the phone rang for a long time inside the Richmond police department's A Squad, the division that worked violent crimes.

"Joe," Andy said, "it's me, Andy Brazil."

"Yo! What'cha know? We still miss your ugly face around here. How are things with the state police?"

"Listen," Andy abruptly said, "can you buzz over to my house? Someone's left something strange on my porch, and I don't want to touch it."

"Shit! You want me to bring the bomb squad?"

"Not yet," Andy replied. "Why don't you come here first and take a look?"

He sat on his front steps in the dark, because his porch light wasn't on a timer and the lights were off inside to save on his electric bill. Richmond police headquarters was downtown but not far from the Fan District where Andy's tiny rented row house was located. Detective Joe Slipper rolled up fifteen minutes later, and Andy realized how much he missed some of his old friends from his former job as a city cop.

"Damn good to see you," he said to Slipper, a short, pudgy man who always reeked of cologne and had a taste for slick designer suits that he got dirt cheap at a local men's discount shop.

"Shit," Slipper said as he probed the trash bag and blank envelope with a Kel light. "This is really weird."

"You got any gloves handy?" Andy asked.

"Sure." Slipper pulled a pair of surgical gloves out of a pocket.

Andy put them on and tugged the envelope off the door. It was sealed, and he slit it open with a pocket knife. Inside was a Polaroid photograph, and Andy and Slipper were stunned as the flashlight revealed a shocking image of Trish Thrash's nude, bloody body at Belle Island. Slipper nudged the trash bag with his foot.

"Shit," he said. "Feels like clothes in there."

He opened the bag and carefully pulled out a black leather biker's jacket, jeans, panties, a bra, and a T-shirt with the logo of what appeared to be a Richmond women's softball team. The clothing appeared to have been cut with a razor blade and was stiff with dried blood.

"Christ," Andy said as he broke out in a cold sweat and thought of what had been carved on the murdered woman's body. "I got no idea what's going on here, Joe."

Slipper quietly and somberly returned to his car and got out evidence bags and tape. He sealed everything inside paper bags and suggested he and Andy talk, neither of them having any idea that Unique was hiding in the shadows across the street, watching the entire drama.

"How about we sit in your car?" Andy suggested because he didn't want Slipper inside his cluttered dining-room office with its research materials on Jamestown, Isle of Dogs, pirates, mummies, photographs of Popeye, and all the rest.

"Sure." Slipper shrugged, slightly puzzled. "What? You hiding a woman in there?"

"I wish," Andy replied. "Nope. It's just the place is a friggin' mess and I'd rather not be distracted at the moment. If you feel better coming inside, that's fine, of course. You can even search the place if you want."

"Hell, no, Andy," Slipper said. "Shit. I got no probable cause to search your house, even if you give me permission. Come on. Let's go sit in that piece of shit the city gives me to drive."

"I don't know what the hell is going on, Joe," Andy kept saying.

"Well, I do," Slipper answered as they climbed inside his old unmarked Ford LTD and shut the doors. "It certainly looks like our killer left this shit and is jerking us around. You know, I worked that fucking scene, and it's obvious to me the photo was taken before we got there. Not to mention, when we responded, there was no sign of her clothes, and we searched the entire island."

Andy was in turmoil. Did the killer somehow know that he was Trooper Truth? Is that why Trooper Truth was carved on the body and now evidence was left at Andy's house? But how could anyone except Hammer possibly know the real identity of Trooper Truth? It made no sense, and Andy feared that if he openly discussed the situation with Slipper, the detective would tell other cops and Andy's literary career would be over and Hammer would be fired by the governor. Worst of all, Andy might become the prime suspect.

"Jesus Christ," he said with a frustrated sigh. "Joe, let me tell you right off, I had nothing to do with this case. I never heard of the victim until you called Hammer earlier today. I'd never seen the victim, and I sure as hell didn't murder her or anyone, if that's what you're even remotely entertaining, and I think we should be really honest with each other, Joe."

"Damn right we'll be honest," Slipper replied, staring out the windshield at the dark, empty street, and Andy could tell by Slipper's refusal to look him in the eye that the detective didn't know what to think and was, in fact, suspicious.

"Do you know anything about Trooper Truth?" Slipper asked.

"I know the name was carved on her body, because you told Hammer and she told me," Andy said. "Certainly, I know about Trooper Truth's website, just like everybody else does."

"You've read his shit?"

"Yes," Andy said. "And I can't see that there's anything in the content of those essays that might be somehow linked to Trish Thrash, do you?"

"Gotta agree with you there," Slipper confessed. "I mean, I don't see any connection between Jamestown, mummies, and all the rest, to what appears to be a blatant hate crime targeted at gay women. And I gotta admit, Andy," Slipper said, finally looking at him, "half the city cops always assumed you was gay, and you never have seemed to care or have a thing about gays."

"I don't," Andy replied sincerely. "I don't have a thing about anybody except bad people."

"Yeah, that's always been my impression." Slipper shook his head, mystified. "But why the hell would the killer leave this shit at your house, for Christ's sake? I'm wondering if it could be some person you've arrested before or somehow had contact with, maybe when you was working for the city? Is your address listed in the phone book?"

"No, Joe, it's not. Mind if I ask you something?"

"Sure."

"Have you considered that maybe the Trooper Truth link isn't that the killer reads Trooper Truth but that maybe the victim did and somehow the killer found that out?"

"You know, I'm kind of embarrassed to tell you that I didn't think of that," Slipper said with interest and a spark of hope. "Damn good thought. I'll follow up on that right away, go back and talk some more with the people she worked with."

"Maybe with some of the people who played on the softball team that's on her T-shirt," Andy suggested. "What you might want to consider is not asking about Trooper Truth directly, because you don't want people knowing the detail about what was cut on her body, right?"

"Hell no. Only the killer and us and the M.E. know that. So we need to keep that to ourselves in case we ever get a suspect and he confesses to it, right?"

"Exactly, Joe."

"So how do you think I could find out about Trooper Truth without mentioning him directly?"

"How about this for an idea," Andy said. "Trooper Truth gets e-mail."

"He does?"

"Yes. It's right there on the website that you can contact whoever he or she is and so on. Why not send an e-mail to Trooper Truth and ask for his or her help? He—let's just go ahead and call him or her a *he*—can post something on his site and see if people who might have known Trish Thrash will respond."

"Like what?" Slipper scratched his chin. "What do we want him to put on his site?"

"Okay," Andy said, thinking. "Try this: *The police are looking for anyone who knew Trish Thrash and might know her hobbies, passions, what she read, and if there was anything or anyone of late that she talked about a lot.*"

Slipper was taking notes and asked Andy to repeat the statement again.

"And I would add," Andy suggested, "that the informers don't have to identify themselves, otherwise some people won't feel comfortable stepping forward. And I'd offer a reward for any tip that leads to an arrest."

Slipper started the car engine and turned on his headlights while Unique crouched behind a tree in the dark, her molecules rearranged into invisibility and her Purpose throbbing as she imagined appearing at the blond cop's door one night.

"My car's broke down," the Nazi scripted. "Can I use the phone?"

The cop would let her inside, and when he turned his back for even a second, Unique would, as instructed, become invisible and slip up behind him, slashing his throat all the way through his windpipe so he couldn't scream and would drown in his own blood. Then, the Nazi said from her dark space, Unique would slash his pretty face, cut out his eyes and tongue, castrate him, carve a swastika on his belly, and photograph the fruits of her Purpose, as usual. Finally, she would take his clothes, which Unique would deliver to whomever the Nazi directed.

"I know you've already thought of this," Andy was diplomatically suggesting, "but I'd get the DNA lab to analyze the envelope, assuming the killer licked the flap, then have the profile run through the DNA database to see if we're lucky enough to get a cold hit. Also have the blood on the clothes checked for DNA. Sometimes the killer cuts himself. I'd also get Vander to do his thing with the Luma-Lite and Super Glue in hopes there are latent prints on the trash bag and the envelope and Polaroid, which he can then run through AFIS. Of course, get trace evidence to check for fibers, hairs, and whatever on the clothes in the bag, and before any of this is done, don't forget to let Doctor Scarpetta see everything."

"Yeah, yeah," Slipper said rather disdainfully, because he was trained in the old days and understood modern forensic science about as well as he did his VCR, which he still didn't know how to work. "I already was gonna do all that."

Thirteen

Trooper Macovich had flown the First Family to the helipad downtown and then returned to the state police hangar where he was now up on a stepladder, cleaning bugs off the 430's bird-proof windshield in the glare of lamps along the tarmac.

Yeah, being a helicopter pilot was glamorous, all right, Macovich sourly thought. Nothing more exciting than hauling around the governor, who was blind as a bat, and that family of his, who acted as if they were royalty. Hell, the Crimms never thanked or praised him, and he hadn't gotten a decent raise in a while, either. It wasn't fair that Andy Brazil could be suspended for an entire year and then dance back to work as if nothing happened.

Macovich hoped Andy got what was coming to him and that everybody else did, too. Macovich wished something magic would happen in his life to help him out of debt and ease his relentless, exhausting sexual cravings. Women and most men didn't have any idea what it was like to have a stallion between your legs that was always kicking, bucking, and snorting to get out of the stall, even when the *horsie*, as Macovich called it, was asleep. His lustful nature had trotted into his life at a very early age, and his father used to chuckle with pride and call his boy Thorlo Thoroughbred, not realizing that little Thorlo was developing a big problem that would eventually dominate his body and his life. He had to have women, and it was expensive. He had to have women who were sexually insatiable and skilled enough to stay in the saddle no matter how hard the ride, and female company like that was hard to find.

Macovich stopped scrubbing away bugs for a moment when he noticed a Land Cruiser boldly pull up and park right in front of the state police hangar. A tough-looking white kid with dreadlocks climbed out and walked toward the helicopter as if he had every right in the world to do as he pleased.

"Hey!" Macovich said sternly. "This is a restricted area."

"And I'm lost as hell," the kid replied. "Can you tell me how to get to the regular airport? I got a flight to Petersburg in fifteen minutes and I'm gonna miss it for sure if I don't get there fast."

"There ain't no flights to Petersburg," Macovich said as he scrubbed a stubborn splat with the rag. "Petersburg's only thirty-something miles from here, so why you need to fly there? Just drive and you can get there just as quick."

The other road dogs had their windows down, listening and tensely wondering what Smoke was going to do. Man, worried Cat, if Smoke skyjacked that chopper, there wasn't a way in the world the dogs were ready to fly such a thing. Cat could see from the backseat of the Land Cruiser that the cockpit looked like a spaceship, with hundreds of overhead switches and circuit breakers and other components unfamiliar to him. He nudged Cuda.

"What we gonna do he shoot that trooper and take the chopper?" Cat asked.

"Maybe we steal a Peterbilt and haul it in the reefer?"

"Won't fit in any reefer I ever seen."

"Yeah. Have to take the top off the reefer with a blowtorch so the propeller would have some room. That the biggest propeller I ever seen."

"They're called blades," Possum corrected them. "Boats and prop planes got propellers. Not helicopters."

"Well, they still ain't gonna fit!" Cat said, annoyed.

"Just go south on the interstate and you can't miss it," Macovich summed up directions to Petersburg.

"How 'bout I pay you to drop us off in this thing?" Smoke nodded at the huge, beautiful helicopter. "How fast could it get us there?"

"Ten minutes, unless we got a head wind. But I can't give you a ride. The helicopter is used only by the governor and his family."

"Yeah? So how's he gonna know?" Smoke was getting increasingly aggressive, standing close to the stepladder and wondering if he should kick it out from under the trooper.

"There's a little Hobb's Meter in the cockpit and every time you pull up the collective, that meter knows it," Macovich explained. "Tomorrow, when I take the First Family on their next trip, the meter will say I flew the helicopter ten minutes, then sat it down, then took off again, then sat it back here at the hangar again, before I picked them up and after I dropped them off from the steak house. How I 'sposed to explain why I flew the state chopper to Petersburg unless the gov'ner think I took him there after dinner?"

"Maybe he won't remember."

This was a distinct possibility, especially after the amount of vodka the governor had consumed earlier this evening, and Macovich was getting tempted. It had been a bad week and a stressful night, and he was certain he couldn't make this month's Visa payment.

"Maybe you give us a quick joy ride in that thing?" the kid with dreadlocks suggested. "We don't really need to go to Petersburg. It's getting late."

"Nope." Macovich climbed down and shook hundreds of dead bugs out of the rag. "It ain't gonna happen, not right this minute."

Smoke was aware of the hard pistol in the small of his back. He was smart enough to realize that a skyjacking might be a little more involved than hijacking a Peterbilt, so maybe he needed to be patient and put a little more thought into this. If he shot the trooper, chances were he wouldn't be able to figure out how to fly the helicopter before someone saw him and his road dogs out here in front of the state police hangar reading instruction books and looking under the many hoods.

"You give lessons?" Smoke tried another approach.

"Yeah, I'm an instructor." Macovich popped open the luggage compartment and tossed the filthy rag inside.

"Tell you what, you give one of my guys lessons, I'll make it worth your while, as long as nobody, and I mean nobody, knows."

Smoke had already decided that Possum would take the lessons. Then, if Possum got caught, Smoke would just hire somebody else and carry on with business as usual. Possum was Smoke's least favorite road dog, anyway, and Smoke really didn't give a rat's ass what happened to him and sometimes regretted kidnapping him from the ATM machine. Smoke gave the trooper his pager number and said to give him a beep if he was interested, but he had better do it soon because Smoke was a busy man. Furthermore, Smoke said, if the trooper was bored with his low-paying, mindless job, Smoke could probably use him on his *pit crew*.

"You got a pit crew?" Macovich was so impressed he stopped locking up the helicopter and stared at Smoke in open admiration.

"Fuckin' A."

"Wooooooo! NASCAR?"

"A driver," Smoke said, thinking fast and sounding impatient. "That's why I've got to be so secretive. Just one mention of my name and I got more fans coming at me than you got bugs hitting your window. It's like being a prisoner if you're as famous as I am."

"Wooo! What's the number of your car?" Macovich knew of no NASCAR driver with dreadlocks, but he could understand the young man's being in disguise off the track to escape his frantic groupies.

"Can't tell you, asshole," Smoke bullied him. "But you want to be on my pit crew," he added as he stalked off, "you give me a fucking call. Soon."

While Macovich was considering the opportunity that had suddenly presented itself, Andy was drinking beer and sitting listlessly inside his tiny row house on the fringes of the Fan District, where marginal people lived in denial of their surroundings.

No matter what the neighbors reiterated when they rocked on their porches at the end of long, hard days, the only thing of historical value about Andy's neighborhood was that it was old. Beyond that, the area was run down with no place to park, and sometimes people recently released from area halfway houses and clinics decided to come into the neighbors' lives without being invited. Andy's one-bedroom brownstone was neither air-conditioned nor properly heated, and it wasn't unusual for him to get power surges and spikes that were threatening to his computer.

At the moment, he didn't care if his power went off completely. A deranged killer had left evidence on his porch, and he wished Slipper would hurry up and e-mail Trooper Truth. Andy got up and shoved a chair halfway across the dining room. He angrily snatched another beer out of the kitchen refrigerator and returned to his computer.

Words began to flow through his fingers as he composed a pithy essay and posted it on the website. Slipper e-mailed Trooper Truth, and Andy answered and then fell asleep at the keyboard. When the telephone woke him up, he was slumped over with his head on the dining-room table.

"Oh, shit," he groaned, looking around, dazed and stiff as the phone continued to ring.

"Hello?" he answered, hoping it was Hammer, and that she'd already read his new essay and liked it.

"Is there somebody there named Andy Brazil?" a vaguely familiar female voice inquired over the line.

"Who wants to know?"

"This is First Lady Crimm."

"Yes, First Lady!" Andy said, startled. "What an unexpected surprise . . ."

"You're to report to the mansion at six for drinks and a light supper. That's six tonight."

"Thursday?" Andy asked, confused about what day of the week it was.

"Why, I guess it is Thursday. I don't know where the weeks go. We're in the big pale yellow house in the middle of Capitol Square on Ninth Street, right before you get to Broad. I know you're relatively new to the city and were suspended for a year and therefore might not know your way around."

First Lady Crimm handed the phone back to Pony and smiled with satisfaction as her daughters looked on from the antebellum breakfast table.

"I still think you should have discussed this with Papa first." Grace nodded at Pony to please add more butter to her grits as wind gusted in from the north and a hard rain began to fall.

"He liked the young man. I could tell," Mrs. Crimm replied. "Your father has a lot on his mind. My goodness! One minute the sun's out, and it's raining the next!"

"He notices more than you think he does. And if he's suddenly flying around with some blond-haired former city cop who's now a trooper who's been suspended before, Papa might remember he had nothing to do with it," Faith said as rain pummeled the old slate roof.

"Do with what?" the First Lady asked.

"With him suddenly flying us."

"Nonsense. We need more pilots. I don't know what's happened to all our pilots unless they're busy with the speed traps and don't have time for us anymore. And you heard what the young man said. He has something important to discuss with your papa, and I, at least, want to know what it is."

Pony was searching for the portable phone base unit. He could never find anything in the mansion and its guest houses when the

151

Crimms lived here, and on especially trying days, he wasn't sure the prison officials had done him a favor by assigning him to the mansion's domestic staff. Other inmates who worked for the First Family were outside repairing things, doing the gardening, raking leaves, and polishing the state cars.

"I don't mean to intrude," Pony said without looking anyone in the eye. "I can't seem to find the base unit for the phone."

Constance, Grace, Faith, and the First Lady were momentarily distracted, just as they always were when someone couldn't find something. Regina was the only member of the First Family who preferred to eat unassisted. If Pony served her, it took too long. She helped herself to toast, grits, eggs over easy, another banana, and sourwood honey that the governor of North Carolina had sent last Christmas to slyly remind the Crimms that the Tar Heel state was far superior to the Commonwealth of Virginia.

"It was here a minute ago." Faith was getting frustrated, her horse-shaped face pale and scarcely visible because she had not colorized it with heavy make-up yet.

The First Family had learned the art of searching all over the house without ever moving from their chairs. Pony had never understood how people could pull this off, but then if he were so special and smart, he wouldn't be wearing a white jacket and waiting on the Crimms morning, noon, and night.

"Excuse me, Miss Faith, but where was *here?*" Pony politely questioned her. "When you saw it last, I mean."

"Just call the number." Regina said with a mouth full. "When it rings, you'll hear where it is."

"That only works if you've lost the phone, not when you lose the base unit," Constance snapped, impatient that phones, base units, and other things did not stay in their proper places.

"The base unit does ring, actually, as you so wisely pointed out yesterday," Pony reminded the First Lady, although she had never pointed out anything to him directly in all the terms he had worked for the Crimm family.

A solution was at hand, but the same problem persisted: Inmates were not allowed to have the First Family's private phone number. So if the base unit were to be located, a member of the First Family would have to dial the number herself, and this was strictly against protocol. The task fell into the job description of personal or administrative assistants, or grade sixes, and at this early hour, no grade sixes were at work yet.

The breakfast table turned into a tableau of the First Family's females frozen in indecision, except for Regina, who was still piling food on her plate and unmindful of protocols.

"Here." She stuck out her hand. "Give it to me, Pony."

He came around behind her and carefully set the phone by her placemat, giving her plenty of body space as if he were serving a flaming dessert. She stabbed out the secret number with honey-coated fingers and immediately the base unit rang under Regina's wadded-up housecoat on top of the mahogany sideboard.

"Hello?" Regina said into the phone, making sure she was the one who was calling. "Hello?" she tried again, crossing pajama-covered legs that reminded Pony of felt-covered tree stumps wearing filthy furry slippers. "Maybe I should sign on with the EPU." She returned the phone to Pony. "I'm bored to death of official duties."

"You couldn't be assigned to us." The First Lady was opposed to the idea and intended to discourage her daughter. "Unless you had yet another EPU trooper assigned to protect you while you were protecting your sisters, Papa, and me."

"Show me that in the Code of Virginia," Regina argued. "Bet it's not in there."

"If I may speak," Pony spoke up as he wiped off the phone and returned it to the base unit. "It's not in there—not anywhere in any section of the Code about the First Family needing to protect itself and be protected at the same time."

"Maybe you can discuss it with that handsome Trooper Brazil, and I'll let him be the one who talks you out of it," the First Lady said to Regina. "Being a trooper is very dangerous and unrewarding, and speaking of troopers, did any of you happen to read Trooper Truth this morning?"

"We just got up," Constance reminded her mother.

"Well, he told the most interesting and mysterious story about who shot J.R."

"Why's he writing about *Dallas?*" Faith puzzled. "That's been off the air forever."

"This is a different J.R.," the First Lady informed her daughters. "But it's a shame *Dallas* was canceled. Your papa never got over it and was just furious when the network took that show off the air. You know, there's nothing good on TV anymore except for the shopping channel."

A WORD ABOUT EATING EAGLES

by Trooper Truth

Quite possibly, a young man the Jamestown archaeologists nicknamed J.R. was America's first white-on-white homicide—loosely speaking, since America wasn't called America back when Jamestown was settled.

But if you visit the excavation site and take a look at the fiberglass cast of J.R.'s skeleton, you can't help but be moved by the plight of a young man dying so far from home and then lying in hard Virginia clay for four centuries before a trowel discovered the stain of his unmarked grave. J.R., by the way, means Jamestown Rediscovery and is the prefix given to every artifact and feature found on the site, which includes graves and the dead people in them. We don't know who shot J.R. At this writing, we aren't even sure who J.R. is.

But through science, J.R. has managed to tell us a thing or two. Results from radio-carbon dating confirm that he died in 1607, possibly just months after the first settlers arrived at Jamestown, so we can assume he was one of the 108 English men and boys who sailed from the Isle of

Dogs and got stalled in the Thames. Anthropology pinpoints that he was a five-foot-five robust male with a rounded chin and small jaw, between the ages of seventeen and twenty-five, had no signs of arthritis and relatively good teeth, indicating his diet did not include sugar. Tests for lead, strontium, and oxygen isotopes show that he grew up in the United Kingdom, possibly in southwest London or Wales.

J.R. was fatally wounded in the leg with a sixty-caliber musket ball and twenty-some shot, which back in those days would be considered a combat load. Forensic testing shows the matchlock rifle that killed him was fired from too far away for the injury to have been self-inflicted. He bled to death quickly and was buried without a shroud in a hexagonal-shaped coffin with his feet turned to the east, according to proper Christian tradition.

If J.R. was, in fact, shot by another settler, and I have a feeling he was, then that leads to theories about motive, which can easily be inferred from historical documentation. A stroll through centuries-old writings and a subsequent commingling of words with excavated artifacts and bones could lead to the following possibilities for why J.R. might have been murdered.

Perhaps he was involved in political intrigue or domestic difficulties, or didn't work and play well with others, or was a thief, or took more than his share of food. Maybe he engaged in cannibalism, like a later settler who was executed after being caught salting down his dead wife. Or perhaps J.R. squabbled with a Natural who somehow got hold of a firearm and figured out how to use it. Or more likely, J.R. got into an altercation with another armed settler who decided the best place to shoot him was in the leg because maybe J.R. was wearing a helmet and upper-body armor at the time. Maybe the settler shot him after discovering that J.R. was spying for the Spanish or was a pirate.

I suspect J.R. was a spy or a pirate or both. Whatever the truth really is, J.R.'s death was not a pleasant one, because quite likely, he was conscious long enough to know he was dying. I envision him lying inside the fort and slipping into shock as he watched himself bleed to death from a severed artery behind his knee, and I can imagine the uproar inside the fort as settlers scurried about with rags and river water and whatever medicinal aids they could muster. Perhaps they were trying to comfort J.R. or perhaps everyone was fighting and shouting and questioning the shooter.

Who knows? But if you imagine this tragic drama, my faithful readers, then certainly you must be asking the same glaring question that I am: Why is there no mention of J.R.'s death in John Smith's writings? Why, to date, is there no reference found in *any* record of a young first settler being shot to death, either by accident or on purpose?

It just goes to show that history is nothing more than what certain people decide that future generations ought to know. I suppose when John Smith was writing his accounts and telling tales for the benefit of King James and people back home, Smith was savvy and shrewd enough to figure that financial backers and prospective settlers might be a bit turned off to hear that people in Jamestown were mutinous, murderous, mad from drinking bad water, constantly under siege by the Naturals, and forced by starvation to eat snakes, turtles, and at least one eagle, based on the trash the settlers left behind.

The beginning of America wasn't exciting, fun, honorable, or even patriotic, but could certainly serve as a model for a reality television show that would make *Survivor* seem like *Fantasy Island*. And sadly, nothing has changed much. Just look at the recent, sadistic murder of Trish Thrash! We don't know who killed her, either, but I ask you, my community-minded readers, to please e-mail me if you happen to have known Trish or knew anything about her life, including her hobbies, interests, what she read, if she used the Internet, and if she might have mentioned anything or anyone new in her life of late.

Be careful out there!

Fourteen

Governor Crimm had been studying the latest Trooper Truth printout for an entire hour, and was fascinated, appalled, and disgusted by it. He repeatedly moved his magnifying glass over every word as Major Trader briefed him on matters of state and offered him a homemade chocolate-covered cherry.

"General Assembly will start up before we know it," Trader was saying. "And we're simply not prepared."

"You always say that," the governor replied as he absently ate the candy. "Who did shoot J.R., anyway? Has anybody pressed the archaeologists about this? And if not, why not? How do you think it makes us look if we can't solve a crime that was committed four hundred years ago and was certainly witnessed? I want you to call Jamestown and demand that the J.R. case be solved immediately, and we'll issue a big press release and show the citizens of Virginia that I will not tolerate crime."

"*Juvenile* crime," Trader added a helpful spin.

"Yes, yes," the governor agreed.

"And I think we can safely suggest he was shot by a pirate—or it might be in our best interest to claim as much, at any rate," Trader added. "We could say it was any pirate—doesn't matter, don't you see? All pirates were bad then and are bad now, so it doesn't make any difference whatsoever if we propose that J.R. wandered outside the fort to get a bucket of water from the river, and all of a sudden he spied a Spanish ship flying a Jolly Roger flag, and next thing he was shot."

"I thought we were avoiding drawing attention to our pirate problems."

"Highway pirates are another matter," Trader replied as he gloated over his secret pirate activities that would soon enough make him rich from booty.

Crimm stopped the magnifying glass on the word *cannibal*. "Imagine some settler salting down his dead wife and eating her," he said in revulsion as he envisioned himself dying of starvation, only to discover his voluptuous wife had passed away.

He thought of her nude, fleshy body and wondered how anybody could eat his wife without at least cooking her first, but he supposed if he cooked Maude, the other settlers would see the smoke and smell the odor of roasting human flesh and would hang him from a tree. Oh, what a hideous scenario, and the governor's submarine lurched and banged into something, sending a painful jolt through his hollow organs.

"That was a capital crime back then," Trader observed as if he were reading Crimm's mind. "The tour guides at Jamestown will tell you that anyone caught eating his wife or anybody else was immediately dragged off and hanged. Then they'd bury him very quickly and in a secret location so another settler didn't salt and eat him, too."

"I'm wondering if cannibalism is still a capital crime, because if it isn't, it ought to be." Crimm's submarine lurched more violently.

"It depends on the circumstances," Trader replied as he imagined his plump, nagging wife and wondered if he could ever be famished enough to consider, even for a moment, eating her, assuming she died unexpectedly and nobody else noticed that she had vanished. "For example, according to state code, there would have to be another serious crime involved," Trader explained. "If the man murdered her first and perhaps included a rape or robbery and then ate her—now that would be a capital offense and he would get lethal injection, unless you blocked the execution or granted clemency."

"I never block executions or grant clemency," the governor impatiently replied as his lens strayed over the printed essay and another shockwave rolled through him. "In fact, I want you to send out a press release and announce that anyone who engages in cannibalism will pay the supreme price, assuming those other crimes are included. I don't believe we've ever addressed cannibalism, and it's high time we did. Indeed, let's draft a bill and put it before this next General Assembly."

Trader was making notes with a pencil, which was his habit because he often found the need to erase whatever he had written.

"Maybe we should say that J.R. was caught in the act of cannibalism and was executed by a firing squad. How about that?" The governor peered up and gave Trader a magnified rheumy eye that was cloudy and bloodshot and getting glassy.

"It's not my understanding that shooting someone in the leg was a preferred form of execution," Trader pointed out. "I don't think the citizens would buy it."

"Of course they would. Everybody knows that guns back then were very unreliable. Now, let's talk about something else."

"Yes, on to other matters," Trader said, flipping a page in his notepad. "What do you want to do about this dentist who's being held hostage on Tangier Island? I'm sure you saw the newspaper this morning or heard the news, or did you?"

"Not yet." The governor groaned and clutched his bloated gut.

"Well, apparently the Reedville police talked to a reporter, and unfortunately, the word is out that this dentist's life could be in danger because the Tangierians are upset about VASCAR. I recommend we suspend our VASCAR initiatives immediately until the matter is peacefully resolved. I can tell you that I, for one, warned Superintendent Hammer about the consequences should the state police start painting speed traps. But of course, she didn't listen, as usual."

"It was her idea?" The governor was confused and lightheaded.

"Of course it was her idea, Governor. Don't you remember when you and I discussed it the other day, I told you this was her latest act of poor judgment and you said, 'Well, good. Then if it causes a stink, make sure she gets the blame and not me.' So I said, 'Good enough, that's what will happen.' "

"Did she ever find her dog?" the governor inquired as he cleaned his magnifying glass with a special cloth and prayed his latest submarine attack would subside.

"It's theorized that one of her political enemies stole it," Trader gravely replied.

"What a shame she has so many people who strongly dislike her," Crimm said as he sat very still and the color drained from his face. "I had no idea when I appointed her that she would become such a hot potato. Why don't you ring her up and she and I will have a little chat? But not right now."

"I strongly recommend against that, Governor—not now or later," Trader was quick to suggest. "You don't want to be tarred with the same brush. She's a political embarrassment, and the more you distance yourself from her, the better."

"Well, I do feel bad about her little dog. I hope she got my sympathy note."

"I made sure she did," Trader lied as he thought of that note and numerous other communications to her that he had intercepted or blocked.

"You know, if something happened to Frisky," the governor wistfully went on with a gasp, "I'd never be the same, nor would Maude or the girls. What a dear, loyal friend Frisky is, and thank the good Lord I have EPU to make sure nobody nabs him for ransom money or to get back at me for some decision that is unpopular."

"Your decisions are never unpopular," Trader said emphatically. "At least not the ones that are your fault."

"Well, I'm sure I'll be blamed for the recent hate crime," Crimm supposed as his submarine plunged into foul waters.

"I strongly advise that we indicate that the Thrash murder is connected to Moses Custer's case, and therefore it's Hammer's fault that neither of the cases has been solved," Trader suggested with confidence and delight. "Maybe we can figure out a tie-in with J.R. being murdered by a pirate, while we're at it, and plant the notion in the public's mind that Hammer is to blame for that case being unsolved, as well."

The governor shot up from his chair and almost fell over as his submarine slammed precariously into submerged objects.

"Leave!" he ordered Trader, lurching and gasping. "I can't think about pirates right now!"

Possum could and was. He had been thinking about pirates ever since reading Trooper Truth early this morning. Possum was watching TV and pondering a very obvious failing on the road dogs' part that he excitedly believed he could use to manipulate Smoke and hopefully save Popeye.

Every self-respecting pirate from centuries past understood the necessity of flying flags from their masts to communicate with those they preyed upon. Raising the skull and crossbones, popularly known as the Jolly Roger, informed the soon-to-be-plundered ship that it had better surrender or else. If the ship ignored the fluttering black-and-white grinning death's head, this was followed by a red flag indicating the *or else* was imminent. If the ship continued to sail about its business, then cannon fire and other violence followed.

Modern pirates seemed to have forgotten the courtesy of flags. These days, when a crew of pirates roar up in a speedboat to overtake a ship or yacht, there is no warning whatsoever before mortars and machine guns open fire. Pirates have become a very cruel, bloody, shameful species of seafaring outlaws who don't believe in giving anyone a chance and are mostly interested in canned goods, electronics, carpets, designer clothes, tobacco, and more to the point, the drugs that hopefully are being smuggled aboard the hijacked vessel. If drugs are part of the booty, the victimized sailors who survive do not report the incident to the authorities.

Highway pirates should return to the courtesy of flags, Possum thought as he perched on his bed with the lamp off inside his tiny RV room that would have looked out over scraggly pine trees in back of the vacant lot if he didn't keep the curtains tightly taped shut. He never missed a rerun of *Bonanza* and constantly fantasized that he had a father like Ben Cartwright and brothers like Little Joe and Hoss. He imagined riding a fine horse through the burning map of the Ponderosa while that stirring theme of strumming guitars and drums galloped through his head.

"*Dun* daw daw *dun* daw daw *dun* daw daw *dun* daw *daw DAW . . . !*"

Just yesterday afternoon he had watched his favorite rerun—the one in which Little Joe's girl gets kidnapped by a carnival and is tied up in the fat lady's closet, several dressing rooms down from the Beautiful Girls of Egypt and the bearded lady. Little Joe convinces Hercules to help him, and they beat up the bad guys, knock the knife out of one bad guy's hand before he stabs the fat lady, and then Little Joe's girl kisses him at the end. Oh, how Possum loved to watch Little Joe swaggering off with his cowboy hat pulled low and that big gunbelt with its ivory-handled six-shooter slung from his hips.

Oh, what Possum wouldn't give to walk out of his cheap, sour-smelling room and find Ben, Little Joe, and Hoss waiting for him instead of Smoke, the other road dogs, and that bizarre girl Unique, when she happened by the RV, which was increasingly less often. Sometimes a tear slid down Possum's face, and he had to glaze himself over when it was time to turn off the TV and emerge from the kinder world he lived in during the day while the other dogs slept off hangovers and late nights of meanness. Possum had never hurt anybody before Smoke stole him away from the ATM machine, and now look at the mess Possum was in.

He had shot that poor truck driver who was minding his own business in his truck, waiting to sell a load of pumpkins when the Farmers' Market opened in the morning. Possum was afraid to sleep ever again, so sure he was that he would have nightmares about what he had done to

Moses Custer and all those pumpkins they hauled over to the Deep Water Terminal and dumped into the James River.

For days, the news had run stories about thousands of pumpkins floating along and getting hung up on rocks. Of course, it didn't take the Richmond police long to put two and two together and deduce that the floating pumpkins might be connected to the ones that had filled the stolen Peterbilt. Possum sure hoped Mr. Custer didn't die or end up a cripple. Possum also dimly realized that the reason Smoke had made him the trigger man was so that Possum could never leave the road dogs without going to jail or maybe even death row. He wished he could send Trooper Truth an e-mail and beg the trooper to save him and Popeye, but what if Trooper Truth turned him in to the police? Popeye might end up in the pound and Possum for sure would end up in juvenile detention with people just as bad as Smoke.

It was dark and quiet as Possum sat on his bed petting Popeye and thinking about a way to convince Smoke to fly a flag from the RV and the Land Cruiser. Why wouldn't Smoke go along with it as long as Possum could figure out how to make him think the flag somehow was his own idea and a good one? The Jolly Roger might be too obvious, Possum considered in the dark, and Smoke probably wouldn't know what it was. Possum went over to the computer, intending to check Captain Bonny's website to see if the pirate had his own colors, and if so, what were they and how did he display them?

But Possum was distracted when he clicked on FAVORITES and accidentally pulled up Trooper Truth instead of Captain Bonny. Possum was surprised to see that Trooper Truth had posted yet another essay.

"Now what do you think of that?" Possum excitedly whispered to Popeye, who was snoring on the bed. "Two in the same morning! Man, that Trooper Truth's up to something."

A Short Digression

by Trooper Truth

The people of Tangier Island are a secretive, sensitive people who know little about the facts of their origin because, unsurprisingly, when one begins to spin legends and pass down misinformation, he eventually forgets what really happened and believes his own distortions.

Throughout the centuries, the people of Tangier hid the truth of their pirate past, preferring to believe their own legends. One afternoon while disguised as a reporter, I visited the island and talked to a local woman who had dropped by Spanky's because things were slow at the gift shop.

"I guess you get fed up with all these tourists invading your island," I commented to the woman, whose name was and perhaps still is Thelma Parks.

"I don't suffer them poorly when they leave us be," she replied, eyeing me with suspicion.

"And I assume they don't."

"Nah, they don't. The other day, they was in my shop with the video camera and they was videoing me and I wanted none of it."

"Did you tell them not to videotape you?" I inquired, taking notes.

"Nah."

Thelma went on to tell me that she now charges a quarter for all photo opportunities while she works the cash register, and the added income makes it somewhat easier for her to tolerate the host of strangers who seem to find her Tangier gift shop exotic and unlike anything they've ever seen, which is inexplicable, she confided. None of the trinkets, such as the plastic lighthouses, crabs, crab pots, lobsters, fish, skiffs, and so on, are made by hand or in America. In fact, she added, lobsters are not common in the Chesapeake Bay and most islanders have never seen one except on TV or in seafood restaurant ads that regularly run in *The Virginian-Pilot* newspaper.

From Spanky's, I continued my wanderings and happened by the medical clinic. I stepped inside and found no sign of a dentist, doctor, or nurse—only a lanky young man with blue eyes and a mop of blond hair. He was sitting in the dentist's chair, staring off, lost in reveries and completely unaware of my presence. I assumed he was a patient and the dentist would return momentarily, not realizing that the dentist was, in truth, being held hostage, since neither his abduction nor the threat of civil war had been made public at that time.

"Hello?" I politely announced.

The boy's eyes were glazed and he was unresponsive.

"Are you there?" I asked.

He wasn't.

"I'm wondering if I might find any medical staff who have a minute to talk to me," I said. "I'm working on a history of our nation's beginning and present condition and believe Tangier Island is key."

"The key is in my pocket." He suddenly blinked to and protectively covered his pocket with a hand. When he didn't recognize me, he was startled and jumped up from the chair. "What for are you doing here? I thought I locked the door!" He ran to the door and threw the bolt across.

I heard muffled sounds coming from a back area and the scrape of a chair moving across the floor.

"The dog's back thar." The young man indicated the area the sound was coming from.

"Why is he making a chair scrape?" I puzzled. "He tied up to it or something?"

"Yass."

The chair scraped some more.

"It must be stuffy and lonely being tied up in there," I worried, not at all pleased by the idea of a dog tied to a chair inside a clinic. "Why don't we let him out so he can get a little air and attention?"

"That's it!" The young man blocked the doorway leading to the area in question as the chair scraped again. "He bites. That's what for he's tied up. He's the dentist's dog."

"Where's the dentist?"

"Tied up, too."

"Oh, he's busy. Well, maybe I can talk to him another time," I replied. "And what about your teeth? I see you have braces and it appears you've had several extractions as well. And I'm noticing that your rubber bands keep flying off when you talk."

"That's it!" Fonny Boy covered his mouth with a hand and looked embarrassed. "The dentist, he better mind his step!"

"While we're chatting," I said, edging closer to the table, where a dental chart was out in plain view, "would you mind if I flipped through this chart and see what all you've had done? I assume this is your chart? Is your name Darren Shores?"

"Ever one on Tanger calls me Fonny Boy."

Fonny Boy and I fell into a conversation and he was very well versed in the lore of the island because of his fascination with the history of shipping, especially in the bay. As we got to know each other better and a level of vague trust developed, Fonny Boy got more specific and began to talk about pirates, or picaroons, as he called them. They used to be everywhere, he told me. At one time, there were so many pirate ships off the shores of Maryland, Virginia, and the Carolinas that cities like Charleston were paralyzed. No one dared set sail out of the harbor for fear they would be seized by pirates who thought nothing of killing people in very unpleasant ways.

Fonny Boy went into elaborate detail about Blackbeard in particular, whose Christian name was Edward Drummon when he was an honest seaman in his home port of Bristol, England, in the late seventeenth century. When he decided to become a pirate, he changed his name to Edward Teach, which has frequently been misspelled in records as Thatch, Tache, and Tatch. After Queen Anne's War, Blackbeard sailed into Jamaica to go after French ships and began to cultivate the most vile, terrifying persona imaginable to entice other vessels to surrender without a second thought, assuming the warning flags weren't enough. He would braid his long beard into little pigtails and set them on fire with slow-burning matches, Fonny Boy said, and strap pistols, daggers, and a huge cutlass to his waist, and wear additional weapons on the bandoleer across his chest.

Soon enough, Blackbeard and his flotilla began to haunt the North Carolina coast and the Chesapeake Bay. The people of Tangier would hoist the Jolly Roger whenever Blackbeard's ship was spotted nearby, and from time to time the ruthless, evil pirate himself would visit the island and drink Jamaican rum and carouse to his dark heart's content. Nobody wanted him on the island or slept much while he was visiting. Women and children hid inside their homes, and Blackbeard began to suppose that Tangier was an island of men only. This made his visits progressively shorter and less frequent. According to Fonny Boy and almost-nonexistent historical records, Blackbeard was most curious as to how an all-male island had survived down through the decades and could continue.

The answer Blackbeard got was lost forever until a three-hundred-year-old account book was discovered. This extraordinary find, according to legend, somehow made it from Blackbeard's ship *Adventure* into the attic of a descendant of Alexander Spottswood, the governor of Virginia during Blackbeard's bloody rampages. The account book focused on the disposition of the loot Blackbeard took and offered details of his sadistic cruelty and lust for chopping people into pieces and shaking his empty rum cup at the heavens and daring God to defy him. Blackbeard's handwritten entries mentioned one hundred and forty barrels of cocoa and a cask of sugar he had stolen and buried under hay in a North Carolina barn. There was a cryptic reference to buried treasure that only Blackbeard and the devil knew the location of, and to this day it has not been found.

I realized it wasn't possible that Tangier could have remained populated without women and pressed Fonny Boy for the explanation Blackbeard was given. Fonny Boy repeated what had been passed down through the generations.

"Damnation seize your soul if you are lying to me!" Blackbeard thundered to a clever but untruthful islander named Job Wheeler, a childless widower who, as the story goes, invited the pirate into his home on an area of the island known today as Job's Cove.

"I cannot spare the truth from you," Job told Blackbeard, who was drinking cup after cup of rum and setting his beard on fire. "Although we had our beginnings in England long ago, we landed on this island by way of North Carolina."

Job offered this blatant lie because he felt certain it would snag Blackbeard's attention, since it was well known that the pirate was in collusion with Charles Eden, the governor of North Carolina. For much of Blackbeard's nefarious career, he had navigated the shallow sounds and inlets of North Carolina with never a fear. Indeed, any plot hatched from other territories to defeat Blackbeard and his seadogs was always foiled by a letter from someone in North Carolina, much to the disgust of Virginia's Governor Spottswood, who was neither friendly with Blackbeard nor inclined for the pirate to remain in business or alive.

"How can this be?" Blackbeard bellowed through curls of smoke, squinting one eye in a threatening manner that suggested Job best be telling "they God's truth or I will cut ye asunder into many pieces and send ye back from whence ye came, which is hell, ye villain!"

"I am neither villain," Job promised. "From whence I came is North

Carolina—not Hell—where ye have many friends and relations. Yet it cannot be known that we on this fair island originally came from North Carolina and managed to escape with our very lives because there was a terrible drought that withered our crops and parched our very tongues and we were short of supplies, so we crowded into bateaus and made our way here, leaving no word except *Crotoan* carved into a fence post and *Cro* carved into a tree to give rise to the expectation that we had gone off to live with the Crotans."

Blackbeard reminded Job that the name of the Crotan Indians was spelled C-R-O-T-A-N as opposed to C-R-O-T-O-A-N, to which Job replied, "Yay, that is God's truth. But it was not I who carved the tree, but another not as well learned as I."

"Are you implying," I probed Fonny Boy, "that the Islanders descended from the Lost Colonists who vanished after Sir Walter Raleigh dropped them off on Roanoke Island? Well," I was talking to myself now, "it is a fact that when Walter Raleigh set out for the New World on May 8, 1587, his plan was to find a location on the Chesapeake Bay, but he was forced by hurricanes to settle farther south on Roanoke Island. So the Lost Colonists never wanted to be in North Carolina to begin with. I guess if you're going to relocate, you would certainly consider your original destination, and Tangier was described as a nice island, with the exception of there being no drinkable water.

"However," I decided, "the chronology makes what Job told Blackbeard impossible, because the Lost Colonists were already lost by the time Smith headed to Virginia and supposedly discovered your island in 1608. So I am forced to dismiss this theory entirely. Furthermore, we can't prove, at least not to my satisfaction, that when Smith landed on Tangier, he wasn't really on Limbo Island, and all of you are therefore not Islanders but Limbonians."

Fonny Boy had the vacant look again as he slouched in the dentist's chair, unfocused and twitching a little. The chair scraped again from somewhere in the back of the clinic and then banged loudly as it crashed to the floor, apparently overturned by the dentist's tethered dog, who may have been dreaming, too, or so I assumed at the time.

"Well, I've got to run along," I told Fonny Boy. "I'll see what else I can find out about your people and why only Job Wheeler and Blackbeard knew the truth or the lies about Tangier's past. And also why, after Job died and Blackbeard eventually met his much-deserved violent end, those secrets and others remained hidden in the account book in the Spottswoods' attic."

Fonny Boy's Rapid Eye Movement was picking up speed as he stared off in a trance, gripping the armrests of the dentist's chair as if he were watching an intense adventure movie. It was pointless to communicate with him further, and I left the clinic. I waved down a golf-cart taxi and headed back to the airstrip as theories and speculations clashed in my head and made little sense because I am neither a historian nor a historical novelist, although I do know people who are. As I set off for home in the helicopter, staying below 3,500 feet to avoid restricted area R 4006, then heading due south to avoid restricted area R 6609, I realized it was only fair and responsible for me to continue my arduous historical investigation on how this country started and what has happened to it since.

"Watch out for that bird over there." My copilot pointed out a seagull that apparently didn't see us until the last second.

"Wow, that was close," I commented as the bird dove under us, clipping its tail on a skid. "I hope he's all right." I nosed the helicopter west a few degrees to get a glimpse of the seagull as it sailed away, appearing to fly backward because we, of course, were going considerably faster than it.

P.S. To whoever is holding Popeye hostage, contact me before it's too late! And many thanks for the tips you, my faithful readers, have been sending me about Trish Thrash.

Be careful out there!

Fifteen

The minute Windy Brees blew into Hammer's office, Hammer knew there was trouble.

"Heavens to Betty! Have you seen what Trooper Truth just put up on his website?" Windy declared.

"Yes," Hammer replied. "I saw what was up this morning."

"No! He's put up something else, and you won't believe what it says!"

"Put up something else?" Hammer was baffled, yet she was not about to let on that she had prior knowledge about Trooper Truth or his publication schedule. "That's interesting," she said. "I suppose I just assumed he posted only one essay a day."

"Well, not so," Windy said. "Whoever he is, he is one proliferated writer. I wonder what he looks like and how old he is. He must be old to know so much. All that history and everything . . ."

"What makes you think Trooper Truth is a man?" Hammer inquired as she logged onto the website.

"Well, he's so smart, for one thing."

When Hammer began reading the essay, she ordered Windy to leave her office and shut the door. She got Andy on the phone.

"That's it!?" she said in an outraged whisper.

"A common Tangier expression," Andy remarked. *"That's it!* means the person saying it is really saying *none of your business.* For example, if I ask you if you're mad at me for not telling you about my secret mission, or will you be mad if I tell you that something awful was left at my house last night, and you say *That's it!*, you mean . . ."

"Meet me at . . . !" she interrupted him as she groped for a location.

There was really no place in Richmond either one of them could go without being noticed, especially if they were together.

"Meet me in the Ukrop's parking lot in fifteen minutes!" she decided angrily.

"Which Ukrop's?" Andy asked over the line. "And I can explain everything."

"Not over the phone, you're not. The Ukrop's at Stonypoint. We'll talk in the car."

Major Trader had just read the essay, too, and he huffed and puffed as he hurried his considerable bulk into Governor Crimm's office.

"Governor!" Trader exclaimed as he burst in without knocking. "Trooper Truth has been to Tangier and claims some island boy named Fonny Boy is the one holding the dentist hostage! He's a journalist who wears a disguise!"

"What?" the governor inquired weakly as he emerged from his private bathroom and straightened his plaid vest, making sure the railroad watch that had been passed down for generations was safely tucked back into the watch pocket. "The island boy's a journalist? What island boy? And what in thunder are you talking about, and you know not to just walk in on me."

"Fonny Boy's his name. Some island boy named Fonny Boy, and we've got a description," Trader excitedly said. "And no. Trooper Truth disguised himself as a journalist, not Fonny Boy."

"He's disguising himself not as Fonny Boy but as a journalist?" Crimm fished his office magnifying glass out of a landfill of papers. "You're supposed to be a bloody press secretary and you butcher the King's English, simply butcher it. Constantly and consistently. And for God's sake, don't you ever take your suits to the dry cleaners? Doesn't your wife complain?" The governor cast an enlarged eye over Trader's slovenly bulk. "You have chili on your shirt and your tie's too short. You look like Big Daddy after he's been on a goddamn bender, and I'm thinking very seriously about firing you one of these days."

"Please, Governor!" Trader cried out. "Don't kill the messenger. I'm not the one leaking all this classified and embarrassing information onto the Internet!"

"I certainly know that." The governor weakly seated himself behind his desk and motioned for Trader to take a chair and lower his voice. "Whoever Trooper Truth is, he's at least a writer."

"Now, I take that very personally," Trader said. "That was naughty, naughty to insult me that way. I think you should apologize for wounding my creative sensibilities."

"The only thing creative about you is your rendition of the truth," the governor retorted. "And if I weren't so preoccupied with important matters, including my health, I would catch you in your lies more often and do something about it."

"How *is* your health?" Trader sweetly asked.

"Did you bring me this latest essay?"

Trader unfolded the printout and smoothed it open on the ink blotter. The governor was silent for many long minutes as he moved his magnifying glass over Trooper Truth's words and grunted now and then and made other inarticulate sounds of disapproval, surprise, and constitutional discomfort.

"There's only one thing to do," he decided in his most sovereign tone. "We're going to have to find a special operative who will finger this Trooper Truth scoundrel and bring him to justice."

"Bring him to justice for what, Governor? I don't believe he's committed a crime."

"Why, I believe he might just be guilty of treason, don't you? Isn't he sticking his nose in state business and referring to my policies as being idiotic? Furthermore, I don't appreciate this tireless obsession with pirates, when we've been working so hard to play down that problem. Now Blackbeard's even dragged into the fray and is on everybody's mind."

"I know, I know." Trader couldn't have agreed with him more as he gleefully thought of his Captain Bonny website. "We certainly don't want the public thinking that Blackbeard was welcome in Virginia or was ever even in Virginia, not even once. What we need to do is emphasize that Blackbeard and North Carolina were as thick as thieves, and it was our own Governor Spottswood who . . ."

"You know how I feel about Spottswood!" the governor blurted out as his submarine went on alert. "I don't want him getting any more credit than he already has, do you hear me? I have to live with his alleged descendants, and I'm sick and tired of being invited to their plantation pig roasts and shad roe plankings and hearing endless apocryphal stories about Governor Spottswood, who was probably a blowhard with gout and the clap." The governor pulled out his railroad watch again. "It's getting late. Why don't you drop by the mansion for supper and we'll discuss this further and come up with a plan?"

Andy already had a plan, but he feared Hammer was too riled up to listen, as he watched her storm out of her car and stride through the Ukrop's parking lot in his direction.

"Unplug the website immediately," she said as she yanked open the door of his unmarked Caprice. "That's it! You're totally out of control. Am I to believe you've been doing undercover work on Tangier Island and you never bothered to let me know? And what awful thing turned up at your house last night?"

"I'm sorry. I was wrong not to tell you about my secret mission. But I was afraid you'd try to stop me," he replied calmly. "And you can't unplug a website. I could close it down, but you don't want me to do that, trust me. There's too much at stake."

"The only thing at stake right now, it seems to me, is my career and good name and the life of a dentist," she retorted.

"A scoundrel of a dentist. You should see the chart I looked at! And what about Popeye?" Andy asked.

Hammer's grief resurfaced and silenced her.

"I believe there was a lot of premeditation involved in her dognapping, and therefore it is most likely the work of someone who has something personal against you," Andy told her.

"That could be half the universe," she dismally replied.

"This isn't about money, not directly," he said. "If it was about a ransom, you would have been contacted long before now. I think someone has something pretty nefarious up his sleeve. And I've been getting some clues because of Trooper Truth—e-mails that are suspicious. I believe if I continue posting my essays and following every lead I can, we're going to get to the bottom of this and a lot of other things. And I swear to God, if Popeye is alive, I'm going to find her for you."

"I refuse to get my hopes up," she stoically said. "Do you really think she's still alive?"

"It's just an instinct. But yes. For one thing, Boston terriers are not a hot item for dog thieves. They have bat ears, bulging eyes that look at the walls, and their little nub of a corkscrew tail doesn't cover anything important, if you know what I mean. Not to mention their flat faces, their tendency to get bald in spots, and their intelligence, which far surpasses that of most of their owners—not including you, of course. I would assume the dogs of choice for thieves are Labs, miniature collies, cocker spaniels, and maybe dachshunds."

"Then Popeye may have been stolen as part of some bigger scheme that we don't know about yet," Hammer deduced.

"Exactly." Andy nodded as their conversation steamed up the glass.

"That was very risky and probably foolish and reckless for you to pretend to be a journalist and go to Tangier Island," Hammer then said.

"Look," he replied, "based on an e-mail tip to Trooper Truth, I knew even before I went there to paint the speed trap that the state police was being set up for a political fall to take attention away from the governor, who is increasingly viewed as a blundering potentate because of that asshole Major Trader. It's just a crime that nasty slob of a press secretary manipulates him so blatantly, but the poor old man can't see it because he can't see anything, period. You wouldn't believe some of the stories I've heard when I've been poking around this past year."

"Such as?" Hammer was getting interested.

"It seems, for example, that every time Trader brings Crimm cookies or candy, the governor soon after gets a gastrointestinal attack that completely debilitates him. And let me add, the goodies are always chocolate or have chocolate in them."

"No. You don't think . . . ?"

"I most certainly do, and I intend to prove it just as soon as the labs complete testing on the chocolates the governor supposedly sent you and what's left of a fudge cake Trader had sent over to Ruth's Chris."

"You sent those to the lab?" She was shocked.

"Of course I did. I'd heard the rumors and the governor never even calls you, so why would he send you chocolates through *guess who*? I think that bastard, no-good Trader is lacing the governor's goodies with Ex-Lax and has been doing it for years. What better way to confuse and manipulate someone than to have that person doubled over with cramps and embarrassment whenever it's time to make key decisions, which, in the case of the governor, is daily?"

"That's criminal!" Hammer said in disgust as she vaguely recalled being interviewed for the superintendent's position, and Trader's offering her a silver bowl of chocolate-covered peanuts, which she refused because she didn't eat sweets or anything else fattening.

"Oh, there's more," Andy ominously said. "I've been doing some pretty thorough checking on Trader. For starters, his mother's maiden name was Bonny."

"I don't see the significance."

"You're about to." Andy met her eyes as the sun began to go down and shoppers hurried to and from their cars, oblivious to the very important conversation that was taking place in their midst. "The Bonnys are originally from Tangier Island. Trader's mother married a waterman named

Trader and Major Trader was born on the island on August the eleventh in 1951. He was delivered by a midwife, who apparently had a very difficult time with the birth because he came out feet first, which sort of seems appropriate since he inverts the truth and upends everything moral and decent."

"So you're suggesting that initiating VASCAR on Tangier Island was a deliberate set-up on Trader's part," Hammer supposed.

"Oh, yes. And one thing is certain, Trader knows the Islanders, all right, and probably still knows people on that island. Yet he's made no effort whatsoever to intervene for at least one very good reason."

"Which is?"

"The Bonny family is descended from pirates," Andy replied. "And I'm afraid I have more bad news," he added, and then he told her about the trash bag and envelope left at his house last night.

Hammer listened to the entire story without interrupting once, which was most unusual for her. But she was clearly shocked and concerned.

"According to some of the e-mail tips Trooper Truth's been getting," Andy went on, "Trish Thrash went by the initials T.T., and of late people had been teasing her about being Trooper Truth. Because of the initials, I'm saying. And she was getting a big kick out of it and often commented that she wished she was Trooper Truth because she wanted to be a journalist but ended up a data entry clerk for the state."

He fell silent, deeply saddened by the thought of the poor woman never realizing her dream and then wishing she were Trooper Truth, and now she was dead.

"So do you think she met the killer and talked to him?" Hammer supposed. "Maybe she told him the same quirky anecdote about people teasing her about Trooper Truth and that she wished she was Trooper Truth, and she then trusted this stranger enough to go off with him somewhere?"

"That's exactly what I think, but I'm hesitating on the gender issue. Other tips I've gotten indicated T.T. wasn't likely to go off with a man and certainly wouldn't let one pick her up unless it was at work, where she lived a lie because she feared repercussions from her bigoted boss. So her M.O. was to dress rather tough and hang out in bars on nights and weekends, looking for same-sex company. She apparently called a friend the night of her death and said she was going to Tobacco Company, which is a very nice place and not the sort of hangout where you'd expect whacko people. So I'm assuming whoever T.T. met, it wasn't anyone people would notice or not trust. Not that I'm saying she met anyone in Tobacco Company. We don't know where she met her killer, not yet. I—through Trooper Truth—have been forwarding all this information to Detective Slipper, by the way. So hopefully he's following up on it."

"But what none of this begins to explain is why the killer left evidence at your house, Andy," Hammer said, her face tense with fear. "I'm worried about your safety, for God's sake! This is a vicious psychopath and now he's stalking you!"

"Frankly," Andy said, "I'm not convinced that the killer is a man or is working alone. Let me remind you that Moses Custer was also cut with a razorlike weapon."

"A woman highway pirate who is committing hate crimes?" Hammer asked dubiously.

"It's such a ridiculous misnomer for people to assume that women aren't violent and capable of the same awful things men do," Andy replied. "Hate is hate. And I think it might be a good plan for me to address that in Trooper Truth soon."

Cat was unfolding his own plan while this steamy conversation was going on miles away on the other side of the James River. The road dog had borrowed the Land Cruiser, which this minute was parked at the state police hangar, inconspicuously tucked between two other civilian cars. After hours of waiting, Cat was finally rewarded when Macovich appeared in the sky and landed the 430 that he had just flown to Tangier Island to pick up fresh seafood.

Macovich had to admit that those Tangierians were the strangest people on earth. Although they had declared war on Virginia and were flying a flag with a crab on it, the instant they realized Macovich had shown up for the single-minded purpose of buying something, they took down the crab flag and hoisted the Virginia flag. Then they doubled the price for the governor's dinner.

"I don't guess you know anything about that dentist you got hid somewhere on this island." Macovich had at least made an attempt to investigate the kidnapping while the lady at the cash register gave him change in pennies.

"The dentist? I haven't seen him of lately," the woman replied. Macovich didn't believe her and couldn't help but notice that she had the worst crowns he had ever seen.

"He cap your teeth?" Macovich asked.

"Yass." The Tangier woman, whose name was Mattie Dize, flashed Macovich a snow-white, chalky smile as he pocketed ninety-two pennies.

"Wooo," Macovich replied, shaking his head. "Glad he ain't my dentist. Now, listen here. I think it would be smart if you folks out here calmed down and let that dentist go on home to his family. What good is it doing to be hiding him somewhere? The rest of Virginia don't want no trouble with you Tangierians."

Mattie's eyes narrowed and she sucked in her bottom lip as she smacked the cash drawer shut.

"The gov'ner don't want no hassle with you folks, either," Macovich continued as blue crabs clattered and a trout flopped in the bottom of the white plastic bucket. "I mean, I could just start breaking down doors until I found the dentist and then lock up every last one of you, but I'm being nice about it. And 'sides, I need to get this seafood on back to the gov'ner before it dies 'cause the First Lady don't like dead fresh seafood."

Macovich had at least tried to mediate, he thought as he shut down the helicopter back at the hangar and noticed a hard-looking youth who was dressed like a member of a NASCAR pit crew and talking on a cell phone.

"He's here," Cat was telling Smoke.

"Who is? It'd better be good, you waking me up in the middle of the afternoon."

"That big black mother cop. He just landed in the chopper."

"No shit?" Smoke was instantly alert. "Well, just get your ass over there and take that lesson, and why isn't Possum there instead of you?"

"He working on something in his room," Cat said.

"I'm going to kick his ass," Smoke groggily said as he rolled over and went back to sleep.

Cat casually strutted toward the helicopter Macovich was refueling with a big hose attached to an Exxon truck with *JET-A* in large letters on it. Cat buttoned up his NASCAR windbreaker and pulled a NASCAR cap low over his eyes, grateful he had gone to every race at the Richmond International Raceway and had already been well supplied with NASCAR memorabilia—such as clothing, cigarette lighters, posters, mugs, pens, and air fresheners for the rearview mirror—long before he knew these items might be important to his work.

Macovich watched the NASCAR man walking toward him and got excited. What he wouldn't give to be part of a NASCAR pit crew! This guy looked like the right stuff: swaggering, rough, strong but small enough to fit inside a stock car. He was smoking a Winston and wearing dark glasses and probably had a beautiful sexy blonde waiting for him at home.

"I'm here on orders of my driver, whose name you still can't know," Cat said, flipping open a colorful lighter with *Winston Cup* and Jeff Burton's signature on it. "Let's get started."

"Get started doin' what?" Macovich eyed the lighter with envy and wondered if the white driver with dreadlocks he met last night might be Jeff Burton in disguise.

"Teaching me to fly." Cat fondled the lighter and took his time firing it up, a cigarette tucked behind his ear.

Macovich looked around to see if anyone was watching. Cat slipped a hundred-dollar bill out of a zippered pocket on the windbreaker's sleeve. Macovich stared at the bill and tried to remember the last time he had seen one.

"I tell you what," he said to Cat. "Let me drop off this fresh seafood first. Meet me back here in an hour or two."

"Wait a fucking minute," Cat said, alarmed. "I ain't taking no lesson in the dark!"

"You crazy, man?" Macovich talked rough with him. "You think a big helicopter like this cares if it's dark? This baby's instrument rated, got autopilot, a traffic scope plus a storm scope, and all kinds of landing lights, and even a DVD player in the back so the First Family can watch movies while I haul them around."

Cat understood the DVD part but nothing else. He was beginning to think he had taken on far more than he could handle, but he wasn't about to let this big mother cop think that.

"Oh yeah?" Cat said. "Well, I seen bigger, better helicopters than this one. What'chu think all them drivers land in at the racetrack?"

"Mostly Jet Rangers and maybe a 407," replied Macovich, who knew firsthand what landed at the racetrack because the First Family was quite fond of stock cars that thunder around and around in circles all night long. "Now I gotta deliver this seafood before it's dead," Macovich said. "I'll be right back and let you get by with paying me only a hundred dollars for your first lesson, as sort of a courtesy. But it gonna cost you more after that. This is a 'spensive machine."

"How much it worth on the street?" Cat eagerly asked.

" 'Bout six mil," Macovich said as he locked the helicopter's doors and baggage compartment.

Possum wasn't allowed to have a lock on his bedroom door, but he could surely use one, he thought, as he worried that Smoke was going to be pissed off when he found out that Possum had wormed his way out of the helicopter lesson. Possum nervously ate a peanut butter and grape jelly sandwich in his dark bedroom as he continued to sketch out ideas for a pirate flag while he watched *Bonanza* and petted Popeye.

"Wish I could do that," he muttered to Popeye as Hoss, who was out by the barn, bent horseshoes with his bare hands.

Little Joe was whipping Hoss in shape to wrestle the infamous Bear Cat Sampson at the Tweedy Circus that had just come to town. All Hoss had to do was pin the undefeated circus wrestler in five minutes, and Hoss and Little Joe would win a hundred dollars. That was probably a lot of money back then, Possum thought. These days, a hundred dollars would barely buy a decent pair of basketball shoes.

Possum sketched a bent horseshoe in his theme book and scratched through it. Then he tried drawing Hoss lifting a wagon full of heavy feed sacks. Next, Little Joe was slamming a board into Hoss's big belly, and Hoss couldn't even feel it. None of these themes worked on paper, either. So Possum tried his hand at the Ponderosa map burning up, and he felt he was at least on the right track.

His door flew open and Smoke was standing there glaring at him. Possum squinted in the sudden light seeping into his room.

"What the fuck you doing?" Smoke said angrily, as if he might just snatch Possum and Popeye off the bed and hurt both of them.

"Nothing."

"Why didn't you go to the hangar? I get a call from Cat while your lazy ass is back here watching TV! You were supposed to take the lesson, not Cat!"

"Cat be better at flying than me," Possum meekly replied. "You was asleep, Smoke, so we didn't want to bother you 'bout it."

"Well, get your ugly ass up. We're going to Wal-Mart to get some NASCAR clothes. From now on, that's our colors and don't let me catch you wearing no more Michael Jordan shit. We're going to the race," Smoke went on. "There's one in town Saturday night, the Winston Series."

"But we ain't got tickets!" Possum exclaimed. "How we get in this late with no tickets? And there won't be no place to park the car."

"We don't need tickets or a place to park," Smoke said, walking out of the bedroom and slamming the door shut.

Hoss entered the ring and was sucker-punched a few times before he locked Bear Cat in a bear hug and broke the wrestler's ribs.

"Let go of him, let go of him!" Possum whispered, even though he had seen this rerun so many times he knew that Hoss wouldn't let go of Bear Cat before time was up, and Hoss and Little Joe would lose the hundred dollars and end up traveling with the circus until Bear Cat healed up enough to wrestle again. "Let him go, Hoss!"

Ben Cartwright and Little Joe cheered from the stands, and Possum started sketching again. NASCAR had given him an idea. Like pirates, NASCAR used all kinds of flags for different warnings and penalties. Possum drew a checkered flag and turned it into a Jolly Roger, coloring the skull and crossbones red.

"Shit," he muttered. "That don't work neither, Popeye."

He turned a checkered flag into a game of tic-tac-toe and still wasn't satisfied, so he drew a black flag that meant it was time to pull into the pits, and he felt a chill creep up to the roots of his hair. He was getting somewhere. Possum erased areas of the black, forming white eyes and a grinning mouth that gave the morbid impression of a smiley-face skull. He crossed the skull with two possum tails instead of bones, and clamped a lit cigarette between the teeth, smoke rising in swirls. A smoking skull, he thought, getting increasingly excited as the Tweedy Circus ran out of money and had to pay Hoss and Little Joe with an elephant that they closed up inside the Ponderosa barn. Ben Cartwright wasn't happy when he opened the barn door and discovered his new livestock.

Possum sadly thought of the late Dale Earnhardt's number 3 black GM Goodwrench Services Chevy, and decided to honor the dead racing hero. *Jolly Goodwrench*, Possum wrote in block letters beneath the smoking skull flag.

"Hey look!" he exclaimed as he ran inside Smoke's bedroom and held up his themebook.

"You come in here one more time without asking and I'll blow your tiny dick off!" Smoke yelled as he sat up in bed and lit a cigarette.

"We got us a pirate flag, Smoke," Possum explained. "I can make one that look just like this and we can fly it at the race and make people think it's our NASCAR flag. We can take Popeye, too, and make sure them two cops show up, right? They never suspect no pit crew might be carrying pieces and are gonna blow their asses away. Then Cat can show up with the helicopter and fly us outta there and nobody can catch us. Then maybe we can 'scape to Tangerine Island, since everybody there's already in trouble and we could hide out with them 'til things chill, you know?"

Smoke sucked on the cigarette and shook several nearby beer cans. All of them were empty.

"Go get me a beer," he said to Possum. "Make sure that fucking flag's finished by Saturday. And get Cat on the cell phone and tell him to make sure we got that helicopter for Saturday. Tell him to tell that big black momma that the famous driver and his pit crew are gonna need it to get to the race and then afterwards to be dropped off at a big party on an island. Once we get there, we shoot that cop, too, and the helicopter's ours, and we got it fucking made in the shade."

Sixteen

Black wrought-iron gates crept open and a stern capitol police officer looked on through the glass window of his booth as Andy approached the governor's mansion.

"Where do I park?" Andy inquired, because the circular cobblestone drive was crammed with the governor's fleet of black Suburbans and limousines.

"Just pull it off on the grass," the officer replied.

"I can't do that," Andy protested as he gazed out at the recently manicured lawn and sculpted hedges.

"No problem," the officer assured him. "The inmates will clean it up tomorrow. It's good for them to keep busy."

Pony was watching all this through centuries-old glass. The butler was not in a good mood. In the past hour, the mansion's kitchen help had snapped at him repeatedly because the Crimm daughters—Regina, mostly—had protested the notion of a light supper, which typically meant trout or blue crabs freshly flown in from Tangier Island. Regina had a nasty habit of stalking the kitchen and peering under pot lids, and when she discovered a trout and several dozen blue crabs in the agonal stages of death in the sink, she pitched a fit.

"I hate fish!" she declared furiously. "Everybody here knows I hate fish!"

"Your mama told us the menu," said Chef Figgie. "We just following her instruction, Miss Reginia."

"My name is not ReGINIA!"

Chef Figgie resisted the impulse to tell her that she might be better off if her name were Reginia instead of the other. He stared at the trout in the sink and wished it would hurry up and die. It had a hook in its mouth and he couldn't understand why it was still flapping around after all this time. The blue crabs kept trying to climb out and were banging around in the huge stainless steel sink, making a racket and training their periscope-eyes on him with resentment and fear.

Chef Figgie resisted killing anything and was opposed, in a religious way, to taking the life from things smaller and less intelligent than him before he cooked them. He preferred food already dead and packaged when it was delivered. Most of all, he was violently against hog farming, and Regina had a passion for pork.

"What happened to ham?" she asked in that rude, loud voice of hers. "Why aren't we having ham biscuits? That's a light supper, and you know it, Figgie. You're just doing this because you don't like me. Look at those crabs staring at me. Let's just put them out the back door and they can wander off somewhere."

"The First Lady wouldn't be pleased if we let them go," he said.

"Who gives a shit?"

The crabs heard every word and climbed on top of each other so the one on top was close enough to the faucet to grab at it with a claw. They froze and pretended to be dead when Major Trader strutted into the commercially outfitted kitchen on the lower level, where, during the

mansion's last restoration, archaeologists had discovered thousands of artifacts, including fish bones and crude hooks, along with numerous ar-
rowheads and musket balls.

"Why are the crabs all stacked up like that?" Trader stared into the
sink. "Looks to me like they're already dead, and the First Lady despises
dead fresh seafood, Fig." Trader always called Chef Figgie *Fig*, for short.
"She likes them scuffling about and banging the sides of the pot as they
boil alive so they're very fresh when she eats them. Here." He set down
a small tin box. "The wife made Toll House cookies for the governor. Nobody else gets one."

Chef Figgie felt sick at the notion of boiling anything alive.

The crabs held their breath, their eyestalks paralyzed in terror as they
stared at Trader. Over the centuries, blue crabs had developed highly refined eyesight in order to spot and evade their natural enemies, which included the watermen of Tangier. The Islanders were a horrible people
who spent all their time on the bay in little boats stacked with crab pots
that they baited with rotten fish and plopped into the water, knowing
full well that blue crabs love rotten fish and have nothing else to eat if
rotten fish or other dead things are scarce.

It happens like this: An innocent crab is scuttling along through the
silt, minding his own business, when this big wire cage descends like an
elevator and settles on the bottom in a cloud of murk. The crab smells
rotten fish and spies chunks of it floating around inside the crab pot. He
calls over several of his friends or family members and says, "Well, I'll
swagger. What do you think?"

"They's potting," one of them offers. "Mind your step."

"God-a-mighty! But I sure has a hunger," Baby Crab complains.

"Keep quite! Hadn't I learned you about potting? You'll get hung up
in that thar thing!"

"Look," Trader said loudly, "these crabs are already dead and the First
Lady won't like it a bit if she finds out when they're on her plate. She'll
have you fired and then all your nidgettes won't have a daddy anymore."

Trader, loathsome racist that he was, thought this was a great idea and
laughed blatantly. Seventeen more little black children out there with no

father figure. They would all grow up to be drug dealers, hanging out in long lines at the methadone clinics, and then end up in the penitentiary just like their daddy. One day, they would work in the mansion's kitchen trying to figure out if crabs were dead or not and whether the First Lady would fire them, too—them being the nidgettes, not the crabs, Trader qualified silently, as all of this seeped into his mind like sewage.

Andy had rung the bell three times now as Pony watched through the wavy old glass. It was essential that a butler give the impression he was very busy and that the mansion was sprawling, requiring many moments to pass through gracious rooms and beneath sweeping archways en route to the entrance hall.

"Coming," Pony said through cupped hands, to make his voice sound far away.

Andy knocked again, crisply rapping the heavy brass pineapple, which was the symbol of hospitality in Virginia. Pony walked briskly in place for a minute, working up a sweat and getting out of breath.

"Coming," he said again, this time without cupped hands to make him sound closer.

He counted to ten and opened the door.

"I'm here to see the Crimms," Andy said as he shook Pony's hand, much to Pony's surprise.

"Oh," Pony replied, his mind going blank for an instant. This young man was polite and nice. He was trying to look Pony in the eye and Pony simply wasn't accustomed to this and had to somehow get hold of himself and play his role. "And who may I tell them is here?"

Andy told him and instantly felt sorry for Pony. The poor man was run ragged by his job, and unappreciated.

"I like your jacket," Andy said. "You must iron it all the time. Looks like it could stand up without you in it." He meant this as a compliment.

"My wife works in the laundry downstairs near the kitchen. She irons it for me and is rather heavy-handed with the can of starch," Pony proudly answered. "We never see each other unless I'm working because the rest of the time they got me in lockup."

"That must be very hard."

189

"It ain't fair," Pony admitted. "The last six governors, including Mr. Crimm three of those times, always promise to have my sentence commuted and then they get busy and never give it another thought. That's the problem with term limitation, you ask me. All people do is worry about what's next."

Andy walked into the entrance hallways and Pony shut the door.

"Exactly," Andy agreed. "The minute they get elected, they're already thinking about what they're going to do next because they have only four years, and half of them must be spent campaigning or going to job interviews."

Pony nodded, feeling encouraged that someone at last understood what it was like to be assigned to the mansion. "You here to see the Crimm girls? 'Cause you sure don't look like their type."

"Not that I'm aware of," Andy said, suddenly suspicious of the First Lady's real motive for inviting him to the mansion.

Regina, too, was suspicious.

"These crabs are not dead!" she yelled. "One of them just looked at me. I just saw its eyes move. How could I possibly eat anything with eyes bugging out of their heads the way they do? It hurts my eyes to watch. You would think stuff would get in them all the time because of the way they stick out and don't have lids."

"It's so they can hide in the sand and still see," Trader explained to her. "There's a reason for their eyes being periscopic like submarines."

He deliberately alluded to submarines to mock the governor's constitution behind his back. Trader was respectful to his prominent boss only when he had no choice, and it was his habit to abuse mansion staff and say whatever he wanted when Crimm wasn't present or was unaware.

"Take them down to the river and let them go," Regina ordered Chef Figgie. "The fish, as well. It's looking at me, too. And take that damn hook out of its mouth first. You let it go with that hook in there, it will get caught on stuff and the poor thing will drown. I want ham biscuits with butter and mint jelly, you hear me? What happened to the rest of that pie we didn't finish? The peanut butter pie?"

She ran tap water on the crabs and the fish, waking them up a little, as she loudly ordered people about.

"There's a bucket in the corner," she said. "The one they came in. Put them in it right now. And don't you ever bring another crab or fish into this mansion. I'm sick of deer meat, too. How do you know the Indians don't poison the deer first to pay us back? They drag this carcass up the steps, thinking we're so lucky they give us gifts."

"You're not supposed to call them Indians, Miss Reginia. They're Native Americans and it's very thoughtful of them to bring us deer." Chef Figgie was offended and not the least bit intimidated by her.

"Native Americans, huh?" Regina's face darkened with rage. "Oh really? That's the same thing as us calling your people *Natives.*"

"It most certainly isn't." Chef Figgie looked directly into Regina's tiny, hard eyes, which reminded him of raisins imbedded in rising bread dough. "And if you ever refer to any of the mansion help as Natives, I'll report you to the NAACP. I don't care if you are the governor's daughter."

"Get these crabs out of there this minute!" Regina screamed. "Or they're gonna die and smell."

The crabs waved their claws in celebration as Chef Figgie gently lifted them and the trout out of the deep sink and set them in the bucket. He got wire cutters and snipped off the hook, sliding it free of the fish's sore mouth.

Pony wasn't so lucky. Nobody had ever let him off the hook for any reason. Oh, how he would love it if Chef Figgie would carry him down to the James River in a bucket and let him go. Pony watched the chef walk through the dining room, heading to a side door, water slopping out of the bucket as the crabs and fish talked to one another, making plans. Regina was close behind and stopped in her tracks when she saw Andy.

"We're not having a light supper, after all," she told him.

"Whatever," Andy politely replied. "I think we need to hook me up with your father as soon as possible."

"Are you making a tasteless pun because of the fish?" She scowled.

He didn't know her well enough to make puns, and Regina had no doubt that this handsome man was not going to be nice to her. None of them were or ever would be.

Andy noticed the fish swimming inside the crowded bucket and realized he had misspoken. "I'm sorry. I didn't see the trout until just this second. Otherwise, I never would have used the word *hook* in its presence. I meant no disrespect. It's just that I sincerely hope I get a chance to speak to the governor tonight."

"You can call me Regina."

No, he couldn't. Andy couldn't possibly say that name without feeling very uncomfortable and embarrassed.

"Do you go by any other names?" he asked. "What about Reggie?"

"No one has ever called me Reggie."

She was knocked off balance by his kind interest and had to steady herself against the polished mahogany bannister that curved out of sight, leading upstairs to the First Family's private quarters, where this minute Maude Crimm was spraying her hair, unhappy with the reflection that was spraying its hair in the mirror.

She had been beautiful once. When Maude and Bedford had first spotted each other at the Fabergé Ball, she had been voluptuous but petite, with a bowed red mouth and expressive violet eyes. Maude was gazing into a showcase at a jeweled egg that had led to the Bolshevik Revolution and the mystery of Anastasia, when Bedford Crimm IV, a freshman state senator, had gallantly appeared at her side and stared through an old magnifying glass at the lovely shapes scarcely covered by her low-cut gown.

"My, can you imagine?" he said. "I've always wondered why an egg. Why not something else if you're going to make things out of precious metals and priceless jewels?"

"What would you have chosen for a theme?" Maude coyly inquired.

She had fallen swiftly for Crimm and his inquiring mind, and it occurred to her that she had always taken the Fabergé collection for granted. All these years, and she had never questioned why.

"Most certainly I would not have chosen an egg," Crimm replied in a rich, important voice that lilted with the rhythm of the Old South. "A

Civil War theme, perhaps." He considered. "Maybe cannons of rose gold or Confederate flags fashioned of platinum, rubies, diamonds, and sapphires—the very stones and metals you should have around your lovely tapered white neck." He traced her throat with a stubby finger. "A long necklace with a huge diamond at the end that would disappear into your bosom." He showed her. "And remain tucked out of sight to tickle you when you least expect it."

"I've always wanted a big diamond," Maude said, looking around rather nervously, hoping nobody in the crowded room was paying them any mind. "You look like you're wearing a big diamond yourself," she said, staring at the front of his tuxedo pants.

"The hope diamond." He chuckled.

"Because you're always hoping. I get it," she said. "You know, I'm quite a collector, too, Senator Crimm."

"You don't say?"

"Oh yes. I happen to know a lot about magnifying glasses." She continued to impress him. "Why, they go all the way back to the caves of Crete and there was once a Chinese emperor who used a topaz to look at the stars. That was thousands of years before the Baby Jesus was born, can you imagine? And I bet you didn't know that Nero himself used to peer through an emerald when he watched the gladiators kill each other. I suppose so the sun didn't hurt his eyes. So I think it's very appropriate that you should have very special optic glasses, too, since you're such an important, powerful man."

"Why don't we slip off to the men's room and introduce ourselves to each other," Crimm suggested.

"I could never!" Maude's *no* was a *yes*, but Crimm would find out soon after their marriage that even a *yes* would be *no* when she was preoccupied with crown molding and cobwebs.

"The ladies' room, then," Crimm tried again.

Beautiful women had always ignored him before he went into politics. Now it was amazingly easy, and he felt he had been given a second chance. Having been born terribly short and homely with deteriorating eyes no longer mattered. Even the size of his diamond made little difference. It wasn't like the old days at the Commonwealth Club, where all the up-and-coming males would sit around the swimming pool naked, making political decisions and discussing unfriendly take-overs.

"Not even half a carat," Crimm remembered one of them whispering. Of course, voices carry across the water, and Crimm, who was sitting on the diving board, heard the tasteless remark.

"It's the quality, not the size," he replied. "And how hard it is."

"All diamonds are hard," said another man, who ran a Fortune 500 company that later relocated to Charlotte.

Crimm discovered in the ladies' room that all diamonds are not hard. Maude's birthmark had caused a bad result. Her bottom looked like she had sat in a puddle of ink. It was hideously stained, and Crimm was afraid to touch it.

"What happened?" he asked as he recoiled and tucked his diamond back into his trousers.

"Nothing happened," Maude said from her position flat against the cold tile wall. "If the lights are out, you can't even see it. Some people find it attractive."

Maude flipped off the light and kissed him hungrily. She mined for his diamond until she could find it again. "Talk vulgar to me," she whispered in the dark restroom. "No one ever has, and I've always wanted to hear lurid things about what people, especially men, want to do to me. Be careful, the wall is hard when you bang me up against it like that. No, don't pull me down on the hard filthy floor instead. Maybe we shouldn't be doing this in here. I'm going to have bruises."

"We could go into one of the stalls." Crimm could scarcely speak. "Then if people walk in, they won't see us. If we make noise, we can cover it up by flushing the toilet repeatedly."

Those amorous days had ended after the wedding. Bedford's eyesight had continually disintegrated, and he had not laid a finger on Maude since Regina was conceived, despite the First Lady's relentless efforts to look desirable, which was for the purpose of teasing and frustrating and camouflaging her true intention of *no*. Maude hadn't fantasized about *yes* in a very long time, and as she thought about Andy

Brazil, it entered her mind that maybe she should try *yes* again and mean it. After all, her husband was being so unfair about the trivets, and she spent all of her time these days relocating them throughout the mansion.

Maybe she should give the governor something important to worry about and keep that gorgeous Brazil boy for herself, she resentfully thought. The hell with her daughters. Maybe if Maude seduced Andy, she would feel better about herself and become sufficiently distracted to cut back on her shopping. She applied another coat of thick black mascara to enhance her violently violet eyes. She slashed vivid red lipstick around her mouth, patted on more blush, and frowned, to see how her Botox was holding up.

"Oh, dear," she said to the mirror when she detected a trace of movement in her forehead.

Her collagen was wearing thin, too, and she dreaded a return trip to the maxillary-facial surgeon. It had gotten to where she simply could not endure another needle stick without a heavy hit of Demerol, and for what? Nobody cared. Nobody appreciated her anymore. Maude unhooked her bra and worked her way out of it without taking off her blouse, a trick she had learned at Sweet Briar College.

"Well, that was a wasted effort," she muttered to herself impatiently as her breasts migrated to her waist.

Sighing, she put her bra back on and changed into an attractive sheer cashmere sweater that had been several sizes too small even when she was much thinner.

"There," she announced to the First Dog, Frisky, who was asleep on the bed inside the adjoining master suite. "You have to admit I look pretty damn good for seventy, don't I?"

Frisky didn't stir. He was a very old chocolate Lab and was tired of the First Lady's talking to him endlessly. It had been going on for nine years, and Frisky believed the First Lady had looked pretty overblown from day one. Now she looked especially bad, with her frozen face and swollen lips, and he didn't intend to open his eyes or interrupt his favorite dream of being a ball boy at Wimbledon. He silently prayed that the First Lady, for once, wouldn't wake him up.

"Come, Frisky!" the First Lady called her sleeping dog as she tried unsuccessfully to snap her fingers.

Mrs. Crimm shimmered with body lotion and her fingers were slippery. "Come!" Her fingers snipped rather than snapped. "Let's go down and greet our company."

Seventeen

The blue crabs and the trout were about to have their luck change yet again.

Major Trader had volunteered to dump them in the river because he had his own secret, selfish agenda. He figured he could find someone fishing and sell the fresh seafood easily and for a pretty penny, and he was scouting for a good location for the drop-off of the waterproof suitcase full of cash that he expected to get from the pirates soon.

Right this minute, Trader was driving his state car, and the bucket was sloshing around in the trunk. Neither the crabs nor the trout could see a thing in the pitch dark, and they had an ominous feeling about the trip as Trader sped and jerked the car into curves and made sudden stops at lights.

"Jiminy Criminy, he must not got a GPS," one crab said as it knocked into another one on the bottom of the bucket. "He's lost. I can tell."

"How?" said the trout as he floated above crabs clashing into one another with each hairpin turn and lurching start and stop. "I think he might have engine problems."

"You ever been in a car afore?"

"Can't say I have," the trout replied. "But I've seen them pull up to the dock, from a safe distance, when the watermen get out to fish. All their trucks and golf carts jump around and careen like this."

The crabs tumbled to one side and landed in a pile.

"Ouch!" a crab complained. "That hurt! Get your claw outta my eye or you're gonna catch it!"

"I'm hungry!"

"There's neither rotted fish until we foller the water. Hold on!"

Trader drove over a curb and parked on the sidewalk, where Caesar Fender was fishing and not catching a thing.

"Hey! You just ran over my tackle box, you motherfucker!" Caesar yelled at the state car. "Who you think you are? I ain't doing nothing. I don't even have a car, so you got no right to pull over with your high beams on and run over my tackle box, like I was speeding or something!"

"I got fresh seafood fit for the governor," Trader announced. "Sell it to you for fifty dollars. Bet you got a passel of hungry nidgettes at home. Bet they never had blue crabs before, and fresh trout."

Caesar Fender was shocked by the big fat white man's slurs. "Just 'cause some black folks is short don't mean they're nidgettes," he lashed back. "And you owe me two dollars for the tackle box and another seventy-five cents for all the hooks you bent and bobbers you busted. You step one foot closer and you're gonna knock my can of worms in the water, and then I'm gonna kick your ass!"

"You lay a hand on me and I'll have you arrested and sent to jail!" Trader threatened.

"Pay me what you owe for all my fishing tackle you ruined!"

"Watch your mouth. You're talking to a very important government official," Trader yelled back.

"I don't give a flying fuck who you are!"

While the two men argued and bickered, the crabs quickly put together a plot to save themselves and the trout. "Play dead," someone said.

Trader popped open the trunk and Caesar peered inside, angry but curious about the fresh seafood. The trout was belly-up with its eyes shut, and all the crabs were motionless, their eyes shut, too.

"You cheatin' motherfucker!" Caesar screamed at Trader. "This seafood's dead as a doornail. How long you had it in your trunk? A month? Peeee-yooo." He waved his hand in front of his face as he lifted the bucket out. "You lying white trash. Here's what I think of your fucking *fresh seafood*."

Suddenly, the crabs and trout were sailing out of the bucket as if they were dashing out a fire. They flew through the air and splashed into the James River, where the crabs sank to the bottom and sat, looking around, stunned, as the trout swam in lazy circles over them.

"Look! I see the trout swimming down there!" Trader pointed at the shadow of the trout deep below the sparkling surface. "They're not dead! You threw away my fresh seafood! Hand over fifty dollars!" he demanded.

"Nope." Caesar gathered up his ruined fishing gear.

Trader's pirate genetic coding was fired up and he punched Caesar in the eye. Caesar turned his fishing pole into a whip and stung Trader's cheek with thirty-test monofilament and several small sinkers that Caesar had attached with his teeth shortly after arriving hours earlier on his bicycle. The two men fought fiercely with each other, rolling on the ground, yelling obscenities and beating on each other. Enraged and bleeding, Trader darted for his car, which Caesar began kicking before he smashed out the front windshield with his damaged metal tackle box.

Frenzied and out of breath, Trader dove into the driver's side and fumbled for the flare gun he always kept hidden under the front seat. He cut his fingers on splinters of glass as he stuffed a .12 gauge flare into the wide barrel of the old flare gun that had been handed down in his pirate family since 1870. He rolled out of the car and pointed the flare gun in

Caesar's direction as the deranged fisherman hurled lead sinkers at him, one of which struck Trader on the nose, causing an instant reflex that twitched his trigger finger.

The flare exploded through the air like a small fiery missile, streaking straight toward Caesar and slamming into his chest. The crabs and trout watched in horror as the fisherman burst into flames and ran several steps before collapsing. Trader fled in his banged-up state car, the trunk still open, the windshield a spider web of shattered glass. When he limped into the governor's mansion a little later, he was pale and bloody, his suit and tie torn. He was agitated, paranoid, and confused.

Regina was confused, too. She had never seen her mother so made-up and heavily perfumed. Had Regina run into her mother in a funeral home, she would have assumed Mrs. Crimm was full of formaldehyde and overlaid in putty and had gotten her clothes mixed up with some other dead lady who was much smaller and fond of fuchsia.

"What the hell happened to you, Mama?" Regina asked as she worked on a thick slab of honey-glazed ham that was tucked inside a huge biscuit dripping with butter and globs of mint jelly.

Mrs. Crimm, running a little late, seated herself at the foot of the table and lifted a fork to signal that everyone could begin eating.

"What do you mean, what happened to me?" Mrs. Crimm shot Regina a threatening glance. "And you're not supposed to start eating before everyone else. As if I didn't raise you better."

Andy cut off the only morsel of lean ham he could find in the mound on his plate as Trader walked into the dining room. Andy noticed instantly that the press secretary was bloody and in shock and smelled faintly of burned chemicals and gunpowder.

"I'd rather know what happened to you," Andy said to Trader.

Mrs. Crimm inferred from this that her handsome young dinner guest didn't think for a minute that anything at all had happened to her. She always looked alluring and thoughtfully put together. It was irrational and Victorian for women to hide their bodies beneath thick layers of loose, long clothing. Andy's attention would find its way down to the foot of the table any minute and linger to wander all over her. After dinner, the two of them would sneak up to the master suite and she would lock the door and say *yes* and mean it. Even if the governor came home, as long as she and Andy were quiet, he wouldn't see them.

"Did you wander into a riot or a hurricane?" Andy's attention remained on Trader, who went into a lengthy, breathless explanation, talking so fast that his words tangled and ran into each other midair.

"What on earth did he say?" First Lady Crimm asked Andy every few seconds. "I wonder if he's had a stroke!"

Trader's story could easily be summed up, although he took a long time to tell it and the facts changed like clouds. The gist was this: He arrived at the river at nineteen hundred hours and an African American male was fishing out by his bicycle. Trader greeted the man and they discussed the weather as Trader dumped the crabs and the trout overboard.

"Oh dear," Mrs. Crimm interrupted. "He didn't toss the crabs into the James, did he? Unless they can find their way back to the bay, they'll die, sure as shooting."

Trader rushed ahead with his story.

"He says there was a shooting, now that you mention it," Andy translated. "A Lincoln with New York plates roared up and a Hispanic male in his twenties started firing a nine-millimeter Sig-Sauer pistol out the window and yelling obscenities. He shot the fisherman at very close range, probably in the chest, and the fisherman possibly caught on fire, possibly from burning gunpowder that was possibly fueled by a Bic lighter that was possibly in the fisherman's shirt pocket."

"How come he doesn't know anything for sure?" Regina reached for another biscuit. "Didn't he even check to see if the poor man just might still be alive or if he was really burning up? Why didn't he try to put the fire out or call for help?" She fastened her eyes on Trader as she ate. "You just rush off and not try to help or anything? What kind of person are you?"

"He shit at me!" Trader raised his voice, not realizing that his sudden speech problem was due to post-traumatic stress that had somehow activated a genetic code that caused him to talk like a pirate.

"We don't talk that way at the table!" Mrs. Crimm fired back at him.

"He shit at me again and again! I was afeared to get near him!"

"I can't stand this." Regina covered her ears. "Someone talk for him. Andy, just tell us what he says. And does he really mean to imply that the Hispanic was doing *number two* at him? Doing it or throwing it?" She scowled. "What does he mean that the gunman *shit* at him?"

"Regina!" her mother scolded her. "We don't talk about bathroom habits at the dinner table!"

Trader started to make the point that he was talking about a shooting, when Andy cautioned him not to say the words *shoot, shot, shooting,* or *shooter,* but to simply simulate by mutely pointing his finger and firing it like a gun. This worked, and the First Family settled down and resumed eating as Trader claimed, through Andy, that he was certain the Hispanic was the one committing the hate crimes and was coming after the First Family next, so Trader had raced back to the mansion instantly to make sure all were safe and protected.

"He say he hated Crimm," Trader blurted out. "And he thinks all Crimms should be put to death."

"You sure he didn't mean criminals, as opposed to Crimms?" Regina considered as she chewed. "Papa's very much in favor of sending criminals to death row and is known for it."

"Honey, that wouldn't make much sense," Mrs. Crimm replied. "The Hispanic is clearly a criminal himself, so why would he be on a spree of hate crimes that target people similar to himself?"

"Damnation seize my soul, the villain meant *ye!*" Trader pointed at each Crimm in an ominous, morbid way. "*Crimm.* Not criminals."

Faith was frightened. "We won't be able to leave the mansion ever again, Mama."

"What if he's out there somewhere?" Constance's eyes were wide, and she kept refilling her wine glass with nervous hands.

"I've never heard of anyone catching on fire when they're shot." Andy pressed Trader on this point. "Did you really see smoke and flames and his clothes igniting? I realize you're saying you didn't hang around long and were frightened and also concerned for the Crimms and may have suffered a small stroke, but I'm having a very hard time with your story."

Trader rather condescendingly replied that it was a well-known scientific fact that people do burst into flames and have cremated themselves unannounced since the beginning of time.

"It's called spontenuous combusting," he said. "Look it up."

Andy didn't need to look it up. He was quite familiar with spontaneous human combustion and the stories of people suddenly bursting into flames for no good reason.

"Well," he said to Trader, "we'll see what the medical examiner has to say."

"You don't think that psycho's gonna come here and set all of us on fire, do you?" Constance worried aloud.

"Why would he hate us?" Grace couldn't make sense of it. "What did we ever do to him or any Hispanic? And we're not a minority except for our practically being a royal family, and there certainly aren't many of those."

"We don't even know any Hispanics," Faith reminded her family as she looked around the table, her horse-shaped face wavering in soft candle light. "And Papa hasn't a single Hispanic working in his administration and never has. So what do the Hispanics have to be resentful about?"

"Probably what you just said," Andy replied.

"Which was what?" Regina asked between chews.

"It's been my observation that the governor's administration could use a little more variety." Andy tried to be diplomatic. "When an entire group of people finds itself excluded, hard feelings arise and can turn to violence."

"But Bedford doesn't speak Spanish," Mrs. Crimm explained. "He sees no reason to."

"He really doesn't see reasons for much of anything, First Lady Crimm." Andy was candid, and he almost added *with all due respect*, but the specter of Hammer had been hovering over him all day. "I'm convinced if he could do something about his vision, his life would dramatically improve."

"His vision is the same as it's always been," the First Lady replied. "He envisions a Commonwealth that is uncommon and committed to the wealth and well-being of one and all, and that from this day forth, there shall be the uncommon goal that the people . . . Oh dear, I'm afraid I can't remember the next line. What does he say?" She scanned her daughters' bored faces.

"The same thing he says at every inauguration," Regina replied in disgust. "He's used the same speech every time he's elected and it was stupid the first time and it's still stupid." She looked at Andy. "He thinks Virginia ought to be renamed the Uncommonwealth of Virginia, because he hates North Carolina and is damn tired of all these Fortune 500 companies and banks and movies going there instead of here."

She reached for the butter, and the silver knife leapt from her buttery, thick fingers and fled across the heart-of-pine floor. Pony appeared out of nowhere and picked it up. He replaced it with a clean one from the silver chest.

"Can I get you anything else, Miss Reginia?" he politely inquired.

"That's not a bad name," Andy said in surprise. "Why don't all of us call you Reginia instead of the other?"

"I don't want to be called something else, and I'm sick and tired of everyone worrying about what I'm called! And I'm even more sick and tired of no one ever calling me to begin with." Tears jumped out of her eyes. "Every time the phone rings it's just somebody trying to find the base unit. I don't have any friends. Not even one." Regina cried with her mouth full, chewing and miserable. "I was born in a coal mine . . ."

"No you weren't," her mother firmly interrupted.

"I was conceived in one." Regina became indiscreet. "I know exactly what happened when you and Papa went down into that deep, dark shaft and you had on that little hard hat with the flashlight. Imagine how I feel knowing his sperm had black dust all over it and swam straight to an egg and decided the result would be me!"

She reached for the bottle of wine, and it slipped out of her grasp and rolled across the table and onto the floor. Pony patiently crawled under the table after the bottle of Virginia Chardonnay.

"I'm so fucking sick of everything!" Regina bellowed.

"You are not to use that word ever again," the First Lady told her severely. "What in the world happened to make your mouth so foul? When you were born, you didn't talk like that. And I think the F-word is filthy and unspeakably degrading and unbecoming to a young lady, especially the daughter of a governor."

"That's the way they talked in the coal mine," Regina smugly said to Andy, and by now no one remembered that Trader was at the table or even in this world.

Then he made the mistake of thinking like a press secretary and speaking like a pirate. "Yay. Better ye use euphetisms like *darnt, doggone it, fudge, rats, for Pate's sake, that's the darntest thing I ever hear, shit, oh shit . . .*"

"Enough!" Andy ordered him. "I told you not to say *shoot* in any tense."

"Why are you talking like that?" Regina was out with it, uncovering her ears and glaring at Trader.

"I was born on the island as was everybody afore me," he said as he dabbed his bleeding face with a linen napkin. "I'm afraid the shock of witnessing the murder has done something to me brain."

"Well, I don't care if you were born on the island. You can just forget the rubbish that what you're speaking is Old English or Elizabethan English or that John Smith said *shit* instead of *shot* or *shoot*. Now he might have said *shat*, but not shit. Does everybody on the island talk like you, or do you have your own special secret vernacular or something?" Regina was brutal but honestly curious. "After all these centuries, why don't you talk so people can understand what the hell you're saying?

"Mama, I insist Papa fire this man. I can't stand him in the mansion another day. I just know I'll hear him in my head all the time and it will drive me to distraction. And I simply can't afford to be driven to distraction because there are so many distractions already and I'm bored to death of being driven everywhere by EPU! I want a car and a license and to go places without security!"

"Shhh!" the First Lady ordered as Pony detected footsteps out front and hurried toward them.

Momentarily, the door shut loudly in the entrance hallway and the tone of murmuring voices suggested that Bedford Crimm had not enjoyed the day much.

"I smell ham!" he announced in dismay. "I thought we were having seafood tonight. I am most decidedly not in the mood for ham. What happened to the crabs I had flown in?"

"Sir, will that be all?" a trooper asked.

"No!" Maude Crimm called out from the dining room. "Don't let him go, sweetie! We need all of the EPU to stay right here!"

This was very much out of character for the First Lady, who was known for getting annoyed with omnipresent security details. At first, she had felt important and admired when squadrons of powerfully built EPU troopers in immaculate suits surrounded her everywhere she went and made certain her every need was fulfilled. Then she grew weary of it. Maude Crimm longed to sit in the garden or the tub or watch TV or shop on the Internet or get her cosmetic procedures without cameras or others taking all of it in. She was becoming increasingly paranoid about her privacy and nurtured a growing suspicion that the troopers saw everything she did—everything, including her endeavors to hide her collectibles.

"What's this all about?" the governor asked as he walked into the dining room and squinted in the candlelight to make out what was on everyone's plates. "Ham," he muttered disagreeably. "I can't stand ham. What happened to the crabs?" He fixed his unhappy, dull gaze on Regina.

"We let them go." She was candid with her father.

"I flew them in on the state helicopter and you let them go?"

"And the trout," she replied, reaching for the mint jelly.

"Sir." Andy was determined to get to the heart of the First Family's difficulties. "There's a situation I think you need to know about. A black male was just murdered while he was fishing in the river, and Major Trader has alleged that you and your wife and daughters could be in danger. Apparently, he allegedly witnessed the crime and is alleging the suspect is the same one who assaulted Moses Custer and killed Trish Thrash."

Crimm reached for his dangling magnifying glass and was visibly startled when his press secretary came into focus.

"Heavens!" the governor exclaimed. "Shouldn't you go to the hospital?"

Trader was afraid to speak and shook his head.

"What happened?" the governor demanded. "I don't mean to sound unsympathetic, but it's not sanitary to bleed at the dinner table."

Trader got up, holding a napkin to his forehead. He mutely stood on the antique Oriental rug, his eyes darting about as he tried to sort out his tangled thoughts and come up with a plan. For starters, he decided, his transient speech disorder was a good thing because under the circumstances, it was smart to talk in a way that made little sense to others. His condition made lying easier, and people were less inclined to question him closely. Not to mention, if he required a second party to speak, then Trader's testimony would be hearsay and not admissible in court.

"It's awful," Faith was describing what had happened. "This monster makes people burst into flames and then speeds off. He's from New York and speaks Spanish and intends to do the same thing to each of us."

"As much as I hate it," Mrs. Crimm said, "I think we need all of the troopers to surround the mansion until this terrible person is caught. Maybe the National Guard ought to help out, too, dear."

The governor pulled out a chair and sat down, not sure what to do and perplexed that no one had briefed him about this emergency before now. Often, he found out bad news when he came home for dinner, and certainly this wasn't helping his submarine in the least.

"Well, someone fill me in," the governor demanded.

Trader wanted to offer many false details, but he knew how the governor would react to their sudden language barrier. The press secretary indicated through sign language that Andy should relay the day's events to Crimm, which Andy did.

"What's your recommendation?" the governor asked Andy after being subjected to the story, which seemed lacking in veracity and rationality.

"I agree in taking no chances," Andy replied. "Keep security tight, sir, but this matter needs to be thoroughly investigated. Frankly, I am concerned that there are important facts we don't know, despite Mr. Trader's alleged eyewitness account. No offense," he directed this at Trader, "but what you supposedly saw and what actually happened may not match up. I have two questions, for example: What happened to the bucket? And did anyone else happen to see the shooting?"

Trader replied through hand signals that the bucket was at large and the only other witnesses may have been the crabs and the trout. Trader felt certain this would settle the matter.

"If the bucket is at large," Andy pointed out, "then this might suggest that you let the crabs and trout go *before* the altercation occurred. Because you certainly wouldn't witness someone burning up and then think to toss the crabs and the trout in the river, now would you?"

Trader shook his head *no* as he recalled the crabs and trout sailing through the air in a cascade of tap water. They splashed into the river and then he and the fisherman began to fight and say ugly things to each other. Trader must have set the bucket back on the ground, or perhaps the fisherman did. By now the police would have found the bucket and taken it in as evidence. He wasn't sure why, but he had a bad feeling that the bucket was going to cause him a problem.

The governor lit up a Cuban cigar. "Tell me," he said to Andy. "If we could locate the crabs and trout, would that help us?"

"That's the stupidest thing I ever heard," Regina retorted. "What good would they do, and how would you know they're the same ones we let go?"

"DNA," Andy replied. "If they left any cellular material in the bucket, even just a trace, it could be matched back to them. For example, people don't realize how many cells their eyes shed. You rub your eyes and have eye cells all over your fingers and then you touch something and deposit these cells. Every living creature has unique DNA, except identical twins."

"So maybe the crabs' eyes shed cells in the bucket?" The governor was fascinated. "How do you know all this?"

"I've always been interested in forensic science and criminal investigations, Governor. My father was a police officer in Charlotte."

"What is he now?"

"He got killed in the line of duty, sir."

This touched the governor deeply. He had always wanted a son and was not at all impressed with his daughters and rarely enjoyed their company. In truth, Bedford Crimm was starved for someone sensible and non-female to talk to, and he had forgotten that he was concerned that Andy and his wife might have an affair.

"Let's pour a little brandy and smoke," he said as he turned a magnified watery eye on Andy. "Do you play pool?"

"Not very often, sir," Andy replied.

"But what about this awful man on the loose?" Mrs. Crimm worried.

"Tell one of the other troopers the story," the governor ordered Andy to tell Trader. "Tell him to get the rest of the EPU on the case and let's have the National Guard fly around, checking for that car with New York plates, and perhaps have a presence downtown, too."

"You may want to consider having us set up checkpoints at the tollbooths, too," Andy suggested. "In case this *alleged* Hispanic serial killer tries to leave the city," he added with a hint of disdain as he stared Trader right in the eye. The press secretary glanced away.

"Excellent idea," the governor agreed, increasingly impressed with this young man. "We need to locate the crabs and the trout. Tell Trader to start looking since he's the one who saw them last."

"Sir, you can tell him yourself," Andy politely said. "He can hear, he just can't talk or at least wants us to think he can't. And I might suggest we have a more objective person look for any witnesses."

Andy had no doubt that should Trader find the crabs and trout, he would make sure they were never seen again. The fat, mendacious pirate–press secretary would probably boil them alive and eat them, Andy thought with disgust as he anticipated the governor's reaction when he read the essay he intended to post as soon as he could find a computer. He gave Trader a harsh, threatening look.

"Stay away from the crabs and trout," Andy warned him.

He waited until Trader limped off before taking the First Lady aside for a private word with her.

"Listen," Andy said. "I hate to impose on you or intrude upon your privacy in any way, First Lady Crimm, but it looks like it may be a long night and I'm wondering if I could borrow a computer for just a minute so I can check something."

"Why certainly," she replied, and she couldn't wait to lead him upstairs to her private parlor where she spent many secret, delicious hours sitting at her antique Chinese desk, shopping the Internet.

She felt a tingle of salacious excitement as she led Andy up the stairs and sat him down in her chair.

"Do you need me to show you how anything works?" she asked, leaning over him and brushing her big, trussed-up bosom against the back of his head.

"No thank you," Andy said as her perfume excited an allergic reaction and he began to sneeze. "If you can just leave me for a moment. I'm afraid this is classified police work and for my eyes only, ma'am." He sneezed three more times.

"What are they doing up there?" the governor jealously asked, looking in the direction of upstairs. "What in thunder are they up to? Who's sneezing?" he demanded as his wife smeared her lipstick a bit and mussed up her stiff hair as she made her way back downstairs.

Andy posted his next essay, which he had finished early that morning. The timing could not be better, and he got up from the desk just as Regina lumbered into the parlor and demanded to know what he was doing.

"Mama's all messed up like you two were making out," she delicately offered. "And it's just a good thing Papa can't see what she looks like!"

"She wasn't messed up a minute ago," Andy replied. "She just showed me to the computer and left. And she looked exactly as she did when we were all at the dinner table."

"What are you doing in here?" Regina's tiny eyes were bright with suspicion. "I bet you're Trooper Truth, aren't you!"

"What a thing to think," Andy said.

"Prove you're not!"

"It's rather difficult to prove a negative," Andy replied as Regina squeezed her way past him and sat before the keyboard.

She logged on to the Trooper Truth website and made a startled sound when she noticed there was a brand-new essay. She clicked on it immediately.

"See," Andy said. "You tell me. Is it possible Trooper Truth could be off writing a new essay and yet be here with the First Family for a light supper at the same time?"

"Well, I guess you're right," Regina said as she eagerly began to read.

A Word About Anne Bonny

The Most Notorious Female Pirate Who Ever Lived
(Note: Many authorities on pirates differ in their accounts of Anne Bonny.)

By Trooper Truth

Her story begins with her birth in County Cork, Ireland, on March 8, 1700, the illegitimate daughter of a successful Irish lawyer named William Cormac and his wife's maid, whose name never made it into the records. When the scandalous tryst was revealed, William had no choice but to flee from Ireland with his new family and settle in Charleston, South Carolina, where he no doubt befriended Blackbeard and corrupt politicians. Soon enough, William became a very wealthy merchant and lived on a plantation just outside the city.

Not much is known about Anne as a child, except that she was a beautiful redhead with a ferocious temper that prompted her to kill one of the servant women with a carving knife after the two of them squabbled. By the time Anne was old enough to pick out her own clothes, she began to dress like a man, and many male admirers began to call on her. Uninvited sexual advances were met with such violence that one suitor ended up bedridden for weeks.

(Note: I pause here to emphasize to you, the reader, that Anne's behavior almost from the start would indicate that she was a sociopath with bad genetic wiring that, unfortunately, she would pass down through the generations to present-day Virginia, where one of her direct descendants is currently employed in a position of great influence and power.)

When Anne was sixteen, she continued on her blighted path by getting tangled up with a poor worthless sailor named James (Jim) Bonny, who was determined to have her family's plantation for himself. He decided the easiest way to do this was to marry Anne, whose attire he either didn't notice or didn't seem to mind. Anne's father did not approve of Jim Bonny, and the newly wed couple did not get the plantation or even a decent room should they have wished to stay with Anne's family.

The young couple left Charleston in a huff and sailed off to New Providence in the Bahamas, where Anne soon became fond of a local establishment called the Pirate's Lair, which was exactly what the name implied. Jim was a weak, pitiful example of manhood and courage, and he began to rat on various sailors he didn't like, accusing them of being pirates, even if they weren't, while his dissatisfied, psychopathic wife spent increasingly long hours at the Lair.

Many of the rough seamen who became her drinking buddies were ex-pirates and bored. One day, Anne, who the ex-pirates thought was a man, was slugging down rum and complaining about the nasty, mean-spirited sister-in-law of Jamaican governor Lawes, who had told Anne she wasn't worth knowing. What isn't clear from the records is whether the woman made this rude comment when Anne was disguised as a man or dressed normally. But it is well documented that Anne's response was to knock out two of her teeth, which was much more serious in the eighteenth century than now, since there were no dentists or prosthodontists to speak of and a gap-toothed smile was irreversible.

"I should have knocked out all her teeth," Anne boasted to the ex-pirates as they drank in the Lair. "Then tied her to a tree and gave her neither bread nor water and let a myriad of fiery stinging ants swarm over her nekkid body."

"Yay, ye should have." Pirate Captain Calico Jack nodded in agreement. "Would ye have her all nekkid, including her privities?"

"All nekkid," Anne replied. " 'Tis better not to cover her privities, making the stings of the ants more fiercely painful."

"Yay, 'tis better."

Anne and Calico got very friendly with each other and she finally made certain he knew she was a woman by unbuttoning her man's shirt one day. He offered to buy her from her spineless husband, Jim, who instantly snitched on both of them to South Carolina Governor Rogers. Anne was ordered to show up for a flogging and then return to her rightful husband, so she and Calico decided they would slip into the harbor, both of them dressed like men, and steal a sloop and begin their lives together as a pirate couple.

Over the next few months, Anne and Calico Jack raided many ships and shore installations. Her gender remained a secret to all but him, until they captured a Dutch merchant ship and recruited a number of its sailors from the crew, including a strikingly handsome, blue-eyed, blond young man. Anne took a liking to him and unbuttoned her shirt to reveal her true identity. The man then unbuttoned his shirt and showed that he was Mary Read. It is not known if both women were disappointed to discover that neither of them was a man, but they became a pirate duo, skilled with rapiers and pistols, and fought bravely whenever their boarding crew stormed onto unsuspecting merchant ships.

Anne and Mary loved being pirates and became well-respected, bloodthirsty buccaneers who swung their blades and boarded ships with more daring than any man. They became pregnant at the same time, and in 1720 suffered a stunning defeat when a pirate turned pirate-hunter raided them while the crew was drunk and hiding below deck, leaving only Mary and Anne to fight furiously in thick cannon fire.

"If there's a man among ye, ye will come out and fight like the men ye are thought to be!" Anne shouted as she furiously swung her cutlass and fired her pistols.

The men below did not answer back, and all were captured and hanged except for the two pregnant pirates, who went to jail. Mary died of a fever inside her tiny damp cell and Anne is believed to have been granted a pardon. She disappeared from the seas and historical records.

My theory of what became of Anne Bonny is based on reviewing written accounts of her life, and then reaching a conclusion that is within the realm of possibility. We can be certain that Anne would not have been welcome back in the West Indies, nor was she likely to return to her husband or to the life of an active pirate. I suspect she had her child and decided on a compromise of breaking the law while avoiding the traditional life of a woman, and doing so in a place that was a safe harbor and agreeable to her need for adventure. She would have known that Blackbeard and other pirates frequented Tangier Island and regularly traded with the Islanders, and that if she continued dressing like a man, she could be a waterman and at least get out in a bateau and teach her child the ways of weather, the bay, and fishing.

This child, I suspect, was a son, and I believe it is from this cutthroat lineage that one certain governmental official descended. And if the governor is reading this essay, I ask him to think back on all of the times a certain disloyal, despicable individual has given him a sweet that is soon followed by an explosive gastric attack.

It is just a shame that this scoundrel, who for now will remain nameless, offered no warnings when he applied for a high-level state position and was subjected to the usual background checks. But background checks are largely ineffective these days. They do not reveal motivation, which in this person's case, like that of his ancestor Anne Bonny, is to have control, adventure, and access to military and police power, and to know the rules well enough to break them whenever he pleases.

Be careful out there!

Eighteen

Paramedics did not try to resuscitate Caesar Fender, who remained unidentified as he smoldered and smoked near his smashed tackle box. The body was charred in a very odd pattern. Only the chest had burned, and there was no evidence of a fire in the local vicinity that might account for his appalling death.

"It's like his heart caught on fire," Detective Slipper said. "Or maybe his lungs. Could smoking do that?"

"You mean, if you was smoking and somehow your lungs caught on fire?" said Treata Bibb, who had been driving an ambulance for fifteen years and had never seen anything like this. "No," Bibb then answered her own question upon reflection. "Not hardly. I don't think smoking's got a thing to do with what killed this unlucky guy." She squatted to get a closer look. "It's like he's got a crater burned in him all the way through, from front to back. Look, you can see the pavement through this big hole. See here?" She touched charred flesh with a gloved finger. "Even the bones in the middle of his chest burned up. But the rest of him is fine." She was amazed and disturbed, wondering who had done this and how and why.

Cars were pulling off the road, and people lined the street as if waiting for a parade. Police were having a difficult time controlling the gathering crowd of sightseers and reporters as word spread that a fisherman had exploded into a ball of fire just off Canal Street, very near where Trish Thrash's mutilated body had been found on Belle Island.

"What's going on?" a housewife named Barbie Fogg asked through the open window of her minivan.

"You'll have to read about it in the paper." An officer motioned with his flashlight for her to move on.

"I don't get the paper."

She shielded her eyes from his waving flashlight and wondered why on earth all these big helicopters were flying around with searchlights probing the city and neighboring counties. "There must be some violent serial killer that broke out of jail or something," she decided with horror as a chill tickled up to the roots of her frosted hair. "Maybe the same one who murdered that poor woman the other day! And now I won't know enough to protect myself and my family because I don't get the paper and you won't tell me the smallest detail. And you wonder why people don't like police."

She sped off, and another car stopped, this one occupied by an old woman whose night vision wasn't what it used to be.

"Excuse me, I'm trying to find the Downtown Expressway," the old woman, whose name was Lamonia, said to the officer with the flashlight. "I'm late for choir practice. What's all that racket up there?"

Lamonia peered up at Black Hawk helicopters she couldn't see. But there was nothing wrong with her hearing.

"Sounds like a war going on," she declared.

"Just a little situation, but we're handling it, ma'am," the officer said. "The Downtown Expressway's over there." He pointed the flashlight. "Turn left on Eighth and it will run you right into it."

"I've run into it before," Lamonia said with a pained, humiliated catch in her voice. "Last year, I hit the guardrail. To tell you the truth, officer, I probably shouldn't be driving at night. I can't see at night. But if I keep missing choir practice, they'll kick me out, and it's really all I have left in my life. You know, my husband passed on two years ago, and then my cat died when I accidentally backed the car over him."

"Maybe you'd better pull over."

Lamonia stared blindly to her left and right and thought she detected a speck of light that reminded her of those eye tests that required her to center her face in a machine and push a clicker every time she saw a little light in her peripheral vision. Last week, she had hit the clicker randomly and often in hopes she could fool the eye doctor again.

"I know exactly what you're doing," the eye doctor had said as he put drops in Lamonia's pupils. "Don't think you're the first one who's tried," he added.

"What about laser surgery again?"

According to the eye doctor, there was no hope for Lamonia's bad night vision. She had been managing all alone only because she had a pretty good memory and knew how many steps led up to the porch and exactly where the furniture was. She could tell by feel which skirt or dress she was putting on in the dark, but driving at night was another matter. The city streets had not changed, but memory could not help Lamonia when cars switched lanes or stopped in front of her, or pedestrians decided to cross to the other side. She was explaining all this to the police officer, who was no longer there.

"So if you can just point your flashlight, I'll follow it and pull over," Lamonia said as another helicopter thundered into a low hover and its searchlight blazed on the crime scene.

She detected an illumination and headed toward it, bumping over a curb and then something that crunched under a tire.

"Now what was that?" she muttered as she hit a stretcher and sent it sailing into the river right before she rear-ended the ambulance.

"Stop! Stop!" Voices all around her Dodge Dart screamed.

Lamonia slammed on the brakes, even though she was already stopped. Confused and frightened, she shoved the car into reverse and backed up through a perimeter of crime-scene tape and felt another bump under her right rear tire.

"STOP!" The shouting voices were more urgent. **"STOP!"**

Hooter Shook sensed something urgent was going on when Trooper Macovich showed up with a trunk full of traffic cones and flares.

"Hey! What you doin' closing off all these lanes?" Hooter called out to him as he arranged the blaze orange cones that always reminded her of the Cap the Hat game she used to play as a child.

"Setting up a checkpoint," Macovich informed her as he dropped hissing, lit flares across 150 North, a busy four-lane interstate that led in and out of the city.

Hooter watched with interest and a little anxiety as Macovich barricaded every lane with a wall of blaze orange plastic and fire, leaving only her Exact Change lane open, forcing all northbound motorists by her window, where they would directly place money in her glove. She was a senior tollbooth operator for the city and remembered the days when she didn't have to wear surgical gloves that were always getting punctured by her artificial nails. In modern times, all the operators seemed to worry about was coming in contact with a driver's fingers, when in truth, cash and coins were far dirtier than some stranger's hands.

Money was touched by millions of people, Hooter knew. It was picked off the ground and rubbed up against other money inside dark wallets and little coin purses. Coins jingled against each other inside pockets that may not have been laundered in recent memory. Cash was porous paper that absorbed bacteria like a sponge, and in local topless bars, men stuffed dollar bills into skimpy clothing and the money came in direct contact with diseased body parts.

Hooter could talk for weeks about all the places money visited and how filthy it was. So she was happy to wear gloves when she finally realized the city didn't mind if she switched to cotton ones that her nails couldn't tear. But it did make her feel bad when she stuck a gloved hand out of her booth, as if the driver were Typhoid Mary. She hurt thousands of feelings every shift and never had time to explain to the driver that in her mind, the glove wasn't about him or her, but about the unsanitary condition of the economy.

"Germs," Macovich said as he smoked, waiting for the next car as he stood outside Hooter's booth and talked to her through the sliding window. "Everything's 'bout germs. Wooo. I 'member learning CPR on those life-size rubber dolls, and you was lucky if they wiped the rubber mouth off before you pinched the rubber nose shut and smacked your lips right over its rubber lips, blowing away. Now, you roll up on a scene and see someone unresponsive and bleeding bad, you got to double glove and drape the face with a sheet of plastic that's round with a hole in the middle, sort of like those 'sposable toilet seat covers you see in public restrooms. You just hope the person don't sneeze on you or puke or start moving around, and you pray they ain't got AIDS."

"Bet you could get AIDS off of money," Hooter said, nodding at her own convictions. "How you know some homosensual don't meet up with another homosensual and have sex in a park and then before washing his hands, he buys a sandwich and pay for it with a five-dollar bill. That same five-dollar bill is shut up inside a little cash drawer with hundreds of other unsanitarian bills, and then goes to the bank and is picked up when some other man dying of AIDS cashes a check. Next thing, that five-dollar bill is smacked down on a filthy bar and the waiter puts it in his unwashed pocket and decides to drive downtown and comes to my window."

"That will be next," Macovich thought out loud, and the conversation was making him uneasy and causing him to wonder if he would ever touch money again. "We'll have to wear gloves morning, noon, and night if we're gonna pay for things. Thank God we don't got to take money direct when we write tickets."

"Yeah, you mighty lucky in that department," Hooter said.

Macovich stepped out into the lane and held up his flashlight at the approaching Pontiac Grand Prix. It was an older model with dents, and his pulse quickened when he recognized New York plates and an expired inspection sticker. He walked over to the driver's door, his hand conveniently touching the snap release of his holster.

"License and registration," he said as the window cranked down, and he shone the flashlight on the frightened face of a Mexican boy who didn't look old enough to drive and was obviously an illegal alien. "You speak English, sir?"

"*Sí.*" The Mexican made no move to deliver either his driver's license or the registration.

"Why don't you ask him if he *understands* English," Hooter loudly suggested from her booth, which had nothing inside it except a stool, a fire extinguisher, and her Pleather pocketbook.

Macovich repeated Hooter's question while the Mexican averted his eyes from the blinding scrutiny of the flashlight.

"No," the Mexican said, getting more frightened by the second.

"No?" Macovich frowned. "Yeah? Well, if you don't understand English, how did you understand it enough to know I was asking if you understood it?"

"*Creo que no.*"

"What he say?" Macovich turned around and looked at Hooter, who was hanging out of her booth now.

"Guess I may as well come on out since the lane's all blocked with you and that big Pontiac," she said to Macovich as she opened the door and stepped outside.

"He said that?" Macovich was baffled. "He said he's getting out of his car? 'Cause it don't look to me like he has any intention of getting out or cooperating in any way."

Hooter caught only fragments of what Macovich was saying as she buttoned her overcoat and slipped a lipstick out of a pocket. She pecked her way over the asphalt in six-inch high-heeled red Pleather boots. One thing about being a toll collector was that it involved a constant exposure to the public. Hooter was fastidious about fashion and fresh make-up and making sure every dreadlock was in place and interwoven with bright, colorful beads.

"It ain't good to not cooperate, honey," Hooter peered through the Mexican's open window. "Now you cooperate with this big trooper. Nobody wants no trouble, 'cause they be looking for a suspect right this very minute who could very well be you. So you best cooperate and not make things worse for yourself. . . ."

"Hooter, don't tell him so much," Macovich whispered loudly in her ear, her perfume rushing up his nostrils and enveloping his brain. "What that you got on?"

"Poison." She was pleased he'd noticed. "I got it at Target."

"How'd you know we was looking for a suspect?" he whispered into her perfume again.

"Why else you be blocking off all the lanes except the Exact Change line, huh?" she replied. "You think I was born yesterday? Well, I been around, let me tell you, and I'm the senior operator at this toll plaza."

"Wooo, I wasn't putting you down or nothing, Senior Operator." Macovich teased her a little.

"Don't you be smart mouthin' me!"

"Wooo, I ain't smart mouthin' no one, least of all a pretty lady like yourself. How 'bout you and me having us a drink after our shifts?" He thought happily of the crisp hundred-dollar bill Cat had handed over after their quick helicopter lesson.

The Mexican was rigid in his seat, his eyes wide and shielded by a hand. He was shaking and gripping the steering wheel so hard his knuckles were blanched.

"*Por favor.*" He glanced up at both Macovich and Hooter. "*No buena armonía.*"

Cruz Morales had a vague understanding of English and was accustomed to tossing out the simplest Spanish phrases that most New Yorkers caught immediately. But there was a sea of incomprehension between him and the cop and the tollbooth lady, and Cruz could not afford further investigation. He was twelve years old with a false ID and had driven to Richmond to pick up a package for his older brothers. Although he hadn't looked at whatever was inside the tightly wrapped bundle hidden in the tire well, he could tell by the weight of it that he was probably transporting handguns again.

"I think the child say he's *poor* and needs a *favor*," Hooter translated for Macovich. "He look too little and young to hurt nobody." Her maternal instincts wafted out on a cloud of perfume. "Maybe he need a soda or coffee. All them Mexicans start drinking coffee when they're little babies."

The tollbooth lady's gold front tooth seemed the only bright spot in Cruz Morales's existence this moment. He made eye contact with her and smiled a little, his teeth chattering.

"See," Hooter nudged Macovich with her elbow, bumping his pistol. "He's relating now. We getting through to him."

She glanced up at miles of parked cars in her lane. Why, it was an endless stream of impatient headlights, and it puffed her up to think they were all here to see her. She felt like a movie star for an instant, and was overwhelmed by sympathy for the little Mexican boy, who clearly was far from home and frightened. He was probably cold, tired, and hungry, too.

Hooter reached into her coat pocket, dug through tubes of lipstick, and produced a napkin that some nice-looking white trooper had given her last year when that man with the paper sack over his head had tried to rob the tollbooth and had run into it instead. Hooter fished out a pen, clicked it open, and wrote down her home phone number on the napkin, which she handed to the Mexican boy.

"Honey, you call me any time you need something," she magnanimously said. "I know 'zactly what it feels like to be a minority and have folks always thinking the worst when you ain't done nothing but collect their unsanitarian money or drive somewhere and probably not knowing your 'spection ticket's espired."

"Get out of the car!" Macovich ordered the illegal alien. "Get out slowly and let me see your hands!"

Cruz Morales smashed the accelerator to the floor and squealed rubber, flying through the toll lane as lights flashed and alarms screamed because he didn't have time to toss three quarters into the bin.

"Shit!" Macovich exclaimed, patting around his duty belt, looking for his keys as he ran to his unmarked car and jumped in.

He flipped on his lights and sirens and flew down the interstate, reminding Hooter of a screaming, flashing Christmas tree. She returned to her custom-fabricated aluminum booth with its vandal-resistant stainless-steel coin basket and shut the Extend-A-Door. The endless river of headlights began to move sluggishly toward her and she hoped people wouldn't be grumpy after the delay.

"What the hell's going on?" the first driver asked from the high seat of his pickup truck. "If I sat here much longer, I was gonna turn into a skeleton."

"Then that pretty lady friend I'm sure you got waiting at home for you won't have as much of you to love," Hooter teased him with a flash of a smile. "I sure do like that rainbow bumper sticker." She nodded at his windshield. "You know, I been seeing more and more of 'em lately, like maybe people is looking for the bright side and feeling hope. I might just get me one of them rainbows and stick it on my tollbooth."

The driver leaned over and popped open his glove box. "Here." He handed her a stack of rainbow bumper stickers. "Be my guest, girlfriend."

"See," Hooter said to the next driver as the pickup truck with the rainbow sticker sped off, "if you nice to folks, it's contagious just like germs is, only being nice don't make you sick." She reached out a gloved hand and took a dollar bill from Barbie Fogg.

"I know why all these cars are stopped," Barbie said. "You heard about that man who got blown up over there by the river? It's all over the radio."

"Oh my!" Hooter returned a quarter to her and dropped seventy-five cents in the toll bin. "I don't got a radio in my booth 'cause they ain't no time for me to listen to it. What happened, baby?"

Cars began to honk, turning the interstate into an endless flock of migrating Canada geese.

"The police wouldn't say. But it will be in the paper in the morning," Barbie replied. "Problem is, I don't get the paper, so I'll never know what happened."

"You just drive through my booth tomorrow," Hooter said with importance. "I always read the paper before I go to work. I tell you all about it. What your name, baby?"

They exchanged names and Hooter handed her a rainbow bumper sticker.

"You put that on your minivan and it will bring smiles and hope to all you pass," Hooter promised.

"Why thank you!" Barbie was touched and delighted. "I'll do it the minute I get home."

Nineteen

Governor Crimm chalked the tip of his lucky pool cue, cigar smoke hanging in a hazy halo around his head as he tried to make out striped balls on the red felt-covered table that Thomas Jefferson had brought back from France, or so Maude had claimed when she'd discovered it on eBay. Every few minutes, one of the troopers came into the billiards room to give the governor updates. The news was not promising.

Checks of vehicles passing through tollbooths had produced only one car with New York plates, and the driver, clearly Hispanic, had fled. So far, he had not been caught, and the consensus was that he—the heinous serial killer—had left the city, heading north. Other disturbing developments included Trooper Truth's latest essay, which accused Major Trader of being a dishonest, self-serving pirate who was trying to poison the governor. As if things weren't grim enough, Regina had planted herself on a Chippendale commode chair, slurping ice cream she had mixed with homemade Toll House cookies she had helped herself to in the kitchen. She was chewing with her mouth open and talking nonstop, distracting the governor as he peered through his magnifying glass at the pool balls he went after.

"Good shot," Andy said when a red-striped ball bounced off the table. He quickly caught it and discreetly tucked it into a corner pocket.

"You aren't letting me win, are you?" the governor said, chalking his stick again.

"Everybody always lets you win," Regina told her father. "Except me. I refuse to let you win."

Regina was a gifted pool player and between her father's terms as governor, when she was at liberty to come and go as she pleased, she was known in area bars for her trick shots and ruthlessness. The only person who had ever beaten her without cheating was that dumbshit, disrespectful Trooper Macovich.

"Here." Andy offered Regina his pool cue. "I'm not with it tonight. You take over. If you don't mind my asking," he said to the governor as Regina racked up balls, "how did Trader come to work for you?"

"A good question," the governor replied. "It was during my first term as governor, and as I remember it, he was a low man on the totem pole, but I got to know him because he used to stop by the mansion to help out with things, such as supervising the inmates, which is not the most desirable job."

Regina broke, and four solid balls whizzed into four different pockets. "Shit," she complained. "I'm having an off night, too."

Pony had just stepped inside to see if anyone needed a touch more brandy, and he caught what the governor said about inmates. He was hurt. It always wounded him when the First Family implied that just because a person was a convicted felon, he could never be trusted with anything ever again.

"Might I get you another cigar?" Pony asked Governor Crimm in a sullen tone as Regina held the cue behind her back and knocked a ball into two more balls, all three of which spun off at impossible angles and smacked into pockets.

"I must admit, I'm very disappointed to learn that he might have been trying to poison me," the governor added. "I think we should go back to having tasters. Huh, make that scoundrel one, as a matter of fact."

"If you can find him," Andy replied. "My guess is, he's going to disappear and probably already has. It's too bad we don't have any hard evidence on him yet or we could have arrested him before he left the mansion."

"Sounds to me like Trooper Truth has plenty of hard evidence," Crimm commented with an insinuation in his tone. "And that indicates to me this renegade columnist may be Trader's accomplice. How else would Trooper Truth know about my being poisoned, now tell me that, unless he had something to do with it?"

Andy hadn't anticipated this turn in the governor's thoughts, and he got a little worried. If Hammer were subpoenaed and asked under oath if she knew Trooper Truth's identity, she would have to reply truthfully and Andy could find himself in a world of trouble.

As if Crimm were privy to Andy's thoughts, he said, "I need to talk to Superintendent Hammer and find out what she knows."

"I'm sure she'd be happy to talk to you, Governor," Andy said. "But she's had a terrible time getting hold of you and never hears from you."

"Never hears from me?" The governor gave Andy a magnified eye. "I've written her a number of notes, not only about her poor little dog, but inviting her to official functions!"

"She's never gotten them, sir."

"So that damn Trader was interfering with everything!" He was getting very put out.

"Seems to me he's been lying to you from the start," Andy agreed.

"A fresh cigar would be a good idea," the governor said to Pony, who was still waiting patiently in the doorway.

Crimm stubbed out his half-smoked cigar in Regina's ice cream dish, which he mistook for an ashtray. He was getting impatient as his unsportsmanlike daughter tapped one ball after another into the pockets.

"That's why I don't like to play with you," he said to her. "I never get to shoot. I may as well not even be in the room. Tell you what I'm going

228

to do, son." Crimm directed this to Andy. "I'm going to assign you to a special undercover investigation. I want you to find out who Trooper Truth is as quickly as possible and see just what his involvement with Trader might be. And while you're at it, let's get the dentist back and make sure those Tangier people aren't up to any other mischief."

"Why don't you put *both* Andy and me on a special mission, and I'll help him solve crimes and get bad people off the streets?" Regina suggested as the last solid ball spun across felt, banked several times, and sank out of sight. "Maybe he can teach me to fly, too."

"Maybe Miss Regina and Mister Andy should help out with that fisherman who just burned up," Pony said from the doorway. "I hear things aren't going too well. Some old woman ran over the body, a bicycle, and a tackle box. The troopers are talking about it. They say a mean Hispanic's on the loose and will probably kill some other poor black person the same way."

"And what way might that be?" the governor inquired.

"Spontenuous consumption."

"Well, I 'spect Doctor Sawamatsu will be the judge of that," was Crimm's response.

He had appointed the most recently hired medical examiner himself, and he had the utmost confidence in the infallibility of Dr. Sawamatsu, who had originally come to Virginia for the sole purpose of studying gunshot wounds. His intention had been to take his training back to Japan, but the traffic was so bad there and he was so tired of living in a crowded house with people he didn't know that he lingered in the Commonwealth well beyond the completion of his internship. Then the governor, who was always trying to attract Japanese businesses and tourists to Virginia, called Dr. Sawamatsu one day.

"Doctor Sawamatsu," the governor said, and the doctor would never forget what followed, "let me get your honest opinion about something. As you know, the chief medical examiner is a woman I'm not especially fond of. All of her staff are Americans, and I'm wondering if I had a Japanese medical examiner in Virginia, would that make a difference?"

"To whom?"

"To these Japanese Fortune 500 companies who keep relocating or never relocate here to begin with—and to Japanese citizens in general who have yet to discover Colonial Williamsburg, Jamestown, our many amusement parks and plantations and resorts and so on. As long as they speak English, and all of them do."

Dr. Sawamatsu had to think quickly. He wanted to be a medical examiner in America more than anything else, but he was keenly aware that his patients were not important players in tourism or the business community and rarely had any influence whatsoever, either before they were carried into the morgue or after they left.

"When you have especially sensational cases, it most certainly would make a difference," was Dr. Sawamatsu's reply. "Because of the publicity and the message it would send if the medical examiner were Asian. In such a case, I believe my people would reciprocate and locate their companies and tourists here, providing you give them a tax incentive."

"A tax incentive?"

"A big one."

"What an unusual idea," the governor said, and the minute he got off the phone, he told his cabinet that he planned to make all Japanese businesses and individuals exempt from state taxes. The result was stunning. Within a year, tourism flourished. Railways and Greyhound had to double their staffs and buses, and camera stores began popping up on every corner. Dr. Sawamatsu became an assistant chief medical examiner and received a personal thank-you note from Governor Crimm, which the young doctor framed and hung in his living room, next to the display case of souvenirs he had collected from dead patients who no longer had any need of artificial body parts, suicide or threatening notes, or the wreckage of whatever they had died in or the weapons that had killed them.

We need to get this body out of here," Dr. Sawamatsu was telling the police as he crouched in the dark, pulling on surgical gloves. "Please do not let anyone else run over it."

"Where's the chief?" asked Detective Slipper, who did not share the governor's high opinion of Dr. Sawamatsu. "Why isn't Doctor Scarpetta here? She almost always responds personally to complicated, sensational crime scenes."

"She went to court in Halifax and will not be back until very late," Dr. Sawamatsu replied rather testily. "Now, we must get this body to the morgue right now."

"I'm not sure we can retrieve the stretcher out of the river," Detective Slipper hated to tell him. "We'd have to bring in divers."

"No time. We wrap him in sheets and carry him to the ambulance," Dr. Sawamatsu ordered. "I look at him in the morning. I can't see anything out here."

"Glad I'm not the only one," Lamonia grumpily agreed.

She was in handcuffs and standing by her dented Dodge Dart, not sure what she had done to irritate everybody so much. Trader, of course, was not put out with Lamonia in the least. He was watching the activity through his shattered windshield after a fruitless hour of standing on a bridge, shining a powerful flashlight down into the water, trying to find the crabs and the trout. Trader was deeply grateful that Lamonia had virtually destroyed the crime scene. He watched the medical examiner and paramedics cover the dead fisherman with sheets and carry him away, tucking him into the back of the ambulance, which had a crunched-in tailgate. How could Trader's luck have changed so dramatically, all in one day?

Major Trader's career and entire life were in shambles and always had been, if he were honest with himself. He looked at himself in the rearview mirror and was faced with a reflection that might as well have been his maternal grandfather, also named Major. All of the men in his mother's lineage had been called Major since Anne Bonny had had sex with a pirate and given birth to a son she named Major because it was a higher rank than captain, and she'd never met a pirate ranked higher than captain.

All the Major men bore a resemblance to one another. They were a sturdy lot with ruddy faces, big girths, pale, shifty eyes, and thinning hair. As a child, Trader had enjoyed a spree of pyromania and had never been caught. To this day, no one on Tangier Island knew that little Major was the one who torched a shed on stilts that turned out to be a soft-crab plantation. Thousands of crabs in the midst of molting had been killed, the year's harvest lost, the economy ruined. To make matters worse, the fire could not be contained and spread up several creeks, incinerating scores of bateaus before the blaze was finally extinguished alarmingly close to Hilda Crockett's Chesapeake House, known for its long family-style tables, crab cakes, clam fritters, home-baked bread, ham, and more.

Young Major Trader also became adept at sneaking the family flare gun out of the wading boot where his father hid his liquor. By experimenting with lighter fluid, gasoline, and bourbon, Major realized he could torch places from a distance by filling a milk jug with a flammable liquid and, when nobody was looking, fire a flare at the jug and cause a small explosion, much like what he had done to the fisherman.

Pony also had led a lawless life as a young one, but unlike Trader, Pony lived with remorse and an overwhelming sense of shame and regret. Having grown weary of watching Regina play pool while her father stood idly by, tapping cigar ashes wherever he thought he saw an ashtray, Pony and Andy had wandered out into the garden. They sat on a granite bench in the cold and began to talk.

"May I get you anything, Mister Andy?"

"No. You're really nice to keep asking, but why don't you just take it easy for a while and tell me about yourself. Why do you call yourself *Pony*?"

"I don't," Pony replied, his breath smoking out and reminding him he longed for a cigarette. "You mind?" He pulled a pack out of his white jacket. "My daddy called me Pony because when my sister was born— she's older than me—she used to tell my daddy she wanted a pony. We couldn't afford a pony, so when I was born a few years later, my daddy named me Pony and says to my sister, 'Now you got a pony.' "

Andy didn't comment as he tried to discern whether the story was heartwarming or simply depressing.

"It's not a name that's helped me out much, you want to know the truth," Pony continued. "The other inmates make comments about it 'til they figure I'll fight 'em if they think for one minute they gonna ride me in the showers, you know what I mean?" He shook his head and grinned, several gold caps gleaming in the dark. "I had my share of scuffles, but I'm stronger than I look. Did some prizefighting when I was younger, know karate pretty good, too."

"How long you in for?" Andy asked.

"Another two years, unless the governor lets me out. And he could, but he won't. Thing is, I do a good job and none of the Crimms want someone else. They're used to me. And if I do a bad job, they'll just send me back to lockup. So I'm kinda stuck." He flicked an ash. "I should never have stole that pack of cigarettes." He shook his head again and sighed.

"You're in jail for stealing a pack of cigarettes?" Andy couldn't believe it.

Pony nodded. "It violated my parole. Before that, it was two pints of apricot brandy at the ABC store. So I pretty much ruined my life over things that ain't good for me anyway. It runs in my family."

"Stealing?" Andy asked.

"Self-destruction. How 'bout you?"

It was rare anyone asked about Andy's life and he had always been cautious about what he revealed.

"Tell me about yourself, Mister Andy," Pony encouraged him to talk. "What about a girl? You got someone special?"

Andy dug his hands into the pockets of his uniform winter jacket and hunched his shoulders against the unseasonable chill as helicopters churned up the night. Clouds had moved on, and the moon was a sliver that reminded Pony of a gold smile.

"Not at the moment," Andy said. "I was on and off with an older woman I met in Charlotte. But we're finished."

"I guess she still in Charlotte?"

"I don't know where she is. I wanted to be friends, but she's not that way. I don't understand women," Andy confessed. "They're always saying men don't know how to be friends, but when I try to be a friend, they act weird about it."

"That is the truth." Pony slowly nodded his head. "You tell it, brother. Women never say what they want or mean what they say or admit to even wanting—unless it's something they don't want or they want you to think they do or don't want. So they can play you, know what I mean? My wife's a sweet woman when she's not too wore out from doing the First Family's laundry or mad at me for going back to lockup during my vacations and holidays. But to look at it from her side, I know I don't always shoot straight with her, either.

"Sometimes I ought to just come out with it and say, 'I sure do love you, baby.' Or 'You sure do look good to me right now, baby.' Or 'I carry this sickness in my heart, baby, 'cause I know I've spent most of our good years behind bars, and that's not fair to you and you got no idea how much I just ache for you when I'm away like that.' And I guess, Mister Andy, I don't want to admit to her or myself that I probably fucked up my life forever, you know what I'm saying?" He sucked on the cigarette. "You know, it's probably too late and I'll probably never get out of lockup 'cause the governor will forget or the next one will or the one after that.

"And I guess I don't got sense enough to cause trouble in the mansion and maybe get fired and then sue the Comm'wealth for discrim'ation, which would entitle me to lawyers who would take me on for a cause and look into my prison record and discover there's some mess-up in the Department of Corrections computer and I would be a free man. As is, I don't got no money for no lawyer and right now I ain't no cause. My point being, if I did the wrong thing, everything would turn out all right for me."

"I know exactly how you feel," Andy agreed. "But you've still got to do the right thing, Pony. Look at Trooper Truth. He did the right thing by telling the truth about Major Trader, and now the governor suspects Trooper Truth of doing something wrong."

"I hear you. I wish I knew Trooper Truth," Pony said with a sigh. "He sounds like one fine person, and it's 'bout time someone blew the whistle on Trader. I've known all along he's a rotten apple up to no good. Yes sir, I wish I knew Trooper Truth. Maybe he could fix my mess with the Department of Corrections."

"Why don't you call DOC yourself and see if you can get someone to look into the matter?" Andy asked.

" 'Cause I ain't allowed to make no personal calls from the mansion. And they don't listen to inmates, anyhow. Everybody in trouble says there's been a mistake, so why should I be any different?"

Regina was hiding behind an ancient boxwood and heard every word. She had lost interest in pool and wished she had thought to wear a coat when she'd decided to sneak out into the garden and eavesdrop. She had a special talent for spying on others, and was hoping to gather a little intelligence that might be useful to her. But as she listened to Andy talk to Pony, she felt herself go soft inside and forgot her original motive. She, too, had been frustrated in her occasional efforts to make friends and often felt wrongly accused.

Regina was shivering uncontrollably, her breath rising in frozen clouds. Her stomach was feeling funny, too, and her intestines were tacking this way and that as they filled with an ominous wind that seemed to have gusted up from the sewer.

"If I were you," Andy was saying to Pony, "I'd send Trooper Truth an e-mail and see if he can get to the truth of why you're still in lockup."

"You think he'd do that for me?" Pony noticed that a boxwood was shaking and smoke was rising from it.

"It can't hurt to ask."

"Well, I don't got access to e-mail, either." Pony watched the shaking, smoking boxwood with growing alarm. He thought of the fisherman and panicked. "I think that boxwood over there's about to blow up!" he exclaimed as a loud, dull detonation sounded from behind the shrubs.

Andy sprang from the stone bench and raced over to the smoking, foul-smelling bush as Regina gave up her cover and rose like a mountain.

"What are you doing?" Andy demanded.

"Practicing investigative techniques," she replied as she clutched her huge quivering gut.

"Well, don't you be hiding behind things and looking like you might explode, Miss Reginia," Pony said, weak with relief. "Lord, you had me going for a minute, thought that crazy man had planted a pipe bomb in the garden and we was all gonna burn up."

"It's time for me to go," Andy said.

"Pick me up first thing in the morning so we can start working this case," Regina said. Even when she wasn't feeling well, she had a manner of making suggestions as if she were ordering an air strike. "I'll be waiting for you early."

"Not possible," Andy replied. "I need to go to the morgue first thing to check on what the medical examiner finds in the case of the man who was killed at the river. You certainly don't want to see something like that. It's very unpleasant."

"Of course I want to see it," Regina said with inappropriate enthusiasm.

"It's very, very unpleasant and upsetting." Andy tried to dissuade her. "You ever smelled a dead animal that has flies all over it? Well, it's much worse than that, and the stench has a way of clinging deep up in your sinuses so that every time you get around food, the smell wakes up and makes you quite nauseous. Not to mention the sights and sounds in the morgue."

"I'm going!" Regina would not take *no* for an answer.

Andy's mood was very dark as he drove through downtown. He was beginning to wish he had never met the Crimms at the steak house the night before. There was no one he would have avoided more arduously than Regina, and now it appeared that he was going to have to be around her constantly. Not to mention, the governor was contemplating that Trooper Truth might be Trader's poisonous accomplice, on top of some psycho's carving *Trooper Truth* into a dead body and then leaving evidence at Andy's house.

"I've gotten myself into quite a situation," he said over the car phone to Judy Hammer.

"Andy, do you have any idea what time it is?" said Hammer, who had been sound asleep when her phone had startled her back into this world. "You sound very discouraged. What happened?"

Once again, Andy happened to be close to Hammer's Church Hill neighborhood, and she suggested that he drop by at the precise moment Fonny Boy decided to drop by the clinic and check on Dr. Sherman Faux, who was shivering blindly in the folding chair.

"Lord, I ask you for a miracle. Not a big one. Just one tiny miracle," Dr. Faux was praying. "Maybe a spare angel could drop by and get me out of here. I promise I'll move quickly and not take unnecessary time, because I know there are so many people and animals who need Your help far more than I do. But I can't do anybody any good as long as I'm tied up here on this island. And I'm stiff and getting sore in this metal chair. So just one angel, that's all I ask. For maybe an hour or two—however long it takes to get me back to the mainland."

Fonny Boy listened attentively without being detected, because he had known since birth not to make sudden movements that might alert fish and crabs that they were about to be caught. Crabs especially were very wily and had excellent vision. If one didn't keep the wire pot perfectly clean, then the crab wouldn't be able to see all the way through it and would get suspicious as to why a piece of rotten fish was inside a box-shaped tangle of eel grass. Fonny Boy kept the family crab pots impeccably clean and could be as silent as a butterfly when necessary.

He would make the dentist think that God was intervening and answering his prayer, when the truth was, Fonny Boy wanted to take Dr. Faux up on his offer of employment on the mainland. Fonny Boy got up and made not a sound as he left the storeroom, then turned around and walked back inside and shut the door so the dentist could hear him enter.

"Who's there?" Dr. Faux said with hope. "That you, Fonny Boy?"

"Yass."

"Oh, thank God. I'm cold and need to go home, Fonny Boy. How's your tooth? The lidocaine wear off?"

"Yass."

"What about the cotton you swallowed? Any problems with that?"

"Yea!" he talked backward, meaning he'd had no problem yet. "I'll carry you ashore," he added. "There's neither time to get the spyglass and searchlight offer my daddy, and it's right airish out, and you don't have a coat. But we need to scud along now afore all the bateaus head out to fish-up the pots!"

"I don't care about a coat, and we can certainly make do without binoculars or a flashlight!" the dentist exclaimed with joy.

He had tears in his eyes, although Fonny Boy could not see them because of the brackish-smelling bandanna that was still tied around the dentist's head. All these years the dentist had been reimbursed for working or pretending to work on that boy's mouth, and never once had it occurred to Dr. Faux that Fonny Boy was an angel.

"God bless you, son," Dr. Faux whispered as they silently made their way out of the clinic.

"Shhhh," Fonny Boy warned him. "Keep quite."

The island's streets were deserted and dark, and there wasn't a light on in a single house as every Islander slept soundly and golf carts recharged. But Fonny Boy knew that soon enough it would be 3:00 A.M. and the watermen would be heading out to their bateaus, so he and the dentist had best hurry along. If Fonny Boy got caught rescuing Dr. Faux, there would be trouble. For sure, Fonny Boy's mother would march him straightaway to Swain Memorial United Methodist Church, and she would rat on him to Reverend Crockett. Fonny Boy had been in trouble with Reverend Crockett before, and was sick and tired of memorizing Scripture to pay for his sins.

The family bateau was docked only several blocks from the church, and with every step, the silhouette of the church steeple seemed to watch Fonny Boy and follow him. The people of Tangier were God-fearing, and disobedience to one's parents was not tolerated. Although Fonny Boy might be an angel to Dr. Faux, Fonny Boy was openly disobeying his father and mother by sneaking out of the house and letting the dentist go. Furthermore, when Fonny Boy's father arrived to putter out to the crab pots, he would have no means of doing so and would be extremely out of sorts because of his missing bateau.

As Fonny Boy and the dentist descended rickety wooden steps leading down to the bateaus, Fonny Boy worried aloud and nonstop. He was having second thoughts and was terrified to go down that last step, which would surely lead to an entirely new, scary world. The dentist tried to comfort Fonny Boy by telling him that he was feeling the same way the men and boys had felt in December, 1606 as they'd filed down the Blackwall stairs on the Isle of Dogs and boarded the ships. Little Richard Mutton of St. Bride, London, was only fourteen, the same age as Fonny Boy, and no doubt froze on the bottom step, too.

"His family, was they with him?" Fonny Boy whispered.

"Little Richard was the only Mutton on the list of settlers, at least that we know of."

"Then what for did he do it?" Fonny Boy whispered as he imagined Richard Mutton all alone and shivering in the dark as he stared out at three tiny ships that were going to sail all the way across the Atlantic Ocean to an unknown, dangerous world.

"Gold," Dr. Faux replied. "The little Mutton boy, like most of our country's first settlers, felt sure they would find gold or at least silver, just like the Spanish were in the West Indies. And of course, they would be assigned great parcels of land so they could begin farming."

"Who learned you all this?" Fonny Boy asked in awe.

"Some of it was in Trooper Truth the morning before you kidnapped me. And I've always loved Virginia history."

Lights were beginning to fill windows in the small houses across the island, and Fonny Boy jumped into his father's bateau and began to imagine gold and treasure as they sped through the bay in the pitch dark. It would have been a good idea for him to have checked out how much gas was onboard and perhaps brought along an auxiliary tank or two for the hour-and-a-half voyage. As it was, they were five miles west of Tangier and inside restricted area R 6609 when the outboard motor began to hiccup and sputter just before it quit.

"Oh, no," Dr. Faux said as he began to fear that God hadn't answered his prayer after all, but had merely thrown him into worse trouble to punish him for his fraudulent life. "What do we do now, Fonny Boy?"

Every waterman kept a flare gun in his bateau, but Fonny Boy couldn't possibly resort to that because he could not be rescued by his own people and then face the unthinkable punishment that would await him for running away with the dentist. He was also mindful of the military restricted areas all around the island and wasn't sure it was a good idea to shoot something up into the air. What if the military shot back?

"You think the current will eventually drift us to Reedville?" Dr. Faux asked as frigid air began to work its way through his inadequate clothing.

"Nah," Fonny Boy replied.

He began digging around in the various compartments in the bateau, moving aside rope, a rusty pocket knife, several bottles of water, and mosquito repellent, which the dentist used liberally, even though it was too cold for insects to be on the prowl. The compartment under the pilot's seat was secured with a padlock, and Fonny Boy tried to conjure up the combination. Anything of true value, including the flare gun, would be inside that compartment, and although he wasn't certain, he was hopeful that his father might have left the handheld radio in there instead of taking it home.

Twenty

Cruz Morales evaded state troopers by cutting through a series of alleyways and parked by a Dumpster behind Freckles, just off Patterson Avenue. He sat in the dark, breathing hard, listening, his eyes nervously jumping everywhere. Country music and the murmur of voices sounded from inside Freckles, which Cruz took to be a small local bar. Suddenly he wanted a beer more than anything else. His nerves were fried, and he was as scared as he had ever been in his life.

He was certain all those huge helicopters flying low with searchlights probing were in pursuit of him. He had no idea what he had done to cause such a manhunt, unless it was that package in the tire well. But how did the authorities know about it? When those white dudes at the automotive shop had taken him in back and given him the package in exchange for another package, Cruz knew he was participating in an event that might get him into trouble, but the dudes certainly wouldn't have snitched on him. What would be the point? And no one saw the transaction, and as best he could recall, it seemed the helicopters were already out before he even pulled into the automotive shop parking lot. So were the authorities looking for him before he did anything? How could that be?

He climbed out of his car, opened the trunk, and retrieved the package from the tire well, which really wasn't much of a hiding spot since there was neither a spare tire nor carpet, and the first place a cop would check for illegal items was under the very conspicuous tire-well door. Cruz was about to heave the package into the Dumpster when the back door of the bar swung open, spilling light and loud voices into the dirt alleyway.

Major Trader was drunk and feeling macho and decided to pee outside, even though Freckles had perfectly adequate restrooms. But relieving himself in the great outdoors returned him to his roots, and pirates and watermen were quite skilled at adapting to inconvenience. Bateaus, for example, did not have heads, and when Trader was coming along, his family had had an outhouse, which he rarely used, unless he had more serious business than peeing to manage. Trader staggered a bit as he struggled with his fly, and stubborn zipper teeth bit into the cloth of his ill-fitting pants and held on for dear life.

"Shit!" Trader swore like a pirate, yanking hard. "Damnation seize my soul!"

The harder he tugged, the deeper the zipper sunk in its teeth. Now he was in a bind, all right, because the zipper was stuck exactly midway, and the more he fought with the zipper, the more his bladder wanted to surrender. He clamped a hand between his legs while he danced and stumbled about, cursing the zipper and trying to rip its metal teeth apart.

Cruz lurked in deep shadows behind the Dumpster, peering out and watching all this in amazement. He had never seen such a display, and what the hell was the language flying out of that fat man's mouth, and why was he hopping on one foot and then the other and holding his privates? In the incomplete light it seemed he was yanking himself up by the crotch, as if trying to break free of gravity and take flight. Now he was panting and cursing like a pirate, and his hopping and jumping were getting more vigorous, and propelling him around the Dumpster in Cruz's direction.

Cruz set the package on the ground and stepped around to the front of the Dumpster just as the wild man hopped around to the back of it. Then Cruz made a run for it. He jumped into his car, cranked the engine, and sped off as Trader grabbed himself and hopped, his urgency becoming unbearable. The zipper had gone from being stubborn to having lockjaw. Those metal teeth weren't going to let go and were clamped with such violence that the zipper felt hot to the touch.

Trader yanked on the zipper and moaned in excruciating discomfort, feeling as if someone had attached a bicycle pump to his bladder and was seeing how many pounds of pressure could be squeezed in before it blew up and went flat with relief and shame. Pirates did not pee on themselves, not even as infants. It was one thing to pee on property and others, but you did not soil yourself, not even if you were in the middle of raiding a ship or torching a crab plantation. Trader was out of breath and exhausted from hopping when he happened to notice a package on the ground and sat on it with his legs tightly crossed.

"Goddamn it," he muttered repeatedly as the back door of Freckles opened, casting Trader in a stripe of light and making him squint.

Hooter Shook had just ended her shift at the tollbooth and had dropped by Freckles for a little male company and refreshment. She had been having such a good time with that big Trooper Macovich that her head had begun to spin, and then, unfortunately, they had gotten into a disagreement.

"Don't believe in getting married," Macovich told her as he threw back his fourth beer. " 'Cause I don't want no bunch of kids jumping on me the minute I walk in the door and then all my money going out the window. I been saving for a Corvette."

"Whaaaat?" Hooter was a bit looped herself, and beer and her basic disposition weren't a good mix. "You just like all the rest," she accused him as she clacked her amazingly long acrylic nails on the Formica tabletop. "Uh huh. I work my ass off and come home to you and you just be out there polishing that 'Vette a yours while the babies are in the house squalling with dirty diapers and nothing to eat. Then you expect sex from me while you drinking beer and you don't even ask me about my day!"

"Wooo! You skipping to the end of the movie, babe. We ain't even held hands yet and already we's married with babies. Why don't we just drink beer and chill, you know?"

She clacked her nails so loudly and erratically that they sounded like ice skates in a hockey game.

"I never did understand why you women got to have these nails three inches long," he confessed. "How you even pick up a penny or a postage stamp?"

"I don't pick up no pennies without gloves," she said indignantly. "You know how I feel about dirt and things unsanitarian!"

This worried him considerably. If she felt that way about money, what kind of exchanges could he ever hope to have with her? For all he knew, she wore a biological hazard suit to bed and those nails of hers could cause him damage in tender places. Woooo, he thought. What if she dug them nails into his horsie? Why did she wear a perfume called Poison, too? He ought to know better than to pick up somebody at the tollbooth. Last time he picked up a woman he knew nothing about, the situation had been similar. Letitia Sweet worked in the Shell Quik Mart not far from headquarters, and Macovich was minding his own business one afternoon when he popped in for a coffee and popcorn. Letitia was built like an old Cadillac and probably had just as many miles and layers of paint, but Macovich was in a mood because of that pool shark Crimm girl.

"What you got on?" he asked Letitia when he stepped up to the counter and impressed her by pulling out a twenty-dollar bill.

"What you mean, what I got on?" She gave him a smirk as she bent over the cash drawer in a way that exposed her bulletlike headlights.

He had to give her credit: That woman was a handful no matter which way he grabbed her, even though their first date was their last.

"Who you think you are?" Letitia yelled at him in the car. "What you think you're doing grabbing at me like that? You think I ain't got no nerves beneath all that flesh? How you like it if I grabbed and twist you like a rag I'm wringing out when I clean up the nacho bin at the end of the day?"

She demonstrated, and Macovich had to admit that he didn't like it a bit. So why did he go from her to Hooter? He was lost in the space of his own dysfunction and bad experiences, and decided it was best not to protest when Hooter said she needed air and if he was lucky, would talk to him briefly next time he came through her Exact Change lane. Typically, she ended the date in a forsaken place and had no ride home, and she was feeling a little sorry for herself when she emerged in the alleyway and spied a fat white man sitting on a package by the Dumpster. For a minute, she forgot her own problems.

"Why honey, you look like you ain't feeling too good," Hooter said, making her way to him on her wobbly heels. "What'chu doing out here in this cold alleyway? Want me to call the ambu-lance?"

"My zipper's stoppered shut," Trader told her, squeezing himself and yanking the slide to no avail. "Damnation!"

"I have that happen sometimes," Hooter sympathized with him, coming closer and getting a good look at him to make sure he wasn't some crazy person. "I tell you, it's a whole lot worse when it's in back." She indicated the back of an imaginary long evening gown. "I had that happen one time when I went to this fancy New Year's Eve Ball at the Holiday Inn, and I couldn't get my dress zipped up and was 'fraid if I yanked too hard, I'd rip that beautiful thing for sure."

She went on to explain in detail how she had finally waited out in the hallway of the motel until some nice Arab man had passed by and helped her unzip her dress so she could start all over again and zip it up without getting snagged on chiffon. But the Arab man hadn't wanted her to zip the dress back up and in fact had insisted that she take it off along with everything under it, so she had had no choice but to beat him up. Hooter lit a cigarette, caught up in the memory, as Trader held himself and begged the zipper to deliver him from captivity.

"Please lit me free. Please lit me free," he begged, near tears, in a dialect Hooter was unfamiliar with.

"Why sure, baby." She bent over and lit a cigarette for him. "You can have all the smokes you want and I won't charge you a cent 'cause I don't touch pennies anyhow. I think it's a sin to let someone bum a cigarette and then charge him for it, don't you? What's that you sitting on, baby?"

Trader was suddenly aware of the hard lumpy package he was perched on beside the Dumpster. He felt for it with his free hand and began to rip off the paper wrapping as he pitched the fresh cigarette in the dirt.

"Guns," he declared, and then he further realized that maybe he could use one to shoot off his stuck zipper, as long as he was careful.

"Oh my!" Hooter exclaimed. "What you be sitting on guns for? That's mighty dangerous, and why you have them to begin with all wrapped up in UPS paper?"

Trader snatched out a nine-millimeter pistol and dropped out the magazine, happy that it was fully loaded, even if he was unfamiliar with firearms, unless it was a flare gun. He tugged and played around with the slide until he figured it was possible a round might very well be chambered. He spread his knees wide and carefully fired.

"Godamighty!" he yelled when the bullet pinged off the brass zipper slide and ricocheted into the Dumpster with a loud thunk.

"You insane!" Hooter screamed, backing up a few steps and almost falling. "What'chu trying to shoot your privates for?"

Trader lined up the zipper slide in the sights again and squeezed the trigger, furious when the bullet ricocheted off the slide and whizzed straight up, knocking out the streetlight. The zipper was indestructible, clenching its teeth in a death grip while Trader fired again and again, ejected cartridge cases sailing and clinking in the dirt as Hooter ran through the alleyway screeching for the police and waving her arms at the big helicopters flying overhead.

"Help! Help!" she hollered up at the Black Hawks. "Get down here and stop this crazy man! He trying to shoot his privates off and keep missing! But soon enough, he gonna hit something! Help! Help!"

A ndy was parking in front of Judy Hammer's house when the call came over the radio.

"Promiscuous shooting in the five thousand block of Patterson Avenue. Any officer in the area. Report of shots fired in the alleyway."

Hammer appeared on the front porch, wondering why Andy wasn't getting out of his car. She came down the steps to investigate.

"What are you doing?" Hammer asked as Andy rolled down his window.

"There's a shooting and nobody's responding," he said, getting excited. "I guess all the city units must be tied up on other shootings and looking for the Hispanic."

"Let's go," she said without hesitation, climbing in.

They roared off with the blue grill lights and siren going full tilt while the city police dispatcher continued trying to raise an officer to respond to Patterson Avenue.

"Three-thirty," Andy said over the radio, using his former unit number from his days with the Richmond police department.

"Three-thirty," the dispatcher came back and sounded slightly confused, because she remembered Andy's pleasant voice and knew he didn't work for the city any longer.

"Responding to Patterson Avenue," Andy said.

"Ten-four, former unit three-thirty."

"You know exactly where in the alleyway?" he asked into the mike.

"Ten-ten, three-thirty," which was the city's way of saying, "Negative, Officer Brazil or whoever is riding around pretending to be Officer Brazil."

Dispatcher Betty Freakley turned around to the 911 operators sitting behind her and shrugged.

"I thought he'd gone and signed up with the state police. What's he doing riding around in the city again?" she asked.

All the 911 operators were busy. Things were hopping in Richmond this night. An intoxicated white male had fallen down in the yard while taking his dog out. A black female was lying in the middle of the street near Eggleston's grocery store. An infant had eaten all the little beads inside a purple Beanie Baby Millennium Y2K bear. There were several car wrecks, and most officers were tied up looking for a Hispanic male suspect driving a Grand Prix with New York plates. But the urgent matter that caught Hammer's attention was the report of a male with a bag over his head who was trying to rob Popeye's Chicken & Biscuits on Chamberlayne Avenue.

"I wonder if that's the same man who tried to rob the tollbooth last year," Hammer said. "What's his name? He ran into the tollbooth because the holes he cut in the bag were in the wrong place and he couldn't see."

"Goes by the street name *Stick*," Andy said. "He's got an endless rap sheet and has tried the bag thing for years."

"You would think he'd figure out his M.O. is obvious and isn't working," Hammer replied, never failing to be amazed by the stupidity of most criminals.

"He hit the Popeye's on Broad Street a couple months ago," Andy recalled, speeding through a yellow light on Cary Street. "Walked in with the bag over his head, tripped over the railing where people wait in line, and made off with an eight-piece chicken dinner, then walked into the glass door and broke his nose. We got his DNA off the blood on the paper bag."

"Does he use a gun?"

"That's the problem. He's never armed, and just walks in with the bag over his head, asking for whatever. So we can't get him on any charges that stick, which is why he never spends much time in jail. According to him, he asks for something and people give it to him without protest, so that really isn't a crime and there's nothing in the Virginia Code that says it's illegal to walk around with a bag over your head. So the judge always throws it out when Stick shows up for arraignment."

"Any officer in the area," the dispatcher came over the air. "Report of a white male with a bag over his head, down in the parking lot of Popeye's on Chamberlayne Avenue. An ambulance en route."

"I guess he tripped again," Andy said.

Stick wasn't the only one to trip that night. When Barbie Fogg got out of her minivan in the carport, she stepped on the Barbie doll of one of the twins. As usual, it had been left where the child had played with it last.

"Oh, my!" Barbie cried out as she picked herself up from the concrete floor and checked for injuries.

Barbie, who very much believed in signs from The Universe, interpreted what could have been a serious accident as a signal that she had misstepped and overlooked something important. Oh, of course! she thought as she remembered the very special thing that had happened before she'd stopped off to visit the nursing home where she made the rounds visiting infirm and forgetful old women she didn't know. Barbie believed The Universe had chosen her to be a healer, and at last, The Universe was about to reward her, which was why Hooter had given Barbie the special gift.

Minutes later, her neighbors, the Clot sisters, watched Barbie apply a rainbow bumper sticker to the back window of the Fogg family minivan. Uva Clot was shocked as she peered out from behind the kitchen blinds.

"Come here and look!" Uva yelled at her spinster sister, Ima, who was watching TV in the living room, the sound blasting. "Lord have mercy, she's falling down drunk and putting that thing on her car with chirren inside the house. What's gonna happen to those little chirren when all the world sees what they momma just put on that minivan a hers? I always wondered about her, didn't I tell you I always wondered about her, Ima? Get on in here and look right this minute!"

Ima shuffled in with her walker and squinted through the opening in the blinds. She stiffened at the sight of Barbie Fogg in her lit-up carport across the street. Ima couldn't quite make out what Barbie was doing, but it looked like she was walking around her minivan and kicking a doll across the concrete, and she kept smoothing something on the back window and admiring whatever it was. Ima barely made out a few bright colors.

"What she up to?" she asked her sister.

"Don't you see what she put on the window, Ima? She got her one of them rainbow stickers! 'Member all them rainbow flags and stickers when we was living in the French Quarter?"

Ima gasped with such a start that she lurched forward with her walker and fell into the blinds. She grabbed them to steady herself, and they crashed to the floor. Barbie Fogg peered at the Clot sisters peering at her through the suddenly transparent kitchen window and waved at them as they scurried out of view.

"Lennie," Barbie called out when she walked through the mudroom into the kitchen, where her husband was rooting around inside the refrigerator. "You'll never guess what happened tonight."

"You're probably right," Lennie testily replied as he popped open a Budweiser. "And I'm not going to guess."

"A figure of speech." She said what she always did.

"What took you so long? I thought you'd be home hours ago."

"Traffic and those poor people in the nursing home," she said. "Oh, Lennie, I made a new girlfriend tonight and have a rainbow on my minivan!"

"What'd you do, drive through a thunderstorm and now you're gonna find a pot of gold?" Lennie gulped the beer and wiped his mouth on the back of his hand.

"Are the girls asleep?" Barbie inquired as she looked inside the refrigerator, too, deciding she would celebrate her rainbow with a Mike's Hard Lemonade. "Wouldn't a pot of gold be wonderful?"

"Yeah, yeah. Listen," Lennie said, "you know, one of my clients has got extra tickets for Saturday night's race, and as you know, I got to be in Charlotte at that real estate conference. So you want the tickets, or should I give them to someone else?"

"I'll get a sitter and maybe take a girlfriend," Barbie replied, failing to add that she wouldn't miss a race for the world and was delighted that her husband couldn't go.

Barbie had a secret passion for driver Ricky Rudd, who had the most flawless creamy skin and cute blond hair. Whenever she saw pictures of him wearing that big Texaco star on the front of his colorful racing suit or watched his number 28 bright red Monte Carlo roar around on TV, she felt tingles all over her body and would send him another letter. She had been writing to him for years, sending him weekly epistles when he lived in North Carolina and then trying to figure out how she might get his phone number after he moved back to his home state of Virginia. He never answered, of course, but she believed he would if she didn't use a pen name and fail to include a return address.

Along with Ricky, Barbie enjoyed an obsession with Bo Mann, whom she'd noticed when he was driving the Monte Carlo pace car at the 2000 Chevrolet Monte Carlo 400 last year. When Barbie made numerous inquiries in the pits and begged for her photograph to be taken with Bo, she was clever enough to trick him into giving her his address.

"If I send you the photo with a stamped return envelope, will you autograph it?" she had said to Bo as they posed together in front of the pace car, after the race.

"Sign the envelope or the picture?" he had asked, and oh how Barbie loved a man with a sense of humor.

"I heard a man got blowed up by the river tonight," Lennie was saying. "I guess that means there's another psycho on the loose. Let's go to bed and have sex."

The lemonade was mounting straight to Barbie's head.

"Oh, dear," she sighed. "I don't think I'm up for it tonight, Lennie. I've got rainbows on the brain and just want to relax a little and bask in it, if you don't mind."

Lenny did mind. Frustrated, he finished the beer and got out another one. He popped the top and eyed his wife's trim figure. She spent so much time taking care of herself, but then she didn't want him to snatch her clothes off and explore what she worked so hard to maintain. It didn't make sense. Why does a woman bother looking good if she doesn't want sex?

"I think I need to check on the girls and go to bed," Barbie announced. "Oh my! This lemonade's making me swoon."

"Glad something does," he muttered as he thought of how seldom he complained about his wife's shopping sprees or what she spent on cosmetic surgery and injections and God knows what all she did when she visited that doctor of hers once a month. Lennie was good about sending her flowers, too, even when there was no special occasion, and he never complained about babysitting the twins, Mandie and Missie, who were almost five. He just wanted his wife to let him touch her and at least pretend she liked it or didn't mind.

Lennie got her another lemonade and helped himself to another beer. Getting her drunk used to work, but now all it did was make her groggy and distant.

"I can't keep on living like this," he said. "I work my ass off selling real estate and half the time come home and babysit while you visit with invalids or your lady friends up and down the street. Then you're too damn tired for me, or maybe you're just tired *of* me."

"A girl needs her girlfriends, you know." Barbie was having a hard time enunciating. "I don't think men understand about our need for our girlfriends. How many extra tickets did you get?"

"Yeah, well, maybe I need a girlfriend, too," he said in a sharper tone.

Barbie began to cry. She simply could not endure his temper or ugliness, and she wilted in the heat of his fury. "I don't know," she sobbed. "I'm sorry, Lennie. I try so hard to please you, honey. But ever since I turned forty, I just haven't felt like it, you know, like doing it at all. It's not your fault. I'm sure it can't be your fault. Maybe I need to see someone and talk about it."

"Oh God." Lennie rolled his eyes. "Now I'm going to pay for a therapist, I guess! And what sense does that make? Here you are a volunteer counselor. Why can't you talk to yourself?"

Sne cried harder and he felt awful. Lennie hugged her and begged her to be happy.

"You need to talk to someone, sweetpea, you go right ahead," he softly assured her. "I got two tickets and could probably get a few more from that General Motors executive who just retired down here and bought that big house on the river."

A ndy and Hammer turned into the alleyway behind Freckles and noticed that all the streetlights were out. Trader, covered in filth, was sitting on a package by a Dumpster that was spilling over with sour-smelling garbage. Trader was out of ammunition and still fighting with his zipper, near hysterics and desperate to pee.

"For God's sake," Hammer said to her least favorite government official. "What the hell are you doing sitting out here on a package and firing a gun? And why is your suit so dirty?"

"My zipper's stoppered shut!" Trader exploded in rage.

Hammer bent over to inspect the problem as Andy noticed a woman lurking in the shadows a safe distance away.

"That's because you've managed to zip your underwear in it," Hammer said. "How'd the little slide get all dented up?"

"I been trying to shit it off!"

"Now settle down," Hammer ordered. "Let me see what I can do."

She touched Trader's zipper slide, careful not to touch anything else. Within seconds, she had unsnagged Trader's underwear and the zipper smiled open. Trader darted behind the Dumpster and began to pee like a horse.

"Jesus Christ," Andy said in disgust.

He inspected the package and shook his head as he counted five high-powered pistols and several boxes of ammunition.

"Looks like he's got all kinds of little businesses on the side," Andy said.

"Huh," Hammer remarked angrily. "What a disgrace."

"Hey!" Andy called out to the woman hanging back in the shadows, unable to make out anything except a silhouette of dreadlocks and high heels. "Come here!"

Hooter wobbled through the dirt, a little nervous that she might be in trouble, too, but not sure for what.

"Oh, I recognize you two," Hooter said in surprise. "You that woman police chief, only you ain't the chief no more 'cause you took over the troopers. And you the nice trooper who tried to help me when that man with the bag on his head tried to stick me up at the tollbooth last year," she declared to Andy.

"What do you know about this?" Andy nodded in the direction of Trader, who was still relieving himself.

"I just know I come out the bar and he was hopping around in the alleyway and then sat hisself on a package. Oh my Lord, look at all them guns! Why he was out here sitting on guns by a Dumpster, I'll never know. I told him it was dangerous, but he wouldn't get off the package and was holding hisself. So I don't know nothing more than that 'cept all a sudden he started shooting all over the place and I ran for cover and yelled for help."

"What were you doing out here in the alleyway?" Andy asked.

"Getting a little air."

"If you were getting a little air, then you must have been inside some place that didn't have much air. So where were you before you walked out here?" Andy inquired.

"Having me a little drink." She nodded at Freckles. "It was mighty smoky in there, 'specially 'cause that big trooper never puts one out without lighting up another one."

Andy immediately thought of Macovich. So did Hammer.

"Check to see if he's still in there," Hammer said to Andy.

He trotted around to the front of the small old neighborhood bar, and scores of bleary eyes turned on him as he walked through the door. Macovich was sitting in a booth by himself, drunk and sucking on another cigarette. Andy slid into the seat across from him.

"We just picked up Major Trader in the alleyway," he said. "Didn't you hear all those gunshots?"

"Thought they was car backfires," Macovich slurred through a cloud of smoke. "And I'm off duty," he sullenly added. "I know Trader was in the area, though. 'Cause he was sitting up there at the bar for a long time, drinking beers all by himself. Now, I didn't speak to him or draw no attention to myself."

"Did you notice him interacting with anyone or talking on the cell phone? Anything that might give you reason to believe he was here to meet someone and maybe buy a package of guns?"

"Wooo! Ain't nothing but trouble these days," Macovich said, turning a beer bottle in little circles on the table. "Much as I don't like that man, I can't say I saw him up to nothing."

"Then we can't prove he had anything to do with those guns," Andy said, disappointed. "At least not at the moment. And it's really not our jurisdiction to charge him with promiscuous shooting. The city police will have to do that, if they are so inclined. Were you in here with Hooter?"

"Wooo, that was a mistake. She don't hold her beer worth a damn and got nasty. That's what I get for picking up a toll lady."

Macovich tried to act as if he didn't care at all for Hooter. She was beneath him—a lowly tollbooth operator. So what if she got ugly and stormed out? He could find women every minute of the day, and he sure didn't need a tollbooth operator, senior or not.

"Guess I'd better give her a ride home," Macovich said. "She don't have a car."

"I think a better solution is for me to call both of you a cab," Andy replied. "But she may have some explaining to do to the police."

Hammer was asking Hooter about the police even as Andy said this.

"Are you the one who called them?" Hammer inquired. "Because somebody must have."

"I yelled up at all them helichoppers." Hooter looked up at a Black Hawk thundering overhead. "So I reckon one of them radioed for help."

"It's not possible that people in a helicopter heard you yelling down here," Hammer pointed out as Trader continued to splash the alleyway behind the Dumpster.

"Well, all I know is I was yelling up at them and waving my arms, so it had to be the helichoppers who called the police 'cause I didn't call nobody. I never heard nobody pee that long before, either." She stared off in the direction of the noise. "That one strange man. I think you better check him out. Bet he done other things that ain't right, you ask me. Maybe he's a homosensual, too, 'cause he was trying to shoot his privates off like he hate his manhood. So that probably mean he got AIDS and lots of dirty money in his pockets. I wouldn't touch him without gloves, you want my advice. I got a pair in my purse, you want to borrow 'em," she offered Hammer. "I figure you gonna have to lock him up," she added as Andy emerged from the back of Freckles.

"Trader was inside drinking," Andy told Hammer. "Macovich saw him. Did you?" he asked Hooter.

"I didn't notice him, if he was in there," Hooter replied. "There was too much smoke hanging over the table."

"I'll call the city police and see what they want to do," Andy said to Hammer. "But I don't think this is our case at the moment. And we need to get you a taxi," he added to Hooter.

"Now you listen," she said indignantly. "I ain't drunk."

"I didn't say you were. But you don't have a car."

"He got a car and is the reason I got here." She jutted her chin in the direction of Freckles, obviously referring to Macovich.

"He's in no condition to drive," Andy said. "He's had way too many beers and is in a bad mood. I think his feelings are hurt."

"Huh," Hooter said as interest lit up her eyes. "He too insens'tive to get his feelings hurt."

"That's simply not true," Andy replied. "Sometimes the biggest, toughest men are overly sensitive and keep everything inside. Maybe you can drive him home in his car?"

"Then what do I do?" she exclaimed. "I ain't staying with no man who still live with his mama!"

Cruz Morales would have given anything for his mother as he sped around half the night. At 3:00 A.M., he glanced around furtively as he shut a pay phone booth door and pulled out the dingy paper napkin the tollbooth lady had given him. She seemed like a nice enough person, and Cruz needed help. He was never going to make it out of the city in his Pontiac with its New York plates—not with cops and helicopters everywhere. Now he at least understood what all of the commotion was about.

While speeding away from the bar where that wild man was hopping around the Dumpster, Cruz heard on the radio that someone had been burned up down by the river and everyone was looking for a Hispanic suspect from New York who might be the serial killer that had been committing hate crimes that could be traced all the way back to a shooting at Jamestown, which was unsolved because some lady police person wasn't doing a good job, according to the governor. Cruz had no idea what all of this was about, but he was Hispanic, and he was at a loss as to how he had suddenly become a fugitive for crimes he knew nothing about. So he pulled into a 7-Eleven to make an urgent phone call. Cruz squinted at the napkin and noticed there were two phone numbers written down—one on one side, one on the other. He could have sworn the tollbooth lady had written down only one number, so what was the other one and which one was the right one? Cruz dropped a quarter in the pay phone and dialed the first number. After three rings, it was picked up.

"Hello?" a male voice asked.

"I look for the toll lady," Cruz said, assuming the toll lady must have a boyfriend.

"Who is this?"

"I can't tell you, but I have to talk to her. She say for me to call," Cruz said.

Andy was sitting at his computer, working on the next Trooper Truth essay, and he had a feeling the toll lady in question was Hooter. But why was anybody looking for her at his house?

"She's not here at the moment," Andy said, which was misleading but true.

Hooter had taken Macovich home, and what happened after that was anybody's guess. Then Andy had called the city cops, who came and got the package of handguns but decided not to arrest Trader with so little evidence to go on, especially since he was an important government official.

"But if we trace these guns back to you," one of the cops had said to Trader, "then you're in a shitload of trouble. I don't care who you work for. So I recommend you go on home and don't try to leave town or anything unwise like that."

"Of course I wouldn't leave town," Trader had lied. Remarkably, wires had reconnected inside his head and he was talking normally again. "I will be at work with the governor tomorrow, as usual."

"Well, I guess you'd better ask the governor that," Andy had told Trader. "He's not too happy with you right now."

"Nonsense," Trader had retorted. "We have always been on good terms, and in fact, he considers me his closest friend."

"Maybe he won't if Regina's blood work turns out in an unfortunate way for you, Trader," Andy had replied. "I understand from the news she was rushed to the E.R. a little while ago with a severe gastrointestinal attack that you and I both know was precipitated by cookies you were witnessed to bring into the mansion kitchen and set down on a countertop. You were overheard to say that the cookies were for the governor only, but Regina got into them anyway when no one was looking."

"No one's ever gotten ill from my wife's cookies," Trader had said.

"When she get back?" the unidentified person with a heavy Spanish accent was asking over the line.

"I'm not sure, but is there something I can help you with?" Andy tried to get this evasive, suspicious-sounding caller to talk.

"It's just I'm concern, you know? They say this Hi'panic kill someone at the river, and I didn't kill no one and the po-lice, they be looking for me." Cruz was out with it as he huddled in the phone booth and noticed a black Land Cruiser parking at the gas pumps.

"What makes you think the police are looking for you?" the man on the line asked.

"Because they stop me at the tollbooth and chase me for no reason. I had to hide and afraid for my life! The toll lady give me her number and say she help me."

Andy strained to figure out why Hooter would have given out his home phone number to a possible fugitive, and then he recalled working the Bag Man case last year.

"Maybe we should meet and discuss this," Andy suggested as he absently clicked the mouse and changed a word in the essay he would post momentarily. "There's no point in running from the police, even if you're innocent, because all you're going to do is create more legal problems for yourself. Why don't I meet you in a secure, safe place and we'll talk about it? I have connections and may be able to help you out."

Cruz was tempted and possibly would have done the smart thing and met whoever he was talking to, but an unforeseen event began to unfold right before his very eyes. Through the expansive plate glass of the 7-Eleven, he saw a white woman walk into the convenience store and appear to be asking the clerk for help. Then a white man with dreadlocks staggered in looking stoned, and whipped a pistol out from the inside of his coat and pointed it at the clerk, who was away from the counter and the emergency button that all convenience stores have these days. Cruz couldn't hear what the white man was saying, but he looked very mean and violent as he mouthed abusive words at the terrified clerk in her orange-checked 7-Eleven jacket. She began to cry and beg as the white man cleaned out the cash drawer. Then, to Cruz's horror, the woman with long black hair calmly took the dude's gun, put it right against the clerk's head, and fired repeatedly. The explosions shook the phone booth and Cruz yelped.

"What was that?" Andy asked, startled by what sounded like gunfire.

"Ahhh! This white dude with dreadlocks! They just shot the clerk!" the Hispanic yelled over the line and hung up.

Smoke? Andy wondered as he recalled the description of Smoke that the prison guard, Pinn, had given after Smoke had escaped. According to Andy's caller ID, the Hispanic had called from a 7-Eleven off Hull Street, south of the river, and Andy called 911 while Cruz jumped into his car and sped off.

Cruz was horrified not a minute later to notice that the black Land Cruiser was right on his rear bumper. He had learned to drive in New York City and swung into several alleyways, gunned through a side street, then another, and roared across a median and threaded his car precariously through others until he ended up on Three Chopt Road in the parking lot of what looked like a huge mansion with tennis courts.

A Brief History of Zippers

by Trooper Truth

A zipper, for those of you who may never have given the subject much thought, is also called a slide fastener and is a simple device for binding the edges of an opening, such as a fly, the back of a dress, or a freezer bag, although the latter is actually sealed by a *zip lock* that is more like gums—rather than teeth—clamping shut. The zipper device of interest to us consists of two strips of cloth, each with a row of metal or plastic teeth that interlock rather much like a railroad track when one pulls up the sliding piece. This railroad track then separates when one pulls down the sliding piece—unless the zipper gets off track or stubborn, which is what happened to that poisonous, lying Major Trader last night.

The first slide fastener recorded in history was exhibited in 1893 by Whitcomb L. Judson, at the World's Fair in Chicago. Mr. Judson called his awkward arrangement of hooks and eyes a *clasp locker*. Within a few years, Gideon Sundback, a Swedish immigrant and electrical engineer, improved the device by substituting spring clips for the hooks and eyes, and in 1913 produced the Hookless #2, although it wasn't called a zipper until BF Goodrich coined the name in 1923, when the company manufactured zip-up overshoes.

It goes without saying that if we happened upon a zipper in what we thought was a colonial grave at Jamestown, then we could at least conclude with some assurance that the human remains were post-1913. Just to linger with this scenario another moment, let's assume that while I was uncovering a grave at the archaeological site, I had indeed unearthed a zipper in the pelvic area of the skeletal remains. I would have immediately pointed this out to one of the archaeologists, preferably Dr. Bill Kelso, who is Jamestown's chief archaeologist and an expert on colonial artifacts, including buttons.

"Dr. Kelso," I probably would have said, "look, a green stain in the dirt that is shaped exactly like a zipper. It's my interpretation that the green indicates a brass zipper that has eroded with time."

The esteemed archaeologist most likely would agree with me and point out that as brass and copper shroud pins erode, they also leave a green stain, but a pin leaves a pin-shaped stain that is easily distinguishable from a zipper shape. He would go on to tell me that the medieval pin might be made of iron topped by a pewter head that was occasionally inlaid with glass or a semi-precious stone. But most pins found at historical sites are made of drawn brass wire with a conical head that is another piece of wire turned three to five times at the top of the shank and then flattened by a blow. This method of making pins continued until 1824, when Lemuel W. Wright patented a solid-headed pin that was stamped out in a single process.

If we found a pin that was at least five inches long, then we would suspect we had a hairpin on our hands, and the person in the grave most likely was a female. If we found a safety pin, then the grave was post-1857. If we found a shroud pin, then the person in the grave had been reverently wrapped in a winding cloth when he or she was buried. Should we find brass wire fasteners for cloaks, then the grave may very well be seventeenth century. As for needles, Dr. Kelso would probably mention, we hardly ever find them because they rust unless they are made of bone, in which case we might conclude the remains were those of a rugmaker.

"What about thimbles?" I might ask Dr. Kelso as I gently brush soil away from the zipper stain in my grave.

"It varies," he could very well reply. "Depending on their usage."

Thimbles of the 1500s and early 1600s were squat and heavy, as a rule, and rarely decorative. Should I uncover a very tall thimble, most likely the grave was mid-seventeenth century, and if a thimble had a hole punched in it, very possibly it had been traded to a Plains Indian who had hung it on a thong as a *tinkler* to spruce up clothing and pouches. The early Native Americans had a great sense of style and very much enjoyed wearing beads, bits of copper, household implements, and heads and body parts of wooden dolls.

Most doll parts available to the Native Americans were cast in pipe clay from a two-piece mold. Highly prized by colonial boys were toy guns and cannons cast in pewter or brass and with fully drilled barrels, suggesting the little boys could shoot up James Fort if they pleased, or if a Native American got hold of such a toy and wore it on a thong, he might accidentally shoot himself in the foot or worse.

Sadly, I did not find any toys or toy parts during my research with the Jamestown archaeologists, nor was it my good luck to find coins or even a button, although I did find a number of musket balls and an arrowhead and the skeletal remains of a woman who had been a chronic pipe smoker and hadn't cut her hair in four to seven years.

In keeping with being a truthful narrator, I will state for the record that I did not find a zipper while excavating at Jamestown. But if I had, I most certainly would have recognized it on the spot and gathered abundant information from it.

To return to that scoundrel Major Trader, he is at large and unremorseful. He was last seen shooting a pistol behind Freckles and quite likely is still in the city, going about his nefarious business as usual. If you click on the small jail icon in the upper right-hand corner, you can view a recent photograph of him with Governor Crimm, who is the gentleman on the left holding a magnifying glass. Please do not confuse the two. The governor is a law-abiding man and I would like to take this opportunity to say the following to him:

I know it is a delicate subject, Sir, but you really must do something about your eyesight, and I'd like to suggest either a guide dog or a guide horse. I actually think the latter is the best way to go because the wait for a minihorse is not as long, they live much longer than a dog, and you already have a dog who might take exception to another dog. I have taken the liberty to inquire as to how you might get a minihorse, and I've found that one is available this very minute. He is housebroken and at ease in sneakers so he doesn't slip on smooth surfaces. He enjoys traveling in the back of the car or van, likes other pets and children, and his name is Trip, because he loves to travel. I have taken the liberty of e-mailing the breeders to hold little Trip for you and call your office with the information, which they have promised to do immediately.

On another subject, Sir, someone should look into your butler's situation with the Department of Corrections. It has been brought to my attention that there may be a computer error and it is past time for your butler to be released from the prison system and work for you as a civilian instead of an inmate. And if I were you, I would look into Moses Custer's condition, too, and make sure he is in protective custody so his assailants don't hurt him again or worse. It is possible these same violent offenders struck again early this morning when a convenience store clerk was murdered, and they may even be connected to the brutal slaying of Trish Thrash.

Governor Crimm, it is time for you to show Virginians that you personally care about them and have no agenda other than what is best for the Commonwealth.

Be careful out there!

Twenty-one

Possum read the latest Trooper Truth essay several times and felt certain that the anonymous web crusader suspected that the assailants he mentioned were Smoke and the road dogs.

"Why wouldn't he figure it out?" Possum whispered to Popeye, who was snoring on the bed. "Everybody knows Smoke's broke out of jail and is up to no good, 'cause he ain't capable of being up to anything else. Oh Lord, Popeye, what if the police somehow find our RV and haul us away, or Smoke gets in a shoot-out with 'em and all of us end up dead?"

Popeye instantly woke up.

"It ain't fair!" Possum went on, getting angrier. "What'd they have to go and kill that Seven-Eleven lady for? Now there's a 'scription of Smoke on the news 'cause somebody saw the shooting!"

Possum took a deep breath and glanced back at the closed door several times.

"Well, it's time I did something," he whispered to Popeye. "And I'm gonna do it and just hope Smoke don't find out!"

Possum typed an e-mail.

Dear Trooper Truth,

That Trader man you just wrote about is a pirate on the web who calls hisself Captin Bonny. I figured it out 'cause of what you said the other day on your web about Trader being relations with that woman pirate who I guess must be dead now.

I think you could trap Captin Bonny by sending him an e-mail and setting him up. Just say you will leave him a waterproof suitcase full of what he's got coming to him and when he shows up, get him! Make up a screen name that's the same as mine so he thinks the e-mail's from me.

P.S. There is a score planned that has to do with Popeye! That Trader man is the one who set her up to be stolt!

Possum clicked on SEND NOW and glanced at the closed door with relief. Thank God, neither Smoke nor any of the other road dogs had seen what Possum had just done. Smoke would kill him for sure if he caught Possum sending an e-mail to Trooper Truth and turning in a source. Smoke would stomp, kick, and beat on Possum, leaving him for dead, just like Smoke had done to that innocent man Moses Custer, who, even as Possum was thinking all this, was being handed the telephone inside his hospital room.

I t's the governor," Nurse Carless said in a blaring voice as the cuff of her nurse's uniform knocked over a cup on Moses' food tray and spilled orange juice all over the front of his hospital gown.

"You sure?" Moses didn't believe her and thought if she caused one more accident, he was going to find the emergency alarm button and push it hard. "I mean, what if it's one of them pirates trying to find me?"

Nurse Carless took the phone away from him, clunking him in the chin. "I'm afraid he's not here," she said over the line as she wiped up orange juice and elbowed Moses in the Adam's apple.

"No!" Moses grabbed the phone back from her. "What if it *is* the gov'ner? I can't be hanging up on him! Who is this, if you don't mind me asking?" he said into the phone. "Before we go looking around room to room for Moses, assuming he's even in this hospital or still alive, we need to make sure who wants to know."

"This is Governor Crimm."

"Which Gov'ner Crimm?" Moses asked, still unconvinced.

"Governor Bedford Crimm the Fourth. There is no other Governor Crimm because each time there's been one, it's always been me. I've been the governor of Virginia three times now. Or is it four?"

"We're still looking for this Moses person," Moses said, not ready to trust the familiar voice quite yet. "But while I got you on the line, you mind I ask the names of your mama, wife, children, and any pets, and their ages and shoe sizes?"

"I most certainly do mind your asking that and anything else personal," the governor replied, deeply offended.

"Okay, okay. Hold on a second."

Moses put his hand over the phone and his heart began beating hard. It was the governor, all right, because no governor was going to answer personal questions like that, and a pirate trying to trick Moses into thinking it was the governor on the phone would have made up the answers.

"Hello?" Moses said in a slightly higher-pitched voice. "Moses Custer speaking."

"Yes, yes," Crimm said with a touch of impatience as he sat in his upstairs mansion office, dimly staring out at the fine view of the circular drive and guard booth. "Things seem very disorganized at your hospital, and whoever answers the phone is very rude."

"I tell you, it's a mess here," the strange, squeaky voice replied over the line. "Ouch!" he said to someone. "You're caught on my cat tube! Don't you be accidentally tugging that out again! It hurts like hell when you stick it back in!"

A muffled argument ensued, and the governor made out that Moses was tangled up in his catheter and refused to let the nurse remove it and switch him over to a bedpan.

"I ain't using no pan!" Moses declared. "Knowing you, that pan will get slopped all over me and the bed! Just leave in my cat tube and take my tray outta here 'fore you spill something else or poke me with that fork! Okay, Gov'ner. I sure am sorry about that. But something wrong with that nurse. I tell you, she got some kind of condition, like Parkerson's or muscular dysentery, and every time she get near me, I get banged up as bad as I was after them pirates beat on me and stolt my truck full of punkins."

"Well, I'll certainly make sure I never go to that particular hospital," the governor said as he scanned the latest Trooper Truth essay with his magnifying glass.

"Oh, no sir. You should never even drive past this place, and for sure, don't never come inside. And it's my heartfelt hope, Gov'ner, that you don't ever need no hospital. I pray daily for your good health and prosperation."

"What?" The governor returned to the advice Trooper Truth had directed personally to him. "What's that about perspiration?"

"Why, I don't know," Moses puzzled, as Crimm assumed that the poor man must be heavily sedated.

"Now, listen here." Crimm got to the point. "The terrible attack on you has come to my attention and I wanted to see how you're doing and let you know that I have a personal interest in your condition and intend to make sure that you are protected when you leave the hospital."

"You do?" Moses's voice went up several more notes as what sounded like a food tray crashed to the floor.

"Of course I do! You're a Virginian and it's my sworn oath to take care of every citizen in this uncommon and magnificent Commonwealth of ours. Now, when are you checking out of there?"

The governor watched as the well-mannered Trooper Brazil drove through the front gates and parked his unmarked car in front of the mansion. Crimm couldn't remember if there was a reason for the young man to show up this morning, but it seemed it had something to do with

Regina, and this was a tremendous relief. Regina needed something to occupy her attention, and the governor needed someone to protect Moses Custer.

"I believe they're saying I can go home 'fore the day out, assuming that nurse don't break my head or give me the wrong medicine," Moses was saying. "I sure do appreciate this. I can't believe I'm talking to the gov'ner hisself! Here I am being beat on one minute and all my punkins gone, then next thing the gov'ner hisself is on the phone saying I'm gonna be protected. And the gov'ner hisself even said he was sorry about what happened, even if it wasn't his fault, and I wasn't going to be in no kind of trouble for all them punkins clogging up the river."

"Of course, you're in no kind of trouble," the governor said as he watched Andy get out of the car and Regina bound down the front steps, dressed in safari clothes.

"By the way," the governor said in an effort to end the conversation and create a goodwill press situation. "Saturday night, you'll fly in the helicopter with me and sit in my box at the Winston Series race. And a state trooper named Andy Brazil will be at the hospital to safely escort you home."

"My Lord in heaven!" Moses was surprised and delighted. "I ain't never been to no real NASCAR race, not once in my life. You got any idea how hard it is to get tickets or find a parking place? I musta woke up in Oz!"

Crimm made his way out of his office, preoccupied with questions about minihorses and what it would be like to be led around every minute. He supposed he might as well give himself up to it. His vision was getting worse daily. This morning, when he had made his way down the mansion's sweeping staircase, he'd had to hold on to the banister with both hands. Then he'd sat in the Windsor chair in the ladies' parlor again and ordered two eggs over easy and a strip of crisp bacon. When no one responded, he had gotten up and wandered across the entrance way into the men's parlor and tried again. Finally, he'd ended up inside the elevator, where Pony had found him moments later as he was carrying fresh linens up to the second floor.

"Where am I?" the governor had puzzled as Pony led him to the family breakfast room.

"Have a seat, Governor," Pony had said as he pulled out a chair and draped a napkin over the governor's lap. "Did you sleep well, sir?"

"I didn't," Regina had answered as she piled butter on a mountain of grits. "I keep having the same bad dream."

Since no one at the table had seemed the least bit interested in her dream, she had decided to tell Andy about it the minute she climbed into his unmarked car.

"It's just like last time," she started in. "I don't know what it is about tires. Why do you think I keep dreaming about tires? One dream after another, there's all these tires rolling down the highway with no cars attached, just rolling all by themselves."

"Where are you while this is happening?" Andy asked her as he fastened his seat belt and indicated she should do the same.

"In my own bed, as if it's any of your business."

"In relation to the tires," Andy rephrased the question.

"I'm jumping out of their way. What do you think?" she retorted.

"You're on foot, then."

"Of course I am! None of us are allowed to drive while Papa's governor. We have to be driven around everywhere, and I'm sick and tired of it."

"I think it's pretty apparent why you're having tire dreams," Andy said. "You feel like you aren't going anywhere. You're like a car with no tires or tires with no car, and in either case, you are stuck on life's highway, helpless and threatened and frustrated and feeling that the world is passing you by."

The governor and the First Lady watched Regina and Andy through the window.

"They seem to be arguing," the First Lady observed.

"We can't have another dog," the governor decided.

"Who said anything about another dog, dearest?"

"I can't get a Seeing Eye dog," the governor said. "Trooper Truth's right. It wouldn't be fair to Frisky to have another dog in the mansion. Maybe a cat, but I don't think they have Seeing Eye cats, and I hate cats."

"I'm sure they can't train cats that way, dearest," Mrs. Crimm said. "I would think they would jump up on things and crawl under other things or simply do nothing, and that would be pretty tricky if a cat did all that while you were tied to it."

"They don't tie you to the animals," Faith said as she walked in on the conversation and jealously watched her dreadful younger sister leaving with the handsome trooper. "You hold on to a little handle. And I just read in Trooper Truth that they have Seeing Eye horses, too, and he wants you to get one immediately. I don't think Frisky would mind a horse, Papa."

"Well, we most certainly can't have a horse in the mansion," Mrs. Crimm protested.

"I want one," the governor decided. "Today."

"I'm not sure how I feel about Regina going to the morgue," Mrs. Crimm worried as Andy and Regina drove out of sight.

"Maybe it would be good for her," the governor considered. "Might make her count her blessings and stop complaining so much."

"I agree," Faith said. "She should be happy she's alive."

The governor walked away and bumped into a life-size portrait of Lady Astor.

"Excuse me," he muttered.

Barbie Fogg was bumping into things as well this morning. Bleary from too many lemonades, she collided with a sharp corner of the bed, cracked her funny bone on the toaster, and just seconds ago, almost bumped into the car in front of her as her attention wandered all over the interstate. Usually, when she drove her minivan to the Baptist Campus Ministry, where she was a volunteer counselor, nobody paid much attention to her. But other motorists were certainly staring at her this morning, and in her stuporous state, she was finding their scrutiny very distracting.

She had always been an attractive woman who dressed smartly but tastefully, and certainly she believed deeply in skin care. Skin was God's gift to women, she often told the female students who sought her advice and guidance. Clothes and accessories make no difference if your skin is bad, and everyone should visit the skin doctor regularly and use good cleansers and moisturizers and stay out of the sun.

Now, it was true that her skin looked especially nice this morning after the glycolic masque she vaguely remembered applying last night after too much to drink. But why were all these motorists staring at her? Some of them were even honking their horns, and a moment ago a man with an earring zipped past in his Porsche and gave her a thumbs up. She slowed down at Hooter's tollbooth and was pleased to see the rainbow bumper sticker proudly mounted on the sliding glass window.

"Why, you must work twenty-four hours a day," Barbie greeted Hooter, who looked a bit under the weather. "We both have rainbows. Isn't it fun?"

"I tell you, I had the strangest thing happen last night," Hooter said as cars lined up behind the minivan.

She told Barbie all about the wild man in the alleyway who was sitting on a bag of guns out by the Dumpster and trying to shoot off his privates.

"Then, you know that big trooper I dated last night . . . ? Well," Hooter interrupted her own story. "I guess you got no reason to know him. But I had to drive him back home to his mama, and he wanted a little loving but I wouldn't give him none 'cause his mama right there in the next room, pro'bly with a glass up against the wall, listening to see what we was doin'.

"So I say to him, 'Why you still living with your mama and if I did what you wanted, what if she walked in?' Can you imagine?" Hooter said to Barbie. "*Can you imagine* riding that big trooper's horsie and right in the middle of it, there's mama in her nightie standing next to the couch. I think that's sick. I'm telling you, that man's a strange one."

"What horsie?" Barbie was horrified and confused.

"Just his little pet name for what I'm telling you is the biggest . . ." Hooter's comment was obliterated by honking horns. ". . . ever saw, girl-friend! Only, I ain't 'zactly seen it in person yet. But based on the com-motion it was making as it tried to bust out of its stall, you get what I'm saying? Uh huh? That's one big . . ." More horns blared.

"Well, you would think I'm causing a lot of commotion myself," Bar-bie confided. "All these people are just staring at me and honking and nearly running me off the road," she added as a huge pickup truck with mud flaps swerved to another line and Bubba Loving flipped a bird and yelled something at Barbie's minivan. "How does he know my name?" she exclaimed to Hooter. "I've never seen that man before in my life and he just yelled my name. I'm good at reading lips."

"You don't say," Hooter remarked, staring after the pickup truck. "I sure do hate it when they got them 'Federate flags on their windshield and *Bubba* on the vanity plate. Good thing he went over to the Smart Tag line 'cause I don't like 'Federate money whether I got gloves on or not! I won't touch it if I got a choice, uh uh! I don't think he say your name, though." Hooter was reluctant to tell her. "Fact is, I doubt he know your name."

"I'm pretty sure he said *Fogg.*"

"Nuh uh. He say something else that wasn't the least bit nice, girl-friend. I think that Bubba redneck call you a *fag.*"

"Well now, if that doesn't take the cake." Barbie was mystified. "You positive he didn't say *Fogg?*"

"I ain't gonna go ask him. He a mean redneck and probably got a hood in his closet, you know what I'm saying?"

Barbie didn't know what she meant.

"You know, a white sheet," Hooter explained. "He probably some cross-burning gran dragon for the Ku Klack Klan!"

"Anyone who burns a cross will go straight to hell," Barbie said with pious indignation.

"I don't care where people like him go after they's dead. I just don't want them stopping at my tollbooth and maybe trying to find out where I live so they can shoot out my windows and burn a cross in my yard. Except I don't have a yard. I guess they could burn a cross in the parking lot, though."

"So many crazy people." Barbie was getting discouraged. "The world just gets worse every day."

"Ever since the new milminimum, everything's worse. Don't see how they could get worser." Hooter could not have agreed with Barbie Fogg more.

A ndy didn't see how things could get much worse, either, as he turned off 9th Street, bound for the morgue with Regina sitting in the passenger's seat smacking gum and playing with the scanner.

"How do you turn on the lights and siren in this thing?" she asked.

"We're not turning on the lights and siren," he told her.

"Why not? You're responding to a murder, aren't you? Seems to me you could turn them on if you wanted to."

"No, I couldn't. We're not pursuing anyone or in a hurry." He worked hard to keep his irritation to himself.

"Well, aren't we in a pissy mood today?" Regina commented as she stared out the window at people aimlessly searching for parking places and waiting in the cold to cross the street.

She did not have to subject herself to common inconveniences, and for the first time in years, she was happy. She could not believe she had escaped the EPU at last and was inside a brand-new state police car, on her way to the morgue with Andy.

"I will make a very good partner for you," she went on. "I know a lot of things you don't and probably more things than that medical examiner woman does, for that matter. I bet you don't know what to do if you get stuck in quicksand, now do you?"

"I don't intend to ever get stuck in quicksand," Andy replied. "I would avoid it."

"Huh. That's easy to say. If it was a simple thing to avoid quicksand, then people wouldn't get stuck in it and sink to death. So what you do is spread your arms and legs and try to float." She showed him. "Then you put your walking stick under your back to keep your hips from sinking, and you pull your legs out and escape. And if you want to break down a door, you kick the lock, and you can pick a car lock with an Allen wrench and a bobby pin. I also know how to survive python, alligator, and killer-bee attacks," she bragged. "And I could deliver a baby in a taxi-cab or save myself if my parachute doesn't open."

"Only because you've obviously read *The Worst Case Scenario Sur-vival Handbook*," Andy replied, to her annoyance and surprise. "And just because you read about a dire situation while you're safely sitting in the mansion doesn't mean you could really save yourself if the worst really happened."

"Papa gave it to me for my birthday," Regina smugly said. "And he's never given that book to my sisters because they don't care about adventure and are cowards. I can just imagine Faith trying to land a plane after the pilot has a heart attack, and Constance would panic to death if she were lost in the desert or adrift at sea."

She rummaged in her knapsack and pulled out the bright yellow little handbook.

"So, what would *you* do if your parachute didn't open?" She tested him as she smoothed open a dog-eared page that was stained with what looked like chocolate.

"I would check my chute before I jumped," Andy replied as his patience tightened like a guitar string about to snap.

"What about if lightning struck?"

"I would avoid it."

"Would you stand under a tall tree?" Regina was determined to evoke a wrong answer from him.

"Of course not."

"What if you were diving a hundred feet down and ran out of air?" Regina asked in a confrontational manner.

"I wouldn't."

Regina smacked the handbook shut and shoved it back into her knapsack.

"When do you think I can get a uniform?" she asked with mounting anger.

"After you attend the academy and graduate. We're talking the better part of a year, assuming the academy accepts you."

"They have to accept me."

"Just because your father's the governor doesn't mean anybody has to accept you," Andy replied a bit sharply. "I don't intend to tell anybody who you are beyond saying that you're an intern who's riding along with me."

"Then I'll tell them," she countered, opening the window and flicking out the gum.

"That would be very unwise. Don't you think it's time you let people like you for yourself instead of for who you are? And don't throw anything out the window."

"What if they don't?" Her mood wilted. "And you know they won't. Nobody has ever liked me even when they know who Papa is. So why would they like me if they didn't know who he is?"

"I guess you're just going to have to see what happens and face reality for once," Andy said as he turned off on Clay Street. "And if people don't like you, you have only yourself to blame."

"Bullshit. None of it's my fault." Regina's voice got louder and more strident. "I can't help the way I was born!"

"It's your choice to be rude and selfish," Andy said. "And I'm not hard of hearing—yet. Lower your voice. Maybe for once you might think about others instead of yourself. How about the poor person back there who steps on that gum you just threw out? How would you like it if you stepped on someone's gum when you were dressed for work, in a hurry, couldn't afford new shoes, and had a sick baby at home?"

This had never occurred to Regina.

"The only reason no one likes you is because you don't like anybody, either. People sense that," Andy went on as he pulled in behind the modern brick building called Biotech II that housed the chief medical examiner's office and the forensic laboratories.

"I don't know how," Regina confessed. "You can't know how to do something if no one has ever shown you. And all my life, everyone has treated me special because of who I am, so I've never had a chance to think about anybody else."

"Well, now you've got your chance." Andy parked in a visitor's space and got out of the car. "Because I'm going to treat you like shit if you treat me like shit. Maybe it's good you're at the morgue. You can practice being nice to dead people and they won't care if you can't pull it off."

"That's a great idea!" Regina enthusiastically followed Andy along the sidewalk and inside the lobby. "Except how do you worry about someone's feelings if they can't feel anything anymore?"

"It's called sympathy, it's called having compassion. Words foreign to you, no doubt." Andy stopped at the information desk and signed in. "Try to think about what the poor people down here have been through and how sad their friends and loved ones are, and for once don't focus on yourself. And if you're obnoxious, that's the end of your internship because I'm not going to put up with it, and I know the chief won't put up with it. She'll throw you out on your ass in a nanosecond."

"Papa can fire her," Regina pointed out.

"She'll eat your papa for breakfast," Andy said.

He handed Regina a small notebook and a pen as electronic locks clicked free and they entered the chief medical examiner's office.

"Take notes," he instructed her. "Write down everything the doctors say and keep your mouth shut."

Regina was not accustomed to taking orders, but the instant she noticed graphic autopsy photographs on desks in the front office, she began to lose her usual bravado and self-absorption. The clerks knew Andy very well, it seemed, and were very friendly and flirtatious with him. Regina was stunned and thrilled when Andy introduced her as his intern.

"Lucky you," one of the clerks said, giving Regina a sly wink.

"Why can't I be your intern?" another one coyly asked him.

"Whoa, baby. I'd be happy to let you teach me a thing or two."

"We're here on the fisherman's case." Andy was all business. "Is Doctor Sawamatsu doing the case?"

"No. He hasn't come in yet."

"What about the chief?" Andy was relieved that Dr. Sawamatsu wasn't in and hoped he wouldn't show up at all.

In the first place, Dr. Sawamatsu's English was poor, and Andy had a very difficult time understanding him, especially when he started throwing around medical terms. Dr. Sawamatsu was also clinical and came across as rather cold-blooded and cynical, and Andy took great exception to anyone who was callous around victims, alive or dead. Worst of all, Sawamatsu had repeatedly bragged to Andy about a secret collection of souvenirs that included artificial joints, breast and penile implants, a glass eye, pieces and parts from plane crashes and other disasters, and Andy doubted that the chief knew about her assistant's unseemly hobby, because the collection was at his home and not at the office.

"Maybe I'll just tell her," Andy thought out loud as he followed a long carpeted corridor to Dr. Scarpetta's office suite.

"Tell who what?" Regina looked around in wonder, pausing to stare inside offices where microscopes were perched on desks and X-rays were clipped to light boxes.

"Don't ask questions, and as we say in bomb investigations, *don't touch or move anything in any way,*" Andy warned her. "And everything you hear and see can never be divulged to anyone, including your family."

"I'll try," she replied. "But I've never kept a secret before."

Barbie Fogg routinely listened to secrets and had a few of her own. Worried that Lennie might have secrets, too, she decided to take the next exit and loop around so she could return to the Exact Change tollbooth and confide to Hooter that Barbie was worried about her marriage.

"Lennie's leaving town and came right out and said he wants a girl-friend! You don't think he's having affairs on the road because I won't have sex anymore, do you?" Barbie poured out her heart to Hooter. "Well, anyway, Lennie sells real estate, meaning he's often at home with nothing much to do, so he usually watches the twins and certainly has plenty of time for affairs. And to make matters worse, he's heading out to Charlotte for an important meeting and I'll pretty much be stuck at the house. Meaning it's possible I won't be seeing you for a whole week."

Both Barbie and Hooter were disappointed. It seemed they had been friends forever.

"Oh dear, I didn't realize how much I'm going to miss you," Barbie confessed.

"Lord, Lord, I gonna have separate anxiety without you coming through my booth! Who I gonna talk to anymore? Why he gotta go to Charlotte? You know, I get so sick and tired of people going to North Carolina. Like it some kind of promise land or something. You know, I never even been to North Carolina. What so special about it, huh?"

"You got any vacation time with the city?" Barbie asked as more cars piled up behind her and blared their horns. "Why don't you come to the NASCAR race with me tomorrow night? I would just love it and you could see all those handsome drivers. But you'd need to take the after-noon off because I like to get there early and hang around the pits and wait for the drivers to come out and climb into their cars. Sometimes they let you get your picture taken with them. Oh, if only you knew what that was like! Standing arm in arm with a handsome stock-car dri-ver in his tight, colorful fireproof jumpsuit!"

"Now, I sure as heck never been to no NASCAR race and I never seen no Afric-American drivers, neither. So I wouldn't know." Hooter paid no attention to the endless line of impatient motorists. "Maybe I take the whole day off! I ain't had no vacation since my sister got married and I was in the wedding. The mattress of honor." Hooter beamed at the mem-ory of being decked out in that long pink dress with see-through sleeves and beads and bows. "That was sure a time, let me tell you, girlfriend."

"Yeah! How about visiting with your fucking girlfriend some other time, you queerbaits, and hurry up!" Bubba Loving was back in his truck with mud flaps.

"What on earth is queerbait?" Barbie asked as she jotted down her phone number on a Post-it. "Something you catch strange fish with? And why is that same vulgar man screaming about fishing?"

"Take one to know one!" Hooter yelled back at Bubba.

"Here, sweetie," Barbie said to Hooter, "you ring me up in the next few hours. I'll be at the Baptist Campus Ministry, and you just call and let me know if you can come to the race so I don't give the ticket to some other lucky person. Please come! Oh dear, I just love having girl-friends to talk to!"

"I just might do it. In fact, I will, I will. Damn right I will." Hooter was getting excited by the idea. "You count me in unless I can't get no one to cover my booth for me. How 'bout you pick me up right here at, well, let's see. What time?"

"Two o'clock sharp."

"I'll slide on home and change and be waiting for you right here at my booth unless something come up. Then we have plenty of time to talk about your rotten sex life."

"Wouldn't that be wonderful." Barbie cheerfully waved good-bye as she drove on and forgot the seventy-five cent toll, setting off the alarms. "The rainbow is working! Magic, magic everywhere!"

"Sweet-talk your girlfriend another time when we aren't waiting until Heck freezes over to go through the tollbooth!" Lamonia yelled from her Dodge Dart.

Lamonia was understandably in a foul mood. First, she had gotten handcuffed because of her bad night vision, now she was stuck in traffic because two interracial lesbians were flirting at the tollbooth and a racist redneck was engaging in road rage. What had gone so wrong in the world? Dear Lord, have mercy, Lamonia thought. The entire planet was self-destructing and it was just a matter of time before Jesus would get fed up and come back, and Lamonia wasn't ready for the Rapture. No, sir. She told Jesus every Sunday to please hold on for a while, because Lamonia had so many friends and neighbors who were going to be left behind if He came in on a cloud and the Rapture lifted up all Believers.

"Give your life to Jesus," Lamonia said to Hooter as she fed a dollar bill into a cotton-gloved hand.

"You tell it, girlfriend," Hooter said, dropping three quarters into the bin and returning a quarter change.

"I'm not your girlfriend or anybody's girlfriend!" Lamonia wasn't the least bit subtle about it. "Ask forgiveness for your sins and pray to Jesus. Ask Him to take your life and do something with it, you hear me? Because He's coming soon, and you don't want to be sitting in that little booth of yours and giving in to perversions with strangers and suddenly find half the cars coming through don't have drivers 'cause they've been Raptured up into Heaven!"

"Tell it," Hooter encouraged the pulpiteer. "You tell it, girl."

Lamonia needed no encouragement. "Two men are working in a field, and suddenly one of them is gone. Two women are doing laundry in the Laundromat, and suddenly, one of them is gone. You'll be taking toll money, and suddenly half the drivers will be gone and you just better hope you aren't still sitting in your booth, because if you are, that means you've been left behind!"

"I ready for the Rapture, girl," Hooter assured Lamonia as the two of them exchanged phone numbers. "Oh yes, I ready and looking forward to it. Always have been looking forward to it! Jesus be coming back. I always knew He would." Hooter stared up at the ceiling of her booth. "You come on now, Jesus. You just come right on. I be waiting for you and won't even charge you no toll when you float down on your cloud!"

"No!" Lamonia protested. "Don't tell Him to come now! There's too much work to do, you silly woman! Look out there at all them sinners! Just miles and miles of them. Pray for them first, child!"

Hooter gazed out at miles of honking cars.

"Yeah, you right, girl. Most them folks out there ain't ready for Jesus. Look how upset and nasty they is. Hmmm hmmm." Hooter shook her head sadly. "So we ask Jesus to hold off a little longer. Just give us a little time, Jesus," she prayed loudly as Lamonia lurched out of the tollbooth and rear-ended another car. "Please, Lord in Heaven, just give me Saturday afternoon off, you got that? Just one little vacation," Hooter prayed. "That all I ask, Jesus."

Twenty-two

"Dear Lord in Heaven," Dr. Faux prayed as he and Fonny Boy drifted in the bateau. "We've been out here all night and half the morning, and I'm so cold and hungry I don't think I'll survive another hour. Please help us."

Fonny Boy had given up on trying to get into the locked compartment and was blowing sour sounds on his harmonica and trying out various methods of hand effects and breathing techniques. He was on the verge of wishing that he and the dentist would be captured and returned to the storeroom, and regretted he had not bothered to carry sodas and food on board. But then, he had assumed they would reach the mainland long before supplies became an issue.

"Lord-a-mercy, I reckon the current's taking us clean back to the island," he told Dr. Faux.

"I don't see land at all. Not anywhere, Fonny Boy. And if we were near the island, we would have been spotted by now and maybe blindfolded and forced to walk the plank. I think we might just have drifted into the sanctuary, and if so, no watermen will be in the area, and we will languish and die out here."

"Nah," Fonny Boy replied. "You can make out the current." He pointed out gentle ripples of moving water. "But nigh as peace, they'll figure we made off in the bateau and if we don't make a hurry now, they'll be on us and we'll have to cite the Bible!"

"Unless they figure we're on the mainland, and you know they won't look for us there. You sure you can't remember the combination to that damn padlock? Maybe there's a flare gun in that compartment or even a mirror for sending signals."

Fonny Boy had known the combination at one time, and he was terribly frustrated as he strained to recall it. He had tried every birthday in his family, Tangier's zip code, and several telephone numbers, all to no avail. He rapped the harmonica on the side of the bateau to knock out excess spit and tried a little straight harp, playing a melody in the key of C, and as usual, starting with hole 4.

"Think hard, Fonny Boy," Dr. Faux tried to encourage him. "Usually people use tricks to remember things, so my guess is your dad used some sort of association to come up with a combination that he wouldn't forget. Are there any other numbers that might be important to your dad? What about your parents' anniversary?"

Fonny Boy couldn't remember that, either. He drew on the low end of the harmonica, trying a little blues jamming, like his hero, Dan Aykroyd.

"Now, I know some of the watermen use compasses," the dentist kept trying. "Possible there is a compass heading your father routinely uses when he comes out to check the crab pots?"

The words *crab pot* floated out of the barely moving bateau, then settled into the water and began to drift to the bottom, where a large collection of *Callinectes* (Greek for "beautiful swimmer") *sapidus* (Latin for "tasty") were enjoying the quiet and security of the crab sanctuary. Clustered together were the fugitives from the bucket, and one of them, an especially handsome jimmy with big blue claws and arms, decided to investigate the human voices and faint strains of a harmonica. He swam up through the murk, leaving his friends behind in a cloud of silt, and some twenty feet below the surface of the bay he spied the bottom of a bateau and heard voices again.

"Nah. He don't use neither compass. Don't need one, noways," a young male said, and the crab recognized the voice as belonging to that skinny blond Islander who was always talking about pirate treasure when he was out potting in the dark early mornings.

"Hmmm. What about your post office box?" another voice asked, and the jimmy didn't recognize this one, but he sounded as if he was from the mainland.

Fonny Boy tried that number, but the padlock wasn't interested.

"A lucky number, maybe? Does your dad have a lucky number?"

The only luck-related number Fonny Boy could think of was thirteen, and the padlock wouldn't budge. He tried playing straight harp style and "Oh Susannah" was almost recognizable.

"What about a favorite food or drink that might have a number in it?" Dr. Faux was not going to give up. "Such as Heinz fifty-seven sauce, Seven-Up, or two-alarm chili?"

"My daddy, he likes the Seven-Up," Fonny Boy said with a glimmer of hope. "He's right fond of it with Spanky's ice cream, drinks more'an it of anybody I ever seen. But the combination, it takes four numbers and seven is only one number."

"What if you added the *up* part?"

Fonny Boy decided to stay in the middle of the harmonica and stick to blow notes.

"Is there a number that might mean *up*, Fonny Boy? Come on, think!"

"The compass, it ain't got neither *up* on it. Only north, south, east, and west," Fonny Boy replied.

"Up could be north, now couldn't it?" Dr. Faux persisted. "You know how people say they're going *up* north to New York or *down* south to Florida. Try three-sixty. That's three numbers and is due north. So maybe he used seven and three-sixty for *seven-up*."

The jimmy's fusiform body propelled itself quickly back down to the bottom, where he warned his frightened friends.

"There's seven of 'em up thar!" he exclaimed. "And they'se breaking the law by potting in the sanctutary and I'm of a mind to get 'em warranted!"

The jimmy assumed that the seven watermen up there in the bateau were a posse looking for the crabs and the trout, although the crabs hadn't seen the trout for quite some time. Or maybe the *Seven-Up gang*, as the jimmy began to think of them, were pirates the governor had promised immunity to if they would find the crabs and the trout and return them to the mansion in the bucket. Blue crabs were quite familiar with pirates and were neither impressed with nor afraid of them. Pirates were too angry and drunk to bother chasing after crabs, and this had been true for hundreds of years. Nor was the life of any crustacean made a whit better by all of the old cannons, coins, and jewels that crabs routinely scuttled over on the bottom of the bay. Crabs frankly didn't give a damn about treasure.

But that blond Islander named Fonny Boy certainly did, the jimmy thought as he scuttled through billowing silt to a shelf in the bay floor, where the wreckage of a sloop appeared in the murk. The old wreck had been blasted with cannon fire and sank in a shoal, and over the centuries the current had nudged the broken vessel along the bottom of the bay until it had settled in its present location. The jimmy rooted around near a rusting anchor and seized a small piece of iron. He paddled furiously with his swimming legs and sculled back up to the bateau, climbed on the small outboard motor, and tossed the piece of iron up in the air. It landed in Fonny Boy's lap right when he was in the middle of practicing a *fish face* by sucking in his cheeks to play cleaner single notes on his harmonica.

"Why, I'll swagger!" Fonny Boy cried out in surprise. "Look!"

He studied the piece of iron and knew it was extremely old and very likely from a sunken ship.

"Treasure's nigh as peace falling from Heaven and it's for to tell there's a picaroon ship down thar!" he exclaimed in uncontrollable excitement as he realized that finally, after such a hard life, he had met his destiny. "We have to mark the spot or we likete lose it!"

285

The only way to mark the location was to drop a crab pot into the water, and minutes later, the fugitive crabs watched a wire cage descend through the depths and dangle well above the bottom, because the rope was too short.

The jimmy crooked his funny mouth into a smile, certain what would happen next because the Islanders were so predictable. The Island boy's greed would excite him into poor judgment, and soon enough, the Seven-Up gang would be in jail.

Possum's scheme was going along well, too, as he cut up different colored T-shirts and sewed and glued the pieces into a pattern that was beginning to resemble a flag.

"See what I'm doing, girl?" Possum whispered to Popeye.

He smoothed the flag on the bed, and Popeye was startled by a grinning skull smoking a cigarette.

"We got us a NASCAR flag for the races," Possum proudly whispered. "See, we hang it up at the pit where we pretend to be a pit crew and I'll make sure somebody look for the flag and come save us. Or if that don't work, maybe Smoke will like the flag so much, he'll be nicer to us, and when we escape to Tangerine Island, I'll find a way to sneak off with you and we'll run to the nearest fisherman's house."

Possum dipped the needle in and out of the flag, sewing on letters that spelled *Jolly Goodwrench*.

"Then I'll give you back to Sup'intendent Hammer, and the police will forget all about me shooting at Moses Custer. Maybe I even get to come see you now and then. Maybe Sup'intendent Hammer give me a job babysitting you. What do you think?"

Popeye thought this was a wonderful idea. Possum continued to piece together the flag with the T-shirt scraps, needle and thread, and Super Glue. The result was not quite what he had intended, because he was realizing that the flag would be one-sided and would have to be mounted rather than displayed from a pole, antenna, or stick. Otherwise, he was pleased with the result, which was not recognizable as NASCAR or a Jolly Roger, but a hybrid of both.

Possum tacked the finished work up on the wall and sat on his bed imagining Smoke's reaction as Possum worried about going to the race on Saturday and wondered what plans and hopes might fly apart. Possum sure didn't want any more trouble. If only he could go back to his family's basement and wander the streets after dark again without any fear of being arrested. Possum had seen on the TV news that Moses was still in the hospital, and thank goodness, his condition was now stable. Possum's heart trembled as he recalled pointing the pistol at the poor man on the pavement and jerking the trigger.

He still didn't understand what had gotten into him, except that he was frightened of Smoke. Possum also knew that if he acted different from the other dogs or seemed to have a conscience, he was going to end up with a bullet in his head one of these days. Oh, how his momma would scream and cry if she heard on the news that Possum had been murdered, his body dumped somewhere along with the carcass of a little black-and-white dog. If only Ben Cartwright or Little Joe or Hoss could help him out. But in all the episodes of *Bonanza* that Possum had watched, he had never seen a black boy on the Ponderosa.

"Maybe he don't like blacks," Possum talked to himself as he envisioned Ben Cartwright with his leather vest and snow white hair. "Blacks was slaves. So who I'm fooling thinking anybody on a horse is gonna ride in to rescue me? Least the Cartwrights don't fly no 'Federate flag, though." Possum gazed at his Jolly Goodwrench flag displayed behind the TV. "Never seen no 'Federate flag or slaves on the Ponderosa neither, just Hop Sing and he's Chinese and could come and go as he pleased, long as he cooked and cleaned."

Possum wondered if there might be something he could do to make it up to the Cartwrights, who certainly must be terribly disappointed in his recent run of criminal behavior.

"I sorry about Moses," Possum was talking to Hoss now.

"Well, little buddy, what you did was wrong," Hoss answered.

"B'lieve me, I know, Hoss. But I was scared and Smoke woulda killed me or beat me bad and maybe drowned Popeye if I hadn't pulled the trigger. I wish I could do it over and run away before it was too late. But it is too late, and here I am in the clubhouse."

"You gotta make it right, Little Buddy," Hoss said from beneath his white ten-gallon hat. "What's done is done, but it ain't too late to make it right."

"How?" Possum asked Ben this.

Ben was sitting high on his horse, ready to ride off to Carson City on an errand. He looked down at Possum and smiled a little.

"Why don't you start with calling Moses and apologizing?" he suggested, flicking the reins. "Then you're probably going to need to turn yourself in to Sheriff Coffey," he added as he galloped off.

Possum sat in the dark and slowly flipped open his cell phone. His heart thudded and he strained to make sure no one was stirring inside the RV. He heard not a sound and called directory assistance and for fifty cents was connected to the hospital where he'd heard on the news Moses Custer was a patient.

"Moses Custer, please," Possum said quietly.

"What's your name? He's only taking calls from people on his list."

Possum groped for a way to trick the lady. "I number three on his list, ma'am."

He heard her checking and hoped Dale Earnhardt's number would prove lucky. It did, sort of.

"It says Mr. and Mrs. Brutus Custer, so which are you?"

Possum had a high-pitched, soft voice that could easily pass for a woman's. He was a bit offended but knew he didn't sound like a Brutus.

"This Mrs. Custer," he said. "I so worried about my daddy-in-law. I can't sleep or eat. Tell him if he don't feel up to talking, I'll try another time."

Possum had given the receptionist an *out*, and was getting cold feet himself. Then Ben Cartwright turned around in the saddle and looked sternly at Possum.

"Hold on," the receptionist said.

"Hello," a male voice was on the line. "This Jessie? How you doin', baby? Why ain't you come to see me yet? I'm going home today."

"Mr. Custer, this ain't Jessie, but I just got to talk to you. So please don't hang up." Possum's heart was beating so hard he thought it might break his ribs.

"Who is this?" Moses was instantly suspicious.

"I can't tell you 'cept to say I'm so sorry for what happened to you. It was wrong, wrong, wrong, and I didn't mean it. But I was forced."

"Who is this?" Moses demanded in an upset voice. "Why you be messing with me? You one of them pirates, ain't you!"

"Yes. But I don't wanna be," Possum confessed.

"The hell you don't wanna be. I knew quick enough you wasn't Jessie, 'cause you don't sound like her."

Possum took a deep breath. "I can't talk long. But I just wanted to tell you I sorry for what I done and if I can find a way to make it up to you, I promise I will, Mr. Custer. And you be sure to keep lots of police around, 'cause them road dogs is already talking about finding you and finishing you off. Their leader's name is Smoke and his girlfriend's Unique and shot that poor Seven-Eleven lady last night, and Smoke say he kill me if I didn't shoot at you when we took your truck and the reefer at the pumpkin stand."

"Sons of bitches! Let 'em show their asses and then they'll see what trouble's all about!"

"I do my best to talk 'em out of it."

"You? Who the hell is this . . . ?"

Moses was yelling, and Possum, beginning to panic, ended the call.

"What the fuck's going on in here?" Smoke suddenly swung open Possum's bedroom door. "Who you talking to?"

Possum tucked the cell phone under the covers just in time.

"Just talking to Popeye about our new flag." Possum thought quickly. "What you think, Smoke?"

Smoke walked in drinking a breakfast beer and looked long and hard at the big flag tacked to the wall.

"What is this shit?" Smoke asked in a hard, mean voice.

"You don't got a flag, and I was thinking that all pirates got flags, just like NASCAR drivers got colors. So I put this together for you, Smoke, like I said I would. Thought you could put it up in the pit when we go to the race tomorrow night. Then, when we escape to the island, you can hang it up there so everybody will know not to mess with you."

"If you're going to talk to yourself, keep your fucking voice down. You woke me up," Smoke said. "Now I'm going to be tired the rest of the day."

Smoke calmed down and looked thoughtful as he studied the flag from different angles. He got an idea and tugged it loose from the wall.

"Maybe I'll just shoot the damn dog and wrap it in this thing. We'll leave a little present on Hammer's doorstep," Smoke cruelly said.

Popeye, who could play possum just as well as Possum could, pretended to be asleep again, and Possum pretended he didn't care what happened to the dog.

"But that wouldn't be as good as getting Hammer and that Trooper Brazil," Possum reminded him because Smoke tended to forget most things these days. "And we need the dog to get them to show up at the race so we can blow them away. Then Cat fly us off in the helicopter, and we live fat lives on the island."

"And how the fuck do you intend to set up all this?" Smoke said, tossing the flag on top of Popeye, who didn't budge.

"That easy," Possum replied. "I send an e-mail to Captain Bonny and get him to do it. We know he got connections, right? So he can get the plan to Hammer and make her think you The Man NASCAR Driver with that pretty girlfriend, Unique, and the rest of us is your pit crew who happened to find Popeye wandering on the road. So we picked her up but ain't turning her over to no one 'less Hammer and Trooper Brazil can ID her for sure. So they show up at the race and come look for us, and the minute she starts screaming 'cause she's so happy to see Popeye, we pull out our guns, shoot everybody, run to the helicopter, and fly away."

"Set it up," Smoke ordered as he chugged the beer and tossed the can on the floor.

Twenty-three

The chief medical examiner, Dr. Kay Scarpetta, was in her office when Andy knocked on her open door.

"Doctor Scarpetta? Hi," he said politely and a bit nervously. "If this isn't a bad time, I'd like to talk to you about the unidentified man who burned up on Canal Street last night."

"Come in." Dr. Scarpetta looked up from a stack of death certificates she was reviewing. "Have we met?"

"No, ma'am. But I've worked with Dr. Sawamatsu before."

Andy introduced himself, and then explained that Regina was an intern with the state police, although he did not refer to her by name.

"And your name is?" Scarpetta inquired of her.

Regina stared at her, wide-eyed and tongue-tied. Regina had never met such a powerful woman before, and she was completely taken aback. Dr. Scarpetta was a very handsome blonde, maybe in her mid-forties, and was dressed in a sharp pinstriped suit. Why would someone who has everything going for her want to work with dead patients for a living? What should Regina say to explain herself, without giving away her identity and causing a stink?

"Reggie," Regina blurted out.

"Officer Reggie," Dr. Scarpetta said with a nod from her judge's chair behind her big desk. "And you'll vouch for her?" she said as a bit of a warning to Andy. "I don't routinely have police interns down here."

"I'll take full responsibility," Andy said, giving Regina a sharp glance.

"Oh, don't worry," Regina eagerly spoke for herself. "I won't talk about anything I see or hear and won't touch or move anything in any way."

"A very good idea," Dr. Scarpetta replied, and she directed her attention to Andy. "The man has been identified by fingerprints. His name is Caesar Fender, a forty-one-year-old black male from Richmond. And we have a full house this morning, I'm sorry to say. Have you ever seen an autopsy?" she asked Regina.

"No, but not because I didn't want to." Regina was desperate to impress this legendary woman doctor.

"I see."

"When I took high school biology, I was the only one in my group who didn't mind dissecting a frog," Regina boasted. "Guts have never bothered me at all. I don't think it would even bother me watching somebody die, like a death row inmate, maybe."

"Well, I didn't like dissecting things in high school," Dr. Scarpetta replied, much to Regina's surprise. "I felt very sorry for the frog."

"I did, too," Andy replied. "Mine was alive and I didn't think it was right to kill it. It still bothers me."

"And I certainly am bothered when I've watched people die, inmates or otherwise. I guess you've never spent any time at scenes or in the E.R.," Dr. Scarpetta said, and she thought Andy's name seemed familiar as she shuffled through the papers on her desk and pulled out a report.

Sure enough, the name of the officer who had submitted the poisoned chocolates to the labs was Trooper Andy Brazil.

"I have something to discuss with you," she said to him. "I think we need a moment of privacy."

It was her way of politely ordering Regina out of the office.

"Please step out for a minute," Andy said to her. "We'll be right with you."

"How can I be an intern if you're always making me leave?" Regina said, a hint of her generally obnoxious personality creeping into her voice.

"I'm not always making you leave," Andy replied, showing her to the door and pretty much pushing her out. "Stay," he said, as if she were Frisky.

He shut the door and returned to Dr. Scarpetta's desk, pulling out a chair and seating himself.

"I just got the lab report for the chocolates," the chief began. "This is serious enough that Doctor Pond wanted it brought to my attention immediately because I'm quite familiar with poisonings by laxatives. I had a case several years ago of a woman whose kids laced her hot chocolate with Ex-Lax—supposedly as a joke. The woman developed multiple organ failure, pulmonary edema, and went into a coma and died."

She handed Andy the report as she went on to explain it.

"Tests were conducted with High Performance Liquid Chromatography, and the chocolates in question are, in fact, positive for phenolphthalein, or Pt, in various concentrations. Normal straight Ex-Lax, if taken in the proper doses, contains approximately ninety milligrams of Pt. But just one of the chocolates in the box you submitted contains in excess of two hundred milligrams, which at the very least would, if ingested, cause fluid and electrolyte loss, which is very dangerous, especially if the victim is older and not enjoying good health."

"Well, that sums up the governor," Andy said with growing concern. "What about fingerprints? Did the labs find anything on the paper the box was wrapped in? And was the handwritten note really written by the governor?"

Dr. Scarpetta sorted through several other reports.

"They did recover a latent by using the Luma-Lite and fluorescing dyes, and the print was run through AFIS," she informed him. "They got a hit, and here is the identification number, which you can check yourself with the state police computer." She wrote it down for him. "As for a documents examination, an exemplar of the governor's handwriting was inconsistent with the note that accompanied the chocolates."

"So the note is a forgery." Andy wasn't surprised.

"That's inconclusive because we need to get an official exemplar. The one we used preliminarily was from a letter the governor allegedly sent to Dr. Sawamatsu."

"Right. And we shouldn't assume that the letter is genuine," Andy agreed with her. "Or that the governor actually signed it himself."

"Legally, we can't assume that."

"Which reminds me," Andy said. "And I hope this isn't out of line, Doctor Scarpetta. But it concerns me that Doctor Sawamatsu collects souvenirs, very inappropriate ones, or at least he brags as much to a lot of us. Do you ever go to his house?"

"No," she replied, her expression turning hard.

One thing she absolutely would not tolerate was disrespect toward the dead. Nor was any member of her staff allowed to even think about collecting mementos, money, personal effects, weapons, drugs, or alcohol from a body or a crime scene.

"Maybe you should drop by unannounced to see him sometime," Andy suggested. "At his house."

"Don't worry," she answered. "I will."

"I'll get on the poisoned chocolates case right away," Andy promised. "And I suppose the documents examiner needs an exemplar of the suspect's handwriting, too."

"I wasn't aware you had a suspect," she said. "But yes. Absolutely. If you can get his or her handwriting, that would be a very good thing. And I suggest you get an exemplar from the intended victim, as well."

"From Superintendent Hammer?" Andy puzzled. "Why?"

"To rule out Munchausen's syndrome," Dr. Scarpetta matter-of-factly stated. "Poisoning with Ex-Lax most often occurs when an individual chronically ingests it to get attention—for example, to gain sympathy from a parent or spouse."

"You're saying it's possible Superintendent Hammer wanted us to think the governor or someone pretending to be the governor sent her poisoned chocolates because she wants attention? I can't believe that for a minute! You don't know her," Andy said politely but defensively.

"No, I don't know her at all," Dr. Scarpetta replied. "But she's new in a very demanding position, and if her experience has been anything like mine, the governor never returns her phone calls or invites her to parties at the mansion. So she may have set up a situation to make it appear the governor was trying to poison her. If he suddenly found himself a suspect in an attempted murder, that would certainly get his attention, I should think."

"Might I quickly ask you about Trish Thrash?" Andy jumped to that subject. "I know it's not my case, but I care about it a lot and as you may know, the killer left evidence on my doorstep for reasons unknown."

"Oh? So that was you?" Scarpetta frowned a little, and it was obvious to Andy that she was upset by the case. "A terribly mean-spirited, brutal death," she added. "But you were very wise to call Detective Slipper and not handle anything. We have recovered latent prints but have thus far gotten no hits in AFIS, and using STR we recovered DNA from the envelope but have gotten no hit on that, either. As for trace evidence, we did find several very long black hairs adhering to blood on the victim's clothing."

"Female hairs?"

"I don't know," Scarpetta replied. "But they could be."

"But no hits? Interesting," he mused. "I'm wondering if you got no hits because the individual is young with a juvenile record, which, of course, would be sealed. And until very recently, we weren't allowed to enter a juvenile's fingerprints or DNA profiles into the databases. So maybe we're looking for a hardened criminal who is young and has long black hair and might just be a female, who kills for sport and may even be associated with Smoke's highway pirates, who possibly assaulted Moses Custer and murdered the Seven-Eleven clerk last night."

"I don't know."

Scarpetta got up from her desk and opened the door, and Regina rushed back into the office, her notepad and pen ready.

"I don't want to take up your time, Doctor Scarpetta, but we are very concerned about this fisherman case," Andy went to the next item of business. "Especially since it's being called a hate crime, and I thought it a good idea to come down here personally to give you the information we have and see what you determine in the autopsy. A certain suspicious individual who witnessed the death claims the fisherman died of spontaneous human combustion that may have occurred when the hot lead and burning powder from a bullet caused synthetic fibers in the victim's shirt to ignite, thus supposedly explaining why he burst into flames. And let me add, this same suspicious individual is a prime suspect in the other case we were just discussing."

"How come you left out the part about my being poisoned?" Regina blurted out. Obviously, she had eavesdropped through the shut door and heard at least some of the private conversation.

"We're not going to talk about that right now," Andy warned her, knowing full well that if she divulged too much, it would become clear that she was not an intern but the pampered youngest daughter of the governor.

"It was awful!" Regina said to Dr. Scarpetta. "I ate these cookies and all of a sudden, I was doubled over with the worst pain I've ever felt in my life. Well, it wasn't really all of a sudden. I didn't feel too bad until I was hiding behind the boxwood in the garden, and then I got cramps and gas.

"Next thing I know, an EPU trooper's rushing me to the hospital where I was subjected to terrible indignities, like peeing in a little plastic cup and then watching a nurse put a little stick in it. They wanted number two also, but I had nothing left in me after that terrible attack. My pee turned pink and it scared me to death! I thought I was peeing blood, but the nurse said it was a chemical test that made it turn pink, but it meant the worst. Someone put Ex-Lax in my cookies and tried to kill me in cold blood!

"Or maybe someone was trying to kill someone else, but I was the innocent one who ate the cookies," she continued, clearly enjoying her own story. "The nurse said that pee usually has a pH of four or six, and the Ex-Lax makes pee turn pink if the pH exceeds seven."

Regina had no clue as to what all this meant, but she reckoned that pH was spelled *pee-h*, and whatever the h-part was, it must be devastatingly affected by Ex-Lax. She was fairly certain her h-factor was still off, since she had been weak and pale when she'd pried herself out of bed earlier.

"I'm just lucky I'm not one of your cases this morning!" Regina said with great drama.

"Yes, you are," Dr. Scarpetta agreed. "We're all lucky we aren't cases this morning or any morning. Trooper Brazil, we've X-rayed the fisherman's body already, and there is no bullet."

"Then what else might have caused him to burn up?"

"Of course, we'll test for accelerants and other chemicals," she said, slipping off her suit jacket and hanging it behind the door. "This is one of those cases when the external examination tells us quite a lot." She put on a lab coat. "For example, there is a great deal of charring that is more pronounced posteriorly, which is consistent with whatever burned him entering the body at about the midline of the chest. A little left of the midline, in the area of the heart, to be precise."

Andy and Regina followed Dr. Scarpetta out into the corridor.

"Then he didn't just burn up for no reason—not if something entered his chest," Andy said as Regina faithfully took notes.

"No weapon found at the scene?" the chief inquired.

"No, ma'am."

"How do you spell *accelerant?*" Regina was struggling, and the chief had not even gotten to the really big words yet.

"This suspicious individual who witnessed the death, did he mention to you what color the flames were or their intensity?" Dr. Scarpetta asked. "If they were an intense white, or blue, or red, for example?"

"Is midline one or two words?" Regina's voice was getting strained and petulant.

"No. I also wouldn't expect him to be reliable," Andy answered the chief.

"One word," she said to Regina.

"How do you spell *posteriorly?*"

"We'll worry about that later," Andy said in a tone that suggested Regina should not butt in again to volunteer indiscretions or to question spellings.

"Most significant is a whitish-gray lumpy residue inside the chest cavity, which is certainly consistent with some incendiary device or other material burning inside the body." Dr. Scarpetta stopped before the ladies' locker-room door. "You'll have to go in through the men's room," she instructed Andy. "Officer Reggie and I will meet you in the changing room and we'll get started."

"Insedentary?" Regina was beginning to panic, and her reaction to insecurity and fear was always unfortunate. "What kind of device? What the hell's a insedentary device?" Her disposition turned ugly. "I can't write this fast and it's not fair! Why should I know how to spell words like this? I'm not used to them. It's not like I hear them every day at the mansion!"

Dr. Scarpetta gave Regina a quizzical look. "Maybe this isn't a good time for you to see your first autopsy," the chief decided.

Andy got on his portable radio and raised Trooper Macovich on the air. "Can you return the package to its origin?" he asked in the code language of the EPU. "And I need you to check out an ID number with AFIS."

"Ten-fo," Macovich's voice came back, decidedly lacking in enthusiasm.

"Ten-twenty-five us in the morgue bay."

"Ten-fo. Be there in fifteen."

"Now you've really done it," Andy complained to Regina minutes later as they waited inside the frigid bay, sitting in plastic chairs by the Coke machine.

Two Swifty's Removal Service attendants were carrying a pouched body on a stretcher, making their way slowly and with difficulty down the ramp. The attendants, a man and a woman dressed in dark suits, seemed to be having a hard time getting the stretcher's legs to unfold.

"I didn't do a thing," Regina retorted. "You're not nice to me!"

"I told you to be quiet and mind your p's and q's and you didn't," Andy said.

The attendants were in a bind. They couldn't open the stretcher's legs, which meant they couldn't set down the dead person, who clearly was very big, and so there wasn't a free hand to open the van's tailgate.

"Look at that," Regina said, pointing at the attendants. "Why don't you go help those poor people instead of sitting here picking on me."

"As long as you stay in your chair and behave," said Andy, who didn't trust Regina for a minute.

He trotted over to the van.

"Here, let me help," he said to the female attendant.

"That's mighty nice of you," she replied, and gave him her end of the stretcher.

"I thought you got this thing fixed, Sammy," she irritably said to her partner as she tugged on the stuck stretcher legs.

"It just needed oiling, Maybeline."

"Then why ain't it working? These legs are froze stiff and one of the wheels was sticking the other day. Bet you didn't get that fixed, neither."

Sammy was silent as Andy held on with one hand and tried the van door with the other.

"How many times I got to tell you, don't say you getting something fixed and then I find out you didn't." Maybeline was furious. "Breaking my back doing this stinking job and you sitting around all the time watching the TV."

"I think the tailgate's locked," Andy said as the stretcher fishtailed and moved around perilously. "I think it's best you forget the legs and let's unlock the van. Then we can just slide the body in. We won't need to roll it."

"Can't roll it anyway, not with that stuck wheel Sammy couldn't bother to fix. What did you do with the keys?" Maybeline yanked at the stretcher's legs.

"In my pocket. I can't get 'em right this minute. I don't exactly have a hand free." Sammy was about to lose his temper. "Quit tugging on the legs before we drop the damn body on the floor!"

Regina, sensing an emergency, made her way over to the stretcher at the same time the buzzer sounded and the bay door began to screech open.

"I'll get the keys out for you," she told Sammy as she began to pat him down the way she saw cops search people on TV.

Regina had no reason to know that Sammy was extremely ticklish. When she started digging in the right front pocket of his pants, he shrieked and jumped six inches into the air. What Macovich witnessed when he drove into the bay was a crazy white man in a dark suit scream-ing with laughter and begging that ugly Crimm daughter to "Stop!" Next, the man grabbed himself, and the end of the stretcher he had been holding crashed to the floor and the huge black body pouch thud-ded on concrete. Andy, meanwhile, was shouting at Regina, and a woman attendant howled in pain as the stretcher pinched her hand and knocked her in the face, leaving her bleeding and holding her nose and a finger.

Macovich thought it wise to remain inside his unmarked car and ob-serve the altercation, which was quickly turning violent. Let's see what the pretty white boy does about this, he unkindly thought. That's what you get for being the teacher pet and babysitting the guv's nasty daugh-ter. Ha. Ha. Yeah, I ain't seen a good fight in a while. Wait 'til Doc Sca'petta sees what you doing out here. Huh. She kick your butt to the moon and complain to Sup'intendent Hammer.

"You idiot!" Andy shouted at Regina.

"You're the idiot!" she fired back at the top of her lungs.

"Now look at what you did!" Sammy bellowed at her. "You better hope this dead lady's family don't see her body all banged up! Wait 'til the funeral home find it with bruises and busted bones!"

"Dead bodies don't get bruises," Andy told him. "And I doubt any bones were broken."

Sammy was enraged by the sight of Maybeline bleeding, and he shoved Regina against the van and snatched his keys from her. She shoved him back and kicked his ankle. Then she socked him in the eye and bit his hand when he grabbed her by the arm. Andy got between them and was putting Sammy in a chokehold as the door leading inside the building flew open and Dr. Scarpetta, dressed in a surgical gown and gloves, emerged to see what all the commotion was about.

"That's enough," she announced in a voice that commanded attention. "Stop it right now!"

Twenty-four

By high noon, Fonny Boy had finally figured out how many turns to the left and right would spring open the padlock if he used the combination 7360, which was nautical, he supposed, for 7-Up.

As he had expected, the secret compartment contained a pint of Bowman's vodka, a pack of cigarettes, and, thank goodness, an Orion flare gun that was made of plastic and had a range of twenty-one miles. There were three cartridges, each with a candlepower of 15,000, and Fonny Boy fired all of them straight up into the air. He and Dr. Faux held their breath for a minute as they drifted in the bateau, still out in the middle of nowhere, the crab pot doggedly following them.

"You shouldn't have shot them all at once," Dr. Faux said, discouraged and peckish. "Why did you do that, Fonny Boy? It would have made more sense to fire one and wait for a while, then try a second round and eventually the last one. Now we're right back where we started from, lost at sea with no food or water. Put that pint of vodka back. All it will do is make you silly and more dehydrated."

What neither he nor Fonny Boy could possibly know at the time was that three Coast Guard pilots and an engineer were out in a bright orange Jayhawk helicopter on routine maneuvers. They were flying at an altitude of five hundred feet when three small fiery rockets streaked past their windshield and startled them considerably.

"Jesus Christ! What was that?" the pilot in command exclaimed into his microphone.

"Someone's shooting at us!" the engineer blurted out over the intercom from his bench seat in back.

"No, no, I think they're distress signals. Flares." The co-pilot calmed down his buddies. "Did you see how bright they were, like they were phosphorous?"

"We're not in a restricted area, are we?"

"No way."

"Gotta be flares, then."

The flares went out quickly but left rapidly fading white streaks across the sky that were easy to trace back to the source, providing one moved fast. The huge helicopter turned on an eastern heading and within minutes spotted a bateau with two people on board, who began waving their arms frantically. The Coast Guard pilots and crew also noticed a buoy that most likely was attached to a crab pot.

"Shit. Tangierians," the co-pilot said.

"Yup. And guess what? They're in the crab sanctuary," retorted the engineer. "Look at that bright yellow buoy. A crab pot."

At the same time they spotted the buoy, Fonny Boy and the dentist heard the unmistakable thudding of helicopter blades. Fonny Boy had been conditioned to resent the Coast Guard, which, he thought, did nothing but persecute watermen. But he was feeling unusually optimistic because of the rusting piece of iron in his pocket. Didn't his mother always say there was a reason for things? Had he not helped the dentist escape, run out of gas, and been rescued by the Coast Guard, he never would have discovered a sunken ship that was plainly marked

with a crab pot that, unbeknownst to Fonny Boy and Dr. Faux, was drifting with the current because the rope was too short.

"Thank God," the dentist said as he stared up at the fast-approach-
ing Jayhawk. "We've been found! And it's a good thing because it
doesn't look to me as if we're moving at all—the crab pot is right here
next to the bateau and it would be farther away from us by now if we
were moving."

"I can't believe the nerve of them to so blatantly fish in the crab
sanctuary," the Coast Guard engineer said, shaking his head.

The pilot steadied the helicopter into a low hover that whipped up
a whirlpool of water around the bateau. The two stranded men lowered
their heads and covered their eyes, their clothing flapping like a scare-
crow in a hurricane as the rescue basket was lowered.

Cruz Morales also needed to be rescued and was becoming desperate. Maybe he should turn himself in to the authorities. At least he
could get out of the chilly morning and eat a hot meal. He was exhausted from walking around Richmond's West End, having wisely decided to ditch his car since all the police in Virginia and the military
seemed to be looking for him. On top of everything else, he worried that
he was going to be blamed for the 7-Eleven robbery and murder he had
witnessed late last night.

Cruz had never committed a violent crime, but as he wandered
around the University of Richmond campus pretending to be a student,
he began to plot and think thoughts that alarmed him. All he had to do
was find someone he could overpower—a woman, especially one who
didn't look athletic or assertive—and he could scare her into giving him
money and the keys to her car. Then Cruz would flee, ditch that car (as
soon as possible), and then steal another one so he could get back to
New York. Or better yet, he reasoned as he approached a small squat
brick building in a wooded area near a lake in the heart of the campus,
he could abandon the car at the Amtrak station and take the train home.

A sign in front of the brick building said BAPTIST CAMPUS MINISTRY. Because Cruz couldn't read English beyond a second-grade level, he made the mistake of assuming that *Baptist* was close enough to *Baptista* to suggest that maybe someone inside spoke Spanish. He ran his fingers through his hair and scrubbed his teeth with his coat sleeve, trying to tidy himself up a bit, and his heart picked up speed. He opened the front door at the very moment Barbie Fogg was walking a female student to the waiting area, where there was a coffee table piled with magazines and an abundance of silk plants that Barbie had picked up for a song at neighborhood yard sales.

"I can only imagine," Barbie was sympathizing with the student, who had acne. "I've always had dry skin, so blemishes have never been a problem, but I can certainly understand how you feel. Just give my doctor a try and I just know he can help."

"I sure hope so, Mrs. Fogg. Like I said, it's all I think about, and I'm so down on myself."

Neither woman paid any attention to Cruz, who quickly sat on a sofa and absorbed himself in a magazine he could not comprehend.

"My mother used to always say that soap does the trick. You dab Ivory soap on the problem areas and it helps dry them out," Barbie went on, patting the young lady's shoulder. "I've never tried it because it would not be helpful in my case. Maybe a peel would do the trick."

"A peel?"

"My doctor does chemical peels. Ask him about it."

"I sure will. Thank you so much, Mrs. Fogg. It helps just to, you know, talk to somebody."

"I'm the world's biggest believer in girlfriends talking," Barbie agreed with feeling. "And don't you worry about none of these college boys asking you out. One of these days you'll find your prince and live happily ever after—with beautiful skin!"

Barbie felt a heaviness settle over her as she said words that rang hollow in her soul. That girl was never going to have beautiful skin. Already it was pitted and dented with angry red and purple scars and would certainly require laser surgery if there was ever a hope of undoing years of damage. As for living happily ever after, Barbie didn't know of anyone who could honestly make such a claim. Life with Lennie was flat and disconnected, and Barbie couldn't wait for a moment of quiet this morning so she could write another letter to her NASCAR lover.

"I'll see you soon," she promised him under her breath.

"See you soon, too," the acne-afflicted student said as she went out the door.

It was then that Barbie noticed the scruffy-looking Mexican boy sitting on the sofa. She frowned a little and felt a prick of anxiety. He certainly didn't look like one of the students, but then young people could be so slovenly these days. He also seemed a little young for college, but the older Barbie got, the younger other people looked.

"May I help you?" she said in a professional tone she had learned on the job and knew never to use at home because it annoyed Lennie.

"*Sí*," he shyly replied, barely glancing up from the magazine.

"I only speak English, I'm sorry," she admitted. "You do speak English, don't you?"

Her anxiety intensified. If he didn't speak English, how could he attend the University of Richmond? And if he wasn't a student, what in the world was he doing here at the Baptist Campus Ministry? Barbie wished Reverend Justice were here today. He hadn't called to say where he was or when he would be in, and the secretary was out with a cold, so Barbie was all by herself in the small building.

"*Sí*," Cruz replied. "I speak a little English, but not so good."

"Do you have an appointment?"

"No. No appointment. I need help bad."

Barbie sat on the other end of the sofa, keeping her distance and realizing it would not be a good idea to take this poorly groomed Mexican boy back to her private office and shut the door.

"Tell me about yourself," Barbie used the line she always began sessions with, and wished Reverend Justice would walk through the door right this minute.

But the reverend had been busy visiting that poor beaten-up truck driver in the hospital, and there were many demands for Reverend Justice to give talks and make appearances on local television and radio shows, Barbie reminded herself. She shouldn't be so selfish as to wish he would tear himself away from truly needy people just because Barbie was a little ill at ease.

"I don't got no money," Cruz told her as his criminal intentions began to weaken. "I not from here and got no money to get home. I just in town on a job, you know? And all these things happen. I scared."

"Well, there's nothing to be scared of at the Campus Ministry," Barbie said with conviction and a touch of pride. "We're here to help people and you couldn't be in a safer place."

"*Sí,* that good. I no felt safe and am very hungry." Cruz blinked back tears.

He also needed to shave the black fuzz off his upper lip, and his hair needed cutting, Barbie couldn't help noticing, and his fingernails were dirty and he had a tattoo on the back of his right hand. This was a child who had endured a hard life. Poor thing.

"How did you find us?" she wondered out loud.

"I see the sign and think maybe you family of Gustavo and Sabina or maybe Carla."

This made no sense to Barbie.

"So I come in." Cruz shrugged. "You know a way I can get home?"

"That depends on how you got here to begin with," Barbie said, confused. "And where might home be?"

Cruz wasn't terribly bright, but he realized he had New York plates on the car he had ditched, and the cops were looking for a Hispanic from New York. So maybe it was best to leave New York out of the equation at the moment.

"I just bet you're from Florida," Barbie said. "A lot of Spanish people live down there. My husband took me to the Everglades on our second anniversary. You know, he'd just always wanted a ride in one of those airboats, and then we spent two nights in Miami Beach in one of the few hotels that wasn't boarded up back then, because I just love Jackie Gleason. You ever watch *The Honeymooners?*"

Cruz frowned and scratched his head.

"Well, I was just thinking, maybe you could take the bus to Florida.

The Campus Ministry has a small discretionary fund we can draw on if a student needs to get home and can't afford it."

Cruz fell into a depression. He didn't know anybody in Florida.

"Maybe I go to New York and look for a job," he then said, hoping she wouldn't assume he was from New York and therefore the Hispanic serial killer who was running around committing hate crimes.

"That's a mighty big city," Barbie pointed out. "And it's very hard to find jobs. But I tell you what I'm going to do. How about I give you some money so you can get a bus ticket and something to eat?"

Something whispered to Barbie that perhaps it wasn't wise to talk about money or imply there might be a discretionary fund inside the Campus Ministry. But she was a bit of a pushover when it came to pitiful people, and although this boy had perfect skin, he was clearly miserable and unlucky. So maybe God was telling her to give him a little miracle, and she thought of her rainbow and felt happy inside.

"Oh *gracias, gracias*, thank you," Cruz said with massive relief. "God bless you. You a nice lady. You save my life and I never forget."

Barbie was fortified by his gratitude and felt better about things. She got up from the sofa.

"But first I've got to clear this with Reverend Justice—if I can find him," she added. "You may have heard of him. He's very famous these days. I just hope I can get hold of him. He seems to have vanished off the face of the planet. You wait right here."

"I be right here," Cruz promised.

Barbie went back to her office and locked the door. She called the secretary, who didn't sound very sick when she answered the phone.

"You got any idea where Reverend Justice is?" Barbie asked as misgivings and fears began to gather inside her again, rainbow or not.

How could she be so sure that Hispanic boy was nice? What if he wasn't?

"You tried him at home?" the secretary asked in an unfriendly way, as if Barbie were a nuisance.

"No one answers," Barbie said in frustration as someone began knocking on her door.

She wished she could call Hooter and get her opinion on giving the Hispanic boy money, but as far as Barbie knew, there were no telephones in the tollbooths.

"Anybody here?" a loud female called out as she knocked harder.

Barbie hurried to see who it was.

"I'm sorry," she nervously shouted through the shut door. "Who is it and do you have an appointment?"

"You take walk-ins? I must talk to somebody or I very well may drown myself in the lake. I'm not a Baptist, but it won't matter if I take my own life and people, especially those who hate Baptists, find out you wouldn't talk to me," the person said in tears.

Regina Crimm's path had led to Barbie Fogg and Cruz Morales in the most extraordinary way, and the timing could not have been better.

Trooper Macovich had been driving through downtown to return the failed Officer Reggie to the mansion, when he got a call over his radio that an old Grand Prix with New York plates had been discovered in the parking lot of the Country Club of Virginia. It was believed that the car had been dumped very recently because an old, beat-up vehicle that did not have Virginia tags would draw immediate attention at the club, and in fact had. A woman on her way to play indoor tennis spotted the Grand Prix while she was parking her Volvo and didn't hesitate to call 911.

"Sorry," Macovich said to Regina as he hit his siren and lights. "We gotta check something out. It may be that Hispanic everybody looking for."

"That's fine. I promise I won't tell," Regina said, cheered by the flashing lights and whelping siren, and excited by the knowledge that it was against regulations for EPU to respond to a dangerous call while protecting the First Family.

"Far as I concerned, you still an intern right this minute," Macovich said as he sped west on Broad Street, weaving in and out of traffic. "So you get some big idea about snitching on me like you already done before when I beat you fair and square in pool, I gonna deny it and say you was officially riding along."

"It's Papa who got mad at you," Regina retorted.

"Huh! 'Cause you such a sore loser and malingered me to him!" Macovich roared through a yellow light.

Motorists were pulling off on the shoulder, certain they were about to get a ticket for something. Traffic had slowed to ten miles an hour as other drivers cowered in terror and prayed they hadn't driven over a stripe on the street and their speed hadn't been checked by some helicopter and now a trooper was after them.

"The governor didn't see me beat you," Macovich irritably went on as he did his best to cut through the barely moving cars. "So you had to snitch, and then suddenly I have to hope he don't remember me."

"He doesn't remember you," Regina reminded him. "He says you all look alike, and he doesn't mean it in a way that's not nice. But Papa can't see most people, and sometimes he calls Constance *Faith* and the other way around, especially if they haven't put on makeup and are still in their robes."

"Would you get outta my way?" Macovich yelled at the cars he was trying to pass.

Within minutes, he was turning off Three Chopt Road into a long driveway that led to the stately country club with its elegant clubhouse, tennis and paddleball courts, and sprawling golf course. CCV, as the Country Club of Virginia was called, was in a very wealthy neighborhood where many of the homes were as big as the governor's mansion. Macovich was in an anxious sweat as he drove slowly over a speed bump. People around here thought all black folks looked alike, too, and poor vision had nothing to do with it.

"I tell you, nothing I hate more than coming over here," he muttered.

"What for? Papa's been a member ever since he was governor the first time. I practically grew up in this club." Regina scanned for the Grand Prix, hoping she would spot it first.

"Yeah. You a member as long as it's a family membership, but the day come you try to get in on your own when your daddy no longer the guv, then you see what happen," Macovich said, spotting the car near the indoor tennis facility. "Folk like you and me don't get 'cepted into places like this, in case you ain't figured that out yet. And most other guv'ners turn down the membership even if it's free, 'cause it go against their conscious."

This was news to Regina. "Why wouldn't I get in on my own? I'm white and from an old Virginia family."

"You still a minority."

Macovich radioed that he had found the Grand Prix and requested a backup as he lit a cigarette. He got out and checked the car, noting that the key was still in the ignition, and when he cranked the engine, he discovered that the gas tank was on empty. It also did not escape his attention that there were no personal effects inside the vehicle or the trunk. He got back on the radio.

"Subject appears to have abandoned the vehicle," he informed another trooper who was minutes away. "I'm going to check the area and let you work out getting the vehicle to the city tow lot."

"Ten-four."

"What do you mean I'm a minority?" Regina resumed arguing with Macovich. "How dare you insult me like that."

"Oh, I get it." Macovich got mad inside his cloud of smoke. "It ain't no insult for me to be a minority, but it is if you're one. Well, let me tell you something, *Miss Majority*. Every time you daddy ain't in office and you don't have EPU following you around, it's well known you hang out at Babe's playing pool."

"Not *every time*. Just the last two times. I was too young before that. And so what?"

"So when was the last time you saw a male in that joint, huh? We all know why you go in there. Maybe you come out with some nice field-hockey player with a shaved head and Dingo boots, or maybe you ride off on a Harley with some other sweet thing you meet in there at the bar. Or maybe you pick up a woman doctor or lawyer who live in the closet until it's cocktail hour and they can hide in some booth inside a nice dark place where they can meet other *Majorities*. Woooo! You live some protected life, all right—acting like you the last one to know."

Regina was crushed. She always assumed that when her father was out of office and not in the news, she could live her life as she wished. All the times she had frequented the women's bar in the Carytown Shopping Center, it had never occurred to her that people were watching and gossiping. Mention of the field-hockey player, in particular, conjured up terribly painful memories of yet one more heartbreaking failed romance. Regina had been desperately in love with D.D., a percussionist for the city symphony orchestra who had waited until Regina's birthday to announce that D.D. was having an affair with a tuba player and never wanted to see or talk to Regina again.

"I hate my life," Regina told Macovich as he turned off into the nearby University of Richmond grounds so he could check with the campus police and see if they might have noticed anybody unusual in the area.

"I can't take this anymore." Regina was more upset than Macovich had ever seen her. "You're mean. Everybody's mean to me. A person can only endure so much cruelty and humiliation."

Macovich pulled into a small parking lot by the lake so he could turn around and head the other way.

"I'm so unhappy, I might just blow up! One of these days I think I'm just going to explode, and they'll find just a little burned spot on the floor!" Regina threatened as she noticed a white minivan with a rainbow bumper sticker parked in front of a small brick building that said BAPTIST CAMPUS MINISTRY out front. "Stop the car!" she demanded. "Stop it now or I'll hold my breath until I die and then you'll have a lot of explaining to do. They won't be able to find out what killed me, and you'll be blamed."

Macovich slammed on the brakes and parked by the minivan as Regina imagined her neglected, unloved body inside a pouch at the morgue. Dr. Scarpetta would spend an inordinate amount of time on Regina and finally admit that there was no apparent cause of death.

"It may be that she died of a broken heart," the famous medical examiner would tell Regina's important parents.

Or better yet, Regina would figure out a way to burn herself up like the fisherman, and then Andy would spend the rest of his life investigating her mysterious, tragic, and untimely death. He would be sleepless, frustrated, and compelled by guilt to somehow figure out exactly what had happened to her. He would think of her morning, noon, and night and wish he had been nicer to her and had not kicked her out of the very morgue where he would visit her after it was too late.

Regina walked past the minivan with its rainbow bumper sticker, heading to the clinic, which she assumed specialized in counseling gay Baptists. How unfair to be born a gay Baptist, and she was surprised that the University of Richmond had enough gay Baptist students to merit a clinic for them. She climbed the front steps and walked into the lobby, where what she assumed was a gay Baptist Mexican was sitting on the couch. She self-consciously averted her puffy, tear-stained face from his curious eyes as she wiped her nose again and another wave of grief racked her massive body. Andy would be sorry, oh yes, he would. He would be devastated when he rushed to the morgue and begged to say good-bye to his former partner, Officer Reggie.

"Please let me have just a moment alone with her in the viewing room," he would ask Dr. Scarpetta. "This is all my fault. I was afraid to show her how much I really cared and needed her, and now it's come to this! The stress of her life and my unkindness toward her were too much and she burst into flames!"

Perhaps it was a touch of clairvoyance on Regina's part, but even as she was fantasizing about spontaneous human combustion, Andy was speeding back to headquarters to post a Trooper Truth essay on that very subject.

The Truth About Spontaneous Human Combustion

by Trooper Truth

Although there is no evidence that people literally blow up without
some mechanical or chemical assistance, it is a fact that living human beings can burn up in the absence of any external fire. I make this distinc-
tion because many of you, my readers, mistakenly believe that *combust*
means to blow up, when it doesn't mean that at all. Now, it is true that
combustion can refer to agitation or tumult, but for the purposes of this
essay, when I mention combust, combustion, or combusting, I am talking about something or someone burning up.

For centuries spontaneous human combustion (SHC) has been written about but not always persuasively. Novelists like Melville and Dickens, for example, use SHC to demonstrate that what goes around comes
around, and if you are evil and unfair to others, then it is poetic justice
if you burst into flames one day while you're minding your own selfish
business in your castle or house.

What may perhaps surprise the reader is that there is a scientific explanation for SHC. Experiments on dead human bodies and body parts donated to The Body Farm in Knoxville, Tennessee, have shown it is possible, given certain conditions, that if a body is ignited, it can continue to burn until it is almost completely cremated. Normally, it takes one to three and a half hours for a body to be reduced to bits of bone and ash, and this only occurs in an extremely hot fire or a crematorium oven.

So I have to admit that when forensic anthropologist Dr. Bill Bass first mentioned to me that one of his graduate students had written her master's thesis on SHC, I thought he was joking.

"People don't just burst into flames," I protested as we ate barbecue at Calhouns in Knoxville. "I can't believe I'm hearing this."

"Not literally burst into flames," he said, drinking iced tea from a jelly jar as the setting sun played across the Tennessee River. "But burn for considerably long periods of time."

This strange conversation over baby back ribs occurred last spring when I happened to drop by The Body Farm to see if the scientists there had ever done any experimenting on mummification. I had just returned from Argentina and was still very interested in mummies, and hoped Dr. Bass might be inclined to attempt an old-style Egyptian embalming on one of the bodies donated to the Farm. He saw no good purpose in this and explained that finding an apothecary shop that sold what we needed would be very hard and probably would exceed the budget.

However, Dr. Bass told me, and I sensed he hated for me to go away disappointed because he is a kind, humble man, The Body Farm was doing some rather unusual research on spontaneous human combustion, if I was interested. I replied that I certainly was, and over a period of weeks, I visited The Body Farm numerous times. It is not a pleasant place, and for those readers who are unfamiliar with it, I offer a brief description.

The University of Tennessee's Decay Research Facility, or The Body Farm as most of us call it, is several wooded acres surrounded by a tall wooden fence topped with razor wire. For some twenty-five years, anthropologists and forensic experts have devoted themselves to studying decomposition, for reasons that should be fairly obvious. Without knowing how the human body changes in different conditions over periods of time, we would have no data to help us determine time of death.

The Body Farm is the only facility I know of that makes it possible for death investigators and scientists to conduct important experiments that are not permitted in morgues, funeral homes, or medical schools. But when bodies are donated to The Body Farm, it is known up front and approved that the remains will be used for research, which in this instance included setting an amputated leg on fire to see if it could sustain almost complete combustion in the absence of external fuel.

I can summarize anthropologist Dr. Angi Christensen's brilliant work by saying that the tissue was ignited by a cotton wick, and the sample continued to burn for forty-five minutes as it was fueled by melting fat which was absorbed by the wick (known as *the wicking effect*). Further experiments on burning bones showed that osteoporotic or thinning bones burn much more readily and completely than dense healthy bones. After many meticulous tests and mathematical calculations, Christensen concluded that in some instances, the human body can indeed burn itself up at a very low heat if it is aided by cotton clothing that serves as a wick.

Obese elderly women with thinning bones and cotton house dresses are most likely to fall victim to this rare but ghastly phenomenon, and I offer here the sad case of Ivy, whose last name I will withhold out of respect for her privacy.

Ivy was a seventy-four-year-old white female who, at four-foot-eleven, weighed almost two hundred pounds, according to her driver's license and descriptions given by people who last saw her in the neighborhood. Up until two years before her strange, fiery death, she worked as a babysitter in Miami to supplement her modest income from Social Security checks and the small amount of cash her husband, Wally, had left her upon his sudden death. Ivy never worked for the same family longer than six months, as she would inevitably alienate the parents after they were subjected to one suspicious situation after another until finally they dismissed the peculiar woman even if they couldn't prove that she had actually done anything wrong.

Ivy had an insatiable need to be needed, and by her way of thinking, no one was needier than a sick or frightened child. She was careful never to take jobs if the children were old enough to talk intelligently and credibly, and therefore the parents never heard the truth about her misdeeds but certainly became concerned when they would return from outings and discover little Johnny or little Mary with stomach cramps, diarrhea, unusual bumps and burns, or in hysterics.

Several former clients of hers called her Poison Ivy behind her back and claimed she doctored their children's food with laxatives and other medicines, and by overspicing. One couple was certain the woman had burned their two-year-old with a cigarette deliberately, although Ivy claimed the child had grabbed the cigarette out of the ashtray and stomped on it, thus explaining the eight burns on the bottom of his tiny feet. Tales and scandals swirled about Ivy, and she finally decided it was best to retire, which was when her real problems began.

Home alone most of the time in her tiny stucco house, Ivy spent her days drinking cheap port, smoking, and eating snacks in front of the television. She was very stooped and round-shouldered from osteoporosis, and her arthritis seemed to flare up more often. No one called anymore or needed her for a thing. She grew to hate her life and everybody who had ever touched it, and never imagined that she was well on her way to becoming a case study in spontaneous human combustion.

As fate would have it, Ivy was in an especially foul mood on Christmas Day, 1987, when she put on a long-sleeve cotton housedress because the weather was a bit nippy. She fixed herself a strong screwdriver after opening the deluxe box of Whitman chocolates that were a gift from her son, who lived nearby but never came to see her and rarely called. She parked herself on the vinyl couch in front of the TV and drank and smoked the morning away. It was here on this very couch that her badly burned body was discovered two days later when the Cuban lady who lived next door became concerned because Ivy had not picked up her newspapers.

Virginia Chief Medical Examiner Dr. Kay Scarpetta worked the case, you, the reader, might be interested in knowing. She was beginning her career as a resident forensic pathologist at the Dade County medical examiner's office and responded to the baffling scene. Fire investigators and the police had never encountered anything like this, which isn't surprising since there have been only some two hundred cases of SHC reported since the 1600s. Ivy's torso was almost completely incinerated, including the bones, yet there was no sign of a fire anywhere in the house. Although not much was known about SHC at the time of Ivy's death, in retrospect it is fairly easy to reconstruct what happened.

Ivy passed out drunk and a lit cigarette dropped out of her mouth, setting her cotton housedress on fire. As her body began to burn, fat melted and the cotton became saturated and served as a wick. Ivy sustained low heat combustion possibly for many hours before the fire extinguished itself long after Ivy was dead. It's just lucky I did research on this rare phenomenon, because I know enough to realize two things about the mysterious death of fisherman Caesar Fender, whose burned body was recently discovered on Canal Street:

SHC is not a paranormal event, nor does Caesar's death meet the criteria in any sense.

In the first place, the grayish-white residue in his chest cavity clearly suggests an external fuel source. Also, Caesar was not very old or overweight, and it is unlikely his bones were thinning. Most significantly, he was not wearing cotton and a wicking effect could not have occurred. Nor was there any evidence that he was smoking at the time of his death, even if a witness, who is now the main suspect, claimed there was a Bic lighter in Caesar's pocket. That alleged lighter or pieces of it were not recovered at the crime scene or the morgue.

This leads me to suspect that a flare gun was used to commit what is clearly a murder, and I have a feeling Dr. Scarpetta is thinking the same thing. This makes Caesar's death quite different from what happened to Poison Ivy, who craved getting attention at the expense of others. Her syndrome is known as Munchausen's by Proxy, which simply means that someone harms another person who can't defend himself or describe what really took place. Victims are often young children or the infirm.

The motivation of the perpetrator is to gain sympathy, attention, or feel needed as he rushes his victim to the doctor or the hospital.

"Oh, I don't know what's wrong with my little baby," the wicked perpetrator will sob to the doctor. "But he's got terrible diarrhea again and is dehydrated and too weak to get out of bed. I'm just so distraught, I don't know what to do. I love my little baby so much, and I've already lost two babies, and if I lose another one I will lose my will to live!"

Another common reaction after the so-called caretaker has harmed someone in his or her care is to wrap the victim in his or her arms and coo and cry.

"Poor little baby," the mendacious, cruel-hearted perpetrator cries out, "oh, my poor little baby! How did you burn your little feet? Oh, don't you worry, I'll take care of you. Don't cry, please don't cry, and don't be mad at me. I didn't do anything, you poor little darling."

Baby wails and shrieks, and in pain and terror clings to mommy, daddy, or the caretaker's neck as the little one is rushed to the doctor, where the parent or caretaker gets the desired attention and compassion.

I think it is entirely possible that Major Trader, in addition to his pirate proclivities, suffers from Munchausen's by Proxy. He poisons others to manipulate and feel needed. If any of you, my readers, run across him or know where he is, please call the police immediately. He was last seen eating a breakfast sandwich as he backed out of his driveway earlier today, and has evaded arrest and is now considered a dangerous fugitive. If you spot him, please do not approach him, as he is violent and incapable of remorse. Nor should you accept any food from him, especially sweets.

Be careful out there!

Twenty-five

That's what I'm considering." Dr. Scarpetta's voice came over the speakerphone in Hammer's office shortly after Trooper Truth's latest essay rocketed through cyberspace. "But I would have preferred not having any information about a flare gun or anything else pertaining to my case published on the Internet."

"No one has any control over what Trooper Truth writes," Hammer replied as she gave Andy a disapproving look. "He's anonymous, assuming he's a he."

"How did he know about my case in Miami?" Dr. Scarpetta inquired.

"Maybe by doing an Internet search on spontaneous human combustion?" It was Andy who answered. "I assume there was a lot in the news about a case as sensational as that one must have been."

"As usual, there was."

"What next?" Hammer asked as she paced.

"I've submitted the grayish residue to the trace evidence lab and we'll see if we come up with oxidized strontium, potassium perchlorate, phosphorous, chemicals like that," Dr. Scarpetta informed them over the speakerphone. "In the meantime, he's a death due to forty percent body burns and I'll have to pend the rest of it, but I think you should work him as a homicide unless we find out he had some sort of flare on his person that accidentally ignited."

"Trader lied. Big surprise," Andy said to Hammer as he hung up the phone. "So much for the Hispanic with New York plates."

Unfortunately, Trooper Macovich had no way of knowing what Hammer and Andy were discussing. As Macovich waited in his car while Barbie and Regina visited inside the clinic, Cruz Morales walked outside to smoke and noticed the unmarked Caprice. His heart jerked and began to pound. That bitch counselor had called the police! He tossed the cigarette and began to run, immediately snagging the attention of Macovich, who recognized him as the Mexican who had stopped at Hooter's tollbooth. Macovich tossed his own cigarette and bolted out of the car in pursuit.

"Stop or I'll shoot!" Macovich yelled as he pulled out his pistol.

Yes, I've thought about shooting myself," Regina poured out her heart to Barbie Fogg, both of them unaware of the foot pursuit outside in the parking lot. "But I don't have a gun."

"I certainly am grateful for that!" Barbie said with relief.

"I don't know what's wrong with me," Regina went on as she wept behind the closed door of Barbie's office, which was furnished with a faux-finished blue desk, a rose sofa, and an abundance of silk arrangements in soothing pastels. "It's like I'm from another planet. I think I'm saying the right thing, and then I piss everybody off. I don't have a single friend, even if I had one . . ." She looked at her watch. "Well, I guess I had one three hours ago but not anymore. I think this is the longest I've ever talked to anyone. For sure, it's the longest anybody's ever listened," Regina added pitifully.

"Who was the one friend you had until three hours ago?" Barbie listened intently from a lavender chair.

"Andy. He let me be his partner and then suddenly he turned hateful."

"His partner? He's your boyfriend or was briefly?" Barbie was a bit surprised.

If ever she had met a woman who was unattractive to men, it was this poor creature. The young woman desperately needed a complete makeover. If Barbie were given the virtually hopeless task, she would start by doing Regina's colors, which were difficult to determine. Regina's pale, ignored complexion and dark hair certainly would be enhanced by bold colors such as charcoal and red, but Barbie believed that only the most feminine of women could get away with any accouterment that hinted of strength and assertiveness.

The last thing Regina needed was to look more aggressive. Maybe if she lost eighty pounds, wore makeup, had a good haircut, and began waxing regularly, her appearance would soften, Barbie hoped.

"No, he wasn't my boyfriend," Regina was saying with an indignation that belied her hurt feelings and overall horrible opinion of herself.

"Do you get headaches?" Barbie inquired.

Regina blew her nose loudly. "Of course, I do. How could anybody in my position not get awful headaches daily?"

Oh dear, Barbie thought. She would have to work on everything about this wretched girl, including quietly dabbing instead of honking her nose.

"You do scowl a lot and have very strong frown muscles," Barbie pointed out. "I think Botox would be a very smart place to start. I can hook you up with my doctor. But first, let's talk about your boyfriend and what happened."

"Andy's not my boyfriend!" Regina cried harder, her face blotched and puffy. "He let me be his intern this morning and we went to the morgue and he got irritable."

"Andy works at the morgue?" Barbie was horrified.

This was going from bad to worse. The last place someone like Regina needed to be was a morgue, and the idea of winter colors only became more distasteful and inappropriate. Anybody who spent time at the morgue should not be wearing bright red and black.

"He's a trooper," Regina explained with mounting impatience. "But that lady who runs the morgue didn't like me, either, and wouldn't let me watch an autopsy just because I couldn't spell."

Barbie listened in perplexed silence.

"You know," Regina went on, "that lady chief."

"Oh yes. I've read about her and seen her on TV," Barbie said. "Now with her blond hair and trim figure, she does fine in winter colors. But I'm beginning to see that we should try something different with you. Maybe summer colors. Have you ever worn a skirt?"

"Winter colors? A skirt? What is this, a Mary Kay Clinic?" Regina was insulted and repulsed. "I came here to talk about my problems! I didn't come here to have you turn me into my mother!"

"We'll talk about your mother another day," Barbie directed her client. "One thing at a time. We're going to need a lot of sessions, sweetie. But I think we should get back to Andy, because clearly he has hurt your feelings."

"I've never had anybody like him pay attention to me, and then I have to be such a big dumb fuck and fall for it." Tears flowed again. "He told me I don't have any friends because I'm selfish and have no regard for the feelings of others, and then he exiled me to the bay and yelled at me when I was trying to find keys and a body fell on the concrete."

"Oh, my!"

This was far more than Barbie could process, and the images flashing in her mind were more than she could bear and would, no doubt, disturb her much-needed sleep tonight.

"I ruined my chance." Regina sobbed. "I realize I did and don't know what to do about it. I want him to respect and admire me for something, but I don't know what."

"All of us women need to work hard for praise and admiration." Barbie understood something at last. "Oh yes, that is very important. So what you need is a little project. What little project could you start that might get you on the right track? Something you do all by yourself that would impress others and give them a higher opinion of you?"

Regina thought hard for a minute, sniffing and wiping her nose.

"What about if we start with waxing and complete skin care?" Barbie suggested. "Then we might chat about dieting and yoga."

If only Regina could prove herself just once.

"Papa needs a Seeing Eye horse," she said, feeling a surge of hope. "Maybe I could be in charge of supervising it. Someone will need to feed and brush it and practice commands with it."

"Does your father have a horse that's gone blind?" Barbie frowned without changing expressions, the paralyzed muscles in her forehead smooth and uncommunicative.

"No. He can't see and wants a minihorse because we already have Frisky."

"Oh. Well, what a sweet idea." Barbie tried to be encouraging. "Then why don't you start with that? Let's work on supervising your father's little Seeing Eye horse."

"He can take it to the race tomorrow night, and I'll make sure everybody sees me supervising," Regina said, her mood a bit lighter. "That will impress everybody, even Andy!"

"What a coincidence," Barbie marveled as she thought of her magic rainbow and how it was making connections in her otherwise vacant life. "You know, it just so happens I'm going to the race, too. Why don't I do a makeover of you before you go, and maybe you'll meet some handsome race-car driver."

"Oh please, sit with us in Papa's box!" Regina got excited and even showed a little appreciation. "That would be perfect. But I don't want to wear a skirt. I refuse to unless you really think it would impress people. Maybe the horse and I could ride in your van. Those Seeing Eye horses aren't any bigger than Frisky."

"I don't know why not," Barbie considered, assuming Frisky was a cat, and therefore a minihorse could easily fit inside a pet-carrying case in the back of the minivan. "Just make sure you tell me where to meet you."

"Meet me at the mansion tomorrow at noon," Regina said, happily. "And I'll let you do the makeover."

Unique, too, was considering a makeover as she sat in her dreary apartment, which was paid for by her wealthy, important doctor-father, whom she accepted help from but hated. Unique was nude on her black bedspread, sorting through Polaroid photographs of various people she had savagely murdered over the years. She wasn't getting the usual excitement and sexual arousal from reliving her crimes, because she was a bit anxious.

When she and Smoke had fled from the 7-Eleven last night, they had noticed a Mexican kid in a beat-up Grand Prix, and Unique had ordered Smoke to chase him. Unique had not bothered rearranging her molecules when she went inside the convenience store because it was very late and although she had noticed the Grand Prix, she didn't realize that its driver was nearby because the lights were out inside the pay phone booth. So Unique wasn't invisible when she blew out the clerk's brains and ran out of the store at the same moment the Mexican bolted out of the phone booth and sped off in his car.

Smoke had not been able to catch the Grand Prix, and now Unique had to consider the possibility that there was someone out there who could describe her to the police. She stared at the gory photograph of T.T. and fantasized about straddling the body and slashing away with the box cutter while T.T.'s warm flesh and blood were consummated by Unique's Purpose and became part of her insatiable Darkness. Every one of Unique's victims became part of her being. The Nazi inside her had directed Unique long ago that this violently sexual transubstantiation, or her Purpose, was essential if the Nazi were to live, and if the Nazi died, then so would Unique.

Unique's frightening eyes roamed around her bedroom, taking in the cheap black furniture, black candles and incense, and the Nazi memorabilia she had begun acquiring through the Internet when she had pledged herself to destroy and consume people who did not deserve human existence according to her Purpose. She picked up another Polaroid and fantasized about the blond undercover cop whose identity she still did not know. But her Purpose would unite him with her soon enough, and although she had been invisible when she had first seen him inside the convenience store and then followed him home, she couldn't take a chance that he might somehow recognize her. What if the Mexican boy gave her description to him?

Unique got up from the bed and looked at herself in the full-length mirror. Her naked skin shimmered, and she shook her long raven-black hair before she began hacking it off with a box cutter. Hair fell all around her bare feet and the Nazi directed her to dye what was left a pale blond that was almost white and change her plan about refusing to go with Smoke to the race tomorrow night. Unique had intended to consummate her Purpose with the blond cop while the road dogs were pretending to be a pit crew, but now things had changed. If only she could find that Mexican boy and slash him into eternal silence. But maybe it was too late. Maybe he had already given her description to the police.

"Show me," she softly said to her Darkness. "Show me the Purpose."

"You will find your Purpose," she answered herself in a different voice that was deep and unearthly.

"Yes." She smiled at herself in the mirror as her craving became intense. "Soon. Soon," she said to the blond cop. "Soon you will have a unique experience."

Twenty-six

I feel right qualmish," Fonny Boy told the pilots through his headset as he and Dr. Faux shivered and felt airsick in the back of the Jayhawk. "I'm of a mind when I scudded along on my losipe and went ass-over-tin-cup and fell in my own spew."

The sad childhood story about Fonny Boy flying along on his tricycle and taking a spill and throwing up on himself was lost on the Coast Guard crew, who had been smart enough to radio NCIC for a record check and had discovered that the dentist they had just rescued was wanted for health-care fraud, money laundering, and racketeering. As for the strange-talking Tangier boy, he was in clear violation of maritime law and also wanted for kidnapping.

Of course, Andy had seen to it that warrants were taken out on Dr. Faux and Fonny Boy after Andy had visited Tangier Island disguised as a journalist and had gone through Fonny Boy's dental chart and later realized that when Fonny Boy had stated that the dentist was tied up, he had meant it literally. Recognizing that the two people the Coast Guard had just rescued were wanted by the state police, the pilot switched to the emergency frequency and radioed for any state police aircraft that might be up.

Macovich, having dumped Regina an hour earlier, happened to be giving Cat a helicopter lesson when the call came over the radio.

"Helicopter four-three-zero-Sierra-Papa," Macovich tensely replied as Cat jerked the twin-engine helicopter into a hover. "I didn't say *lift* the pedal, I said *left* pedal," Macovich admonished him through their headsets, and in Macovich's confusion, he pressed the transmit button on his cyclic and his instruction was heard by hundreds of area pilots, including the Coast Guard. "If you lift the left pedal, it's the same thing as pushing the right pedal, and how many times I gotta tell you that? And see what happens? The chopper noses 'round to the right, 'cause what you just did was give it right pedal since you lifted the left pedal. Don't you remember what I told you about torque?"

Cat was sweating and not at all interested in aerodynamics. He just wanted to learn whatever was necessary to fly the helicopter himself. He didn't give a damn about getting his license or abiding by any FAA regulations, because he was fairly sure that once he and the road dogs escaped to Tangier Island, they would sell the Bell 430 to pirates in Canada and never have another worry. Six million dollars, he thought as he over-controlled and caused the helicopter to oscillate precariously over the tarmac.

"Helicopter zero-Sierra-Papa." A voice came back to Macovich. "You're on one-twenty-four-point-five," which was the emergency frequency. "Switch to one-twenty-five-nothing."

Macovich switched as he struggled with the controls and yelled at Cat while unwittingly pressing the transmit button again. "Set it back down. Easy, easy! Don't hunt for the ground. Just let it settle. Jesus Christ, don't jerk the collective up at the last second!"

The helicopter popped back up into the air and then set down again hard, bouncing on its wheels as the tail boom swung around and almost hit a power cart. Macovich yelled for Cat to take his hands and feet off the controls.

"It's my ship!" Macovich fought to steady the aircraft. "It's my ship! Let go of the fucking controls, you son of a bitch! That's it! I ain't giving you another lesson ever! It ain't worth it!"

Cat shoved the cyclic forward and pressed down on the right pedal, causing the helicopter to taxi along the tarmac in a hard right turn, heading straight for the hangar, the rotor blades chopping at full power. Macovich had no choice but to haul off and slug his NASCAR student in the side of the head, knocking him out cold. Macovich pressed down both pedals and stopped the helicopter before it taxied into the back of a Cessna Citation. He cut the throttle back to flight idle and blew out a big, stressful breath of stale tobacco-smelling air.

"Man," Cat groaned as he slowly came to. "Why'd you fucking hit me, man?"

"You tell your fucking driver when he needs to go somewhere, I'm flying and you can park your dangerous motherfucking ass in back," Macovich angrily said. The near-disasters of the morning were compounded by his throbbing hangover and bad memories of Hooter's dissing him in Freckles and then refusing to have sex with him on the couch when she drove him back to his mother's cluttered single-bedroom house.

"Man, we gotta go to the race tomorrow night," Cat said as he rubbed his head.

"Yeah, well, the guv'ner got to get there, too," Macovich said as he flipped switches to the off position. "So I'm gonna have to fly you dudes in shifts, 'cause I got no choice about it. I can't just tell the guv that he's gonna have to go by car."

"What'chu talking about?" Cat hotly replied. "Look at all them helicopters."

He stared at the fleet of shiny new helicopters inside the hangar.

"We don't care which one you fly us in, as long as it cost as much as this one," Cat said.

Macovich figured the NASCAR pit crew had an important, powerful image to maintain, and puzzled what to do. He supposed he could recruit Andy to fly the First Family in a smaller but equally luxurious 407, which would leave Macovich free to transport the thus-far anonymous NASCAR driver and his pit crew in appropriate style for a handsome price that would enable Macovich to get his own apartment so the women he picked up would feel more comfortable about having sex with him. He would just lie to the governor and say the 430 was in for maintenance, assuming the governor even noticed.

"Uh, helicopter Sierra-Papa? You got company?" the Coast Guard pilot tried again as he choppered at a hundred and seventy knots toward the Richmond skyline.

"Sierra-Papa. Who's trying to contact?" The breathless voice came back, and the Coast Guard pilots glanced at each other and nodded, which was their way of signaling that it was no bloody wonder state police pilots were always quitting.

Stories had made the aviation rounds, and the accepted version was that no one wanted to fly for the state police because the First Lady was always trying to matchmake her ugly daughters with the pilots who flew the First Family to dinner and shopping. Well, maybe not. Most likely it was because the entire state police department had gone whacko ever since it had been taken over by the woman superintendent the Coast Guard needed to contact about two fugitives.

"We're a Coast Guard HH-sixty," the pilot radioed back. "Have two subjects on board and need a state police contact. Uh, the situation's sensitive. You got a freq for the superintendent?"

It's just like a movie!" Windy Brees exclaimed as she blew through Hammer's door a minute later and excitedly informed her and Andy that a Coast Guard helicopter had just picked up the kidnapped dentist and his harmonica-playing abductor. "They're in a helicopter and had to lift them up in this huge basket with waves crashing everywhere and the wind storming, just like in *The Perfect Howl*! Did you see that with Keanu Clooney? Oh, if only he were older!"

"All right, all right," Hammer said. "See if you can get the Coast Guard back on the air so we can talk to them."

Hammer swivelled her chair around to the radio on the table behind her desk as Andy switched to 125.0, a rather generic frequency shared by small airports and often not very busy.

"Tell them we're on one-twenty-five-nothing," Andy told the secretary.

Soon enough, they had the Coast Guard pilots on the air.

"This is the state police," Andy said into the microphone. "Are you on *crew only?*"

"Roger," was the comeback.

"Roger," Andy said. "Can you relay the circumstances?"

"Roger. We spotted two subjects in a boat and brought them on board. Appears they were fishing in the crab sanctuary and ran out of gas. They fired flares at our aircraft, and a post SAR boarding showed they were not in compliance. No fire extinguishers or life jackets."

"We need them here." Superintendent Hammer got on the radio. "What's your present location?"

"Eleven-point-three miles east of the Richmond airport."

Hammer asked the Coast Guard if they could transport the prisoners to state police headquarters for questioning at the very moment Dr. Faux was saying into his headset that it would be most helpful if the pilots would drop him and Fonny Boy in Reedville, not realizing that the radio was turned to *crew only* and no one in the cockpit could hear him.

"I don't need to return to Tangier at this time," Dr. Faux said into his microphone as the helicopter thundered across what a pilot would call severe-clear skies. "And I want to make sure that you understand that Fonny Boy was simply being kind enough to play his harmonica for me while he showed me around the bay when the bateau experienced engine problems. As for the crab pot, we have no idea where that came from."

"That true?" asked the engineer, who was in back with them and could hear the dentist's transmission but not what was being said in the cockpit.

"Nah!" Fonny Boy made the mistake of talking backward as the helicopter choppered west, toward state police headquarters.

"Oh, it's *not* true?" the engineer said harshly. "I thought as much. So you were crabbing!"

"I'll call my wife and she'll come get us," Dr. Faux nervously rattled on. "And I sure am sorry for all the trouble, but you certainly saved our lives. If you ever need any free dental work, please call me. Here's my card."

He held out a business card, which was caught by air rushing past the helicopter's open door. The card sailed out into the bright afternoon and was shredded by the tail rotor.

"Oh, dear. That was my last one. And this doesn't look like Reedville," Dr. Faux said in alarm as the Jayhawk made its approach to a helipad in what looked like Richmond.

Y ou've got a lot of explaining to do," Andy said to Fonny Boy and the dentist after they were handcuffed and led into an interrogation room.

"It's all a mistake," Dr. Faux said, deciding he would deny being kidnapped and anything else that might stir up a bigger mess. "I had simply extended my stay on the island, and Fonny Boy was taking me home when his bateau ran out of gas."

Fonny Boy's attention wandered down to the rusting piece of iron in his pocket. No matter what, he had to get back to the crab pot and follow the rope down to the sunken ship, which by now he was convinced was filled with treasure. He wasn't entirely sure why the buoy had remained only two feet from the bateau's stern as they drifted with the current, but assumed he had gotten disoriented and the bateau had not moved at all. He couldn't face the possibility that he had lost the location of his destiny, and all that awaited him in life was returning to Tangier Island or maybe finding himself behind bars.

"Have they taken anybody else hostage on the island?" Hammer asked the dentist as Windy took notes.

"I know nothing about any hostages," Dr. Faux said. "And it's outrageous that you are detaining me here in handcuffs like a common criminal. I'm a dentist who helps the poor!"

"Yes, you help them all right," Andy aggressively said, playing bad cop. "By ruining their teeth with unnecessary, lousy, and nonexistent dental work—such as substituting cheap materials for expensive crowns and fillings, and billing for bogus *behavior management* of pediatric patients, who end up with more steel crowns than they have baby teeth. Last year alone, thirty-two patients of yours endured some one hundred and ninety-two tooth removals, and in at least a hundred instances you billed for bringing in anesthetists when in fact, you were sedating the patients yourself.

"I could go on," Andy sternly said as he stared hard at Dr. Faux, who was feeling faint. "Just so you know, I've mounted a joint investigation that includes the Virginia Medicaid Fraud Control Unit of the attorney general's office, plus the FBI and IRS. There's been an outstanding warrant out against you for two days because the sheriff couldn't find you to serve you, and guess why that is?"

"I don't know," Dr. Faux's voice squeaked as Fonny Boy ran his tongue over his poor-fitting braces and a rubber band shot across the conference table.

"Your only address is a post office box, and your home and office phones are answered by a machine," Andy berated him. "And you've never allowed friends and family to take photographs of you, so the sheriff has no idea what you look like, and you were being held hostage on Tangier Island anyway, and no sheriff is going to try to find you on the Island, because the Islanders aren't likely to cooperate with anyone in uniform, especially if he's trying to serve a warrant."

"That's your opinion," Dr. Faux said, and his real nature began to show itself. "You'll have to prove everything you're saying and what the reasons are. A lot of people use post office boxes and are shy about having their picture taken. I was not a hostage and there are no hostages."

"Listen, Doctor Faux, we need your help," Hammer said, playing the good cop. "The last thing anybody wants is another civil war. The Islanders are citizens of this Commonwealth just the same as you and I, and to fight us is to fight themselves. It's like getting angry and shooting yourself in the leg. Any civil uproar on the Islanders' part will only prove self-destructive, and it is the contention of the Coast Guard that when you fired the flare gun three times out in the bateau, you weren't signaling distress but were making a blatant attempt to shoot down the helicopter."

"Say what?" Dr. Faux exclaimed.

"I'll tell you what," Hammer replied, changing to the role of bad cop now. "When an island declares war on its own government and takes down the state flag and commits a kidnapping, what is anybody supposed to think when suddenly one of these Islanders starts firing at a law-enforcement aircraft? Not to mention, aircraft are part of what the Islanders are upset about because of VASCAR."

"Fonny Boy shot the flares, not me, and I'm not an Islander," Dr. Faux quickly pointed the finger. "I told him not to do it. And he's the one who dropped the crab pot into the sanctuary, too, so he could find that pirate's ship."

"Pirate's ship?" Andy asked.

Fonny Boy tuned in at this and gave Dr. Faux a menacing look.

"You hadn't orte do that! Doncha be talking about my picaroon ship!" Fonny Boy said in protest. "I knew you was not much count!"

"I count for quite a lot," the dentist said huffily. "And you didn't find a ship. What happened, exactly, is a piece of old metal found you."

"What are you, a magnet?" Andy sarcastically said to Fonny Boy. "I think it's about time someone told the damn truth around here. Let me see the piece of metal."

"Yass!" Fonny Boy talked backward, scraping his handcuffs over the tabletop and protectively moving his hands toward a pocket.

"Don't make me pat you down for it!" Hammer helped Andy gang up on Fonny Boy.

"It's mine!" Fonny Boy refused to cooperate. "It fell out from the sky and landed on my leg as I was playing the juice harp."

"Please, let me see the piece of metal," Andy said, switching to good cop and getting up from his chair. "I promise I'm not going to keep it un-less it's related to a crime or an accident investigation, okay?"

"That's it!" Fonny Boy was adamant, clutching the right side of his windbreaker, and feeling an unexpected hard lump near the broken zipper.

Curious, Andy dug into the pocket, worked his fingers through a hole and discovered the key to the clinic in the lining.

"Ha!" the dentist blurted out. "The key he took when he locked me inside the clinic after hitting me in the nose for no reason!"

"I thought you said you weren't kidnapped." Hammer caught him in a lie.

"I'm an innocent victim," Dr. Faux said. "I demand to be released im-mediately and I fully intend to press charges! Those violent, untrust-worthy people on the island held me against my will and probably are the ones who have framed me for fraud!"

"I've seen the teeth out there," Andy said. "And all I have to do is look at Fonny Boy's teeth, too. How many fillings, root canals, crowns, and ex-tractions has he performed on you, Fonny Boy?"

Fonny Boy couldn't recall or count that high. He squeezed a pocket of his jeans and felt the piece of metal. Realizing he was in big trouble because the dentist had just ratted on him, Fonny Boy thought it wise to give the trooper what he wanted. The metal probably wasn't worth much, anyway, and all that mattered was that Fonny Boy get out of here so he could return to the crab pot and find the sunken ship and the treasure.

Andy reverently held the old, irregular, rusting bit of iron, studying it in amazement as if it were a priceless antique.

"We need to carbon-date this," he said to Hammer. "It could be very important."

Twenty-seven

The day was running out on Andy, and there was still much to do.

Next on his agenda was to pick up Moses Custer at the hospital and make sure he got home safely. Then he had that waterproof suitcase to deliver to Canal Street, where Captain Bonny—a.k.a. Major Trader—had agreed through e-mail to show up so he could get what was coming to him.

You'll get what's coming to you, all right, Andy thought as he packed an old, battered aluminum suitcase full of weights from his cramped, makeshift gym in the basement of his row house. How about getting your ass arrested for murder, attempted murder, conspiracy to murder, obstruction of justice, and whatever else I can think of, you son of a bitch?

Andy threw the suitcase, a disguise, and fishing gear into the trunk of his car and hurried downtown to the hospital.

"I'm sorry I took so long to get here," he apologized as he walked into

Moses Custer's room, a large private one the governor had ordered him moved to, even though Moses was on his way out.

"He's all ready to go, and it's about time you showed up, because we need the room," said a nurse whose nametag read A. CARLESS.

"Do you pronounce your name *Careless* or *Car-less?*" Andy politely inquired of the woman, who was built like a wrestler and had eyes that looked in two directions at once.

"People pronounce it both ways," she replied as she began to help Custer out of the bed and into a wheelchair.

"I don't need no wheelchair," Custer nervously said. "Ouch! You just hit my mouth with your elbow! Hold on. My gown ain't closed in the back! Lord help me, Mr. Trooper! Please get this woman away from me! I'm more banged up now than when I got here!"

Moses Custer was a pitiful sight. His head was black and blue, one eye was swollen shut, and he was missing teeth, although it was unclear how much of it was related to the assault. One arm was in a cast that Nurse Carless managed to knock against the bedside table as she tried to force him from beneath the covers into the wheelchair that she had forgotten to secure with the brakes. Before Andy could intervene, she lifted Custer off the bed and set him down hard in the wheelchair, which took off on its own and crashed into a chest of drawers. Custer shrieked as the chair bounced backward and slammed into the bed, his bandaged right foot catching the handle of the bedpan on the floor and sending it flying as the chair spun uncontrollably and threw Moses out.

"Don't touch me!" he screamed as the nurse lifted him up by the front of his gown, thereby exposing his backside and other parts that were nobody's business but his own.

"Whoa!" Andy said, gently taking Custer by the elbow, closing the gown and blocking Nurse Carless to prevent further physical harm to the patient. "Where are your clothes, so you can get dressed?"

"My son brought me over some. In that drawer there," Moses said. "Don't you get them!" he snapped at the nurse. "Let the trooper get them!"

Andy helped Moses dress over the protests and attempted interventions of Nurse Carless, and then helped him into the wheelchair.

"I'll wheel you out to the car," Andy said. "We don't need your help," he warned the nurse, who was getting put out and more aggressive.

"It's hospital policy that a nurse must roll the patient out," she protested.

"And it's state police policy that someone in protective custody will be transported by an officer of the law," Andy replied. "I suggest you don't interfere, Nurse Care-less."

"It's Car-less!" she declared, defiantly putting her hands on her big hips.

Big nurse's shoes sounded after them as Andy rolled Moses swiftly through the hallway.

"I'm reporting you to my supervisor!" Nurse Carless called out as she shoved an intern out of her way and caused another nurse to swerve and almost crash an IV stand that rolled precariously into a potted corn plant.

Major Trader was not the sort to ride the bus unless he was desperate. But when he read the latest Trooper Truth essay, he thought it might be a good idea to stop by the Trailways station and get a one-way ticket to Key West, where he had relatives who shared his pirate heritage and would never turn him in to authorities. Clearly, an intensive investigation was underway that would reveal many facts that would not serve Trader well.

Governor Crimm would be no friend when he learned for a fact that Trader had been poisoning him for years. Nor would the governor be happy to learn that Trader had, as a matter of course, lied, withheld and blocked information, forged notes when needed, been lazy, framed colleagues, manipulated news releases to his egotistical and financial advantage, used an Internet alias to conduct illegal business with pirates, was in fact born of pirate stock, was a pyromaniac as a child, and had murdered the fisherman on Canal Street, to mention but a few of Trader's failings.

He left the bus station, the ticket in his pocket assigned to an assumed name, flagged down a taxi, and headed to Canal Street. Realizing time was running short, Andy had asked Moses if he minded riding along with him on an assignment.

"That nurse slowed us up," Andy explained. "And I'm supposed to meet a suspect at two-thirty, which is just fifteen minutes away."

"I'll be glad to go with you," Moses replied. "I been cooped up for what seems like a month. A little fresh air and activity would do me good. Can I help with anything?"

"Can you remember anything else about being assaulted?"

"Nope. All I recollect is an angel saying her car broke down and promising me something unique."

"Unique?" Andy puzzled.

"That what she say."

"Do you know how to fish?" Andy then asked.

"Is a pig's ass made of pork?" Moses replied.

Andy parked several streets down from the predetermined location, which just happened to be the place where Trader had murdered Caesar Fender. When the so-called Captain Bonny had exchanged e-mails with Andy, who was really signed on with Possum's screen name (although Andy didn't even know Possum's real identity yet), Andy had suggested the location of the drop. He thought it might add insult to injury if he not only lured Trader back to the scene of his crime, but rewarded his evil deeds with a suitcase full of iron and a free ride to the city lockup. Andy popped the trunk and lifted out the suitcase. He put on the same fake beard, ponytail wig, and frumpy clothes he'd worn undercover on Tangier Island and handed Moses a fishing pole.

"All you got to do is fish," he told Moses as they walked in the direction of the retaining wall at the river's edge. "You just fish and don't pay any attention to me. What will happen is a man will show up and try to pick up this suitcase, as if it belongs to him. He won't be able to move it an inch and will struggle with it. I'll volunteer to help him, and next thing he knows, he'll have on handcuffs and will be on his way to jail."

"Uh huh. Sound good to me," Moses said.

"Then I'll get you home safe and sound."

"Yeah." Moses limped along. "That sound fine."

Tatters of yellow crime-scene tape fluttered in a stiff cold wind and Moses looked around a bit uneasily and stared at a burn mark on the concrete and an overturned plastic bucket.

"Well, look at that," Andy said in annoyance as he picked up the bucket. "Yeah, real good policing. I can't believe they just left this thing lying around out here."

He set the bucket on the wall and placed the heavy suitcase several feet away. Moses tied a plastic worm on his fishing line and attached a bobber.

"This ain't where that fisherman blowed up, is it?" he worried.

"As a matter of fact, it is," Andy replied, preparing his own fishing gear.

"I hope you ain't meeting no killer here," Moses said. "I had my share of mean people for a while."

"Don't be alarmed," Andy assured him. "Just mind your own business and fish. The person who'll show up isn't going to do anything to you. All he wants is to grab this suitcase and run."

"Got to admit, no one would ever recognize you in that getup," Moses said, smoothly casting his line into the sluggish, rocky river. "You look like a leftover hippie, one of them types that drives an old VW with big flowers stuck all over it."

"Good. And make sure you don't call me Andy or Trooper when this dude shows up."

"Not me," Moses said. "I ain't tipping my hand with no killer around. Why'd he blow up that poor black fisherman, and what makes you so sure he won't take one look at me and decide to do the same thing? You gonna need to put a bobber on or your worm's gonna sink straight to the bottom and get hung on a rock."

"This guy just wants to take the money and get the hell out of Dodge," Andy said as he clipped a bobber on his line and cast it into the river. "Besides, I'm here, and if he tries anything, he'll have a big problem on his hands."

"You packing?"

"Got my friend right here in the back of my waistband," Andy said as he felt a slight tug on his line.

Major Trader rolled up in a Blue Bird taxi and told the driver to wait or he wouldn't get paid. Trader spied two bums fishing on the wall and a beat-up aluminum suitcase sitting all by itself. His loaded flare gun was in his coat pocket just in case anybody tried to give him a hard time, and he strode right up to the suitcase.

"This belong to either of you fellows?" Trader asked.

"Never seen it before in my life," Andy replied, because it was perfectly acceptable to be deceptive when one was undercover.

"Me neither," Moses echoed. "Was sitting there just like it is when we come here to fish."

"Someone stole my car and my suitcase was in it, which is why I had to take a taxi," Trader lied. "I had a feeling whoever the culprit was, he'd probably dump the suitcase somewhere because there's nothing in it but clothes and a few books."

"Help yourself," Andy said.

Trader took a good look at the two fishermen to make sure they weren't paying him any mind and would not be able to identify him later, should they ever get questioned. Both of them were obviously losers and probably had never held a real job in their lives. Why else would they be out fishing on a Friday afternoon while decent people were at work? Trader grabbed the suitcase handle and his shoulder practically came out of the socket as he yanked.

"Shit!" he muttered in surprise.

The damn thing must weigh two hundred pounds! He imagined hundreds of silver dollars and stacks of bills and maybe gold. The pirates must have made quite a score. He tried to lift the suitcase again and couldn't get it an inch off the ground. Then he tried to open it, but the combination was set and the locks wouldn't budge. While he was deliberating what to do and furtively glancing about and starting to sweat, the old black fisherman, who looked as if he had been in a bad car wreck, jerked up his pole and started reeling hard.

"Got me one," Moses announced for all to hear. "Yes sir, this baby ain't long for the water."

"How do you always do that?" Andy played his role. "Every time I come out here with you, you catch a bucket of fish and I go home with nothing."

It was then that Trader noticed the familiar white plastic bucket, and his adrenalin kicked in and an internal alarm went off.

"That your bucket?" Trader asked as he tried different lock combinations.

"Sure is," Moses replied.

"Then how is it the bucket has *Parks Seafood* on it, which is a Tangier Island fish shop?" Trader was getting suspicious and felt for his flare gun. "That bucket came from the governor's mansion, so don't be telling me it belongs to you."

"Wouldn't know. Never been to the gov'ner's mansion, but I'm going tomorrow 'cause the gov'ner taking me to the NASCAR race. Someone left that bucket out here," Moses said, reeling in a fish. "Didn't seem like nobody wanted it. And I don't mind returning it to the mansion when I get there."

"Well, if it's yours now," Trader said, walking over to get a closer look, "then why is it you have no water in it? Seems to me, if you intended to use it for the fish you catch, you would have bothered to fill it with water. And I know for a fact you're not going to the race with the governor!"

The fish broke the surface of the river as it fought for its life, and Andy thought it looked familiar.

"A trout?" he asked Moses as Trader frantically tried to lift the suitcase again and groaned in exertion.

"Sure is," Moses said. "A nice one, too."

Becoming more desperate and a little wary of the two ragged fishermen, Trader tried to drag the suitcase and began cursing. Moses held up the flapping trout, and Andy noticed an old hook wound in its lower lip. The trout looked at Trader and played dead.

"Let it go," Andy said to Moses. "We don't need a fish or crabs or anything else to ID this big fat piece of lying shit."

He pulled off his fake beard and ponytail wig and whipped out his pistol.

"Hands up in the air, Trader," Andy fiercely ordered as Moses worked the hook out of the trout's mouth and tossed him back into the river.

"Free at last," Moses said to the trout as it swam away.

"You're under arrest!" Andy shouted.

Regina was giving orders and shouting as well, and not having a good result. Trip the minihorse had been delivered to the mansion an hour earlier, and Regina had paid little attention to the trainer's instructions and had not bothered to watch the training videotape. How hard could it be to tell a tiny horse to turn right, left, sit, come, or lie down? But she had been barking commands at the guide animal nonstop and Trip just stood in the middle of the ballroom and stared at her.

"Move," Regina said, snapping her fingers and stamping her foot.

Trip blinked and didn't budge.

"Come here right this minute," Regina tried again in a harsh tone as the First Lady hurried down the winding staircase, clutching a box of trivets that she intended to stash in the butler's pantry.

"You stupid pony!" Regina yelled.

"Regina!" Mrs. Crimm paused, panting hard from exertion. "You know not to talk to the help that way!"

"Oh, she isn't talking to me, ma'am," Pony said as he appeared in his starchy white coat. "Can I assist you with that box?"

"What's all the commotion about?" the governor inquired as he stepped out of a parlor, peering through his magnifying glass, obviously befuddled. "Where am I? I walked into my office and I couldn't find my desk. Did someone move my desk? What are you carrying, Maude?"

"Just some things that need to be tossed," she quickly made up a story. "I was cleaning out one of my closets and came across that revolving shoe tree I bought on an information commercial. I don't suppose you know which one I mean, but it's never served a useful purpose, and most of the shoes on it are out of style anyway."

"Your desk is in the same spot," Pony told the governor. "May I help you upstairs, sir?"

"What's this?" The governor spied the minihorse and was instantly smitten. "What a pretty little fellow you are! And such a handsome harness with a nice little leather handle, and my goodness, he even has shoes!"

"He has to have shoes or he'll slide all over the hardwood floor," Regina impatiently explained as the First Lady dashed downstairs to hide the trivets. "But he's worthless. He won't do a thing I say, so I certainly can't see what good he's going to do, Papa. Come here!" Regina clapped her hands at the indifferent tiny horse. "You idiot, get here right this minute or I'm sending you back and you can just go live with some other blind person who probably lives in a dump and has no household staff or limousines or cooks or important people visiting!"

"Perhaps you're not saying the right words to him," the governor considered as he moved closer to Trip and patted his thick red mane. "Sit," he said.

Trip did nothing.

"Fetch." The governor tossed an imaginary stick across the Oriental rug. "Well, leave it then."

Trip did.

"Sir," Pony said. "What would you like for your midafternoon snack?"

"I believe two eggs and a piece of toast would be nice," the governor replied as his magnified cloudy eye scanned his new guide horse.

"Over or under?" Pony politely asked.

"Under," the governor decided, and Trip suddenly crawled under an inlaid mahogany Federal card table.

"Now isn't that strange," the governor commented as he got down on his knees and tried to coax Trip back out. "I think there's something wrong with this horse. Or maybe you've confused the poor thing and intimidated him with your rude voice," he said to Regina.

"Right," she said sarcastically, and Trip backed out from under the table, turned right, and started walking across the ballroom in his Velcro-fastened tennis shoes. "Everything's always my fault. I'm so sick and tired of being blamed for whatever goes wrong. I'm an excellent supervisor, and it's the retarded horse who's screwing up, not me . . . !"

"Wait," the governor snapped at his daughter, because he had heard quite enough.

Trip stopped.

"Sir?" Pony was back. "Would you like hollandaise sauce, butter, salt, pepper, or anything else on your eggs?"

Crimm paused to check on his submarine, which had been blissfully still in the water since he had stopped eating Major Trader's sweets. Well, maybe he didn't need such a bland diet anymore. Dear Lord, wouldn't that be a blessing?

"I might even try ham again," he thought out loud.

"I can put ham on the eggs, as well," Pony suggested as Trip continued to walk across the ballroom, his driverless harness flopping.

"Well, why not?" the governor happily said. "Load up!"

Trip stopped in his tracks and then headed toward the elevator.

"Look at that," Pony marveled. "That horse is headed right toward the . . . where's he going? He's going to the . . ."

"Lift!" the governor interrupted with excitement, finishing Pony's sentence and using the English word for elevator, because he preferred all things English and always had.

Trip stopped and lifted a hoof.

"I believe there's a pattern developing," the governor announced as he went to Trip and patted his head. "You can put your foot down, little fellow."

Trip didn't move.

"Seems like to me he only listens to one or two words," Pony observed. "Load up," he said to Trip.

The horse lowered his hoof and headed to the elevator again. Intrigued and challenged, Pony followed and pushed the down button. The doors opened and Trip boarded.

"We'll just ride along with him and see what he does," the governor said, enjoying himself more than he had in quite a long time.

He and Pony rode the elevator with Trip, and when the doors opened on the kitchen level of the mansion, the minihorse stood still, waiting.

"Let me see," the governor pondered. "I suppose the opposite of load up would be unload. Unload," he said to Trip.

Trip clomped off the elevator.

"Right!" Pony exclaimed, hoping that the governor had figured out the pattern of commands.

Pony turned right and walked through an open door, where the First Lady was struggling to set the heavy box of trivets on a shelf. When she heard the minihorse's sneakers and glanced around and saw her husband, she shrieked and the box crashed to the floor. Trivets clanked and banged and scattered across centuries-old heart of pine.

"Wait!" Mrs. Crimm tried to explain as her thoughts and fears tumbled together nonsensically.

Trip stopped.

"What are all these?" the governor asked her, perplexed, as he eyed the trivets through his magnifying glass. "Okay," he said.

Released from the wait command, Trip stood inside the pantry surrounded by trivets and listened for what he was supposed to do next.

"So that's what this is all about!" the governor declared. "Shopping. Huh. You've been hiding trivets again, and all the while I thought you were entertaining immoral men in the mansion."

"How could you think such a thing?" the First Lady cried out as she stooped to gather up her beloved trivets, or at least the most recent batch of them she had ordered over the Internet. "Why Bedford! I would never cheat on you!"

"Leave it," the governor ordered her to stop picking up the trivets, and Trip obeyed the command by not bothering to do anything, not that he was doing much at the moment anyway.

"What do you mean, *again?*" Mrs. Crimm asked in amazement. "You know I've been hiding trivets?"

She gave Pony an accusing look, and he shrugged as if to say, *He didn't find out from me.*

"Oh, I've run into your trivets here and there," the governor explained. "Frankly, I just thought they were junk, possibly left by previous governors in the last century."

"They most certainly aren't junk," Mrs. Crimm said indignantly. "And they're very expensive," she unwisely added.

"Send them back," the governor ordered.

"Back? Back!" the First Lady raised her voice angrily and Trip took a step back inside the pantry, clanking a horseshoe trivet into a lacy one that featured a dog.

"Goodness me!" Pony was startled. "You think he recognized the horseshoe and that's why he decided to step on it? That's one smart little horse! Maybe he recognized the dog, too. Maybe that's his way of saying he wants to knock Frisky out of the way and be your only pet."

"We must keep them separated," Mrs. Crimm said, dismayed that she had yet one more thing to worry about. "Oh, poor Frisky. He'll be heartbroken if we pay more attention to this little pony than to him."

It was unfortunate that she planted this thought in her husband's head, because from that point on, he began to refer to the minihorse as the *pony*, which was very confusing to Pony the butler.

"Come here, pony," the governor tried to coax Trip out of the pantry, and Pony responded by stepping inside the pantry, where he, Trip, the First Lady, and the governor crowded one another and began to step on trivets. "Be good, pony, and come on out of here," the governor said as if Trip were Frisky and might expect a biscuit.

Pony stepped back out of the pantry, and Trip didn't budge.

"You're being very obstinate, pony," the governor said rather sharply.

"I'm sorry, sir," Pony said, and by now he was thoroughly confused. "I didn't mean to do nothing to upset you. I guess you want your eggs under. And let me see. Load up? I believe that's what you said."

"Right," the governor abstractedly answered as he peered through his magnifying glass at Trip as the minihorse walked out of the pantry and under a harvest table before he headed to the elevator and took a right, which led him into the kitchen.

"That's the most amazing horse I ever seen!" Pony marveled. "Look at that, sir. I think he's going to fix your eggs. Now listen up," he said to Trip. "Under. And load up. That's how your master wants his eggs."

Trip walked under a butcher's block and headed back to the elevator.

"I was just having a little fun," Pony sheepishly said to the First Couple. "I know there ain't no horse on this planet that can cook. If there was, you could just have all these little horses in the mansion and you wouldn't need inmates no more."

"I, for one, wouldn't eat anything a horse cooked," Mrs. Crimm said with disapproval. "Think how unsanitary that would be."

"That reminds me," the governor said, following Trip. "We need to get you straight with the Department of Corrections. I'll give them a call."

"So you must've read that nice thing Trooper Truth said about helping me out," Pony remarked with joy and amazement. "I sure do wish I knew who he was, 'cause I'd like to show my 'preciation."

Twenty-eight

Hey! Shut the fuck up!" The hostile voice came from inside a cramped, stinking, dark cell. It was late at night now, and the lights had been turned off inside the city jail.

"Shut yourself up!" Major Trader snarled back at the tedious bandit who called himself Stick and had ended up in jail after supposedly bumping his head, which had been covered with a bag, and then faking unconsciousness, assuming he would get a free ride to the hospital and then escape. It hadn't worked.

"Shut up!" another inmate chimed in, and Trader wasn't certain, but he thought the offensive voice belonged to Slim Jim, a repeat offender whose specialty was picking car locks and stealing toll money and sunglasses.

"*You* shut up!" Trader answered back. He was in far too foul a mood to be intimidated by anyone.

"No! *You* shut up, you motherfucker!" And it was Snitch who was awake now and irritable.

"*Sí*," the Mexican boy piped up. "Everybody shut up, *por favor.*"

"Stay out of it, spic," Trader warned.

"Huh!" the Mexican boy replied, offended. "I seen you jumping around the Dumpster."

"Whoa," Stick said. "I knew that man was crazy as shit. What he be jumping around a Dumpster for?"

"I think he was jerking off," said the Mexican boy, who had yet to reveal his real name to his cellmates or admit to the police that he was a juvenile. "See, I'm hiding from the police behind this bar, you know? And I seen him jumping around in the alley and he's holding his dick and jumping and making all kinda noise. So I run off 'cause he's *loco.*"

"Ain't you lucky as shit to end up in the same cell with him," Snitch sarcastically said as he shoved the flat pillow under the back of his head. "Ain't all of us lucky to have some crazyass stinking fat loco in the cell with us?"

"Yeah, what you jumping around for, huh?" Stick prodded Trader.

"None of your damn business. But I have a reason for everything and do nothing without a motive."

"Whoa. Loco-motive," Slim Jim said in a mocking voice. "We got Locomotive on the next bed."

"Please. Let's not fight. It's bad enough to be in here. For the love of God, let's show a little consideration and pray for peace," said Reverend Pontius Justice, who had dropped off several videotapes at Barbie Fogg's house last night and then had made the mistake of negotiating for a blow job on his way out of her neighborhood, only to discover that the woman he had decided to solicit wasn't a hooker but a spinster whose car had broken down after the battery had died in her cell phone.

"What would I want your twenty dollars for?" the spinster had inquired in a strange accent as Reverend Justice motioned her to come closer to his Cadillac. "If you offering me taxi money, babe, that sure is nice, but I don't take no money from strangers."

"I don't care what you spend it on," replied Reverend Justice, who was intoxicated and worn out and unfulfilled from promoting his new neighborhood watch program that so far had not prevented a single crime. "You climb in and take care of me for a minute, and you can do what you want with this brand-new twenty-dollar bill I'm holding. See?"

The spinster, who turned out to be Uva Clot and was infinitely older than he had thought when he'd first spotted her in the distant darkness, approached his Cadillac, wrote down his plate number, and started yelling for help. As Reverend Justice sped away, the police were on his butt with their sirens screaming and lights throbbing like his head.

"So, what you in for?" the reverend asked the dark area of the cell where Trader filled up the bed like a huge sack of potatoes.

"I'm a pirate," Trader said in an ugly tone.

"Lord protect us all!" the reverend exclaimed in shock. "You ain't one of them pirates that beat on that poor truck driver and stolt all his pumpkins, I sure hope?"

"None of your business!"

"Lord help us!"

"And I take pleasure in harming small animals," Trader added, for he knew enough about psychopaths to be aware that all of them began their monstrous lives of violent crime by tormenting helpless creatures.

He, for example, had never felt a hint of remorse when he'd torched the crab plantation, murdering mothers and little babies and other molting crabs who were temporarily without their protective shells. He didn't care a bit about the bateaus that had burned up, and it wouldn't have bothered him at all if Hilda's Chesapeake House had gone up in flames or if most of Tangier Island had. Nor had his peace of mind been disturbed when he had set up Hammer's Boston terrier to be stolen by Smoke and his ruthless road dogs. Trader hoped Popeye had long since been put to a cruel end. It would serve that bitch-superintendent right.

"Whoa," Stick's disapproving voice sounded in the dark cell. "That one thing I never done and never would. I think we should drown him in the toilet," he said to the others. "Two of us hold him and whoever's hands is free can shove his head in."

"Someone run over my puppy when I was still in the eighth grade."

Slim Jim sounded sad and upset. "I never did get over that, and the ass-hole who done it didn't even stop."

"What'chu mean, *still in the eighth grade?*" Snitch was curious as he sat up in bed and shoved the pillow against cinderblock to support his cramping back.

"You know, I just couldn't get out," Slim Jim replied. "Kinda like this place, you know? Every year, they said I had to repeat the eighth grade, all 'cause of that Mrs. Knock, my homeroom teacher."

"Bet they was all kinds of *knock-knock* jokes flying around the eighth grade," Stick observed.

"Un huh. That was one of the things that pissed her off," Slim Jim replied as he drifted back to that frustrating time in his failed life. "Knock-knock?"

He waited for a response from his cellmates. Finally the reverend caught on.

"Who's there?" he asked.

"Shut up!" Trader blurted out in disgust.

"Shut up, who?" the reverend asked, relieved that a distraction had presented itself.

"Shut up the fucking pirate in the toilet bowl and flush his fucking brains out!"

"Yeah, how I know it wasn't you who run over my puppy?" Slim Jim accused Trader's bed.

"Because, for one thing," Trader's voice coldly replied, "it is highly unlikely I frequented your trashy neighborhood. No doubt you lived in federally subsidized housing and spent all of your time on the street eating free cheese and wearing stolen sneakers."

"You dis me one more time," Slim Jim threatened, "and I'm coming over there and popping you in the head before I stick it in the toilet and flush your soul to the sewer where it belong!"

"Please!" the reverend protested. "This is a time to pray for forgiveness and seek peace and love thy neighbor as thyself!"

"Ain't never loved myself," Snitch admitted, getting morose.

"Me, neither," Slim Jim said sadly. "When my puppy got smashed in the road right in front of me, I quit loving myself. I 'cided never to love nothing again after that, 'cause if you love something, look what happens."

"Tell it," Stick chimed in.

Possum was alone inside the RV, because Smoke and the other road dogs were out cruising, and Possum had used the excuse of adding finishing touches to the Jolly Goodwrench flag so he could stay in with Popeye.

"You've got mail!" his computer suddenly announced.

Possum's adrenaline surged in excitement. Most of the people he e-mailed were other pirates who were usually drunk, stoned, and away from their computers at this late hour. Possum got up and sat on the wooden crate, clicking the mouse to see what was in the e-mail box. He was thrilled and nervous when he saw that the sender was Trooper Truth:

Dear Anonymous,

You must be a good person to provide me with the important information you sent. I've been waiting to hear back from you, and since I haven't, I decided to try to contact you now. You will be pleased to know that Captain Bonny (a.k.a. Major Trader) was apprehended earlier and is now in jail. I made sure this was accomplished, and now must ask you to hold up your end of the bargain.

What is the big plot that involves Popeye? And how do I know you're telling me the truth? I'd like to believe you don't intend for anyone else to be hurt. Where can we meet to resolve this, and how can we rescue Popeye?

Trooper Truth

Possum sat for a moment, excited but afraid for his life. If he set up Smoke and the road dogs and failed, he would be dead and so would

Popeye. Possum petted Popeye, who had jumped up in his lap and seemed to be reading Trooper Truth's e-mail, although Possum knew this wasn't possible. No dog could read. Most people Possum knew couldn't read, including the other road dogs. Even Smoke and his weirdo, nasty girlfriend had a hard time reading and usually got the information they wanted either from Possum or the TV news.

"What do I do, Popeye?" Possum whispered.

Popeye grabbed the pencil with her teeth and tapped the keyboard. Possum watched in disbelief as three words appeared on the screen in bold: JUST DO IT.

"Why didn't you let me know you can read and write? You even know the Nike ad!" Possum whispered as he hugged Popeye.

Popeye licked his neck. Oh, please save me, she silently begged.

"What you want me to do?" Possum asked again as the three words seemed to pulse on the screen like emergency lights that were roaring in for the rescue.

Popeye jumped out of his lap and up on the bed and began pawing the Jolly Goodwrench flag.

"You think that will really work?" Possum asked her. "I mean, that was my idea, too. How'd you know that was what I made that flag for? But what if it don't work, Popeye? What if Smoke end up shooting all of us?"

Popeye curled up on the flag and went to sleep, as if to suggest she wasn't worried in the least. She knew what Possum did not. Trooper Truth was really Andy Brazil, and Andy was fearless and would always prevail over evil. Popeye's owner would, too. What Popeye wasn't sure of was what might happen to Possum. She didn't want him locked up or punished in any way. She woke up and jumped off the bed. She pawed at the bedroom door, indicating Possum should open it, which he did. Popeye trotted into the living room and dug through a pack of crumpled cards until she found the ace of spades, which she carried back to Possum.

"I ain't sure I understand," Possum whispered to her. "Oh, wait a minute. Maybe you telling me I got to have a card up my sleeve?"

Popeye just stared at him in a way that suggested he was getting warm but was missing the point.

"Or maybe I should play a game?"

Popeye didn't react.

"I should bluff?"

Popeye was getting impatient. Why did humans have such a hard time understanding animals? Animals were explicit and didn't lie or even shade the truth. Unless animals were sick or had been treated savagely, they had no agenda beyond surviving and being respected and loved. Popeye snatched the playing card out of Possum's fingers and tossed it on the keyboard repeatedly, as if she were dealing.

"Deal?" Possum scratched his head, and Popeye licked his bare foot, voicing her approval. "What you saying? I make a deal with Trooper Truth?"

Popeye jumped back up in Possum's lap and licked his face with enthusiasm. Possum blew out a loud, tense sigh and began to type, just in time, because Andy was about to give up on getting a response.

> Dear Trooper Truth,
>
> I swear you can trust me. But my problem is, is I gonna get in trouble if I help you out? See, I'm sort of trapped by Smoke and the road dogs and if I set them up and even if it works, I'm afraid I'm gonna end up in jail.
>
> See, it was me who shot Moses Custer in the foot, knocking his boot off, 'cause I had no choice or I would have been hurt bad by Smoke and maybe shot, too. And Smoke always be saying he gonna hurt Popeye if I don't do what he say.
>
> I don't know what to do.

Andy read the e-mail and realized for the first time that the son of a bitch Smoke was behind Popeye's dognapping. Andy knew that Smoke was not to be taken lightly. Andy also realized with relief that he was in a perfect position to make an honest bargain with whoever this anonymous road dog was, so he fired back an e-mail to him.

Dear Anonymous,

The bullet you say you fired at Moses missed. He was in the hospital because the road dogs beat and cut him up so badly. Did you beat on him, too? Or cut him?

Trooper Truth

Dear Trooper Truth,

No! All I did after trying to shoot him was help dump the punkins in the river. As for the cutting, that was Unique. I sure is glad that bullet missed! Maybe now I can forgive myself and Hoss won't be mad at me no more.

Andy was unclear about the Hoss reference and didn't understand what Anonymous meant by the cutting's being *Unique*, but he decided to take a risk.

Dear Anonymous,

Surely you must know that Hoss would want the road dogs caught so nobody else, including Popeye, is in harm's way. I doubt very much that Hoss has been mad at you, because he would know that bullet missed Moses. Hoss knows everything. He's possibly been disappointed in you for not turning in Smoke and the road dogs. Now is the time to make things right, and a place to start is to tell me how I can find Smoke and the other pirates without them figuring anything out. By doing so, you will be granted immunity in exchange for your assisting the police. And I think you know by now that I always tell the truth.

Trooper Truth

A reply landed in the mailbox moments later.

Dear Trooper Truth,

Go to the race and look for a pit crew with a Jolly Goodwrench flag. That's us pirates. I'll have Popeye and do my best to stay out of the way, but you should know that Cat been taking helichopper lessons from the state police and plans to fly all of us to Tangerine Island after Smoke kills a lot of people.

"Jesus," Andy muttered as he stared at the message. There was only one state policeperson he could think of who might be giving anyone flying lessons right now, since the state police were so critically short of pilots at the moment. "Macovich. You stupid son of a bitch!" Andy said out loud. "What the hell are you doing?"

Macovich wasn't a saint, but he wasn't terribly bright, either, and Andy tried to work through Macovich's motivation. He dug through his briefcase until he found the paperwork on the Bag Man case he had worked last year. He dialed Hooter Shook's home phone number.

After much clunking and groping and coming to, Hooter groggily answered, "Hello?"

She assumed it was Macovich, who had been calling her a lot and stopping at her tollbooth, even when he didn't need to. That man was sex-addicted, she angrily thought. She had never seen anything like it. Most men she dated for the first time gave her at least an hour or two to figure out whether she might be remotely interested in holding hands or digging tongues halfway down each other's throats. But Macovich had kept grabbing at her under the table when they were drinking in that booth at Freckles. It was a shame, really. Hooter had liked him a fair amount when they'd chatted out by the traffic cones.

"I told you to quit calling me!" Hooter snapped over the line before Andy had a chance to say a word.

"I haven't called you recently," Andy replied. "Let me guess, you think this is Trooper Macovich."

"Well, you don't sound like him," Hooter said, calming down.

"This is Trooper Truth," Andy boldly said.

"Naw . . . You pulling my leg," Hooter replied with suspicion. She didn't recognize Andy's voice because most white folk sounded the same to her. "Ain't no way Trooper Truth be calling me."

"Well, I am," Andy said with confidence. "And the reason is because I need your help. It has come to my attention that you had drinks with Macovich at Freckles the other night."

"Yeah. That was the night from hell, I tell you."

"Did he take the check?"

"I didn't see no check," Hooter replied. " 'Cause I left to get me some air in the alleyway, then this crazy man started trying to shoot his privates off . . ."

"Yes, I'm aware of that," Andy politely interrupted her. "But I'm wondering if you ever saw Macovich pull out his wallet?"

"Uh huh. He paid for each round, 'cause we was the only Afric-Americans in there, and I'm assuming they didn't trust us enough to start a tab."

"I sincerely doubt that was the case," Andy reassured her. "The people in Freckles aren't like that, and it's easy to assume the worst if you've ever been treated unfairly. Maybe Macovich didn't ask for them to run a tab because he likes to flash his money, especially if he was trying to impress you."

There was a pause on the line as Hooter pondered this.

"Well," she finally conceded, "I guess you must be right, 'cause he sure was flashing his money, which I didn't like a bit 'cause money's just full of germs and he knew how I felt about it and then kept trying to grab at my legs under the table when we was drinking in the booth. But now that I think of it, I don't remember his asking for a tab, so maybe you right and I was jumping to 'clusions. You know, I got people at the tollbooth who never say 'Thank you' or 'Have a nice day,' even after I say it first. And I just always assumed it's 'cause of my non-white status."

"Many people are simply rude and consumed with themselves," Andy pointed out.

"Yeah, I guess that's so," Hooter said. She had softened considerably and seemed wide awake now. "But he did have money he was flashing around," she added, returning to the subject of Macovich. "Now you gotta understand there was a lot of smoke in there, but he was flashing away and I caught a lot of twenties and at one point, what I could swear was a hundred-dollar bill, which I never seen in the Exact Change lane and ain't never had in my entire life."

So Macovich *was* giving Cat helicopter lessons and possibly being paid a hundred dollars in cash for each one. Macovich was probably doing this at night or off hours when he knew no one else would be at the state police hangar. Andy walked into the kitchen to check the time. It was a little past 1:00 A.M. He dressed in civilian clothes, took his gun and portable radio, and went out to his car.

It was just as he'd suspected when he arrived at the airport. The Bell 430 was not inside the hangar, and there were what appeared to be fresh Salem Light cigarette butts all over the tarmac, even near the fuel truck. Andy switched his radio over to the state police aviation frequency.

"Four-three-zero-Sierra-Papa," Andy said over the air.

Macovich was startled and unnerved when Andy's voice filled his headset, as Cat, dressed in NASCAR colors, tried to fly the helicopter level and steady in a pattern around the nearby Chesterfield airport.

"Thirty-Sierra-Papa," Macovich replied, trying to sound innocent and busy.

"Who's calling us?" Cat demanded to know.

"Stand by," Macovich transmitted to Andy. "It's the tower," Macovich told Cat over the intercom because he didn't want to make the same mistake of broadcasting what he was saying in private.

"Let me talk to 'em," Cat said as he missed his approach. "I need to practice the radio."

"Not now," Macovich said through his mike. "You're gonna have to do a flyover 'cause you was way too high for that approach, and I got a feeling the tower's gotten a complaint about the way you're flying, so the best thing is let me deal with them and you just take your headset off for a minute, 'cause it ain't gonna be pleasant, whatever the tower's got on its mind, I can tell you that! Don't get so damn close to the fence! Pull it up to eight hundred feet and just fly the damn helicopter while I deal with this!"

Cat took off his headset and squinted through his Oakley sunglasses, trying to make out the very dark shape of trees looming ahead.

"Thirty-Sierra-Papa," Macovich transmitted to Andy. "I'm busy right now."

"Roger. I'm well aware of that," Andy's voice came back, and his tone boded that he knew exactly what Macovich was doing. "Your student is in violation," Andy used aviation vernacular.

"What you mean?" Macovich was getting increasingly alarmed and pulled up on the collective to clear the trees, a reflex he scarcely noticed anymore because he had to fight for the controls routinely when giving this NASCAR dumbshit a lesson.

"Just inform your student that the tower needs you to return to the ground ASAP," Andy ordered Macovich.

"Roger," Macovich reluctantly replied, and he tapped Cat's headset, indicating for him to put it back on. "We gotta problem," Macovich told Cat. "It's my ship. Don't make me tell you again to get your hands and feet off the controls! We got us a big mess with the FAA and I'm gonna have to deal with it so you don't get in any trouble and we don't end up grounded."

"Shit!" Cat exclaimed. "The race! There better not be any fucking problem! The world-famous driver I work for ain't gonna put up with no problem, and he's good friends with the gov'ner and the president of the United States and will get your ass fired!"

"Don't you worry," Macovich said, speeding back to the Richmond airport. "I'll handle it."

The only thing that got handled was Cat, who within the hour was in the city lockup, crowded inside a dark cell full of inmates who kept telling each other to *shut up* and continued to go on and on about some puppy that had gotten flattened in a hit-and-run. Andy called

Hammer the minute he got home. He informed her of everything that was going on, including the reassuring news that Popeye might be alive and would be rescued at the Winston Series race.

"That rotten snake," she said of Macovich. "He can just turn in his gun and badge when he gets to headquarters. You call him and tell him to report to my office at eight sharp."

"I respectfully disagree," Andy said. "Smoke and the other road dogs don't know Cat's identity has been revealed and he's now in jail."

"And he's also missing in action, as far as they're concerned," Hammer reminded him. "Don't you think they're going to be a bit suspicious when he doesn't show up to fly them to the race?"

"I think I've got a way around that."

"Let's hope so."

"I'll fly the governor in a four-oh-seven and make sure he, Moses Custer, and whoever else, get safely in their box," Andy laid out his plan. "And we'll have at least twenty troopers and EPU in plain clothes strategically stationed. Macovich needs to fly Smoke and his road dogs as expected. Don't worry, I'll get it all arranged."

"Balony, Andy!" Hammer wasn't convinced. "There will probably be a hundred and fifty thousand fans at that damn race. Twenty troopers can't begin to protect the governor and his guests and manage such a crowd if something bad goes down. The first shot fired and there will be a riot and people will get crushed in the stampede. Cars will run off the track and crash. It will be a terrible disaster, and I just don't think we're equipped to control it.

"And what if Tangier Island decides to be a problem, too? I don't think anything will dissuade them of the ridiculous notion that NASCAR plans to take over their island, and a perfect time to launch some sort of hostile move on their part would be during the race," she continued to paint negative scenarios. "We ought to have troopers posted on the island, too. Frankly, I wish you could write something in an essay that would convince those people to behave and settle down, but I doubt anyone on Tangier even has a computer."

"I've received no communications from anybody on the island," Andy informed her. "So you're probably right. No one there is reading me. But based on all the satellite dishes I noticed, they certainly watch TV. So why not create a diversion on the island? I can plant something in my next essay that will end up being broadcast in the news before the race."

He thought of Fonny Boy and the rusting piece of iron, and decided that nothing captured an Islander's attention more than items of value that they feared outsiders might try to take from them. Andy began to write a carefully worded e-mail that instructed his anonymous pirate friend to leave his or her computer logged on to Trooper Truth and watch for the next essay. In addition, the anonymous pirate was to inform Smoke that Cat was busy *practicing autorotations* and getting his *check ride* and would meet them at Tangier Island after the race so he had time to do a *high recon* of the area and set up their new headquarters.

"Tell Smoke and the others that Cat got word of a huge stash of treasure, and his instructor was going to drop Cat off on the island early and would fly Smoke and the dogs to the race as planned, then whisk them to Tangier Island where Cat would already be out in a boat, securing the treasure before anybody else found it," Andy e-mailed the anonymous pirate. "Assuming Cat doesn't have a computer or know how to use one, just say that the e-mail alerting them about all this came from the helicopter instructor, Trooper Macovich, who has decided to throw in his lot with you road dogs and be your pilot and get you guns and scuba gear, set up money laundering, and make runs to Canada and whatever else you need, in exchange for his being cut in on a modest share of the treasure."

Possum was slightly confused and a little frightened when he got Trooper Truth's latest communication, but he would do as he was instructed and leave the computer logged on to the website and pass on the information to Smoke. But Possum did have one final question:

Dear Trooper Truth,

This is the last time I write you but I was wondering if you could take that picture of Popeye in her red coat off the front page of your web. See, if Smoke see that picture, it will be the end of Popeye 'cause

he don't know anybody still looking for her except the lady supinten-
derent Popeye got stole from.

    P.S. My name is Possum but I use to be Jeremiah Little before
Smoke made me join his road dogs or else kill me, he said. Can you
call my mama and tell her I'm o.k. and ain't in any trouble and find
out if she still living with my daddy, 'cause if she is, I can't go back to
the basement and won't have no place to go when I get free of Smoke
and move out of the RV?

    P.S. P.S. Don't forget your promise!

Andy replied with an Instant Message assuring Possum that Popeye's
photograph was being removed right that minute, and of course, Trooper
Truth would call Possum's mama and keep all promises. Andy also wrote:

When you are about to leave the racetrack, be the first one to climb
into the back of the big helicopter that Trooper Macovich will be fly-
ing. Then slide across the seat with Popeye and rush out the other door
and run as fast as you can toward a camper that is flying a Virginia
flag and has six traffic cones in front. The camper will be easily visi-
ble on the other side of the fence surrounding the helipad, and I will
be sitting in a lawn chair in front, disguised as a drunk NASCAR
fan. Please stay clear of the tailrotor!

                                                            Good luck!
                                                         Trooper Truth

DISCOVERY OF TORY TREASURE HOURS AWAY!!

by Trooper Truth

The recent arrest of Dr. Sherman Faux (a mendacious dentist who should be avoided by all) has resulted in a shocking revelation that is exciting maritime historians, archaeologists, and treasure hunters around the globe.

If you, my faithful readers, are wondering why you have never heard of the famed Tory Treasure, I now offer you a fairly obvious explanation. The notorious and untrustworthy Major Trader is known for manipulating all official news that circulates throughout the Commonwealth and goes out over the wire to other states and nations. So clearly, the imminent recovery of shipwrecks in the Chesapeake Bay, which will no doubt lead to the discovery of the remarkable Tory Treasure, is information that Trader and others would not want the general public—and especially the Islanders—to have.

During the American Revolution, the most notorious and dangerous Tory raider was Joseph Wheland, Jr., who began his violent, greedy career in 1776 by seizing and plundering on behalf of the British crown. Soon enough, Wheland commanded a small fleet and struck wherever he pleased, burning plantations in Chesapeake Bay country and making off with livestock, slaves, furniture, family silver, jewelry, and any other valuables that he and his men could find—their true motivation having little to do with military victory or loyalty to the crown. In short, Wheland became an out-and-out pirate and chose Tangier Island as his winter quarters.

From his pirate's lair on Tangier, Wheland would set sail with his growing flotilla of gunboats and board other ships to steal and slash and shoot. There is insufficient documentation as to how much loot he amassed or how many vessels he sank or how many of his own sloops went down off the shores of Tangier and neighboring islands, but it is safe to say that for more than two centuries, a fortune of undiscovered Tory Treasure has lurked in the silty bottom of the bay. The reason for this deduction is one of pure logic.

Pirates as desperate and ruthless as Wheland not only preyed upon the innocent, but they gave no thought to raiding and slaughtering each other, provided they could get away with it. So if another pirate vessel laden with plantation loot was in the area, Wheland most certainly would have gone after it, unless he feared he might be overpowered. In this regard, Wheland and his pirate crew were no different from the drug dealers of today. When drug dealers stop off in Virginia during their travels from New York to Miami, it is not uncommon for one drug dealer to buy handguns or heroin from another, and then pull out a pistol and open fire. The point is, whoever wins not only gets the booty, but also the money or contraband that was the intended payment. Extra bonuses include cash and drugs from the victim's pockets, his gold chains, diamond-encrusted watch, rings, and means of transportation.

Drug dealers, like modern highway pirates, are simply land pirates. If you can imagine, for a moment, a band of drug dealers spinning back in time to the eighteenth century and waking up on a gunboat off the coast of Tangier Island, then you can pretty much envision what an encounter with another ship would have been like back then. You can be assured

that an ensuing battle between seafaring drug dealers would be no different from Wheland's attacking another pirate vessel in days of old.
Let's even go so far as to cast Wheland himself in the role of a time-
traveling drug pirate. The story would go something like this:

On a crisp October night, Joseph Wheland set off in his black Mer-
cedes with its spoiler, purple-tinted glass, gold mag hubcaps, fleece seat
covers, souped-up sound system, and dangling air fresheners. Smoking a
cigarette and nicely buzzed from pot, he left New York and headed
down to Richmond with several other vehicles and armed crew serving
as his convoy. Wheland was known on the street as *Wheelin' Bone*, because he was always in his car, didn't play hoops or lift weights, and was
bone-thin and physically unimpressive. But his appearance did not di-
minish the terror he struck in the hearts of his victims and other land pirates when they learned that Wheelin' Bone was in the neighborhood.

Arriving in Richmond in the early morning hours, Wheelin' Bone
and his mates parked along a trash-cluttered street in the federal housing project Gilpin Court, and proceeded to an apartment that was the
lair of a local drug dealer other land pirates called *Smack*. When Smack
looked out the window and spied Wheelin' Bone dressed in a long black
coat, black Nikes, and a black warm-up suit that had skulls and bones all
over it, Smack got a little uneasy.

"Shit, I don't know," he said to several of his lieutenants. "Man, he look
bad. Look like he might be packing an Uzi under that black coat a his,
'cause I can see the barrel poking out."

"You sure that ain't a buttonhole?"

"I say we don't take no chances."

"Shit no, we ain't taking no chances," Smack agreed. "I say we shoot
'em through the door."

Pistol slides snapped throughout the lair, and then the inexplicable
happened. Wheelin' Bone and his crew were about to knock on the door
when suddenly they vanished with a strange crackle of static and a flash
of intense white light. This frightened Smack and his pirates, and they responded with a salvo of gunfire that ripped up the door and shattered
lamps and beer bottles. They fired until magazines were empty. When

the smoke cleared, they peered out in astonishment at the dark, empty street.

Wheelin' Bone and his crew spun through the Third Dimension, passing through the Wrinkle in Time, and landed softly on a gunboat called *Rover*, which was loaded with eighteenth-century antiques, jewelry, and sacks of gold dust and silver coins.

"Where the fuck are we?" Wheelin' Bone asked as he stared out at the peaceful waters of the Chesapeake Bay and the distant shadowy shape of Tangier Island. "Man, I ain't never seen a boat this old. It don't even have a motor or a flashlight."

"Shit, look at these guns!" one of his mates exclaimed, as he inspected a huge cannon. "I sure would like to shoot one of these at a police car!"

Wheelin' Bone and his crew laughed at the image, and set about to figure out how to safely handle cannons, make homemade grenades, and sail. As days and weeks passed, they were indiscriminate in seizing other ships and celebrated with drunken nights of Madeira wine and rum, because they had quickly run out of pot and crack cocaine and could find no one who had ever heard of either. Wheelin' Bone and his men became expert at attacking other pirate ships and setting them on fire after they had been pillaged and their crews shot, hacked to pieces, and dumped overboard to be eaten by crabs.

Years passed and the American Revolution ended, but Wheelin' Bone became only more powerful and lustful. He terrorized the bay and the shores of Maryland and Virginia, and became even more feared than Blackbeard was in his day, although there is no record that Wheelin' Bone ever had a beard or set it on fire. His modus operandi, which he no doubt learned from stories about Blackbeard that were passed down from pirate to pirate, was to blast his cannons at the broadside of an unsuspecting vessel, which was followed by the hurling of Blackbeard-style grenades that were case-bottles filled with powder, small shot, slugs, pieces of lead, and iron—rather much like modern pipe bombs, except the grenades were ignited by a small, quick match that the pirates lit before quickly tossing the massively destructive devices into enemy ships. Wheelin' Bone and his mates would then board the disabled ship, step over the dead and finish off the wounded, and raid to their hearts' content.

Wheland or Wheelin' Bone (whatever you prefer to call him) faded from historical documentation toward the end of the eighteenth century, and by 1806, piracy had pretty much come to an end in the bay, although those otherwise peaceful waters and neighboring shores became vicious and volatile again six short years later during the War of 1812. Indeed, the Chesapeake and the nearby Patuxent River to this day remain a focal point of military activity, thus explaining the inconvenient restricted areas I mentioned in an earlier essay that make it so difficult to fly to Tangier Island.

One can only imagine the number of ghostly, broken hulls of ships and chests of loot that have littered the bay floor since John Smith settled Jamestown. Antiquities Law clearly states that found pirate treasure belongs to the location, which in the case of the Tory Treasure is Virginia. Of course, if the treasure can be traced back to the vessels from which the loot was originally seized, then the vessel's point of departure is highly likely to unfairly claim the treasure, and there will be a long, drawn-out battle in court. I strongly suspect that Wheland's remarkable stash will be claimed by North Carolina. But all of this is moot if individuals can find the treasure first and quickly pass it off to dealers at a very high price. I am stating the obvious to mention that no one is more capable of rapidly locating and seizing the Tory Treasure than the descendants of pirates who now live on Tangier Island and know the ways of the bay better than any other human beings.

It is my contention that the treasure belongs to the watermen, and we should allow them to have it. Tangier's economy is depressed. There are strict limits on the number of blue crabs they can trap, and the crab population has been shrinking for years. I am asking everyone, including the governor, to stay away from that crab pot marked by a yellow buoy that is approximately 10.1 miles off Tangier's western shore. Let decency prevail and greed vanish as you consider that most of us don't suffer the hard, often unrewarding lives of the watermen. Since their ancestors suffered so much when Joseph Wheland set up his winter headquarters on their island long ago, it would be only fair and right for today's Tangiermen to profit from that evil pirate's ruthlessness. It may very well be a perfect example of poetic justice.

Anne Bonny and Wheland never met the punishment they deserved. Even Blackbeard didn't get what was coming to him. Hacking him to death and impaling his severed head on a gunwale was light punishment compared to the way some pirates were dealt with in other parts of the world. Before piracy was first romanticized in modern times and then mundanely reduced to armed robbery, it was taken with grave seriousness in past centuries. All you need to do is flip through the pages of the two-volume 1825 edition of *The Terrific Register: or Record of Crimes, Judgments, Providences and Calamities,* and you will be shocked and sickened to see what I mean.

By way of example, I offer what was the typical fate of Russian pirates on the Volga, which in centuries past was so infested with pirates that merchants stopped transporting any cargo of value down the river unless the ships were accompanied by an armed convoy. These Russian pirates, who were not nearly as cold-blooded as Bonny, Wheland, or Blackbeard, were taken alive and no doubt became quite unsettled as they observed soldiers building a float and erecting gallows on it that were equipped with huge iron hooks.

The captured pirates were stripped naked and hung by their ribs on these hooks, and the float was sent slowly drifting down the river, allowing one and all to view the ghastly sight and hear moans of pain. If anyone in the bordering villages and towns the floating gallows passed showed a whisper of pity by offering the wretches water or liquor or a merciful death by gunfire, the punishment for being a Good Samaritan was to suffer the same slow, tormenting death as the pirates. This threat was sufficiently severe to prevent the public from intervening, and in fact, when one pirate managed to escape from his hook and, nude and trembling from pain and blood loss, came upon a simple shepherd, the shepherd's unsympathetic response was to beat the pirate's brains out with a stone.

I'm sure the shepherd was quick to loudly boast throughout the village about the unkind thing he had just done, otherwise the story would never have made it into historical records. This is not to say that I believe in vigilantism or torturing prisoners on death row. Nor should you assume I approve of the way the Russians dealt with piracy. But my point is that Bonny, Blackbeard, and Wheland, and their bloodthirsty sea dogs were just lucky they weren't caught in Russia.

It is quite likely that a piece of iron from one of Wheland's grenades has led to the discovery of at least one of his sunken ships, and one can only imagine the mysteries and treasures that have rested for centuries at the bottom of the bay in the area of the yellow buoy I previously mentioned. I realize that some maritime historians will insist that there is no evidence of a Tory Treasure, but I must remind my readers and Governor Crimm that Wheland "Wheelin' Bone" did not leave a list of all the ships and plantations he raided, and we can't be certain what ships sank, including his own, and what was on them.

Be careful out there!

Twenty-nine

Possum didn't notice the essay when it was first posted on the website because Smoke and the road dogs had returned to the RV not even an hour before, and dread had seized Possum by the back of the neck.

"I just wish you was here with me," Possum was praying to Hoss. "I know I ain't always done the right thing, but I'm trying to now. You be sure you tell Little Joe, Mr. Cartwright—and maybe Adam, if he ain't left the show yet. Okay? If you hear me, Hoss, please round up a posse and meet me at the race. I'm real scared—the most scared I ever been in my life. I don't know, but I got a bad feeling something ain't gonna happen the way Trooper Truth thinks it will.

"And I can't stand giving up Popeye. She's the only thing warm and alive I can trust, Hoss. Think how you'd like it if you had to give away your horse or was worried a bunch of outlaws was going to ambush you when you wasn't expecting it and shoot your horse! I know Popeye don't belong to me and it ain't fair for her to be locked up in this RV. I know I gotta do the right thing. But I need some help, Hoss."

"Now listen up, little buddy," Hoss said as he sat high on his beloved horse. "Outlaws are outlaws, whether they're horse thieves or truck thieves, and you *do* gotta do the right thing. Me and Pa and Little Joe ain't sore at you, and you gotta believe that. We're mighty sore at Smoke and his pack of gun-toting outlaws, though. Each and every one of them ought to be hung from a long rope. Now you do exactly what Trooper Truth told you, and don't be scared 'cause we're pulling for ya."

Hoss faded from Possum's mind and Possum dried his tears on the Jolly Goodwrench flag and sat up, noticing the Trooper Truth website glowing on the computer screen. He went over to his crate and clicked on the newest essay and read it with great interest, not certain but guessing what Trooper Truth had in mind. Taking a deep breath and telling Popeye to *stay* and *be a good girl*, Possum dashed out of his room and banged on Smoke's door.

"Smoke!" Possum yelled. "Smoke, get up and look at this! You won't believe it!"

Smoke was sitting cross-legged on his bed as he filled a hypodermic syringe with a poisonous mixture of solvents and rat poison that he had stolen from the hardware section of Wal-Mart when he had taken the road dogs out to find NASCAR colors.

"What the fuck do you want?" Smoke shouted at Possum. Smoke was high on beer, crack cocaine, and meanness after robbing another convenience store and discovering there was only eighty-two dollars in the cash drawer. "You seen Cat? Where the hell is Cat?" Smoke shouted again as he stuck the orange plastic cap back on the tip of the hypodermic needle.

Possum cracked open the door and peered through the space, his heart hammering.

"Smoke, I don't mean to bother you none, but there's something on the Trooper Truth web you got to see!" Possum said in a small, intimidated voice. "It's got to do with a whole lot of treasure and we can get it if we think quick. What you doing with that needle?"

Smoke jumped up from the bed, his bare chest covered with tattoos and beaded with sweat. His eyes were glassy, and the only thing worse than Smoke was Smoke when he was high and needed to sleep it off.

"Pop-eye," Smoke said with a cruel laugh as he pretended to inject Popeye with the syringe.

"Forget the fucking dog for a minute," Possum said, faking the bad act he had gotten fairly good at.

"Don't you fucking tell me to fucking forget anything, you little retard," Smoke said, pointing the needle at Possum as if he might just inject him instead of Popeye. "See, this is how Smoke makes assholes pay for their sins. Right when that bitch Hammer and her fuckhead sidekick Brazil come rushing up to the pit to save the stupid dog, I whip out this syringe and inject Popeye with rat poison right in front of them. While they're busy trying to save the dog, which will instantly go into convulsions and be in terrible pain, we shoot them in the head and run for the helicopter."

The scenario was unspeakably horrible, but Possum played up to his name and had no reaction. In fact, he looked half asleep and inattentive to everything except the opportunity to seize the Tory Treasure before anyone else got it first.

"Or if one of them fishermen gets the treasure 'fore we show up after the race," Possum said, "then we just wait for them back on the island and blow their brains out and dump their bodies in the bay and take the prize for ourselves. And Cat will already be there with everything set up, which is why he ain't here now, and we even got our own trooper working for us, too. Man, everything's phat, Smoke," Possum bragged.

Regina felt everything was fat, too, but not in a good way, as she made her way down to the breakfast table later that morning. She had suffered another terrible night of tire dreams and was at last facing the truth: Andy's interpretation was right. Life was passing her by. She was disgustingly fat and had a rotten personality. For the first time in her life, Regina's conscience stirred and she felt a twinge of shame and regret.

"Good morning," Pony said as Regina sullenly pulled out a chair and plopped down in it.

"Are you telling me it is or wishing it or just saying words that are meaningless?" Regina muttered, eyeing the steaming food Pony was setting on the table.

"Seems like a good morning to me," Pony replied cheerfully. "I'm on my way to being a free man, Miss Reginia! Only thing is"—he served scrambled eggs and link sausage on a plate shining with the gold Commonwealth of Virginia seal—"turns out I been in prison three years longer than I was s'posed to be 'cause of that Mr. Trader. Seems he did some messing with certain officials 'cause he didn't want me let out."

Regina stared at her food and realized with surprise that she wasn't hungry. She couldn't remember the last time she hadn't been hungry, unless it was when she had been sped to the hospital after eating Trader's poisoned Toll House cookies. But her loss of appetite then had been transient and medically based and couldn't be related to her present condition.

"You aren't eating, Miss Reginia," Pony worried, standing across the table from her in his stiff white jacket, a linen napkin draped over an arm.

"You shouldn't have been in prison, anyway," Regina surprised herself by kindly saying. "I've never seen you do anything wrong and have never been afraid of you."

"Why, thank you, Miss Reginia." Pony smiled but was puzzled. He was unaccustomed to Regina's having any opinion about his welfare or even noticing that he might have a life of his own. "I 'preciate that, and I think I can help you with Trip. What it's looking like is, he only respond to one- or two-word commands. If you start trying to conversate with him, he gets confused and don't listen."

Regina perked up a bit.

"How 'bout I write up a list of commands and maybe you can help out with him at the race tonight?" Pony suggested. "I been reading some of the papers the trainer left, and that little fella is quite the traveler. All you gotta do is put a diaper on him and you can stick him right in the limo or helichopper. My wife's down in the laundry room this very minute fixing a fancy blanket with the Comm'wealth of Virginia seal on it that he can wear under his harness."

Regina's mood continued to improve, as if anger and depression had been a stationary front all of her life and suddenly the oppressive, solid layer of unhappiness was moving away. She thought of Andy and his lecturing her about showing compassion, and she rehearsed an empathic line or two in her head as Pony continued to tell her about Trip's being housebroken and how to put on his tennis shoes and that he liked to snuggle when he wasn't working.

"I'm glad Papa's straightening out your prison mess," Regina repeated what she had rehearsed several times in her mind. "But I hope you'll still work for us, Pony, even if you don't have to anymore."

Pony was startled and wondered if Regina had a fever. She did look a little pale this morning and wasn't touching her food, and it sure wasn't like her to be nice.

"I would like it a lot if you wrote down that list of commands for me." Regina continued to baffle Pony with kindness. "Papa will need some help with Trip at the race, and I want to make sure I know everything I should. I'm glad Papa has a Seeing Eye horse. Maybe he won't need all those magnifying glasses anymore."

Regina got up from the table and neatly folded her napkin as Pony looked at her as if she had magically turned into someone else.

"Thank you, Miss Reginia," Pony said. "I'll make you that list and maybe show you a few things, if you want."

"Thank you, Pony," Regina said as she headed upstairs to her parents' master suite.

The First Lady was seated at her ornate Chinese desk, scrolling through something on the Internet, her attention rapt.

"Where's Papa?" Regina asked, pulling up a chair to see what her mother was so engrossed in.

"I believe he's in the garden with the pony," Mrs. Crimm said, tapping the down arrow.

"We shouldn't refer to Trip as a pony," Regina replied in an unusually thoughtful tone. "He's a minihorse, not a pony, and when Papa starts calling out *pony* this and *pony* that, Pony thinks he's talking to him and gets confused and it probably hurts his feelings, too."

The First Lady gave Regina a perplexed glance and said, "Well, I suppose you're right. You seem in a strangely pleasant mood this morning. I don't believe I've ever seen you like this. Are you sick?"

"I don't know what's wrong," Regina said, staring over her mother's shoulder at what appeared to be a new essay by Trooper Truth. "But I dreamed about tires again, Mama, and it started me thinking about what Andy said to me on the way to the morgue. Then I started thinking about the morgue, too, and wondering if I would have ended up there if I'd eaten any more of those cookies Major Trader tried to hurt Papa with. And suddenly I started feeling a little bit of hope. You know, I've never thought there was any hope."

"Of course there's hope, dear," Mrs. Crimm absently said as she wondered if those Tangier watermen would indeed find the Tory Treasure, which most certainly would include trivets from raided plantations—not that she assumed pirates used trivets, but they might have. Certainly, they cooked on their ships, and it would make sense to set a hot pot on a trivet to prevent wooden surfaces in the galley from getting burned.

"How long do you suppose a trivet could be on the bottom of the bay before it would rust away?" she questioned out loud as she peered through antique wire-rimmed glasses that were attached to a long, gold chain. "You should read this. It's quite interesting, about an old piece of iron that most likely will lead to the Tory Treasure, and I'm assuming if a piece of iron would still be intact after hundreds of years of being under water, then why wouldn't a trivet fare just as well? Many of them are iron.

"But I must say, your papa's not going to be pleased when I read this to him. I can't imagine he won't insist that the Commonwealth is the rightful owner of the treasure. It doesn't matter who Wheelin' Bone stole it from. What right does North Carolina have to anything found in the Chesapeake Bay? What matters is that the treasure is here in Virginia and therefore belongs to Virginia, and therefore any trivets found should be given to the mansion."

Regina got up to take a closer look at what her mother was reading. Although Regina had always been a strong advocate for *finders-keepers*, she wasn't so sure what she thought in this case. If the Islanders found the treasure and did whatever they wanted to with it, then the rest of the world would never have the pleasure of viewing old cannons and coins and jewels in the Virginia Museum.

"Those old cannons and jewels should be shared," Regina said as two sets of sneakers accompanied by slippered feet sounded behind them.

"What?" the governor posed his usual question as he caught the tail end of Regina and Mrs. Crimm's conversation. "Go ahead and keep walking," he said to Trip, who was already going ahead and didn't need to be told.

"Papa, I think he does better if you use fewer words," Regina tried to help.

"Okay," the governor considered, and the word *okay* released Trip from any commands and he came to a standstill near the First Lady's black-lacquered, mother-of-pearl-inlaid desk. "I didn't tell you to stop, but that's what I wanted you to do," the governor chatted on to his mini-horse and fondly rubbed his soft nose. "I think he understands far more than you might imagine, Regina."

"He might," she replied, "but what he understands and what you want him to do may be two different things."

"I see. What's this about cannons and jewels that should be shared?" the governor inquired as he dipped into a robe pocket for his magnifying glass, because no matter how much help the guide horse might prove to be, it could not assist Crimm with reading.

Regina paraphrased Trooper Truth's essay and again offered her opinion that the treasure should not be squandered by whoever finds it, but should be shared with the public.

"As long as certain pieces would come to the mansion," the First Lady was quick to add.

"Maybe a cannon or two in the garden and out front," the governor considered, and his spleen was acting up a bit at the thought of that damnable state of North Carolina. "As awful as that pirate Wheland was, he's part of Virginia history, and I'll be damned if those watermen are going to get the treasure first and sell it to some antique dealer or, worse, to North Carolina."

"Oh, Bedford," Mrs. Crimm pleaded, "you must do something right away, before it's too late! Can't you send in an aircraft carrier or something, so those Tangier people don't haul all of the treasure away? They have no right to it!"

"No, they don't," Regina agreed, and it was the first time she had not been in concert with what Trooper Truth had to say. "How weird," she added. "Whose side is Trooper Truth on, anyway? He's always made sense in the past and been on the side of truth and justice."

"He could very well be in collusion with Tangier Island and is trying to influence me to let them have the treasure," said the governor, who was seeing matters far more clearly since he had stopped listening to Trader and eating his sweets. "I'll issue a press release immediately that warns all treasure hunters to stay clear of that crab pot with the yellow buoy," the governor declared. "Let those fishermen just try to go near that sunken ship and think they're going to"—he patted Trip's neck—"load up. Right, little fella?"

Trip pulled away from his owner and headed toward the elevator and then took a right.

"Right!" Regina said, proud of her father's power and decisiveness, while Trip made another right and stopped before his reflection in a gilt Chippendale mirror.

"How far down do you think it is?" the First Lady pondered as she imagined chests of gold, family silver, and jewelry fit for a queen.

"Down?" Regina puzzled. "How far down what is?" she asked as Trip lay down in front of the mirror and continued to stare at himself, a bit puzzled.

"Based on the location in this Trooper Truth propaganda," the governor replied, "I'd say the treasure's down pretty deep, because it's in the crab sanctuary, which is in a trough of the bay, if I'm not mistaken."

"Well, that's good," the First Lady said with relief. "The deeper the better, because it will make it all that much more difficult to find. I doubt those Tangier people have the proper gear to dive down and bring a big cannon to the surface. Why, it would sink one of their little boats."

Within the hour, news of the Tory Treasure screamed over the wire and blared over televisions and radios throughout Virginia, the U.S., and in particular, bombarded North Carolina. Commentators speculated that the people of Tangier would be excited into a furious frenzy because of the governor's order that any waterman seen within five miles of the crab pot with its yellow buoy would be arrested by the Coast Guard, which had rushed to patrol that area of the bay. Treasure hunters and their vessels were on notice that they would be seized, the airspace between the Virginia coast and Tangier was restricted to all except authorized aircraft, and Naval vessels were preparing to form a blockade around the island.

Fonny Boy and Dr. Faux heard the news over the car radio after posting bond and leaving Richmond as quickly as possible. They sped toward Reedville, where the dentist intended to hop on the mailboat and bribe the captain to help them find the crab pot Fonny Boy had dropped in the water.

"The Coast Guard won't be suspicious of the mailboat," the dentist reasoned as Fonny Boy stared tensely out the window, watching telephone poles fly by.

"That's poor! It ain't fittin'! The treasure, it's mine!" Fonny Boy said every other minute.

"We'll split it fifty-fifty," Dr. Faux reminded him. "You owe me for bond and whatever I end up paying the mailboat captain. We'll need gear, too, which will be expensive. There's a bait and tackle shop near where the mailboat docks, but we've got to hurry, and for God's sake, don't do anything to cause trouble, Fonny Boy. If the police know we've left Richmond, we'll be arrested again for jumping bail, and then the judge is really going to throw the book at us."

"They wouldn't do nothing to us!" Fonny Boy's backward talk meant that if they got caught while finding the treasure, they were really in trouble this time.

"And if the mailboat gets seized, who cares?" Dr. Faux replied. "It doesn't belong to us. If questioned, we'll just blame everything on the captain and say that we boarded the boat to mail a few letters and dental bills back to the island, and next thing we knew, the boat was speeding toward the treasure before we had a chance to get off."

"No!" Fonny Boy excitedly meant the opposite.

Major Trader and his cellmates learned the news, too, because one of the guards had a habit of wearing a Walkman with the sound turned up so loud prisoners could hear every tune, advertisement, and news release that leaked from his headset.

"Now listen here," Trader said. "Instead of wasting all your time trying to drown me in the toilet, let's band together. If we can figure a way out of here, we can find that treasure first."

"You think so?" Slim Jim asked with nagging doubt. "I mean, even if we could get outta here, how we gonna find that crab pot and then haul all the treasure outta the bottom of the bay?"

"I can't swim," Snitch added.

"Uh uh, I never could swim," Stick confessed.

"You don't have to swim, you idiots!" Trader impatiently replied.

He had traded beds with the Mexican boy because if there was one thing Trader understood, it was office psychology. His maxim was fairly simple. If you wanted to feign friendship and sympathy, you sat the person you wished to manipulate in a nice living area with nothing between the two of you but a coffee table. If the objective was to intimidate, you sat at your desk, which became an imposing barrier between you and the individual you intended to terrorize. If you wished to confuse and humiliate, which had always been his preferred tactic with the governor, you poisoned the person with Ex-Lax and then insisted on having important discussions while walking through buildings or driving.

The Mexican boy's steel bed, as it turned out in the light of morning, was in the center of the cell. By appropriating it while he was using the toilet, Trader had gained the leadership role he wanted, although the other cellmates weren't sure why they suddenly viewed him with a bit more respect. Realizing the power of violent gastric attacks, Trader directed that when the guard was strolling past, on cue Reverend Justice would double over in agony and make loud moans and shrieks while the other cellmates gathered around him in a panic and screamed for help and shouted for everyone to give him air.

"The guard will burst inside the cell to render aid," Trader explained. "And when he does, you"—he said to Stick—"poke him in the eye, and you"—he said to Cat—"grab his radio, and you"—he said to Slim Jim—"grab his keys so you can unlock all the doors, and you"—he pointed to the Mexican boy—"put your finger in your pocket and pretend it's a gun and start threatening to shoot because no one in this place understands Spanish, and you"—he nodded at Snitch—"stay right here in the cell and when questioned later, claim that our jailbreak was an inside job and you overheard us saying we were escaping in an awaiting getaway car that was taking us to Charlotte."

"But we don't got no getaway car," Stick said, and he didn't like the thought of sticking his finger in anybody's eye.

"That's where you come in," Trader said to Reverend Justice. "The guards treat you far more respectfully than the rest of us and have even asked you religious questions and told you to pray for their various problems. I fully believe that if you ask to use the pay phone because one of your parishioners is dying and needs last rites over the phone, the guard will give in."

"Baptists don't do last rites," the reverend protested. "And I'm not so sure I want any part of this. I'm already in a world of trouble for trying to solicitate that old Clot woman."

They fell silent as the guard with the headset loudly passed by, his eyes glazed as he snapped his fingers and hummed to a rap tune.

"When you use the pay phone," Trader resumed, "you call someone of lesser intelligence who works for you and is submissive and naive, and order that person to pick you up on the street. Just say you'll have a few

381

friends along for the ride, and then we'll get the hell out of town. In the immense unlikelihood that we're apprehended, I'll just claim that you were abducted and had nothing to do with the plan."

Reverend Justice was a little more at ease when Trader put it to him that way. After all, Reverend Pontius Justice was a local celebrity who had devoted his life to saving souls and stopping crime. Even if he released his pent-up needs of the flesh now and then by picking up ladies of the night, he always paid them and gave thanks.

A ndy had yet to receive any thanks from Hammer, and it was getting on his nerves that all she seemed interested in was pacing the carpet in her headquarters office and complaining.

"You should have run this by me first," she kept saying behind the closed door, even though there were very few people at headquarters on a Saturday morning. "For God's sake, Andy, where was your brain when you wrote all this nonsense about a so-called Tory Treasure? Look at what you've stirred up! By encouraging the Islanders to seize the alleged loot because it's rightfully theirs, you have succeeded in prompting the governor to issue threats and send out the military. If there wasn't a civil war before, there certainly will be one now. And frankly, I'm in agreement with the governor. The Islanders do not have a right to the treasure. It belongs in a museum."

"That's what I'm trying to tell you," Andy tried to get through to her. "My only intention was to cause everyone to think everybody else is trying to take something away from them. And in order to make Tangier Island really angry at Virginia, it was necessary for me to excite Virginia into being really pissed off at the island. Then, when Macovich arrives tonight in a state police helicopter filled with NASCAR guys who are really Smoke and his road dogs, just what sort of reception do you think they'll be greeted with? Our undercover troopers will hardly be needed."

"You're making no sense and you're scaring me!" Hammer blurted out. "And I thought the entire point of Trooper Truth was to always tell the truth. It seems to me in these latest essays all you're doing is manipulating everyone, even if it's for a good cause. Or even if you mean it as a good cause. Damn it! I'm so confused."

"I understand exactly how you feel," Andy said. "I promise I know what I'm doing. We both know how ruthless and dangerous Smoke is. If that helicopter sets down on the island and he sees the first hint of people who don't exactly look like watermen, even if they're dressed like them, he very well may open fire the minute he steps out on the airstrip. We've got to introduce an element of surprise to make him pause just long enough for us to surround him and take him down without incident."

"Let's get on with this and mobilize the troops," Hammer decided. "The governor will just have to return by car to the mansion after the race. You and I are flying the helicopter to Tangier Island to see what we can do to bring closure to this mess. And by the way, what makes you think a Tory Treasure really is in the bay?"

"I don't necessarily think it," Andy replied. "But that old piece of iron clearly came from a battle, possibly involving pirates. And that Tory turncoat Joseph Wheland certainly must have amassed a fortune during all of his years of plundering plantations and other ships, so what happened to all of his loot?"

Barbie Fogg had never been on a real plantation, but she got a sense of what that might be like when she pulled up to the front gates of the governor's mansion at noon, just in time to see a very odd sight.

Two powerfully built EPU troopers were shoveling woodchips into the back of a long, black limousine. Barbie drove through the opening gates and parked on the circular driveway. She collected her makeover products, which fit nicely in a large toolbox, and grabbed a bag of clothes out of the trunk.

"What are you doing?" she asked the troopers. "I don't mean to pry, but why are you piling all these woodchips on the back floor of this beautiful limo? Are you planning to plant flowers inside? If so, I think that's a wonderful idea. Then the governor can ride around in a garden."

The troopers sternly replied that the information was classified, and then the mansion's front door opened and a black butler in a stiffly pressed white jacket greeted Barbie with a smile.

"Do come in," he warmly said. "Miss Reginia is expecting you. Here, let me take your coat, and can I help you with your toolbox?"

"Thank you," Barbie said, slipping out of her coat and revealing a rather sexy tight leather outfit that did not seem in keeping with her daintiness or soft voice. "I need the toolbox and the bag so I can work on Regina."

Pony knew that Regina's appearance required a lot of work, but it saddened him to think things had deteriorated to the point that tools were required. He escorted Barbie up the winding staircase to the First Family's private quarters, where Regina was rummaging through her bedroom closet, pulling out painter's paints and sweatshirts and getting increasingly discouraged.

"Oh!" she said with relief when Barbie walked in and set the toolbox and bag on the bed. "I'm so glad you're here! I can't find anything to wear and I looked in the mirror a little earlier and scared myself. Do you really think you can make me pretty in time for the race?"

"Of course I do," Barbie assured her as she looked out the window at the EPU troopers shoveling more woodchips into the limousine.

"That's for Trip's trip," Regina explained.

"Trip-trip?" Barbie was baffled. "What's a trip-trip?"

"No, *Trip's* trip, not trip-trip," Regina said. "Trip's Papa's new little minihorse that's specially trained to guide blind people. Papa has to take him everywhere he goes, you see, and since I'm supervising, I did a little research on the subject and found out that minihorses do better in the car if they have woodchips."

She paused to see if Barbie understood the point. Barbie didn't.

"Sort of like being in a stall," Regina offered a hint. "You know, like a litter box."

"Oh," Barbie said in amazement. "And here I was thinking they were planting a nice little mobile garden. Silly me. But I would think if a little horse does his business inside a limo—woodchips or not—it might prove a little unpleasant for whoever else is riding along."

"Horse doo-doo doesn't smell as bad as dog doo-doo," Regina reminded Barbie. "And the minute Trip uses the bathroom, you just scoop woodchips over it and you don't even know it's there."

"Then what happens when you get up in the governor's box at the race?" Barbie worried as she opened the toolbox and began to arrange bottles of foundation, blemish cover-up, nail polish, hair treatments, and dyes, along with dozens of other cosmetics, on top of an antique walnut high chest.

"If he needs to go out, he'll paw the door," Regina replied. "Then I'll take him down in the elevator and find a patch of grass somewhere. What are the scissors for? Are you going to cut my hair?"

Barbie told Regina to sit in the Shaker rocker and be still for a moment. Barbie circled her most challenging project, taking in the overall scene and deciding that Regina's long frizzy dark hair with its split ends had to go.

"Let me see your teeth," Barbie said.

Regina opened her mouth wide and curled back her lips, revealing yellowing teeth that, ironically, could very well belong to a minihorse, Barbie thought.

"I brought some tooth bleach," she said with more optimism than she felt. "So let's put the bleach on now and give it a chance to at least begin working. As for your hair, dear, it has no color at all, really. I suppose it's sort of a brindle—a splotchy mix of brown and black. And I think the solution is to dye it black and cut it just below your ears, layering it, of course, and this will help to soften your nose and chin.

"I also thought to bring along a nice tanning solution that you'll put on after your salt scrub, Dead Sea soak, manicure, pedicure, and mud mask. You'll turn a nice golden brown without exposing your skin to even one ray of damaging sun. Isn't that exciting?"

Regina wasn't sure. For one thing, she had not anticipated that Barbie might expect Regina to strip completely naked and allow an almost-stranger to rub salt, mud, and lotions all over Regina's corpulent body.

"Now, I know what you're thinking," Barbie said as she draped a towel around Regina's neck and began snipping away huge clumps of hair that reminded Barbie of tumbleweeds in old Westerns she sometimes watched with Lennie. "I'm aware from our counseling session that you have a very poor self-image and hate your body, and probably are just a wee bit nervous about being naked and having things rubbed, peeled, scraped, and scrubbed over every inch of you, but you'll be fine and just so pleased when you see the result."

"Nothing you scrub me with will get rid of all this fat," Regina candidly pointed out as more hair tumbled across the floor. Under ordinary circumstances, the idea of having her body so completely manipulated would have been secretly pleasant.

But Barbie Fogg wasn't Regina's type. Not at all. Barbie wasn't robust enough and struck Regina as the sort who could probably touch and knead another woman all day long and experience not the slightest tingle or desire for more. Regina doubted that Barbie had much interest in anything physical from anyone, and in that regard was probably similar to Regina's mother, who for as long as Regina could remember had been far more interested in collectibles, such as cast-iron banks, old coffee and tobacco cans, and trivets, than in wild, erotic same-sex or opposite-sex or even self-sex.

"We'll start you on a diet immediately," Barbie said as she snipped, snipped. "Which means you'll need to stay clear of the buffet tables at the race, okay? A nice salad, and lots of celery, carrots, and radishes will have to tide you over, but in the meantime, don't be so negative. You know what they say, *clothes are a girl's best friend*, and I went to the trouble to pop by a sweet little boutique and pick out something just perfect for you."

"What?" Regina was almost afraid to ask as Barbie began to layer strands of hair with a razor.

"Oh, it's just the cutest thing. To die for, really. I intuited what you might feel comfortable in and what suits your overall face, figure, and personality, and came up with this simply perfect denim outfit! I couldn't believe it when I found it! Now, hold still and try not to rock. Such a lovely rocking chair, by the way, but I don't want to cut you with the razor as I shave the back of your neck before we do a nice waxing of your upper lip and chin, and maybe clean up your eyebrows and sideburns.

"Anyway, what I found is a pair of stonewashed overalls that have a cute skirt instead of pants, and you can wear it with this darling long-sleeved silk shirt that's designed to look like a lumberman's shirt, only it's got a lace collar and will show off your bust, which will really be enhanced by the push-up bra I found. I had to guess, but you look like a forty-four D, am I right?"

"I don't usually wear a bra," Regina replied through a shower of shredded hair. "I hate bras and wear undershirts most of the time because nobody really sees me through sweatshirts, anyway."

"Well, people will certainly see you tonight," Barbie cheerfully piped. "You'll have so much cleavage you could pack a picnic in it! As for shoes, because no outfit is complete without them, I found an adorable pair of bright red patent leather high-top tennis shoes. Can you imagine? They have a Converse seal on the ankles made out of sequins, and white leather laces, and you'll wear them with designer socks that are supposed to look like old-fashioned tube socks, but these are made of silk! Now let me guess, your shoe size is a twelve? And your dress size is a sixteen?"

"Men's or women's?" Regina asked, holding very still as Barbie worked away with the razor, cleaning up the back of Regina's neck. "I always wear men's stuff, so I don't know what size I wear in women's."

"Don't you worry for a minute. I'm very good at guessing people's sizes," Barbie promised as she stepped back to admire her work. "I suppose it's because, as a professional counselor, I have to be good at sizing people up. There."

Barbie held a hand mirror so Regina could admire her new hair style.

"I don't know," Regina said with misgivings. "It's shaped exactly like one of those helmets the race-car drivers wear."

"The newest rage," Barbie beamed. "It's called a *NASCOIF.* Isn't that just too chic? And you'd pay a pretty penny if you got one in a salon, assuming you could get an appointment or even on a waiting list during the race season."

"If it's so chic, then why don't you have a NASCOIF?" Regina wanted to know.

"Oh, my features are far too delicate," Barbie said. "Now let's get you in the tub."

Thirty

Hooter was also devoting the day to getting ready for the race. She had spent hours unraveling her dreadlocks and processing her hair, which this minute was cooking under a snug head-rag as she glued on new acrylic nails that looked like long, curled American flags. Then she struggled into skintight black imitation-snakeskin stirrup pants, and over these she pulled on a pair of puffy silver boots that fastened with velcro and were designed to have an astronaut look.

Completing the ensemble required much careful deliberation, and she decided on a simple black tube top, and for the pièce de résistance, the beaded jacket with Kodak, DuPont, and Pennzoil logos in bright colors that she had found in the NASCAR section of a knock-off fashion boutique on East Broad Street, between the Affordable Gun Store and the Nocheck Check Cashing and Pager Shop.

* * *

A ndy was paying close attention to his attire as well, but not for reasons of vanity or sex appeal. He had never been to the Richmond International Racetrack and wasn't exactly sure what a drunk NASCAR fan might wear, but he figured the less conspicuous and more heavily protected and armed he was, the better. So he put on scuffed cowboy boots and baggy jeans that easily concealed a pistol in an ankle holster he fastened at a boot top, and over his body armor he wore a Redskins sweatshirt and leather jacket. He had been smart enough not to shave this morning, and with his stubble, ponytail wig, mirrored sunglasses, and a nine-millimeter pistol tucked out of sight in the back waistband of his pants, he felt secure in his appearance. Smoke wouldn't recognize him. In fact, nobody would.

He had just begun the process of splashing himself with beer when his doorbell rang.

"Who the hell . . . ?" he muttered, slightly alarmed, because he certainly wasn't expecting company. "Who is it?" he gruffly said through the locked front door.

"It's me," a muffled female voice replied, and at first, Andy did not place it and thought of the serial killer who had left the evidence on his doorstep.

"Who's me?" he asked.

"Hammer."

"Wow," he said in surprise as he opened the door. "I'm sorry I sounded rather unfriendly, but I had no idea it was you. I mean, I didn't at first. So I almost didn't recognize your voice, because I . . ."

The blood didn't seem to be flowing to his brain as he looked her up and down. Hammer was dressed like an Outlaws motorcycle gangster, all in black studded leather, black Dingo boots, and a Harley jacket. Slung over her shoulder was a Harley tote bag that no doubt contained a small arsenal. She had hardened her handsome face with gaudy layers of make-up, and her hair was teased.

"Don't give me a hard time," she said right off as she walked inside the house. "The last thing I want to look like is a cheap motorcycle slut, but I had to do something. I'm just worried about our arriving by helicopter looking like this," she added as she took in his disguise. "And we can't get any undercover troopers out to Tangier because the only pilots I have are you and Macovich, and both of you are busy, and the ferries aren't running because of the goddamn restrictions the governor has imposed because of your Tory Treasure essay. That's why I decided to drop by right away and ask you to consider if maybe we should reconfigure what we're doing."

She followed him into the dining room, and they sat in his makeshift office. As Hammer noticed the computer, printer, filing cabinets, and piles of research materials, it gave her a strange feeling to realize this was the secret headquarters of Trooper Truth, even though she knew very well who Trooper Truth really was and where he worked and lived. It oddly occurred to her that even she had begun to bond with the fantasy writer and to wish she could meet him.

"This is ridiculous," she said.

"I know," Andy agreed. "I look pretty stupid and I'm sorry I smell like beer and haven't shaved, and you're probably right. A state police helicopter may not fit with our disguises."

"What I meant was, it's eerie sitting in the place where you write your essays. I feel as if I've just walked behind the curtain and discovered the Wizard of Oz or am in the Bat Cave or something. And I must say, a part of me is very disappointed because I think I must have started believing in Trooper Truth, too. Oh good God, don't tell me I was becoming a fan!" She shook her head and sighed. "I must be losing my mind. In the first place, I'm a fan of no one and think being a fan of anything or anyone is irrational and silly. Why would a rational human being inflate someone to Mount Olympian proportions, think they're a god, and hang up posters of them?

"How does it make sense for someone to adore and even want to go to bed with a perfect stranger?" she went on as Andy stared down at his hands, ill at ease and hurt that she had, perhaps, liked Trooper Truth better than him. "I guess what this means is there are probably thousands, if not millions, of perfect strangers out there who read Trooper Truth and worship him and entertain sexual fantasies about him," Hammer continued. "I know Windy certainly feels that way, only in her case, she's convinced that Trooper Truth is at least eighty years old and has to use a walker. I guess the gig is up," Hammer announced by slapping her hand down on the table.

"What gig?" Andy replied with a hint of pain and anger. "There's no gig and never has been. It doesn't matter what nom de plume I use or if I use one at all. I'm still the one who has written the essays. I *am* Trooper Truth!"

"Trooper Truth doesn't exist," Hammer said.

"All right, let me ask you this," Andy said, trying to regain his composure. "If you never thought of me as Trooper Truth, then who was Trooper Truth to you? Did you have some fantasy about him, huh?"

"We need to disengage ourselves from this pointless, inane conversation right this minute," Hammer said. "We've got a major operation about to happen and need to focus on that, for God's sake."

"You're absolutely right," he said in a steadier tone. "It truly doesn't matter to me that you are or aren't a fan of Trooper Truth or anyone, including me. I'm not a fan of anybody, either. Never have been," he added as the telephone rang.

"Wooo! We got us a real problem, Brazil," an excited Macovich said over the line. "The guv don't want to take the helicopter to the race!"

"You're kidding," Andy said. "Why the hell not? You'll just have to talk him into it. Tell him for security reasons he must fly in . . ."

"It won't work. Seems like he's all of a sudden got it in his head he's gotta have a big litter box for this little horse he just got. I think that damn ugly pool-shark daughter had something to do with it. I ain't never heard something so stupid in my life, but there's nothing we can do. He's got troopers to fill the back of his limo with woodchips and we can't talk him out of it. So he and the First Family are going by limo and that's final. I got to drive him. I'm real sorry, I don't know what else to tell you."

"But what about Smoke and the road dogs?" Andy protested. "What are they going to do when the helicopter doesn't show up to take them to the race? And they've got Popeye!"

"All I know is they're supposed to meet me at the MCV helipad, and I ain't gonna be there."

"Shit!" Andy exclaimed as he slammed down the phone.

He explained what was going on, and it pained him to see the anguish flicker across Hammer's face as she realized that Popeye might not be saved and their entire plan had just crashed and burned. Smoke and the road dogs were still at large unless she could think of a way to lure them into a trap. Now it was unlikely they'd show up at the race.

"If they wait for the helicopter and it doesn't come, they're going to figure out that something's up," Hammer said, dejected. "They'll figure out that Cat has probably been grabbed by us and we've got half the state police force waiting for them at the racetrack. All because of a goddamn minihorse!"

Andy was silent. Both of them knew that it was Andy who had planted the minihorse in the governor's mind by suggesting it on the Trooper Truth website.

"I don't know what to say, I'm . . ." Andy started to say.

"It's too late for apologies," a crestfallen Hammer replied. "And you don't need to apologize anyway, Andy. It's not your fault. I was the one who went along with this Trooper Truth charade, never realizing the repercussions it might have. I just hope Popeye . . . Well," she said, her voice breaking. "I just hope she doesn't suffer . . ." she blurted out in grief as tears welled in her eyes. "Damn it all!"

"Wait a minute," Andy said as an incredible but simple idea occurred to him. "Donny Brett flies a four-thirty!"

"Who?" Hammer asked as she dug in her Harley bag for a tissue and handcuffs clanked against a pistol.

"You know, number eleven! He's got six wins so far this year, including Martinsville and Bristol, and the reason I know about his bird is Bell has used it in a lot of ads. It's painted with Brett's colors and he always arrives at the races in it, so it's probably sitting at the racetrack helipad even as we speak. Yes!" Andy's thoughts flew so fast he was scarcely making sense. "Family of one of the drivers. That's it! And we'll just show up at MCV in Brett's helicopter and fly that son of a bitch Smoke and his road dogs ourselves!"

"But how the hell are we going to get whatever-his-name-is-Brett to let us use his helicopter at this late hour?" Hammer said. "It's impossible."

"Simple," Andy replied. "We walk into the fantasy and turn fiction into fact."

"Now is not the time to talk like a writer!" Hammer warned as she blew her nose.

"You can be up front with me in the left seat and pretend to be my girlfriend," Andy relayed his plan as it unfolded inside his head.

"And who will you be?"

"I'll go as Donny Brett's brother," Andy said. "What we've got to do is let Smoke and his road dogs think Macovich couldn't make it to pick up the so-called Jolly Goodwrench pit crew and got Brett to help out. We'll pick up the assholes, have undercover guys everywhere, and the minute we land, we'll nail them. Now come on. We've got to get to the racetrack."

The only way that was going to be possible, in light of traffic jams that spanned virtually the entire Commonwealth as a hundred and fifty thousand NASCAR fans fought their way to the racetrack, was for Andy to overfly the gridlock in a state police helicopter. Then he and Hammer would hurry to find Donny Brett, who had always been described as an all-American boy and family man who collected police badges and guns. Brett also believed in security, and when Hammer and Andy pushed through the crowds and showed up at Brett's luxurious trailer on the racetrack grounds, big men blocked the door and looked as if they didn't mind hurting overly enthusiastic fans and stalkers.

"We must have a word with Mr. Brett," Hammer announced.

"He's resting, so please go away," one of the bouncers said in an unfriendly way.

Hammer's wallet was in the back pocket of her leather pants, attached to a chain, and she flashed her badge as she said in a low voice, "We're state police involved in a huge undercover operation. Lives are at stake!"

Andy dug into his jeans and flashed his badge, too.

"We don't want to disturb Mr. Brett and realize he needs peace and quiet before he gets into his car and hopefully wins the race, but we must see him," Andy explained.

"I sure as hell hope he wins, too," the second bouncer said. "He gets pretty upset when he don't win, and he always likes to get a little shut-eye and meditate before he races. But let me tell him what's going on and we'll see what he wants to do."

"You're joking, right?" Donny Brett said moments later when the motorcycle mama and her redneck younger boyfriend were escorted inside the plush trailer. "I'm not doubting you're cops, but you must think I'm pretty stupid to let you or anybody else just fly off in my chopper. And how would I get out of here after the race?"

"We can get you the state police four-thirty," Andy said to the handsome, famous driver, who looked rather sleepy and unassuming when he wasn't wearing his colors. "As soon as the governor is safely returned to the mansion in his motorcade, an EPU trooper named Macovich will fly here and pick you up. I promise."

Brett considered this for a moment as he popped open a Pepsi.

"Oh yeah?" he said. "So what does the state police bird look like? What kind of paint job does it have?"

"The state police paint job," Hammer replied.

"So if I win the race, it will look like I'm getting a police escort out of here?" Brett rather liked the idea.

"Even if you don't win, you will," Hammer said.

"But you will win," Andy added.

Brett sat at a table and blew out a big sigh. He suddenly looked small and uncertain and not at all like his heavily endorsed, highly exploited self.

"Truth is, I'm not so sure," he confessed, hanging his head in shame. "Everybody says I'm the favorite, which only puts more pressure on me, and truth is, Labonte's taken a whole lot better advantage of the season than I have. You know, he took over the points race from Jarrett in the third race in Vegas, and that ol' boy's held a real strong position since. See, my problem is, I like trophies. Like 'em way too much. And that means I don't rely on consistency like Labonte does. And if I'm honest about it, Richmond's not my favorite track. Hell, I finished eighteenth in the Pontiac Excitement Four Hundred last spring, can you believe it?

"That really shattered my confidence, even if the general public don't know it. I think that's one of the reasons I had to go out and get me that big chopper. You know, the crowds go wild when I fly in and out in that thing, and it helps my confidence and maybe makes the fans think I'm the Big Guy even if the way I'm heading, I'm not gonna be big for much longer."

Hammer was getting impatient as she glanced at her watch and Andy pulled out a chair, listening intensely to what Brett was saying.

"Look," Andy said, "There are twenty or twenty-five cars out there and every one of them, including number eleven, has the capability of running up front."

"Yeah, now you are right about that," Brett said, sipping his Pepsi and looking pretty miserable. "Anybody could win. The competition's about as tight as it can get, and that's why my confidence just cracked when I came in eighteenth last time I was on this damn racetrack."

"On any given race weekend," Andy went on, "any driver can make a big move and win, and I think you're the one to make that big move tonight. You can do it, Donny. You're a Bud Pole winner just like Rudd, Labonte, Skinner, Wallace, and Earnhardt, Junior, are. You sat on the pole for the Daytona Five Hundred and had a starting position in the Bud Shootout, right? And don't forget, you still lead in the Raybestos Rookie of the Year standings and you grabbed the checkered flag at The Winston in Charlotte."

"But I came in eighteenth, man . . ." Brett obsessed. "That's the only thing I'm thinking about as I get ready to go out there tonight, and when you start choking, that's when you start beatin' and bangin' off the corners or get nudged into a spin 'cause you aren't really focused and are misjudging which way someone's going."

"You've always been known for your instinct and judgment," Andy reminded him. "Remember the Busch Series in ninety-nine?"

"We've got to go," Hammer said as her tension mounted to a screaming pitch. "If we don't go now, it's going to be too late!"

"How could I forget?" Brett replied with a shake of his head. "That was one of my best."

"Exactly," Andy encouraged him. "And why? You had to work for every piece of the track you got, and there were wrecks and door-banging tussles going on everywhere. And what did you do? Right after an accident in Turn Four took out number forty and caused a seven-lap caution, and Hamilton spun off Turn Two and took out Burton and Fuller, you were smart enough to get off the gas and get on the brakes, and then you shot out ahead on the back straightaway and just stayed in it."

"Yeah," Brett said, looking up and greatly fortified, "I sure as hell did."

"And that happened right here," Andy concluded, measuring his words by tapping the table with his finger. "That was right here at the Richmond racetrack."

"I know, I know. I guess it's my nature to dwell on poor performances," Brett said with a grin. "And guess what? I'm just not going to do that tonight, and if you want to use my bird, you go right ahead as long as someone knows how to fly the damn thing."

"You bet I do," Andy said. "And when you're out there tonight, remember what I said. Make your Big Move. You'll know when."

"What in the world was that all about?" Hammer asked Andy as they flew toward downtown Richmond in Brett's glorious 430, which was painted black and emblazoned with his car number and endorsements in brilliant yellow, purple, and red. "I thought you didn't go to races."

"I don't, but I watch them on TV occasionally and study strategies, whether it's of race-car drivers or tennis players or Navy SEAL snipers," Andy replied through his mike as he pushed ahead at a hundred and fifty knots and overflew I-95, which was a solid line of barely creeping cars for as far as he could see. "Glad we're up here and not down there," he added.

B arbie Fogg had so far avoided the backed-up traffic caused by the masses headed to the racetrack. It wasn't that Barbie was wise in the ways of shortcuts and alleyways, but after she had picked up Hooter at the tollbooth, the unexpected had occurred. Barbie's cell phone had rung, and she had been surprised and relieved to hear Reverend Justice's voice on the line.

"Where on earth have you been?" Barbie said as Hooter flashed her nails in the passenger's seat, admiring her little acrylic flags.

"Been busy with the prison ministry," the reverend replied. "And my car's broke down, so I need you to come over and pick me up quick as you can. I'm gonna have a few brethren with me, so you need to have room for, let me see, six of us, including me."

"Oh my, that's a tight squeeze," Barbie said while Hooter ripped open the velcro straps on her astronaut boots and readjusted them, admiring her stylish outfit and imagining herself in the governor's special box at the racetrack.

Hooter wondered if that big, bad Trooper Macovich would show up and figured he would. He sure did brag a lot about how dangerous and important his job was. Everything was the *guv* this and the *guv* that when Hooter and Macovich had been drinking beer the other night, and Hooter felt a twinge of regret. It was true that Macovich was fresh and had one thing on his mind, even when he was going on and on about the governor and what it was like to work in that big mansion in Capitol Square while beating everybody in pool, but Hooter was lonely.

"I tell you, girlfriend, maybe I been too rough on him," Hooter said with a sigh as Barbie pulled into a boarded-up gas station and turned around. "I kinda hope he'll be there tonight. You think he'll admirate my style?"

"I think you look fabulous," Barbie assured her as she worried about getting to the race on time, if at all.

The reverend's phone call was out of the blue and very peculiar, Barbie thought as she headed toward a rundown part of the city, just northwest of downtown, where the reverend had instructed her to wait across the street from the city jail, in the back parking lot of the juvenile courts building. He and his brethren would be hiding in a small wooded area and would jump in the minivan the minute she showed up, and then she was to speed away and not ask any questions.

"Maybe you should ring up that trooper and tell him we might be a little late," Barbie suggested with growing anxiety, "and ask him to make sure they don't give away our seats in the governor's box."

"What'chu mean, *late?*" Hooter exclaimed, because she had not paid much attention to whatever Barbie had been saying on the cell phone a few minutes ago. "Girlfriend, we can't be late! Uh uh, we're late, you gonna totally miss seeing all them race drivers come outta their trailers and get into their cars! You won't get your picture took with none of 'em! This is the opportunity of a life, and we can't be late!"

As Barbie drove faster, Hooter noticed a big, colorful helicopter hovering in the area of the Medical College.

"Why, look at that helichopper!" Hooter leaned forward to get a better look. "Now, that would hang the moon, wouldn't it, girlfriend? To ride on a helichopper? Must be some poor person they's rushing to the emergency room, but I ain't never seen a med-chopper that look like that."

"Oh my Lord," Barbie exclaimed and almost ran off the road. "That's Donny Brett's colors! And look, his number eleven's painted on the door. Oh dear Lord, he must've been in a wreck already!"

"But the race ain't even started yet," Hooter pointed out. "Maybe he had a heart attack or something. You know he must be feeling a lot of stress after comin' in eighteenth last spring when he was here."

Thirty-one

ndy and Hammer were feeling far more stress than Donny Brett was.

Despite Andy's apparent confidence when he promised Hammer he knew exactly how to handle Smoke and the road dogs, the truth was, he had no idea what to expect, and the headset kept rearranging his ponytail wig, and pretty soon it would be too dark to wear the Ray-Bans. He held the helicopter in a rock-hard hover and turned the nose into the wind as he spotted Smoke, a fragile-looking woman with short platinum hair, and two road dogs climbing out of a black SUV parked in the lot on the other side of the fenced-in helipad. The thugs were dressed in NASCAR colors, and the smallest one was holding a small bundle wrapped in what looked like a folded black flag.

"That must be Possum," Andy said to Hammer over the mike. "And it looks like he might have Popeye."

Hammer did her best not to react. She knew it would be unwise to show that she had any interest in whatever was in the folded flag, because she was supposed to be Donny Brett's brother's girlfriend and had no reason to know who Popeye was or care.

"Stay tight," Andy said as he set down the helicopter on the concrete surface and cut both engines' throttles to flight idle. "I'll go talk to them. If something happens, just cut the throttles all the way off and start shooting through your window. It slides open."

The road dogs and the woman were gathered at the fence, staring in awe at the glorious helicopter and looking a bit perplexed as they watched the redneck with a ponytail headed their way.

"Who the fuck are you?" Smoke asked as the little bundle moved in Possum's arms.

"My brother sent me to pick you up," Andy said, rewriting his script yet again.

"Your brother's Donny Brett?" Cuda asked with wide eyes. "Whoa, man, he's phat! I sure hope he pulls it off tonight, 'cause I know he sucked last spring, coming in eighteenth."

"Shut up!" Smoke ordered. "We're supposed to be picked up by the state police," he said to Andy. "Why the shit would your brother send his chopper after us?"

Andy detected Smoke's twitching fingers over a pocket on his bright red Winston Cup jacket, where he probably had concealed a high-caliber gun. Andy eyed what he assumed was Smoke's trailer-park-looking girlfriend and something about her eyes gave him a creepy feeling. She seemed familiar.

"All I can tell ya," Andy said, "is me and my girlfriend-copilot was just with Donny in his trailer, giving him a pep talk, when this big black trooper shows up in a panic. He starts telling this story about the governor's helicopter getting a chip light and the thing's grounded, and he's got a pit crew he's supposed to pick up downtown, and he don't know what to do, but maybe Donny could help out because his helicopter's just sitting there. I assumed you're the Jolly Goodwrench pit crew," Andy added, feigning sudden doubt and suspicion to buffalo them a bit.

"Yeah," Possum shouted above the thud-thudding of the helicopter blades, and he managed to unfold the flag enough for Andy to make out part of a skull smoking a cigarette, and the word *Jolly* and part of *Goodwrench*. "Come on, let's go!" Possum exclaimed.

"Wait a minute," Smoke said, staring menacingly at Andy. "How the fuck do you know about Jolly Goodwrench?"

"Yeah!" Cuda agreed.

"Because it's on your flag," Andy replied, pointing at it and grateful Possum had been sharp enough to unfold it just in time.

"And I put something about Jolly Goodwrench on the NASCAR web," Possum added an untruth to firm up the story.

"Right," Andy said, sending a secret signal to Possum. "I saw it."

Possum caught on and hid his shock. The blond guy with the pony-tail wasn't Donny Brett's brother but Trooper Truth undercover! Trooper Truth had changed the plan! Possum had been suffering from a bad feeling that something was going to screw up at the last minute, and he was right. Otherwise, Trooper Truth wouldn't have shown up in Donny Brett's helicopter!

"Listen, we can't stand here all day talking," Andy said loudly. "We've got to get off this helipad before Medflight shows up to drop off a heart for transplant surgery. So either get in, or I gotta get out of here and back to the racetrack."

"Come on," Smoke said. He, his girlfriend, and the road dogs climbed over the fence and held on to their MAC Tools, M&M, and Excedrin baseball caps as they ran through gusting rotor wash toward the 430.

Barbie and Hooter saw the bright helicopter pop up over the tops of buildings and speed away as Barbie turned into the empty parking lot of the courts buildings. She drove to the back, and instantly six desperate-looking men, including the reverend, rushed out of a wooded area and ran like hell toward the minivan, jerking open the doors and piling inside. It did not escape Hooter's attention that the men smelled unwashed, were unshaven, and had neither belts nor shoelaces. She knew inmates when she saw them, and froze in fear. Oh, oh, oh, what had she gotten herself into now? And wasn't that Mexican boy the same one she'd met at the tollbooth the other night?

"Drive!" Reverend Justice shouted.

"Yeah, get the fuck outta here!" Slim Jim screamed.

"Duck down!" Trader yelled.

"Man, you're crushing me!" Cat complained.

The men ducked down on the floor as Barbie shot out of the parking lot and noticed cop cars with flashing lights rushing toward the gloomy brick jail across the street.

"Just drive normal," Hooter said, because somebody had to have a clear head and take control. "You be whizzing around like this and the police will stop us for sure. Then we gonna get arrested for helping convicts escape from jail."

"What?" Barbie panicked, clutching the steering wheel in both hands. "Convicts?"

"We was unfairly arrested, Barbie," the reverend said from the floor in back. "It's the Lord's will we got out and you're helping us. And I had no choice about it 'cause these other inmates forced me to act like I was rupturing something in my belly and when the guard burst inside the cell to help, I smacked him over the head with a food tray, just like Pinn had done to him when he used to work as a prison guard.

"So I got the idea from being on *Head to Head with Pinn*. Ain't it wondrous the way the Lord works?" Reverend Justice preached on. "If I hadn't been on that show, all 'cause of Moses Custer and the Neighborhood Watch I started down there near the Farmers' Market, well, I never would' ave thought to smack someone with a food tray. 'Course, if I hadn't been so over-stended and stressed out from all the publicity I suddenly was getting, I might not have tried to pick up that old woman for purposes of releasing myself, and then I never would'ave had to smack nobody with a food tray."

M aybe it was just a superstition, but Moses Custer had always heard that if his ear itched, it meant someone was talking about him. As he rode in the governor's motorcade, Moses's right ear was itching something fierce beneath bandages, and he wondered if it might indicate that a lot of people out there knew he was a VIP guest in a long black limousine, and destined to sit in the governor's box at the race. He stared out tinted glass at backed-up traffic as the governor snored and his peculiar daughter with her jet-black helmet haircut kept staring down at her quivering cleavage while that tiny red horse stood in the woodchips and now and then stepped on Moses's foot.

Macovich, meanwhile, was trying to weave through traffic as he talked over the radio to Andy, who had turned the helicopter's intercom to *crew only* so the road dogs couldn't hear what he was saying.

"To make everything worse," Macovich said into the mike, "six inmates just broke out of jail and cop cars are everywhere, so I'm telling you, it's a mess out here. I don't know when we'll get to the racetrack, but we gonna be late."

"Look, I've got to go to Plan B," Andy transmitted as the mobbed racetrack appeared a thousand feet below, in the distance.

"Wooo, seems like we should be on Plan G or H now, at least."

"I'll do a high recon over the racetrack and just keep circling until you can get a bunch of uniformed cops to swarm onto the helipad so Smoke will change his mind and order me to take them to Tangier Island," Andy came back.

"But we ain't got no undercover backups down there, man!" Macovich worried.

Andy looked down at thousands of fans waving wildly up at the helicopter and fighting to get close to the helipad.

"I wasn't expecting this and should have," he said, "but Brett's fans are recognizing his bird and are going to storm us on the ground. Someone may get hurt or Smoke's going to get away. No way I'm setting down at the racetrack."

"Ten-four," Macovich came back. "I mean, roger."

The stands were filling up as Andy switched on pulsing landing lights and began to slow down. He turned the intercom back to *all* so everyone in back could hear him through the headsets.

"We'll be landing in a few minutes," Andy announced. "Now it's very important you follow instructions, for reasons of safety. When we set down, just keep your seats and the ground crew will get you out."

Smoke was staring out his window. When the helipad came in sight, he noticed dozens of cops crowding onto it. Smoke also detected that there was something odd about the pilot's ponytail. It seemed to him that a minute ago, the ponytail had been centered, and now it was cock-eyed.

"What are all those cops doing?" Smoke said into his mike.

"Don't know, but they'll clear out of the way as I get closer," Andy replied, and Hammer tensed up and wanted desperately to turn around and check on Popeye.

"Oh yeah?" Smoke countered as meanness crept into his voice. "Well, maybe something stinks about this."

"Man! Look at all them people down there," Cuda marveled. "And look how all of 'em are pointing up at us and pumping their fists! They must think we're Donny Brett!"

"Bullshit," Smoke's voice filled Andy's headset, and suddenly the ponytail wig was yanked off from behind and the Ray Bans were knocked askew.

Andy remembered what Macovich had drilled into him when Andy was learning to fly: *Just fly the helicopter.* No matter what happened or how desperate the situation, Andy must simply fly the helicopter, and he held it in a steady descent as he felt the hard, cold barrel of a gun at the back of his neck and Smoke yelled obscenities at him and threatened to kill the dog.

"Calm down." It was Hammer who spoke. "Do you want us to crash, you idiots? Now shut up back there so we can handle this huge machine because none of you knows how to fly, and that means you're going to have to depend on us!"

". . . Fucking cops!" Smoke was ranting and raving. "I know who you are, you motherfuckers! And I've got your fucking dog back here, you bitch, and if you don't do what I say, I'm gonna pump her full of rat poison!"

Hammer assumed and sincerely hoped Smoke was bluffing, but Possum saw the syringe Smoke had just pulled out of a pocket. Possum held Popeye and could feel her shaking through the flag as Unique sat very still, as if in a trance, her eyes filled with an eerie light.

"Don't do nothing like that right now," Possum told Smoke. "You stick the dog and she's gonna start having cavulshuns and jumping everywhere, and if she dead, you ain't got nothing to threaten them with no more."

Smoke fell silent for a moment, and decided Possum was probably right, as Hammer's heart was seized by fear, because she realized Smoke might really have a syringe full of rat poison back there. The bastard. If they ever got back on the ground alive, she might just kill Smoke even if it was a bad shooting and she ended up professionally ruined or charged with manslaughter.

Unique slid a box cutter out of a pocket, her surreal stare fixed on the back of the blond cop's neck. The Nazi had directed that she would find her Purpose, and she had. She rearranged her molecules and then arranged them back to normal as she realized that the cop she had been stalking, who had turned out to be Andy Brazil, had already seen her when he picked them up in the helicopter. So there was no point in being invisible, and he wasn't going to recognize her, anyway. Her groin throbbed as she anticipated cutting his throat from ear to ear. Then the copilot would take over, and after they landed, Unique would cut her throat, too, and spend some alone time with the body.

"Get us out of here!" Smoke ordered Andy. "Now! Take us to Tangier Island! And don't you say anything I can't hear in the back!"

Thirty-two

Macovich spotted the white minivan with the rainbow bumper sticker two cars ahead, and he recalled the rainbow sticker on Hooter's tollbooth. Just as Hooter entered his mind, he realized with surprise that she was sitting in the front passenger's seat of the minivan and turning around to talk to people in back, none of whom Macovich could see.

"Wooo, girl, what's going on here?" Macovich muttered to himself as he noted that the minivan was driving a bit erratically, slowing down and speeding up, swerving and trying to switch lanes to pass.

Macovich flipped on the specially equipped limousine's blue grill lights and got on the bumper in front of him, forcing the motorist to pull off on the shoulder. He did the same thing to the next car, and was now on the minivan's rear, his emergency lights strobing.

"What's going on?" Regina asked as she tried a few pats of the face powder Barbie had given to her.

"I'm just trying to get us through all this traffic," Macovich said as he managed to nudge into the left lane and get parallel to the minivan.

He started waving at Hooter, trying to get her attention, and when she finally looked over and saw him, after Barbie brought him and the limousine to her attention, Hooter made a face of distress and mouthed *help!*

"Shit!" Macovich said, because he was not allowed to make traffic stops or get involved in incidents while he was driving the governor.

He shrugged, as if to tell Hooter there was nothing he could do. He pointed toward the back of the limousine and drew a box in the air to indicate he was carrying The Package. Hooter rolled her eyes and mouthed *help!* again as she pointed to the back of the minivan and held up six fingers and then wiggled two fingers to suggest six people running. Macovich frowned and wondered what she was trying to say. *Six passengers in back who were running?* Wooo, he thought. Didn't six inmates just break out of jail not too far from here, and if normal, innocent people were in back of the van, then why were they ducking out of sight?

Macovich got on his radio and called for backup units while he motioned for Hooter to get her ditzy-looking driver to somehow pull off the road.

Girlfriend," Hooter said loudly to Barbie. "I is so sorry, but I got to use the lady's room, and I mean *got to*."

"Forget it!" Cat's urgent voice drifted up from the floor in back. "We're not stopping until we get outta all this traffic and to some place where there ain't no police!"

"Let me tell you something," Hooter tossed over the seat, "when a lady say she gotta stop, then she gotta stop, you understand what I'm saying? Didn't your mama raise you right, huh? Didn't she teach you nothing about ladies and their monthly spells, and how a lady can be riding along minding her own business when all a sudden, she feels her fertility waking up when it wasn't expected for two more days?"

The men on the floor in back fell silent.

"So, girlfriend, you just pull over right up there at the Hess station and I'll run in. I'll be quick, but I sure hope I ain't gonna get the cramps. Oh Lord, please don't let me get the cramps."

Barbie was so concerned she momentarily forgot the inmates inside her minivan. Barbie had suffered terribly from cramps when she was younger, and she understood completely how unbearable and debilitating they could be. She flipped on her right turn signal and reached over to pat Hooter's arm.

"Just drive!" Trader ordered.

"Do you have any Midol?" Barbie asked Hooter.

"Uh uh, ohhhh," Hooter replied with a groan as she held her belly. "Ohhhh! I didn't bring nothing 'cause I wasn't expecting my periot. Ohhhhhh! Lord, why this have to happen on today of all days?"

"I am very sorry," Reverend Justice said with feeling as he inhaled a mouthful of dust from the carpeted floor and shoved Cat's foot out of his face. "I'll pray that the Good Lord deliver you from The Cramps. Dear Lord"—he sneezed twice—"please deliver this woman, your servant, from The Cramps. I claim your powers of healing in the name of Je-sus!"

"Ohhhhhh," Hooter moaned louder as the minivan crept ahead in the barely moving gridlock of race fans, all of whom were getting out of sorts and worrying about missing the start of the race, when the pace car would roar out onto the track and Air Force F-16s would fly over in formation.

"All right, okay, all right," Slim Jim's voice sounded, and if there was one thing he couldn't stand, it was hearing a woman with The Cramps and then having to brace himself for the rotten moods and mean-ass behavior that were sure to follow. "Pull over and you make it quick and don't talk to nobody or do nothing to 'tract attention!"

Macovich was intently watching Hooter as he drove beside her. Clearly, she had been injured and needed to be rushed to the hospital, and Macovich was beginning to panic. How did he know one of the inmates hadn't stabbed her with a shank and she was bleeding to death right before his eyes?

"Sir, excuse me," Moses raised his voice to the governor.

"What?" the governor asked, waking up.

"That little horse's got his hoof on my foot and I can't move it," Moses said, trying not to cause an inconvenience, but he feared his foot might be broken and he was in terrible pain.

Regina tried to remember where she'd put her list of commands and realized she had left it at the mansion. She knew there was a command for picking up a hoof, and she searched her memory. What was it?

"Closer," she said to Trip.

Trip responded by moving a foot closer to his handler, who in this case, was the governor.

"Ahhhh!" Moses yelled when the minihorse knocked against the cast on his arm and then stepped on his other foot. "I don't mean to complain, but I'm getting as banged up back here as I was at the hospital!"

"Right!" Regina began to panic and all of the commands she had glanced at tumbled together in her head. "I'm sorry."

Trip turned right and banged Moses's bandaged head against the window. He screamed and begged for someone to let him out of the car.

"I'll just get me a cab and go on home to bed," he said as he tried to push the minihorse away.

"Can you pull over?" Regina yelled to Macovich as she tugged on her denim skirt, which was a bit snug and tended to creep up her enormous thighs. "Mister Custer's not feeling well and needs to go!"

"Needs to go where?" Macovich said as he crept along with the minivan.

"Back," Regina shouted, and Trip stepped back and rested all of his weight on both of Moses's feet this time.

"Ayyyyyyy!" he shrieked.

"Ohhhhhh," Hooter moaned as Barbie finally, at long last, turned into the Hess station, and the governor's motorcade pulled in right behind her.

Other race fans who also had decided to take advantage of a pit stop stared in amazement at the lead limousine with flashing blue lights and the other three black stretches that followed. Shiny black doors opened and the governor, a fat girl with awful hair and bizarre taste in clothes, and what looked like a hospital patient, in addition to a tiny red horse, and plainclothes drivers who had guns under their jackets, and the rest of the First Family, climbed out to get a little fresh air.

The governor grabbed Trip's harness and took a few uncertain steps as Macovich rushed toward the minivan just as Hooter climbed out and began to wave her arms and yell.

"We've been abducted by convicts!" she shouted, and immediately, every NASCAR fan who had stopped to buy beer, and relieve himself from beer already consumed, began to cheer.

Slim Jim, Stick, Cruz Morales, Trader, Cat, and the reverend boiled out from the back floor and scattered. Two of them were tackled by Bubba Loving. Macovich snatched Cruz and Stick up by the backs of their shirts, and Cat zigzagged and dodged and ran straight at the governor, whom he intended to hold hostage. Regina, remembering that she was still a police intern, decided it was up to her to control the situation and yelled at Trip, "Sic him!"

The minihorse was unfamiliar with the command and did nothing as Cat ran past, and the governor squinted about in confusion and patted for his magnifying glass. Regina, who as a child had annoyed and injured mansion staff and family by butting them in tender places, lowered her NASCOIFED helmet-head and pawed the ground with her red patent-leather high tops, building up steam as she suffered a violent atavistic throwback to her primitive programming. She rushed the inmate and butted him in the groin, knocking him off his feet and sending him sailing through the air and body-slamming into Trader. Then she pounced on both of them, sprawled across their chests, and hollered as she banged their heads together and strangled them. Hooter hurried over to assist, while cheering NASCAR fans encouraged the fat girl to *slam into them again* and *stomp their pedals to the metal* and *blow their asses off the track.*

S moke continued to bump Andy's head with the pistol and threaten to kill Popeye if Andy and Hammer didn't do exactly as they were told.

"I know you got guns, so hand them back here," Smoke ordered over his mike.

Just fly the helicopter, Andy told himself.

"Hand them back here now!" Smoke's cruel voice sounded in Andy's headset.

"I'm flying," Andy replied. "It takes both hands and feet to fly and I'm not about to start rooting around for any alleged weapons until we're on the ground."

"I don't have a weapon," Hammer answered as she wondered if she dared turn around and shoot Smoke with the nine-millimeter pistol inside her Harley purse.

She supposed this was not a good idea. Nailing Smoke wasn't the problem at such close range, but if he happened to fire his gun because she'd fired hers, then Andy might be wounded or killed and it would be up to her to fly and she didn't know how. Not to mention, if her bullet passed through Smoke and penetrated the helicopter, severe damage might be the result and they could crash. She looked out at the dark waters of the James River as it opened up into the mouth of the Chesapeake Bay and remembered her fear of drowning.

"Sit back and shut up," she told Smoke in the severe tone she reserved for suspects. "We're over the bay now and the last thing you want is for us to lose control of the helicopter. If we go down, everybody drowns. You'll be trapped inside, beating on the doors, trying desperately to open them, but you won't be able to because of the vacuum. So you'll struggle in the frigid pitch dark as water fills the cabin and you'll die slowly."

"Chill," Cuda begged Smoke. "Just chill, man. I don't want to drown!"

Possum kept Popeye snugly wrapped in the flag and hugged her hard. Smoke sat back in the seat, playing with the syringe while Unique stared weirdly at Trooper Truth's neck, a box cutter wrapped so tightly in her delicate hand that her nails had pierced her palm and drawn blood. She felt no pain, only the blast of heat and intense frequencies and vibrations rolling up from her Darkness.

Andy checked a flight chart and entered Patuxent's frequency on the radio, and minutes later raised the military tower on the air. "Helicopter zero-one-one-Delta-Bravo," Andy said over the radio.

"One-Delta-Bravo," the tower came back.

"Are restricted areas six-six-oh-niner and four-zero-zero-six hot?" Andy inquired.

"Negative."

"Permission to transition through them at one thousand, en route to Tangier Island," Andy said.

"Permission denied." The tower said exactly what Andy thought it would.

"Roger," Andy said as he entered code 7500, for hijacking, into the transponder and then gave Hammer a thumbs-up.

He was going to transition through the restricted areas anyway, and now that Patuxent had him on their radar and knew his tail number and realized there were hijackers on board, the military would respond. He pulled in more torque and was grateful for a tailwind that propelled them along at a ground speed of one hundred and seventy knots, and fifteen minutes later entered Patuxent's airspace.

Andy took a deep breath and switched the 430 over to automatic pilot. Smoke had no way of realizing that Andy's hands and feet were now free, and Andy slowly reached down and slipped the pistol out of his ankle holster. Following his lead, Hammer withdrew the nine-millimeter from her bag, and both of them tucked the guns under their legs so Smoke wouldn't see what was happening should he climb back up on his seat and glare into the cockpit again.

Fonny Boy and Dr. Faux didn't know what was happening, either, when they walked along Janders Road in plain view and couldn't find a single sign of an Islander. Lights in many of the small houses were off, and not a single golf cart or bicycle rattled past in the chilly dark. The island had been deserted this way ever since Fonny Boy and Dr. Faux slipped off the mailboat after an unsuccessful attempt at bribing the captain to look for the crab pot with its yellow buoy.

"I swanny! Maybe the Rapture done come," said Fonny Boy, who had heard about the Rapture all of his life. "And we've been left 'cause we ain't fittin' for Heaven 'cause of all wer sins!"

"That's silly," the dentist replied in frustration.

He was hungry, cold, and tired, and he was imagining all of the watermen out in their bateaus, finding the Tory Treasure. He wondered if the Coast Guard had rounded up all of them and placed them under arrest, or if the watermen had found a way to extort cooperation from the authorities. Plain and simple, Dr. Faux didn't know what was going on, but he was spooked and wished he had never been so foolish as to pad his dental bills, lie to Medicaid, take advantage of children, and ruin people's teeth for the sake of profit.

When they eventually reached Fonny Boy's house, no one was home there, either.

"My mama, she should be in thar raisin' a fire and renching the dishes. She never goes out after dark," Fonny Boy marveled as his fears grew. "I'm of a mind Jesus come down on His cloud and everybody's gone, save us!"

"Stop it," the dentist insisted. "Nobody's gone up in a cloud, Fonny Boy. That's a fairy tale. Now there must be an explanation for why the island is deserted, so let's just get your family golf cart and drive around. I suggest we head over to the airport and see if anything's going on over there."

But the golf cart's battery was dead, and this just increased Fonny Boy's feeling of foreboding and damnation.

"I guess we'll walk," Dr. Faux decided, turning around and heading in another direction that cut through a marsh. "I will admit this is strange. If everyone's out in the bateaus looking for the treasure, then why did we see so many bateaus at the docks when we got off the mailboat?"

"Shhhh!" Fonny Boy said with a finger over his lips. "I hear a helichopper! It must be the Guardsmen!"

The dentist strained to listen and detected the distant thud-thudding, and he heard something else, too.

"Singing," he said. "Do you hear it, Fonny Boy?"

Both of them stopped on the footpath, the brackish air stirring their hair as they listened hard to the faint sound of gospel singing that was carried almost imperceptibly by the wind.

"It's coming from the McMann Leon Methodist Church over thar on Main Street," Fonny Boy said with breathless excitement. "But I don't have neither notion why. The church, it don't have neither meetings on Saturday night."

Fonny Boy and the dentist began to hurry in that direction as the sound of helicopter blades got louder and they spotted two bright moving lights high up in the star-scattered sky, coming in from the west. Fonny Boy broke into a run and didn't care if he left the dentist behind.

"Hey! Wait for me!" Dr. Faux called after him. "Well, never mind, I'm heading to the airstrip to see if I can fly the hell out of here on one of those helicopters coming in!"

Fonny Boy ran as fast as he ever had in his life, and was panting and drenched with sweat when he bounded up the church steps and threw open the door. He couldn't believe what he saw inside. Every single person on the island must have been crowded together in the church, the lights were out, and the Islanders were holding candles. They were singing "Amazing Grace" without accompaniment, and Fonny Boy stood still, staring in confusion and fear. Something terrible must have happened, he thought. Or maybe something wonderful. Or maybe they knew the Rapture was coming for sure and they were waiting for Jesus on his cloud. This was crazy, Fonny Boy silently protested. Why wasn't everybody trying to find the Tory Treasure, and didn't it concern them that helicopters were flying in? The sound of their engines was loud enough so that Fonny Boy could hear it inside the church. He pulled his harmonica out of a pocket, cupped his hands airtight around it, made a fish face, and began bending and tonguing, stomping his foot to the rhythm as he jammed the blues.

The singing instantly stopped and Reverend Crockett stepped up to the pulpit. He scanned the sea of small flickering flames.

"Who's playing the juice harp?" he asked.

"I ain't adrift nei-ther more." Fonny Boy sang improv and bent a few notes. "I ain't prinked up in nei-ther Sunday shoes with my pockets puffed out, but a freehearted boy, he ain't never been poor!"

Gasps sounded all around him and voices called out *praise Jesus* and *thank you, Jesus* and *it's a miracle!* Then Fonny Boy's mother was stumbling out of a pew and clutching Fonny Boy in her arms, and next his father was lifting him up in the air, tears streaming down his weathered face. Everyone on the island figured Fonny Boy was dead when they heard about the Tory Treasure and the capture of the dentist. Since there was no mention of Fonny Boy in connection with this news, the Islanders assumed the poor young man had been pushed overboard by the greedy Dr. Faux.

"Grasp hands in a mazy dance of praise!" Reverend Crockett proclaimed. "The Lord is dealing out grace and has blowed the breath of life back into this drownded boy!"

"Praise God!" Fonny Boy's mother cried. "He's brought wer baby back from the dead!"

"I'm a die if I was dead!" Fonny Boy said, confounded and deeply moved as it began to occur to him that the entire island had been gathering in the church, perhaps nightly, to pray for him because he was lost at sea. "The dentist, he returned me right 'fore dark."

A rumbling stirred throughout the congregation as helicopters thundered overhead, shaking the roof of the church.

"That's it!" Reverend Crockett boomed in disapproval. "The dentist is back on Tanger?"

"No!" Fonny Boy exclaimed backward.

"Whur's he at?"

"He's follering his way to the airstrip!" Fonny Boy replied.

"That bad man from the main, he pulled ever one of my teeth!" Mrs. Pruitt said loud enough for all to hear.

"And mine."

"And mine."

"Yass! Mine, too."

"He must be fixin' to escape on the helichoppers!"

Loud, outraged voices ran together into a deafening rumble before Fonny Boy could explain, and the island's entire population streamed out of the church and moved in a determined, united candlelit front toward the airstrip, which was only a five-minute walk away, because nothing on the island was far from anything else.

S oldiers dressed for combat were climbing out of two Black Hawk helicopters when they saw a cloud of small flames floating in their direction. Andy picked up the strange display of light as he thundered fifteen hundred feet overhead at the same moment Unique pushed a button and zipped open the box cutter's blade.

"What's going on down there?" Hammer said before she could restrain herself.

"You better not try anything or all of you are dead!" Smoke threatened as he looked out the window at the moving sea of lights and the big Black Hawk helicopters. "What have you done? What the fuck's happening? Tell me now!"

Possum's attention was riveted to the syringe in Smoke's hand, and he knew Smoke well enough to figure out exactly what would happen next. The instant the helicopter was safely down, Smoke was going to stab Popeye through the flag and inject her full of rat poison, then he would shoot Hammer and Trooper Truth and keep Cuda and Possum as his road dogs on this forsaken island forever. Suddenly, Possum noticed Unique twitch as if she were having a seizure as she unfastened her seatbelt.

"Bye-bye, Popeye!" Smoke said in a mean, mocking tone as he pulled the protective orange tip off the syringe.

"*No, Unique!*" Possum screamed, and Andy instantly remembered Possum's saying in an e-mail "It was Unique" in reference to whoever cut on Moses, and Moses talking about an angel who promised him a *unique* experience. Andy yelled, "*Mayday!*" into the mike as he slowed down, lowered the helicopter's nose, and shoved the cyclic to the right, rolling the 430. For a hair-raising second, they were upside down, then warning alarms went off and emergency lights began to flash and the helicopter suddenly flared like a rampant stallion.

"Crash position! Crash position!" Andy yelled over the intercom as he cut the throttles back to flight idle, shoved the collective all the way down and glided the helicopter with nothing but air moving up through the blades to keep the helicopter from dropping like an anvil.

There was nothing special about deliberately cutting the throttles midair. Andy practiced autorotations regularly and not only was good at them, but he loved the excitement of landing a four-ton machine without the help of its engines. Another little trick he liked was to wait until he was thirty feet off the ground before pulling in power again and flying off, which was what he did now, and suddenly the helicopter was thundering into a high performance takeoff that shot it straight up into the night. At five hundred feet, Andy cut back the throttles again and smiled at Hammer as the warning bells began screaming again and he started down in yet another autorotation. He went through this perilous routine three more times for good measure, and was not at all surprised when he finally lowered the landing gear and set down that Smoke, Cuda, and Possum were ashen and doubled over in fetal positions, and Unique was on the floor, out cold.

"I'll get Smoke, you get the girl!" Andy yelled at Hammer as they flung open the back doors while the blades turned and rotorwash gusted like a gale. "Watch her! She's our slasher!"

Andy pointed his pistol at Smoke, who was dazed and had long since lost his gun. Andy yanked the monster out of the cabin and tossed him on the tarmac like a sack of rags while Hammer grabbed Unique. The sea of candles drifted around them in a circle as soldiers rushed over to see what the hell was going on.

"Pirates!" Andy announced to the stunned Islanders as he snapped handcuffs on Smoke's wrists and Hammer Flexcuffed Unique's ankles and her hands behind her back as she drifted in and out of consciousness and drooled.

"I'm sorry," Andy said to the soldiers. "I had to violate your restricted areas because I was being held at gunpoint as I suppose you determined from the code I squawked. If you wouldn't mind helping me by grabbing that other pirate out of the back, the one who's throwing up in a bag? But leave the smaller fellow alone. His name is Jeremiah Little and he's an innocent hostage. We'll take him back to Virginia with us."

"I know four-thirties. Want me to shut her down for ya?" one of the soldiers asked.

"Thanks," Andy replied as Popeye covered Hammer's face with kisses, and Dr. Faux crept near and gave Hammer an insincere, patronizing pat on her black-leather-covered back.

"I don't know what happened, exactly, but I certainly am glad your dog is all right. Isn't it amazing how pets are like children? I know how much I love my cats. If you don't mind," Dr. Faux said to Hammer, "I think it best I ride back to Virginia with you. I assume you're leaving right away?"

"Yass, cart him away!" commanded Reverend Crockett. "We don't want neither contact with him ever. Warrant him!"

"*No!*" The island's entire population talked backward in unison, their voices rising above rotorwash and the chop-chopping of slowing blades. "Return him to the main!" they began to chant.

DONNY BRETT TRIUMPHS!!

By Trooper Truth

Well, race fans, what a night!

I suppose the bad news is there was no Tory Treasure, or at least not in the spot marked by the yellow buoy, which apparently had done nothing but drift with the bay's current until the water got shallower and the crab pot finally got snagged on eel grass about a mile off the Virginia shore. But what matters is the only treasure the Islanders cared about was Fonny Boy, and way to go, Officer Reggie, for singlehandedly catching the escaped inmates!

But how about our boy Donny? Now, I'm sorry to say I was caught up on a case last night and missed the race, but I watched TV and the endless replays of his Big Move when he was running side by side with No. 4 and an accident on Turn 4 took out the No. 33 Chevy and caused a seven-lap caution with a restart on lap 94. Darned if Donny didn't take advantage of a perilous situation by making his Big Move.

That's right, sports fans. You saw him get off the gas and get on the brakes, just like he's done before, and then he just bulleted past No. 4 on the outside of the back straightaway, and he stayed with it the rest of the race.

"I just dug deep inside me," an exuberant Donny Brett said as he took a slug of champagne. "I just tried to enjoy it again and not worry so much about losing, you know? And I want to thank that cop who took the time to talk to me in my trailer. I don't know your name, but hey, thanks, man. And I want to tell everybody out there the same thing he told me. It's not about being good, it's about knowing when to make your move."

And now it's time for me to make my Big Move and say to you, my faithful readers, that there's a time to speak and a time to be silent. I'm going to sign off now, and this will be my last essay. Maybe I'll be back one day, but I don't know. So much has happened lately and there is a lot for me to finish up and a lot to figure out.

I will continue to welcome your e-mails and appreciate all you do to enlighten me and make the world a better place. But if I don't answer you, please don't feel bad or think I don't care. Remember the Golden Rule, and that even the smallest life and everything on this earth has a story, if only we take time to listen.

Be careful out there!